What readers are saying about
Steve Mosby's gripping thrillers

'Steve Mosby has become one of a handful of writers who make me excited about crime fiction'   Val McDermid

'Intense, creepy and deeply disturbing. Mosby stabs right to the heart of one of our deepest fears'   S. J. Bolton

'Steve Mosby is one of the most consistently and innovatively creepy writers working right now'   Eva Dolan

'Shocking and gripping'   *Evening Telegraph*

'Steve Mosby should be up there with the Mark Billinghams of the crime-horror genre'   *Metro*

'Mosby has become renowned for thrillers that reach into dark places where most British crime writers are afraid to go'
    Sunday Express

'Steve Mosby has been quietly producing some of the most exciting and dark-drenched serial killer novels of the decade'
    Catholic Herald

Steve Mosby was born in Leeds in 1976. He studied Philosophy at Leeds University, worked in the Sociology department there, and now writes full time. He is the author of ten psychological thrillers which have been widely translated. In 2012, he won the CWA Dagger in the Library for his body of work, and his novel *Black Flowers* was shortlisted for the Theakston Old Peculier Crime Novel of the Year. He lives in Leeds with his wife and son.

www.theleftroom.co.uk
 @stevemosby
/theleftroom

Also by Steve Mosby

You Can Run
I Know Who Did It
The Nightmare Place
Dark Room
Black Flowers
Cry for Help
The 50/50 Killer
The Cutting Crew
The Third Person

STILL BLEEDING

STEVE MOSBY

ORION

First published in Great Britain in 2009 by Orion
This paperback edition published in 2019 by Orion Fiction,
an imprint of The Orion Publishing Group Ltd
Carmelite House, 50 Victoria Embankment
London EC4Y ODZ

An Hachette UK company

1 3 5 7 9 10 8 6 4 2

A CIP catalogue record for this book
is available from the British Library.

ISBN 978 1 4091 8877 3

Typeset at The Spartan Press Ltd,
Lymington, Hants

Printed and bound by CPI Group (UK) Ltd,
Croydon, CR0 4YY

www.orionbooks.co.uk

For Lynn

Acknowledgements

Thanks, as usual, go to my agent, Carolyn Whitaker, and all the people at Orion who have contributed to this book with their insights, advice and, most of all, patience. Especially Genevieve, Jon and Jade, and all the people – genuinely too numerous to name, but you all know who you are – who helped make the previous books such a success. I really can't thank you enough.

In addition, thanks to a few people I forgot last time around: Sophie Hannah, James Nash and Tom Palmer. And Val McDermid for kind words and support.

More personal thanks for general support and friendship go to the usual crowd: Neil and Helen; Keleigh and Rich; J and Ang; Gill and Roger; Ben and Megan; Cass and Mark; Emma Lindley; the Sociology lot; Mum, Dad and John; and everyone who wrote to me over the last year to say they liked the other ones and were looking forward to this.

Most of all – as always – thanks to Lynn, for your love and encouragement.

Residents of Leeds will notice a few key locations have been mangled to fit the entirely fictional geography of the city in the book, and one conversation within refers very loosely to the activities of a real Art collective, the 'Leeds 13'.

On a much darker note, aside from key plot elements, it should be recorded that the videos and images Alex encounters in the book are based on actual footage freely available online. It can be a scary world out there.

Prologue

The last time I saw my wife was one evening in January, two and a half years ago. Marie was twenty-six years old, wearing a black jacket and dark-blue jeans, and she was on her way to buy a bottle of wine to go with the dinner I was stirring. She walked through the kitchen and opened the front door, casually swinging her car keys, but then hung back and said:

'Do you need anything else while I'm out?'

I shook my head. 'Just you to come back to me.'

She didn't reply, but I could hear it in the silence:

Are you sure that's what you need?

We'd had a difficult couple of weeks. For as long as I'd known her, Marie had been prone to bouts of depression: periods of time where everything I said or did was wrong, followed by periods where all she'd do was apologise, hate herself and wonder what I saw in her and why I stayed. I wasn't sure which of the two I found hardest, but we were between stages right now. Everything seemed much better than it had for the last few days, but the atmosphere between us was awkward.

I looked at her and the blankness on her face made me ache inside. *I wish you could see how beautiful you are*, I thought. *I wish you could just see that.* But I didn't say it, because I knew she wouldn't accept the words. They would drift past, and the frustration of not getting through would only make me feel bad, which would then make her feel worse. Sometimes, she was so determined not to be loved.

'Just that,' I said.

She nodded, her face still blank. 'Quick kiss, then.'

I left the spoon balanced and walked over.

'You want me to go instead?'

'No, it's fine,' she said. 'I love you.'

If I now remember those words being grabbed at – said a little too quickly – then I didn't notice it at the time.

'I love you too.'

She closed the door behind her. A minute later, I heard the car start up and drive away.

I was an introspective man back then. Prone to worrying. I'd imagine scenarios, always turning them around in my head to find the worst possible angle, then forcing myself to explore it. Whenever Marie was late back from work, I'd start to think that something terrible had happened to her. *What if she doesn't come back?* The minute hand on the kitchen clock would become a key turning slowly in my head, unlocking one awful possibility after another, so that they fell into my mind like coins. Late at night, I'd lie next to her and wonder what it would be like for one of us to lose the other.

I don't know why I was like this, because nothing bad had ever really happened to me. Perhaps that's why.

On that day, she should have been ten minutes at most. The shop she was heading to was only up the road, and for some reason I wasn't worried at all. You like to think you'd know, but the truth is that you don't. So the food simmered gently, and I kept on stirring it, the wooden spoon knocking against the base of the pan, and I was oblivious to the fact the world had quietly shattered without my noticing.

I can't remember when I started to think bad thoughts, but I know it was exactly forty minutes after she left when I decided *right, that's enough,* and called her mobile.

It was answered by a policeman. In the background I could hear sirens and a rush of traffic, and, straight away, I knew that this time something really had happened. In times of crisis, some part of your subconscious often takes charge, and I was shockingly calm as I spoke to him. It was only afterwards, as I grabbed my coat, that I realised I'd barely taken in a word he'd said, and that the ones I had didn't make any sense.

Marie had been hit by a truck, he'd said, on the ring road that circled the city. I'd taken that to mean there had been a car accident, but then I realised she shouldn't have been anywhere near the ring road. And some other phrase he'd used implied she wasn't in her car when it happened. Later, at the police station, I got the full account, and those things clicked into place. It hadn't been the truck that killed her. Most likely, it had been the fall from the bridge, fifty feet above, where they found her car.

The police always described it as the fall, never the leap, but that word was generally there in the tone of voice of whoever was speaking to me at the time. I heard the judgement attached to it. The sense that my loss was somehow not as great as the loss suffered by others.

In general, people talk about suicide in two different ways. Either they have sympathy for the person who kills themselves and think it's a tragedy, or else they see it as the ultimate in selfish behaviour. Some people probably do a bit of both. I know all that, so I found it easy to understand the attitude of the police. The truck driver, they told me, could have been killed. As things stood, he might never recover from what he'd seen that day.

I empathised. But I couldn't bring myself to share that feeling. I didn't blame her. I was never angry with her. And I never hated her for what she did to us, not even for a second.

Because I remembered the expression on her face when she left that day: full of regret for all that she imagined she'd put me through; full of that spiralling self-hatred. I remembered the last thing she said to me: *I love you*. And I knew that, whatever anyone thought, Marie hadn't been acting selfishly at all, or at least not when it came to me. In her head, however misguided her intentions, she was doing what she thought was best for me. She thought she was saving my life, rather than destroying it utterly.

The understanding was brought home six months later.

At that point, I was in the process of selling the house, and it had forced me to go through papers – things I'd been putting off for a while, reluctant to face. That was when I learned about the additional life insurance policy Marie had taken out. It had cost her twenty pounds a month. Almost unbelievably, it now equated to a single lump-sum payment of nearly half a million pounds.

The suicide clause in the contract had become null and void after the first two years of the policy. Marie had waited for two years and eight days. She had been planning what she did, without me knowing or suspecting, for that long.

Like I said, I never blamed her. It always felt like there were far more deserving targets to aim for on that level.

So, that was the last time I saw my wife alive.

But it was not the last time I saw her.

Part One

One

Her father talks to her about death.

The whole time, his eyes are very serious. They look like someone has drawn a perfect outline round them in red pen.

She tries to understand, but sometimes she can't and they both get upset. *Death is a monster,* her father says, just like in the thin fairytale books she has in her bedroom. *Like a dragon?* she asks, but he shakes his head. *It's bigger than that, and far more frightening. A dragon can only be in one place at a time, but Death can be anywhere it wants. It doesn't breathe fire. It breathes sadness.*

Sarah sits cross-legged in the corner of the settee, clutching a cushion against her stomach. Her father crouches down in front of her. It's evening, and the room around them is dark and gloomy. He reaches out and pinches his finger and thumb together tightly, like he's plucked a speck of Death from the air. Then he opens his fingers.

He has explained all this so carefully that Sarah sees it fall.

Death has ripples, he says.

She squints at the rough fibres in the carpet and imagines the ripples of Death spreading out from it in wavery circles, like a stone dropped into water. In one of the books at school, there is a picture of a lifeboat angled on a wave, the yellow-jacket sailors holding their hoods in the spray. But she doesn't have to go to school any more.

Death is contagious, Sarah. That means it spreads like a disease.

That knowledge frightens her the most. Because Death has already bloomed once in their home, and if you can catch it like a cold then either of them might be next. Or both of them. Her father seems afraid of that too. It's partly why he stares at her, she thinks, and why she stares back. As though looking into each other's eyes is casting a spell to keep the monster away.

Her father always breaks the spell first.

He shuffles away from her afterwards. Sometimes, he looks frustrated. She heard him crying once, which made her even more scared because fathers don't cry. The thing is, her own mind is as full of Death as her father's, and she knows he's only trying to help her. It's like the way they used to read difficult sentences together, working patiently through each word until it made sense. When she hears him cry, she's determined to try harder next time.

It's difficult, because she wants to cry too, and it doesn't feel like she should. Last week, she woke up in the night and thought she saw her mother shining, bright as a saint, in the corner of the bedroom. It was only a dream, but she told her father the next morning because she thought he might like to know, and because she wanted him to tell her that maybe it was real. But he said:

Was she still bleeding?

No, Daddy, Sarah said. *She was smiling, I promise.*

Instead of being pleased, he searched the house. Even now, he still looks for her. He crouches down by his bed, lifts the duvet to look underneath, then talks to the space.

Death is a monster, Sarah.

She says: *But how can we fight it?*

Well, this seems important. Her father thinks about it for a moment, and then he begins to explain, as best he can. She hangs on every word.

There are some people, he says, *who are so afraid of the monster they try to make it happy.*

Like sucking up to a bully? she asks.

Yes, he says, *and the man who hurt your mother was like this. But then there are others who turn their backs and run away, too frightened to face it.*

We can't be like that.

Her father grips her shoulders gently, so that she understands how important this is.

We have to stare it in the eye. We have to see. Do you understand?

She nods. But he hasn't answered her question, and now she's even more scared than she was before. Because it doesn't feel like her father is fighting anything, and the only thing he ever stares in the eye is her.

Sometimes, she sees him squatting by the front door, talking to people through the letterbox, telling them he's fine, and go away and leave us alone. She knows it's her aunt, because one time her father made her come down the hall and tell her that everything was all right. But he never opens the door.

Every day, Sarah wakes up to hear him pacing in the kitchen. The house smells of his cigarette smoke. She can see it hanging in rooms where he's been, like blue silk. In the mornings, while she's still in bed, he only does it in the kitchen. She stays in bed until she hears the window opening then closing.

She wakes up today and the house is quiet.

It's the kind of silence that hums in your ears, like you've banged your head on something and now it's ringing like a bell. It's the sound somebody makes after they've gone.

Sarah slips out from beneath the covers, quiet as a whisper, and moves down the corridor. Her father isn't in the kitchen. There's no smoke in the air. Straight ahead, his bedroom door is closed. She walks up and taps on it. Nobody answers.

Daddy?

Nobody answers.

She turns the handle and pushes the door, but it only opens a tiny fraction. There's something behind it, blocking it. Stopping it from opening.

A second later something crushes Sarah inside. She understands what has happened. While she was sleeping Death has bloomed again in her home. Through the slight gap in the door, she can smell the sadness of its breath.

At first she is frozen in place. Then she wants to run.

But she mustn't turn away. Sarah begins to push the door harder, with all her small might, because she knows that she has to see.

She is nine years old.

And now she was thirty.

Life had moved on, but those memories felt more recent than things that had happened yesterday. More *present*. But the past was a blueprint, wasn't it, for a drawing of the future. As time went on, you added new lines – or else they were added for you – but the old ones remained, and sometimes it was those that became the most pronounced. You just had to go over them enough times.

And so the determination her father had left her with – that you always had to *look*, no matter how horrible or difficult it might be – had never left her. Instead, it had matured and grown, and it was still visible now, in the same way the little girl's features remained there in her adult face.

Sarah shook her head, and then folded up the letter from Alex. He'd sent it two years ago, on the day he left Whitrow, and she'd read it so many times since that the paper had become worn. She even knew sections of it off by heart. *I appreciate everything you've done for me, and how you tried to help me. I hope you can understand and forgive me for this.* But she'd read it again anyway, because today it seemed appropriate. Today, two years on, she was leaving too.

As always, it had set off her memories.

You were right, he'd written. *Death has ripples.*

She slipped the letter into her pocket.

It was one item, at least, that she would not forget to pack.

The rest of her things were proving a little more difficult to sort, and time was running out.

Outside the window, the evening was just beginning to settle in, and the room felt drab and grey. She checked her watch. It was nearly seven o'clock, which meant the taxi she'd booked would be here in a few minutes. She wasn't organised at all.

Without realising it, she'd started biting her fingernail.

Did she have what she needed? The bag in front of her on the bed was only half full. There were enough clothes to be getting by with. Her real concern was all the personal items she couldn't bear to be without: the small gifts and photographs that were inconsequential in themselves, but had memories tethered to them. You never remembered things like that until you either saw them or wanted them.

She'd spent most of the afternoon searching the house for what she wanted to take. It upset James – obviously – and she'd suggested it might be easier for both of them if he went out for a while. But he refused. He just sat there, ignoring her. Pretending it wasn't happening. His expression was set like stone, but waves of sadness had been escaping him, and the guilt she felt might have caused her to overlook something important.

A *clatter* from downstairs.

Sarah listened, still worrying at her fingernail. James was washing up, she guessed. Or rather – throwing plates into the sink, deliberately loud enough for her to hear. It was generally his way. He'd never been good with words, but could usually make himself clear when he wanted. You needed to work out the precise shade of the anger, and then translate it, but she'd become used to it. What he was saying now was:

Don't leave me.

James had his own blueprint: his own lines that had been gone over too many times. His earliest memory, he'd told her, was of his father leaving. The man was clambering into his car to drive away, and James had been stood by the side of it crying, begging him not to go. His father had moved him gently backwards so that he could close the car door.

Another *clatter*.

I'm sorry, James.

Last night, he'd asked if she loved him, and she'd said that she did. It was true. When he asked why that wasn't enough, she had no idea what to say. The question had hung in the air for days before he'd eventually asked, and it had remained there since. She was almost afraid to go downstairs and see him now. But she had never been one to turn away.

Outside, a car beeped: the taxi was here.

The sound was immediately followed by a *smash* from downstairs. James had broken a glass. Either dropped it, or, more likely, thrown it across the room.

Sarah took a deep breath, trying to find some resolve, and then picked up the bag and walked out onto the landing. The door to the spare room was open. All her articles were boxed up in there, sitting on the shelf. Maybe she should take those? But you could go on for ever, couldn't you?

She hitched the bag up on her shoulder and made her way carefully down the thin stairs.

James had been drinking already. Most likely he was drunk by now. That wasn't unusual, but it concerned her today, as he could be unpredictable and volatile. There hadn't been a scene yet – not unless you counted the silences – but she suspected there was going to be. Perhaps he would beg her not to go. Christ, she hoped not. It wouldn't change her final decision, but it would make things harder for both of them, and for him most of all.

But deep down, Sarah thought, he did understand. He just loved her more than anything and didn't want to be without her. That was why it was so hard for him, and it was why, ultimately, he wouldn't stand in her way.

It'll be OK, she told herself.

Drunk or not, he wouldn't try to stop her.

Two

It sounded like a gunshot.

The noise came from somewhere overhead, echoing around the empty square.

I glanced up. It wasn't a gunshot, of course; it was an old woman, three storeys above. Her face was like a wizened fist wrapped in a handkerchief, and she was holding a faded red blanket out in the late afternoon sun, a cloud of dust descending towards me. She gave it another ruffling *crack*, then glared down at me and shouted something in Italian.

I had no idea what she was saying, but, clearly, she wasn't impressed. Perhaps she was wondering why I wasn't down at San Marco with everyone else, rather than cluttering up her piazza and getting in the way. Tourists. It had been two years since I'd left England, and I'd been travelling the whole time, collecting a deep tan and uncut, sun-bleached hair along the way. But wherever I went I was still immediately pegged as English. And that was before I even opened my mouth.

'*Dispiace*,' I said.

She didn't acknowledge the apology. I stood up and walked away across the square. A moment later, I looked back to see the old lady pull the shutter closed with an indignant *pock*.

And then it was blissfully silent again.

I'd been in Venice for nearly a week. Most of that time, I'd been walking around on my own, searching out little places like this. It was the same wherever I went; I always did my best to avoid the standard attractions. What I enjoyed more than anything was exploring the background – the smaller streets, away from the floods of tourists. I wasn't out here on holiday, as such, so my aim was never to collect photographs or gather memories. It was more a case of finding somewhere fresh and different, then kicking my heels for a while and allowing myself to become lost.

After a few days in a place, when I began to recognise its people and paths, the urge to move on grew steadily more insistent. It was as though I'd used up the strangeness of whatever city I was in and needed to seek out a new one. Either that, or I'd have the vague sense of a shadow falling slowly across me, cast by something enormous approaching from the distance. Each time that happened, without considering the matter too deeply, I packed my small rucksack and left as soon as possible. On those occasions, even though I understood there was nothing physical pursuing me, I tended to travel the furthest.

I headed away from the piazza now, breathing in the warm air.

Venice was one of the first places I'd visited that was threatening to hold onto me. I liked it a lot: its small, shaded alleys and dry, hidden squares; the dusty arches and secret walkways. Over a hundred separate islands, split by water, and stapled into a patchwork maze by the bridges. You walked through it, and it seemed like something coherent and whole, but it wasn't. You stepped down too heavily and the city creaked, like the deck of an old ship.

I was staying in the north, in a hostel. In truth, I still had more money than I knew what to do with, but this was the general standard of accommodation I sought out wherever I went. There was something simple and spartan about hostels, which was all I needed, but they also managed to be both anonymous and familiar at the same time, like coach seats. Wherever I'd gone, I'd learned to expect the same rough cloth on the beds, the same showers, the same *clack* of pool balls coming from slightly different lounges. You shared a room with someone that kept changing but somehow staying the same, about as variable as the wallpaper.

Currently, I was sharing my room with an American guy called Dean. He was travelling with a group of friends and was the unlucky odd-number in terms of room allocation. He was a bit talkative, but he seemed basically all right. The whole bunch were back-packing across Europe over the summer, aiming to end up in Pamplona so they could run in front of the bulls. From my point of view, bulls running down a street at me would be a good indication I should be somewhere else, and since the event was world-famous there was no real excuse for failing to avoid it.

But he was only nineteen, and ten years makes a big difference. Maybe that's part of being young: challenging your mortality; sneaking up to Death and smacking it around the face a bit, then running away and feeling invincible because it ignored you. The truth is that when mortality means business it'll steamroll straight over you no matter how fast you fucking run. But I quite liked Dean, and I hoped he came out of it with whatever affirmation of existence he thought he needed.

He wasn't there when I got back. The window was slightly open, and I could hear the call of seagulls drifting in with the breeze, and smell air that had skimmed the scent off the water.

I shrugged my T-shirt off, sprayed on some deodorant, and then picked a fresh top from the small pile I kept under the bunk.

Before I put it on, I looked at myself in the thin mirror on the wardrobe door. I saw a thirty-year-old man with long blond hair, rough stubble, and a solid tan. Bare living had stripped a lot of excess weight from my body, so that it looked functional and strong, like a piece of rope designed to carry something, day after day. Anyone who had once known a young man named Alex Connor would barely have recognised him standing here. Even for me, it felt like I was looking at a stranger, or at the reflection of somebody who wasn't really there.

I slipped the T-shirt on, then headed down for a drink.

The lounge in this hostel was how I imagined a rec-room in a prison: a high ceiling and drab paintwork, with lots of tatty old armchairs dotted around. There was a pool table at one end, and a small television mounted on a spike in the wall at the other. Halfway between, glass doors were propped open onto a patio overlooking a particularly effluent stretch of canal. I bought myself a bottled euro-beer from reception then headed in.

A few groups of young travellers were sitting around talking. A girl was holding her hair back from a beaming red tan, brushing it into a ponytail with her hands. Everyone seemed excited, keen, eager. It was the same with most of the young travellers I'd met over the last two years. If they stepped off a building, they expected a safety-net to have been erected the night before. As with Dean's potential suicide-by-cattle, perhaps it should have annoyed me, but it didn't. I remembered feeling that way myself, and I missed it. I certainly didn't want to kill anyone's joy, like some bitter old grandfather standing at the edge of the playground shouting obscenities.

I went out onto the patio, resting my elbows on the flaking paint, and watched the water slap gently against the side of the canal. The evening sun cut against it, highlighting the dense water. Everything was still and peaceful, and I closed my eyes for a second, breathing it in. When I opened them, an immaculate woman in sunglasses and high heels was clicking past on the cobbled walkway opposite. She had a big square bag and a sense of purpose. Behind me, back inside, I could hear people laughing.

'Who are you?'

It was a man's voice, from right beside me, and it sounded slightly disgruntled. I turned my head, and there was nobody there.

I took a swig from my beer and watched as the woman headed up some steps and disappeared around a corner, out of sight; she might have been moving into a different world altogether. Behind me, the laughter sounded much further away than it had before, as though I wasn't only separated from the people in there by distance or age, but by something more profound. The sadness was like a grey curtain, unravelling quickly down inside me.

It was time to move on. *Tomorrow*.

I went back into the lounge, figuring I'd take the bottle up to my room. Head out for some food in a bit, maybe, then turn in and try to sleep through the cycle of chart hits pounding dully through the walls. Get an early start—

Instead, halfway across, I stopped.

I wasn't even sure why at first. There was something on the TV. I knew that much. But it took me a second to recognise it and find a frame of reference in which to fit it.

Sarah is on the television.

A photograph of her was taking up the left-hand side of the screen. It was an old picture, and one I half recognised. She was outside somewhere, squinting against the sun, with her bright red hair and a slightly lop-sided smile. Her face took up most of the image, but I could see grass in one corner, and she was leaning back against the shoulder of someone behind her on the left.

The red banner at the bottom of the screen said:

FIELD SEARCHED AFTER FIVE DAY HUNT

The right-hand side showed an aerial shot of a field. The footage appeared to be live, taken from a helicopter that was circling overhead. On the ground below, a large tent had been constructed next to a hedge, and small white figures were moving around it. Some were picking through the grass a little distance away. There was no sound.

I stepped between some armchairs by the television, and looked down at the girl sitting nearest.

'Is there any way of turning the volume up?'

'What?'

'The volume?'

I tried the side of the set. The cheap plastic creaked, but I couldn't find any controls. It filled me with an absurd sense of powerlessness.

'What,' the girl said, 'you know her?'

I started to answer, but then the screen changed.

The right-hand side now showed a reporter talking into a microphone. Behind him, I could see a country lane, and a gate with a policeman stationed in front of it. And on the left-hand side, Sarah's photograph had now been replaced by another.

This one showed my brother, James.

Three

Two and a half years ago, on the day of Marie's funeral, a strange thing happened. I woke up and absolutely nothing was wrong. It lasted for a couple of seconds. Then I noticed the empty bed beside me, registered the silence of the surrounding house, and I remembered what my wife had done.

At that point, I swung myself out of bed and away from everything. It was still early days, but that was already how I'd learned to deal with things: by hiding from them or running away. I'd never been like Sarah, determined to face problems head on. Instead, I kept myself moving. It was as though the impact of what had happened was genuinely physical, a punch I could slip if I ducked quickly enough. One that, if it landed square-on, would knock me flat.

I showered, then went downstairs and made coffee with a dash of vodka in it, and then put on my suit. From eleven o'clock, I started going through the motions of opening the door to welcome friends as they arrived, enduring all the well-meant words and hesitant pats on the shoulder.

And then, at some point, I went through the kitchen and out into the back garden, ostensibly for a cigarette, and I walked away.

It was easier than it should have been, but I suppose there wasn't much to it physically, and it seemed to happen almost on auto-pilot. I just started walking: slowly at first, then moving faster, until, by the time I reached the end of the street, I was running, my heart thumping in my chest.

I felt absolutely exhilarated.

At two o'clock, when the service was due to start, I was sitting in the beer garden of a small pub called The Cockerel. It was a rough, old drinkers' pub on the arse edge of the Grindlea estate. The winter's day was clear and sharp, but it felt precarious. The rain last night had been heavy, landing against my bedroom window like handfuls of stones, and there were still dirty puddles of rainwater in the gutter now. The air remained damp from it, and the world itself seemed like it was quietly shivering, as though it had been soaked through and then left out in the cold.

I sat at a rickety wooden bench and drank beer after beer, vodka after vodka, observing the minute hand of my watch with an almost professional detachment.

The minister will be telling them how wonderful Marie was.
And she was.

A minute later: *he'll be using the word 'tragedy'.*

The whole time, my attention kept being drawn to a house across the road. Cars flashed past in between. On the face of it, it was an innocuous building, with nothing obvious to distinguish it from its neighbours. Just another red-brick semi with the curtains shut tight and the paint peeling from its old front door. The small garden out front was unkempt and bedraggled, like hair the owner didn't see a point in combing any more.

Eventually, my latest glass was empty and it was time to get another. After I'd paid and gone back outside, I found Sarah sitting at my table.

She had long, bright-red hair, a pretty face covered in freckles, and she was wearing a black jacket, with a black blouse and trousers beneath. I paused, then walked over and sat down, putting my beer and vodka on the table between us.

'I didn't know you were coming,' I said. 'I'd have got you a drink.'

She picked up the vodka.

'This one's fine. Fancy seeing you here.'

'Yeah,' I said. 'Imagine.'

'Cheers, anyway.'

Sarah raised the glass, then winced as she took a sip.

'Neat. Well, I did have a hard time finding you, to be honest. I drove around a while. Tried the usual places.'

'There'd be no point hiding in one of those.'

That, at least, got a grim smile. 'Any reason for this place?'

'Just fancied a change of scene.'

'Lovely scenery.' She glanced around dubiously, then back at me. 'People are worried about you. I guess you know that.'

'It's none of their business.'

'OK. So your friends and family aren't important.'

I sipped my beer and said nothing. The harsh truth was that my friends and family meant absolutely nothing to me right then. But I hadn't quite reached the point where I'd say so out loud. After all, Sarah had come looking for me, just as I should have known she would. That had always been her nature: to go looking for people; to pick them up when they fell. As shit as I felt, I wasn't about to throw that back in her face, and so it was safer to say nothing at all.

Sarah tapped the bench.

'J's really annoyed at you for running out.'

That didn't even deserve a reply. Seeing my brother at the house that morning had been the day's most awkward moment, this current one notwithstanding. It was stupid and unfair, but I couldn't help thinking that, deep down, James might be secretly pleased Marie was dead. After all, his little brother had always been the one with the grades, the good job, the girlfriends, whereas all James had collected was minor criminal convictions – fighting, mainly – and a string of abandoned jobs and broken relationships. From his perspective, life had treated him pretty badly, while everything had gone lucky for me. *Finally,* he was probably thinking. *Your turn.*

'He's right, though,' Sarah said. 'You can't just . . . run away from what's happened, you know. You need to face up to it.'

Again, I said nothing.

'I wish you'd talk to me, Alex.'

'What would you like me to say?'

'I don't know. It's hard for me as well. She was my friend too.'

I nodded, feeling even worse now.

Sarah had actually known Marie longer than I had, and they'd been very close. I imagined she was taking it badly, partly for the same reasons as me, and also because Sarah's relationship with death had always been a strange one. I first met her when she came to live with her aunt in Whitrow, after her father's suicide. We were both ten. But even now, when I looked at her as an adult, I could still see that same little girl in her face. There had always been this odd mixture of sadness and determination to her, as though life had presented her with a painful problem that she was absolutely intent on solving.

I could never decide whether that was a good or bad thing: to be that young and to have already found your calling. These days, Sarah worked as a crime correspondent at the *Evening Paper*, and it suited her down to the ground. Death was something she'd always been driven to confront and understand. You couldn't deal with anything, she thought, by turning away from it. I had no doubt that right now she was dwelling on all the things I was too scared even to allow in my head.

So a part of me felt bad for this selfish behaviour of mine. However, a larger part was far more apathetic. My wife had died. Could people please leave me the fuck alone?

'And *you're* my friend too,' Sarah said. 'So talk to me.'

'I don't know what to say.'

'Tell me what you're thinking.'

I shrugged. Most of the time, I didn't dare think anything. Because, when I did, it felt dangerous. I'd picture myself standing in the middle of the street and screaming so loud that it levelled the place. The sound I'd make would strip leaves from the trees. It would pulverise houses and scatter brick dust and glass for miles. Shatter streetlights and knock birds from the sky. And none of it would achieve anything because, at the end, when I closed my mouth, I'd still be there.

I said, 'I miss her.'

And then looked down at the bench and got a grip on my tears. How flimsy I was: just saying it out loud had been enough to puncture my resolve. I was disgusted with myself. Back then, I didn't even know about the insurance policy, but the feeling of guilt was already overwhelming. How could I have let her down so badly? How could I not have *known*?

Sarah reached out and rested her hand gently on mine.

'Me too,' she said.

'I miss her so much.'

'But you've got to hold on to the good memories, Alex. That's where Marie is now, and you need to try to remember her smiling. I know it seems impossible at the moment, but you've got to believe that it won't do for ever . . .'

She looked at me, then sighed.

'Let's get out of here, OK?' she said. 'Go somewhere else.'

'I don't want to see anybody.'

'You don't have to. We'll just go together. You and me. I'll leave the car somewhere, and we'll disappear off, get pissed out of our minds. Talk about whatever. And if you don't want to, then I'll talk *at* you and you can pretend to listen.'

I almost smiled.

'But I'm not leaving you on your own, Alex.'

That was for certain. I knew her too well to think I'd be able to shake her off now. To Sarah, tragedy and loss were contagious, and she wasn't about to lose me too.

I nodded. 'All right. Thank you.'

'It's nothing,' she said. 'We're always there for each other, aren't we? Always have been. Always will be.'

'Yes.'

'And if it was the other way round,' she said, 'you'd be there for me too.'

*

I didn't know exactly what I'd been planning on doing that day, but I think it's very possible that Sarah saved me. Not in a dramatic way, but in the ordinary and everyday sense – by just finding me when I was stumbling, then hooking an arm round, determined not to let me fall. And she kept doing that. She had a knack for reading between my lines and knowing when I needed her, and, on those occasions, she'd come over and be there for me.

Looking back, it reminds me of when someone is seriously injured, and a friend sits with them, determined to keep them awake until help arrives. *Come on*, they say; *stay with me*. If I let you slip away now, you might never come back.

But in the end, that's what happened. As hard as she tried, she couldn't save me for ever.

The last time I saw Sarah was six months after the funeral, just after I'd learned about the insurance policy Marie had taken out. It was the middle of the night, and I turned up at her house drunk out of my mind, and wearing only a T-shirt and jeans, even though it was pouring down with torrential rain. At that moment, I simply had no idea where else to go.

Only a few weeks after that, I was sitting in a hotel room, writing her a letter. I was trying to explain. I told her that she'd been right all along: that death has to be faced down, or else it spreads and destroys your life. I told her I couldn't bear what my life had now become, and that I had to get away from it: to try to find a new Alex Connor. I told her I was sorry and that I hoped she could forgive me.

Then, in the morning, I left for the airport.

You could sum up those six months with a single image: my friend's fingertips brushing against mine as I stubbornly refused to take her hand. As we fell slowly, sadly apart, until I wasn't touching her any more. Until I wasn't touching anything.

Four

The guy at reception shrugged when I asked him about the TV volume. It was remote control only, he said, and he didn't know where it had disappeared to.

'Somebody has perhaps . . .'

He made a throwing gesture, and I made a mental note to be less forgiving in future of the young, care-free spirits in the lounge.

I headed out to the railway station round the corner. It was full of frustrated international travellers: guys with shades balanced on their heads talking into mobiles, and girls sitting on luggage, knees together, looking forlorn. There was a magazine stand at the far side of the station, and I bought an English newspaper, took it back outside and sat down at the top of the steps.

My hand was shaking as I flicked through the pages, one by one. I was searching for any coverage of what might have happened. Already, I was doubting what I'd just seen on the television. Only a few minutes had passed, but that was long enough for it to have become surreal.

It couldn't possibly be . . .

But on the fifth page, there it was.

MAN CHARGED: POLICE APPEAL FOR HELP IN HUNT FOR WOMAN'S BODY

by Barry Jenkins

The boyfriend of a woman he confessed to killing appeared in court yesterday and was charged with her murder.

James Connor, 32, was remanded in custody. He is accused of killing Sarah Pepper, 30, his partner, who was living with him in Whitrow at the time of her death.

Outside Whitrow Crown Court, police continued to ask for help in locating Ms Pepper's body.

Det. Geoff Hunter, who is leading the murder inquiry, appealed for farmers and ramblers to report anything unusual they saw in fields and woodland.

He said: 'This is obviously a very distressing period for Sarah's friends and family, and we need the public's help in locating her remains as quickly as possible.'

Officers have conducted extensive searches of the Whitrow countryside since Mr Connor approached the police on the morning of 2 June. The unemployed man claimed the couple had argued over his drinking and Ms Pepper was planning to leave him. He confessed to killing her at their home on 1 June, but was unable to remember where he had hidden her remains.

A local taxi driver confirmed he had been booked to collect Ms Pepper from the couple's home address, but upon arrival was told by her boyfriend she had already left.

Ms Pepper's body is thought to have been left in woodland, and may be partially concealed under leaves and branches.

Det. Hunter said: 'We would ask the public to be on the lookout for a wooden gate set in a drystone wall. Our information leads us to believe there may be two empty vodka bottles nearby.'

Mr Connor appeared in court accompanied by a police guard. He gave his name, date of birth and confirmed his address. There was no application for bail.

I looked up. The top of the steps was shaded by the station building, and a slight breeze rustled the pages of the newspaper. Below, an expanse of bright, sunlit stone spread out, dotted with people. As I watched them all, my heartbeat was visible in front of me: a red pulse appearing like silk at the edges of my vision.

Living with him, I thought.

The newspaper had yesterday's date, so this report was from the day before, when Sarah had still been missing. According to the television back at the hostel, she had just been found. That wouldn't appear here in the papers until the day after tomorrow.

Her *body* had just been found, I reminded myself.

Not Sarah. Sarah was gone.

I wasn't sure what I was feeling. It wasn't grief exactly. There was the same initial sense of disbelief – the same slap that knocks you off-kilter – but it still didn't seem real and I couldn't fit the facts into my head. Sarah was dead and my brother had killed her.

Ridiculous. Couldn't be happening.

But then, I thought about it some more. One of the earliest memories I have is of my brother. In it, James is red-faced and *screaming*, the cords in his neck standing out as he throws a cushion at our mother.

Put like that, it doesn't sound so bad. It was only a cushion, after all. But she was a small woman, and the frightening part was that it wouldn't have mattered what he'd been holding at the time. The cushion had just been the nearest thing to hand. If he'd been able to reach a knife, he would have thrown that instead.

I was three or four years old at the time. I remember pushing the heels of my palms into my eyes and screaming, trying to make it all go away. My mother said something, James shouted back, and then a door slammed. Then I felt my mother's arm around me, holding me close. Afterwards, she was upstairs in James's room, talking softly. I could hear him crying, and perhaps she was too.

That had always been my brother's way, and he'd kept it up well into adulthood. He got angry, lost control and struck out at the world. Acted without thought, and then said sorry afterwards.

So I tried to imagine it: James squatting down beside Sarah's body, knocking back vodka to numb the panic and remorse from what he'd done. At first, he would probably have been blaming her. Then he would have begun to panic as he drank more and more, and the realisation hit that he'd gone too far to say sorry this time. Making some stupid attempt to hide what he'd done, then waking up the next morning and knowing there was no way to carry it off.

Horribly, it wasn't so hard to do.

Five days.

I felt that inside me. Sarah had been missing for that long: the days flicking on and off as she lay there, discarded and forgotten. I'd gone about my business without the slightest inkling that anything had happened to her. And back at the hostel, I'd been watching real-time coverage of the scene. Breaking news. Which meant that, hundreds of miles away, my friend's body was lying beneath the white tent I'd seen on the screen *right now*.

At least I'd seen it. My plan after Venice had been to head South towards Rimini, with a possible eye to catching a ferry. If I'd missed the report today, it might have dropped from the schedule by the next time I caught any international news, and I would never have known.

And that would have been better.

The thought came from nowhere.

For a moment, I didn't do anything. I could hear the gulls reeling overhead, and the *trick* of wheeled cases pulled along by travellers. Ordinary people going about their ordinary lives. The warm air smelled of the sea.

It wasn't an actual voice in my head, more of a feeling inside me, roughly associated with the small curl of panic that had appeared close to my heart. But if it was a voice, it would have had the no-nonsense edge of someone being practical about something that might look unpalatable but was, actually, very important to get right. The kind of voice that said: let me take charge of this delicate matter. You go put your feet up. When you get back I'll have done what needs doing and you won't need to think about it again.

These people are not part of your life anymore.

And no. They weren't.

In the letter I sent to Sarah before I left, I wrote: *At the moment, I'm not sure where I'm going. All I know is that I have to get away.* It had been true. But in the time since, I'd slowly lost touch with my old life entirely. The visits to Internet cafés had fallen by the wayside. If there was any guilt attached, I'd shrugged that away too. I hadn't thought about Sarah for weeks, if not longer. Losing touch and cutting yourself off can look remarkably similar, assuming they take place so gradually that you never have to look too carefully.

You don't want to remember how bad it was.

The panic throbbed gently inside. On one level, I knew it was justified. Because it was easy, with two years' distance, to forget how hard something had been. The weeks before I left had been so difficult I found it hard to remember them now, but I knew that leaving had stopped them from destroying me, and travelling ever since had kept me one step ahead. If I had cut off my old life, I'd been doing it to save myself.

But it also struck me now that leaving had never properly worked. Could I carry on like this for ever? Everywhere I went, I felt nothing but emptiness, waiting to be filled; every few days, I still found myself packing up and moving on. It was as though staying in one place for any length of time provided me with an address there, and then mail I'd left behind began to be forwarded on. However painful it had been, I hadn't escaped those feelings. They'd trailed after me.

Maybe it was everything else that I'd lost.

I opened the newspaper again. Beside the article, there was the same photograph they'd used on the television, only this time in black and white. Sarah looked so unguarded in it, caught almost by surprise. The tilt of her head, her smile: they were instantly familiar, just as I would have pictured her.

And I recognised where it had come from now.

It was from when we'd all gone away to the Lakes years ago: six of us crammed into a camper-van we rented for the week. Me and Marie. Julie and Mike. And Sarah had been with some randomer called Damian at the time. We'd arrived at Coniston on the first day, and that was where this photo had been taken. It was my wife who was holding the camera. The shoulder that Sarah was leaning back against, in that checked shirt, would be mine.

The memory brought a wave of guilt. How could I have forgotten this? Even Marie – I remembered her holding my hand back then as we walked slightly behind the others. Her grip had felt tentative, but it had been there, and it had been determined in its own way: a small expression of hope. At that moment in time, whatever happened afterwards, I'd made her happy.

I sat there for a while, staring blankly at the photograph, carefully prodding at the memory and checking for any signs of pain. There weren't any. The only thing that came was a terrible sense of sadness, not just for the things that had been taken from me, but for all the things I'd given away afterwards. All the things I realised now that I missed so badly.

Sarah . . .

And most of all, I remembered how hard she'd fought to help me in the months after Marie's death. She'd always come searching, determined not to let me slip away as well. And yet, when she'd needed me in turn, I'd been deliberately looking the other way.

We're always there for each other.

I closed my eyes.

If it was the other way round, you'd be there for me too.

Five

Rebecca Wingate was standing right there in front of him.

She was wearing the black trouser suit he recognised from the photograph, and it stood out, clear and sharp, against the swirl of mist around them both. One strand of her hair was loose, hanging down beside her ear like a ribbon. He watched her stare anxiously to the left and right, as though she couldn't quite remember what had happened for the last few hours and didn't know where she was.

Kearney took a step forwards.

He'd found her.

'Rebecca,' he said. 'It's OK now.'

She turned at the sound of his voice. That was when the man emerged from the mist behind her. He was emaciated and his skin was jaundiced and hazy with fuzz, like the forearms of an anorexic. But he moved quickly, wrapping his arm around Rebecca Wingate's neck from behind and yanking her backwards. She screamed.

Kearney started running towards them. But the man was impossibly strong. Rebecca was disappearing into the mist, with one hand reaching out for him. He gritted his teeth and *concentrated* on that hand. When he reached the place it had been, everything around him was simply grey, and all he could hear was screaming, so far in the distance it might just have been an echo in his head.

And then he was half out of bed, one of his feet stamping

uselessly against the rough carpet, like he was trying to kick-start a motorcycle.

Jesus Christ.

His heart was bouncing.

Just a dream. Deep—

But his breath caught as he saw the yellow man was crouched at the end of the bed, the knuckles of his spine standing out, like some bony creature hunkered down at the edge of a pool. A split-second later, the yellow man resolved himself into the outline of a washing basket, full of old clothes.

Kearney stared at it. He was a grown man and he was trembling. It took a few more seconds before he managed a quiet, humourless laugh at his own expense. The details of the nightmare were already fading, the way they always did, leaving behind only the knowledge they had been awful.

He rubbed his face. Damp with sweat.

A wedge of pale blue morning light was cutting in through a gap in the curtains. Around him, the pipes in the walls had already begun their early morning creaking and clicking. The alarm clock at the side of the bed was silent, the red numbers bright in the gloom. It was nearly half-past five. That was too late to bother with any more sleep, assuming he could even have managed it, but he was still shaking a little, and so he simply sat there.

On the other side of the bedroom, his computer monitor – old, grey and lifeless for the moment – was balanced on a cheap plywood desk. The bookcase beside it was full of his files, printouts and carefully written notes. He'd stayed up there working last night, bathed in the soft light of the screen, and then fallen into bed about two or three hours ago. As always, it was no wonder the bad dreams had been able to find him so easily. They only needed to follow him across the room.

Never again.

But he thought that every day, and it never worked. Every evening, he still found himself sat across there, trawling online for answers. And then, every morning, he woke up with the same sense of futility. This determination to stop. It was the way he imagined an alcoholic might feel after a long night alone in a bar.

And in between, the nightmares. He had always suffered, but this year they'd become far worse: horrific, breathless, and endlessly inventive. Sometimes he dreamed there were ghosts crowding him, watching, their features as stern and frozen as the faces in sepia photographs. There were shadows that crawled in flickering stops and starts. And of course, there was the yellow man.

Still looking at the computer, he was angry with himself.

You're making yourself sick. You know you are.

That was true. But he felt that every morning, and it wasn't enough to make him stop.

Kearney was well-known in the department for getting too involved: for demanding answers to the questions that other cops had long since learned were more sensible to avoid. They just wanted the who and maybe the how, but Kearney always needed to search out the why. He felt compelled to look at something until it made sense. Until he could comprehend it.

That was exactly the problem.

Todd Dennis, Kearney's partner, had told him once that police work was dangerous in the same way the sea was. From a high enough altitude, Todd said, it looked calm and peaceful. But however tempted you were, it was always a mistake to head down for a closer look. Because the waves didn't care about you, and they carried on regardless; you wouldn't find answers to make sense of them. All you'd find down there was a million identical places to drown.

Kearney got up and headed for the shower.

Then he put on his suit and ate breakfast slowly, thinking of the investigation that was waiting for him. The one that had, in a roundabout way, started him on this descent.

Operation Butterfly had been running at various speeds for the last four years, with the number of men assigned to it ebbing and flowing in an irregular heartbeat. The peaks represented the confirmed killings of three women and the disappearance and suspected murder of two others.

In all five cases, the abduction scenario had been almost identical. The women had been taken late at night on their way home, and their cars were found abandoned along quiet stretches of road, the passenger doors left hanging open and the interiors bright in the darkness. It looked as though the women had pulled over for some reason, and the killer had emerged from the undergrowth and stolen them away.

In serial enquiries such as this, Kearney found himself remembering the first and last victims most vividly. The others mattered just as much, but the first and last circumscribed the investigation. They held it in place like bookends.

Linda Holloway was the first. In life, she had been a solicitor, married, successful and happy. In death, her killer had dumped her body in a wooded gully north of the city. When they found her, she was bright white and lying face up in the mulch of autumn leaves, with coins of wet mud on her skin. There was no blood at the scene, and none remaining in her body; the autopsy revealed a number of insertion points on her right arm, the bore and bruising consistent with that of an industrial syringe, and the cause of death was ruled to be exsanguination. For reasons unknown, Linda Holloway's abductor had bled her over a period of days until the process eventually killed her.

Six months afterwards, the second known victim, Melissa Noble, was taken. Her body had never been found. Next was Kerekes, then Slater at the end of last year. Both were eventually found lying on riverbanks. Price, abducted in January, remained missing.

Five victims. Three bodies.

And the other end of the investigation was Rebecca Wingate. Over the last few days, Kearney had spent a long time staring at one particular photograph of Rebecca. She was young and attractive, with her hair tied back, and she was wearing a black suit that she looked a little nervous and unsure in. Every time he saw it, Kearney felt a desperate urge to reach into the picture and take her hand.

Rebecca Wingate's car had been discovered four days ago, abandoned by the roadside. One door was hanging open, and the indicator light was still blinking, as though in shock at what had happened.

Somewhere, Kearney told himself, she was still alive.

It wasn't just in his dreams.

Half-past eight.

Fully composed now, he parked up. In front of him, the police department's new building was enormous and imposing: a block of shining steel and glass, glinting in the sun. It was ten storeys high. The bottom three floors were wider than the ones above, and then the top slanted to a point in one corner. It looked like a sword piercing the sky. Kearney had a vague idea it was meant to.

He drummed out a quick solo on his knees.

First things first.

That meant finding Simon Wingate in reception.

Wingate was wearing a black suit and sitting with his elbows resting on his knees, hands clasped in front of him, staring down at the floor. For the last four days, since his wife had gone missing, he'd presented exactly the same figure, exactly the same pose. He kept almost perfectly still.

Kearney had worked traffic accidents before. He'd sat with the relatives of victims outside hospital wards at two in the morning while they waited for news, their fingers twitching anxiously, and so he recognised a vigil when he saw one. The difference was that people in a hospital could at least expect news of some kind, but nobody could guarantee Simon Wingate anything.

Wingate must have known that, but he continued to turn up regardless, and that made other cops nervous. They couldn't quite figure out what he wanted. Todd had actually started coming in the side entrance to avoid him.

35

He's like a fucking . . . angel of death, or something.
I think you mean 'judgement'.
Whatever.

Every day, Wingate faced the world with the top of his bowed head. He was thirty, but he looked older. Rebecca Wingate was slightly younger: only twenty-seven. Kearney pictured her face again now and felt sad as he sat down beside her husband.

'Good morning, Simon. How are you holding together?'

Wingate just shook his head. He rarely looked up or spoke more than a few words. Nevertheless, Kearney made a point of sitting with him like this every morning. It felt wrong to leave him alone.

'Can I get you anything?' he said.

'No.' Wingate shook his head again. 'I'm sorry. I don't want to bother anyone.'

'You're not. I promise.'

'I just don't know what else to do.'

'I know.'

'Where else to be.'

Kearney nodded. He understood. There was no point Wingate being anywhere right now, because his wife wouldn't be with him. This place – horribly – was as close as he could get to her until she was found.

'You can sit here all day, Simon. The moment we have any news, I'll let you know.'

Wingate nodded. 'Is there anything I can do?'

Every morning, he asked that question. The man was self-educated and ran a small but successful security business that he'd built up from scratch. This was impossible territory for him. He was used to being in charge – tackling and solving the problems that came his way – and now he felt suddenly disabled.

Where possible, Kearney made an effort to spend these short periods of time with the relatives of victims, and he'd seen this reaction a number of times. There was always pain. There was always fear. Ultimately, there was usually grief. All of those took their turns at being unbearable, but the sense of being powerless was constant, and often the hardest thing of all for people to deal with. So Kearney felt for Wingate, but all he could offer him was the same answer he always gave.

'You can stay strong.' He rubbed his hands together slowly. 'You can keep yourself in one piece. And you can keep believing that we'll find Rebecca. Because we *will* find her. Look at me, Simon.'

Wingate did look at him. His gaze moved up slowly, revealing eyes that were pink and tired. Devoid of hope. Life, even. Kearney kept his own face firm, his expression resolute.

'We *will* find her,' he repeated. 'I promise you.'

Wingate stared back. Kearney was a slight man and looked younger than he was, but his eyes were piercing and serious. Kearney's ex-wife, Anna, had told him he was a reassuring presence. *People believe you, and they trust you to help them.* She said he looked capable and dependable. And that was true. Whatever turbulence was going on below, the surface remained calm.

Wingate nodded carefully. A delicate gesture, as though he was scared it might break. Then he looked back down at the floor.

'Thank you, Detective.'

Kearney stood up. 'Take care, Simon. I'll see you soon.'

Wingate didn't reply, so Kearney said nothing more. He keyed himself through behind the reception desk and waited for the lift to arrive.

A stupid thing to say.

That was another observation his colleagues would have made. Detective Paul Kearney – always making stupid promises he couldn't keep. He knew full well that what he'd just told Simon Wingate was absurd. There were no guarantees they would find Rebecca at all, never mind alive. And given the way he felt himself disintegrating, Kearney couldn't even be sure he'd still be around if they did.

37

But he'd made the promise anyway. Because it was what the man needed to hear right now. Because there was nothing else worth saying.

The elevator doors *hushed* open. He emerged into an open office full of cubicle desks and people talking on headsets. The air hummed with the subdued murmur of phone conversations, and he could smell the clean carpets and polish. At the far side of the office, sky-bright windows looked out over the city. In the distance, the ring road, with all its bridges and underpasses, looked like a series of drab, grey ribbons, tied loosely in bows.

Kearney made his way across, then down the corridor to the office he shared with Todd.

His thoughts returned to Anna.

She'd always said he was dependable, yes, but her perspective on that had changed. The marriage had ended last year, as a result of Kearney drifting – slightly helplessly – into a brief affair. It was a painful memory, but thoughts of both Simon Wingate and his own nightmares kept leading inexorably back to it.

When Anna found out what he'd done, she told him that the worst thing wasn't the affair itself, but every single false 'I love you' he'd uttered to her while it was going on. Afterwards, she'd gone over them in her head, and felt each one as a separate stab of betrayal. Promises that he had known could never be kept, but which he'd made in an attempt to fool them both.

That was the worst thing, she said – far worse than what he'd done. It was the deception that hurt her the most.

Six

I wasn't expecting a fanfare when the plane landed and I didn't get one. But I did feel something as I stepped off the plane onto the tarmac. It wasn't electricity, exactly, just a tingle that passed from the soles of my feet up my legs and into my chest – and then seemed to drift away on the light breeze. As though the sensation had been checking it was me and had now hurried away to tell someone I'd arrived.

It was a warm day. Nowhere near as dense a heat as I'd left behind in Italy, but the sky above was clear blue, with a flock of birds heading across, the formation rippling like a fingerprint pressed on water. At ground-level, an enormous expanse of tarmac and yellow lines, with a low, flat terminal in the distance.

I was home.

After a few moments, a single-decker bus arrived, beeping quietly, and I boarded it, taking hold of a rubber strap hanging from the roof. It jolted and sped off, and I watched the plane recede through the back window. At baggage collection, I stood by the conveyor belt, arms folded, foot tapping, watching the luggage pass. I was travelling light, as always. When my small rucksack appeared, I picked it up and walked away quickly.

Two minutes later, I was standing in the throng of the main airport, helpless as a rock in a stream. All around me, for the first time in two years, there was English conversation. It was almost overwhelming. It felt like I'd been sitting in silence for a long time and someone had just turned on twenty televisions.

After finding a cash point and buying a newspaper, I went outside and found the taxi rank.

'Where are you going, mate?'

'Town centre.' I closed the door.

As he drove, I turned my attention to the newspaper. With the crime being local, I'd expected Sarah to be front page news, but she wasn't. Instead, there was a photograph of a different girl below the headline:

FEARS GROW FOR MISSING REBECCA

I scanned it briefly, then opened the paper and found the article on Sarah relegated to the third page:

POLICE SEARCH FIELD IN HUNT FOR BODY

I read it through, but it only confirmed more-or-less what I'd learned yesterday. A walker had spotted the discarded vodka bottles by a wall and called it in. Forensic teams had been on site since yesterday afternoon. And so on.

Something about the wording bothered me though. The whole article seemed a little more non-committal than the report I'd watched yesterday. There had been no official confirmation, for one thing. No further comments from Detective Hunter. And then there was that headline. Police were *searching* the field. And saying *hunt* implied it was ongoing.

I leaned forward.

'Have you been following that murder case?' I said. Then I glanced at the paper's front cover and figured I'd better clarify that. 'The girl in the field, I mean?'

'Everyone has.' The taxi driver shook his head. 'Terrible.'

'They've found her, haven't they? It's definitely her.'

'Yeah. They've not said, but what else can it be?'

I sat back, still uneasy. But he was right, of course. The gate, the bottles: it matched the description James had given. So what else could it be? The police might not have confirmed it yet, but maybe they took their time with things like that. The headline might just be worded cautiously.

'You know what gets me the most?' the driver said.

One of his hands was resting lazily on the steering wheel, and his tone of voice suggested he'd mentioned this to a few people.

'What?'

'That she was lying out there all that time.' He shook his head again. 'Sad to think of that.'

Lying out there for five days. Yes, it was sad, and I felt that guilt again. It was irrational, because even if I'd been here, I doubted I could have done anything. But it still felt like I'd let her down somehow. Perhaps it was just because it was sad, and when something like that happens you automatically think of all the ways you could have stopped it. Sadness blurs things, like tears, and it's all too easy for *could* to become *should*.

'Well, at least someone's found her now,' I said.

The driver nodded.

'Yeah,' he said. 'Does look that way.'

Two years is a strange length of time to be away from a city.

As we closed in on the centre, I started to recognise the areas we were passing through, and it was an odd sensation. I'd expected the streets here to be filled with old memories, almost as though they'd been waiting around for me, but the opposite was true. In my absence, the place seemed to have become slightly unfamiliar, and I found myself observing it from a distance, noticing the changes and then feeling unsure whether they were real or I'd simply forgotten how it always was.

There certainly wasn't any obvious justification for the sense of dread I'd been feeling. Returning here wasn't anything like as painful as I'd worried it might be.

See? I told myself. *This isn't so bad.*

Maybe it was even good.

I had the driver drop me by the train station, and then went to a slightly seedy hotel behind it called the Everton. Apart from the vertical neon sign hanging down, it looked more like a bland, grey office block than a place to sleep. I had no idea if my lack of permanent residence was going to be a problem, although I could give the address of the storage unit I'd rented if

41

I needed to. But if anywhere in the city was going to rent a room no questions asked, I figured this would probably be the place.

The receptionist didn't bat an eyelid.

'How long will you be staying?' he asked. His tone of voice suggested they took bookings from one hour upwards.

'A week,' I guessed. 'We'll take it from there.'

He raised an eyebrow.

'Payment up front for that.'

I clicked my card down on the counter.

Top floor. I looked around my room. It was small, containing little more than a single bed at one end, a wash-basin at the other, and a thin shelf running along at waist-height that was intended to be a desk. I opened a door – found a toilet and shower cubicle – and closed it again. There was a small window out onto a fire-escape, but nothing to see through it apart from a saw-blade silhouette of industrial roofs.

I put my bag down on the bed and went for a shower.

Half an hour later, I was washed, changed and in a different taxi, heading across town to my first port of call. I'd known Mike since university, and, with Sarah gone, he was the closest thing I had to a friend still living in the city. Under normal circumstances I'd probably have been round there right now. That's what friends do when something hits them hard: they congregate and band together. But when the taxi driver dropped me off outside, I realised this had probably been my first mistake.

The house looked almost the same from the outside – a red-brick semi with a small garden out front, a brown wooden car-port over the drive – but there were a few telling differences. The smart white family saloon in the driveway, for one. No way was that fast enough for Mike. And the buzz-cut on the front lawn was, by any stretch of the imagination, far too much effort.

Most of all, I'd always recognised the house from the stickers in the front window: DayGlo pink and yellow stars taped to the inside of the glass. He'd had them at uni, then got hold of a new set when he bought this place shortly afterwards. They weren't there any more. Those stars were so indelibly associated with him that if they were gone I was sure he must be too.

I hesitated on the pavement as the taxi pulled away – then decided I could at least knock. Whoever lived here now might at least have a contact address for forwarding on post.

When he opened the door, it took us both a second to recognise each other.

I got there first. Mike had cut his hair and was wearing an untucked work shirt and suit trousers, but he hadn't changed all that much because he hadn't tried to. From his point of view, though, God only knew what he saw. I was tanned, un-shaven, unkempt, and dressed in clothes that probably still had at least a patina of dust from abroad. It seemed that what I'd thought in the hostel was true. People who'd known the old Alex Connor wouldn't recognise him now.

'Mike,' I said.

His eyes went wide.

'Alex? Jesus Christ, man.'

He glanced back into the house, then looked at me again and shook his head, unable to believe he was seeing me. For a moment, neither of us knew what to do.

Then he stepped out and threw his arms around me.

The physical contact was a shock. My hands hovered for a second, and then I hugged him back, a little uncertainly. He stepped away, but kept his hands on the side of my arms, and peered intensely at my face, as though it had done some kind of magic trick and he was trying to figure it out.

I felt helpless. 'How are you doing?'

'How am *I* doing? Fuck that, man. How are *you*?'

I opened my mouth to answer – somehow – but he'd left the question hanging, and was already dragging me inside, calling up to the landing above.

'Julie! Come down!'

I had time to look around the corridor and think *well, he's decorated,* and then I heard Julie coming down the stairs.

'Shhh,' she said quietly. 'There's no – oh my God.'

She stopped near the bottom and just stared at me.

'Julie,' I said.

'Alex.'

Her hair was shorter and blonder than it used to be, cut in a neat bob now, and she was wearing a light blouse and a dark skirt. As with Mike, there were small changes, but she seemed far more surprised at the sight of me. In fact, she looked like she'd seen a ghost, and I was worried she was going to drop the baby she was holding.

Mike walked over and took the child from her, then glanced down at it with an expression on his face I'd never seen before.

'And this is Josh,' he said, turning his body so I could see.

I said, 'Wow.'

Josh looked to be only a few months old and he was sleeping peacefully right now. I looked from Mike to Julie, then back at the baby. I realised I didn't have the faintest clue what I was supposed to do next.

'Congratulations,' I said.

Seven

Half an hour later, I was sitting on my own in their front room, cupping my hands around an empty coffee mug. I didn't know quite what to do with myself. I was trembling slightly.

More than anything, it was the reaction I'd had to Mike hugging me outside that had upset me. Even back in uni, he'd been a tactile guy, and it had never bothered me before – but it had *jolted* me just now. It was strange to realise just how much I'd frozen up over the last two years. When I thought about it, aside from an occasional handshake, I honestly couldn't remember the last time I'd been that physically close to someone. I almost wanted him to try again so I could have another stab at it. The worst thing was that I wasn't sure I'd manage it any better.

And looking around the front room wasn't helping matters.

In my head, Mike's house was ramshackle. He'd been with Julie for a while before I left, but still – this place had always been *his*, remaining entirely and no doubt frustratingly resilient against her repeated attempts to civilise it. But now, it was tidy and grown-up. There were new carpets, new paint, new matching units. Even the settees were plush and spotless, positioned at careful angles to the beetle-black plasma screen mounted on the wall.

I should have expected things to change, and been prepared for this. People's lives move constantly, and it's only when you step out of them for a while that you become aware of the motion. But I hadn't seen the friends I'd left behind for such a long time now, and in my mind they'd remained static: sealed in place as the people I remembered, like faces in a photograph. But of course, in reality, they'd carried on without me, becoming different people, in exactly the same way as the city had changed. Just because you don't look at something, it doesn't mean it's not there.

Right now, Mike was busying himself in the kitchen, and Julie was putting Josh down in his cot upstairs. Following that single, brief exchange at the door, it was clear she had no idea what to say to me, and felt at least as awkward as I did. Typically for Mike, he was coping by acting as though I'd never been away at all, and it was the most natural thing in the world for me to have turned up on his doorstep. But I could tell that even he was a little lost. At the moment, he seemed to be finding things to do so as not to have to come through and talk to me. And that brought me full circle, back round to feeling miserable.

What did you expect?

A few minutes later, I heard Julie coming downstairs. Mike must have, too, because he emerged from the kitchen and passed me a glass of wine.

'Thanks.'

'No problem, mate.'

He dodged out again. As Julie walked into the room, he returned with another two glasses.

'Thanks, sweetie.' She took it, then held the back of her arm against her forehead for a second.

'Big effort?' Mike said.

'Mmm. He didn't want to settle tonight.'

'Sleeps for Britain.' Mike smiled at me. 'Well, after a bit of persuasion anyway.'

Julie raised her eyebrows: *an understatement.*

'Like his dad,' she said.

Then she sat down on the buffet stool by the fire, put her glass down on the hearth and clasped her hands between her knees, as though warming them. Mike sprawled at the opposite end of the settee, his arm resting halfway along the back, and then stared at me as though he still couldn't quite believe what he was seeing.

'It's *good* to see you, Alex.' He nodded. 'Really good.'

'You too,' I said.

But it was uncomfortable as well. I felt a little like I was standing in the dark outside a house, looking into a bright room full of people I used to know. It *was* nice to see them, but there was something in the way that stopped me being part of it. Something I wanted to remove, but wasn't quite sure how.

'How old is Josh now?'

Julie said, 'Nearly six months.'

I tried to think where I'd been six months ago.

'Well, I'm really pleased for you both.'

She nodded once. 'Thank you.'

Now she'd had a chance to gather herself together, she sounded a lot more formal than she had before: professional and polite, but not friendly. The undertone of that was clear enough. She gave us all a chance to sip our wine and then said:

'So. Where have you been all this time?'

'Just travelling, really.' When there was no reply, I glanced between them. 'You knew that, didn't you?'

'Yes.' Julie frowned. 'We knew that. That's not really what I meant. It's that we didn't hear from you for so long. None of us.'

I didn't reply.

'You didn't answer emails,' she said. 'Or let us know how you were doing. Or anything.'

She spread her hands. *Explain this to me.*

'I know,' I said. 'I'm sorry.'

'And now suddenly, you're back. It feels very strange.'

'It feels strange for me too.'

Her face went blank. Quite clearly, any strangeness here was of my own making, and she wasn't going to have much in the way of sympathy. We were not negotiating the choppy seas of this conversation in the same boat.

'What happened?' she said.

My wife died, I thought. *Could people please leave me alone?* And perhaps a blankness settled in my own expression then, because Julie shifted slightly.

'Well, I know what happened. What I mean is, why did you never get in touch? None of us knew where you were. You just vanished.'

'I'm sorry,' I said.

'But it's like we meant nothing. Sarah was really hurt by it.'

'Ah, Julie,' Mike said.

'No.' Her voice jabbed at him like a finger. 'You were too.'

My glass clinked gently as I put it down on the coffee table. *This was a mistake, Alex.* And the voice was right: it had been a stupid thing to do, coming here. Unlike all my other mistakes, however, at least there was an easy way to rectify this one.

I was about to stand up and leave – but then I stopped myself. Was it really what I wanted to do? I'd known it wasn't going to be easy being back here. Julie couldn't understand what it was like for me when I'd left, and I hoped she never would, but at the same time, she had every right to be annoyed. And maybe running away again at the first reminder I'd done something wrong wasn't the best way of handling things. It hadn't worked for me so far, had it?

I settled back down. 'OK.'

And then I waited them out, aware that Julie was watching me. It seemed to take a long time for her to come to her decision, but eventually she sighed to herself.

'Well,' she said quietly. 'I suppose you're here now.'

Mike had never been a big fan of awkward silences, and he only let this one ride for a few seconds.

'So,' he said. 'Where have you been?'

'Europe mainly.'

'Oh yeah? Anywhere nice?'

I smiled. The way he said it, anyone would think it had been weeks rather than years. I picked up my glass of wine.

'Just travelling around: going place to place. I've not been anywhere in particular.'

I reeled off a few cities, finding it hard to remember now it came to it. But then, I hadn't been gathering snapshots, or not deliberately anyway. My mind had taken a few, but they weren't filed in any real order; they were more like quick pictures, taken at random by someone just testing the camera still worked.

Mike nodded along anyway.

'Have you got somewhere to crash?' he said.

'Oh – yeah. I'm fine.'

'Because we've got the settee. I mean, it's not much, but it's yours if you want it.'

I smiled again. The offer was just like him, and I was genuinely touched. There was no way I'd have taken him up on it, of course, even if I hadn't already booked the hotel. I suspected Josh would be growing up in a broken home if I did.

'Thanks, but I've got a room in town.'

'Are you staying, though?'

'I'm not sure. I heard about Sarah on the news – I haven't really thought much beyond that.'

'That's why you came back?'

'Partly. I don't know. I'll at least stay for the funeral.'

'That might be a while.'

'I guess so.'

'What did you see on the news?'

'Not much. Just that something happened between James and Sarah . . .' I trailed off for a second. Saying it out loud had just made it seem more real. 'I saw that they'd found her body.'

'But they haven't.'

'*Mike*.' Julie glared at him.

I frowned. 'I thought they had?'

'No. They've found the field, but not her.' That got Mike

another glare, and he raised his hands at Julie. 'What? He's got a right to know.'

'Has he?'

'It's his brother we're talking about. And one of his best friends.'

'Hang on,' I said. Mike had thrown me a little, so that even the sudden third-person hostility didn't make the impact it might have done. 'But I saw it on the news. And in the newspaper report. The gate, the bottles . . .'

Neither of them answered.

'What's going on?'

Julie was still looking at Mike. It was her that eventually turned to me.

'We've been in touch with Barry Jenkins,' she said.

The name rang a bell. I'd seen it in the newspaper.

'The guy who wrote the report?'

'Yes,' she said. 'Sarah's editor.'

'OK.'

'The press have more information, but they're not releasing it to the public yet. The police have asked them not to print it until they're sure what's happened. But Barry's kept us in the loop.' She glanced at Mike. 'Confidentially.'

'And what *has* happened?'

'They know they've found the field where James left her. It's the right place. There's physical evidence at the scene. So they know Sarah's body was there.'

'I don't understand.'

She took a deep breath.

'Alex, they gave the description of the gate and bottles days ago. People have been looking out for it ever since. A walker found it, but obviously he didn't go and investigate. And when the police went in—'

Julie stopped suddenly, and looked up at the ceiling. My first thought was that she'd heard a noise from Josh, but then I realised she was trying not to cry.

I looked sideways at Mike.

'And when the police went in . . . what?'

Mike looked at me for a second. It wasn't that he was reluctant to answer. His expression was more like he didn't quite know how. As though what he could bring himself to say wouldn't be enough.

'Mike?'

'Sarah's body wasn't there any more,' he said. 'The police think someone else must have . . . found it first.'

For some reason, it was the taxi driver's words that came back to me then. *You know what gets me the most? It's that she was lying out there all that time.* The police had given a description of the scene and the wrong person had followed those instructions and found it before they did. Her body was there, and now it wasn't.

She had been lying out there all that time, and . . .

'Someone has moved her body?'

Mike said nothing

And I shook my head, because I suddenly understood what that silence meant. It was almost incomprehensible, but it was right there in the expression on his face. He was just unable to speak the word out loud.

Not found, he was saying. *Not moved.*

Taken.

Part Two

Eight

At first, traffic officer Carl Webster couldn't work out where the screaming was coming from. It made the hairs on his neck stand up. Even though he knew it must be coming from a human being, there was something primal about it, as though he wasn't hearing a man in pain at all, but the anguished cries of an animal.

He'd just parked up a little back from the intersection where the crash had taken place. At first glance, the accident before him didn't appear serious enough to warrant such a sound. Maybe that was what disturbed him. Even as he stepped out of the patrol car, he had a sense that something was off-balance here: out of the ordinary. Every nerve inside him was on edge.

Three cars rested across the junction. The furthest vehicle – facing him – was angled to one side, its front crumpled like a ball of paper, the windscreen shattered. Nearest to him, another car was pointed towards it, the red hazards blinking on its sturdy back end. The driver and passenger doors were open on both vehicles, and a few people were standing hesitantly nearby.

A couple of them were peering into the third car, a black estate that was turned sideways in the middle of the inter-section. The front was slightly buckled and the back had popped open.

Immediately, Carl could see what had happened. The driver of the black car had lost control and swerved into the oncoming lane, hitting the furthest vehicle. The car behind had then smacked into it and flipped it round. But the damage to all the vehicles looked relatively minor.

That was what made the shrieking that pierced the air so incongruous.

What the hell is that?

In the distance, at least, he could hear sirens.

'Please,' Carl said, 'step away from the vehicle.'

He made a mental note of the faces around him in case anyone decided to disappear. It wasn't likely. The screaming seemed to have frozen them in place, like rabbits in headlights. Everyone was just looking at him helplessly.

Carl moved between people to get a better look at the black estate, hanging back slightly.

'Who are the drivers here?'

He couldn't see inside properly – the windows were blacked out. A gangster-mobile. But a cheap one, with old, rusted bodywork. It reminded him of a hearse.

He turned back to the people.

'Who are the drivers?' he repeated. 'What happened?'

An ashen faced man in a suit actually put his hand up.

'You're not in school,' Carl said. 'What happened?'

'I'm so sorry. He just . . . swerved in front of me. I'm not sure why. It looked like he had a wasp in his car or something.'

A young woman was hugging herself. 'I didn't have time to stop.'

That was what he'd thought. 'A wasp?'

'He was waving at something.'

Carl glanced back at the estate. The screaming was awful. He'd attended more accidents than he cared to remember, but he'd never heard anything like it. In his experience, as odd as it sounded, the more badly injured a person was, the less noise they made. Like death was a vulture circling, and people kept quiet out of instinct, so it wouldn't know they were available. *Or just in shock*, an old partner had told him when he mentioned it. Whatever: it generally held true.

It didn't sound like this person was injured. It sounded like their fucking soul was on fire.

'Wait on the pavement, please.'

The people dispersed to either side, and Carl moved closer to the estate. At any other accident, he would have been there already, but he was nervous here. The shrieks were degenerating into wretched, inhuman sobbing, and he couldn't shake that feeling that it wasn't a man in this vehicle at all, but a wounded animal that might snap at him if he tried to help.

'Sir?'

He tried to peer in. Actually, he *could* see into the front – the windows weren't made of darkened glass after all. The windscreen itself was tinted, but the side windows had been covered on the inside: decked out with black fabric. The driver had decorated the whole interior of the car with awkward, home-made curtains, stretched across the glass like bats wings. But they had fallen away on the passenger side, and Carl could see the front seats.

There was nobody there.

He could still hear the noise; the driver must have crawled into the back. Now that he was closer, he could hear the man was talking to himself. Repeating something. Although not in any language Carl had ever heard before.

'Sir?'

He pulled open the back door of the estate. The man was curled up in a foetal position on the back seat. As the light hit him, he began *screaming* again, pulling himself into an even tighter ball. Pressing himself against the far door of the vehicle.

'Sir, are you injured? Can you tell me if you've been hurt?'

It felt like a stupid question, but the man didn't appear to be wounded. He was dressed in black suit trousers and a dark blue raincoat, so it was difficult to tell for sure, but he was moving OK. Nothing looked to be broken. Carl glanced through into the front of the car. Everything seemed to be intact. What the hell was wrong with the guy?

'Sir—'

But then Carl looked down at the ground and saw the blood he was standing in. A large pool of it was expanding out from behind the back tyre of the estate.

He took an involuntary step back.

Then he crouched down. He couldn't see much detail beneath the vehicle, but the pool was black and wide. He watched as a tendril crept slowly down the slope of the road. It hit a small pebble, parted, and then overwhelmed it.

What the hell?

His mind put the screaming together with the blood and that made sense. But the man was *inside* the car and, apart from the noise he was making, he wasn't hurt. Carl leaned in and tried to see. The driver had gone still now; he was just keening softly to himself. But there was no blood visible on the back seat. None dripping down into the footwell.

And there was too much of it.

Everything inside him began to tingle at that.

There really is . . . far too much.

Carl moved round to the rear of the vehicle, where the boot lid was bent in two, pointing up in the air like a hooked metal claw.

Don't touch anything.

He didn't. He just looked. And it was enough. Not enough for him to understand immediately what he was seeing, but certainly to justify the feeling he'd had since parking up. Something was terribly wrong here; he understood that much at least.

The inside of the boot was soaked red. But it was bare metal in there, and the base was rusted through, which had allowed the blood to pour out onto the tarmac below the car. There was broken glass in there, and he recognised the handled top of what might, before the crash, have been a demijohn. And then another. At the back, a saucer-shaped slab of glass that was crusted red. Slivers glinting in the sunlight like tiny knives

The driver had been carrying bottles of blood.

The man was silent now. Even the keening had stopped. The only sound was the sirens in the distance.

Carl looked down the street, willing the back-up to arrive.

Nine

My brother's house was on the opposite side of town, at the end of a small cul-de-sac that curled down from a busy main road. The property might have belonged to him now, but it hadn't always. This was where the two of us had grown up.

When my mother died, she left the place to James. She fought a long battle against cancer, approaching it with the same quiet dignity with which she handled a number of other battles through her life. Towards the end, she sat down with me, just the two of us, and explained what she wanted to happen to her things when she was gone. I was to receive a small share of her savings, but the bulk of everything she owned, including the house, would go to James. On the surface, she was simply explaining this, but I knew she was also making sure I understood. And that if I disagreed or was hurt by her decision she might change her mind.

Perhaps I was a little of both, but I didn't show it. At that point, the actual money felt like one of the least important things in the world, and anyway, it did make sense. I didn't need those things. I was settled with Marie, and we already had a home together. I had a steady job. Whereas my brother was existing – as he always had – on a hand-to-mouth basis, finding it difficult to cope with life. He flitted from jobs and homes and partners, or else they flitted from him.

You'd think the fact he was older would have made him more capable, more mature, but it also meant he remembered our father leaving. For as long as I could recall, there had been an air of resentment to him, as though he believed he was somehow entitled to things and shouldn't have to work at or earn them. When he didn't get something, it was the something's fault. My mother indulged that attitude better than I did, perhaps because she remembered my father leaving too.

So I told her it was fine. But it annoyed me, afterwards, the speed with which James accepted everything, just as he always had, without even mentioning it afterwards.

Looking back, I know that was stupid of me. What was he going to say? And yet, in my head, it was one of the many things that added up against him over the years. Maybe the worst part was that, with a bit of distance and a bit more maturity of my own, I could see that from his perspective those same figures probably added up against me as well.

The police might not have known where Sarah's body was now, but they appeared to be satisfied about the circumstances of her actual death. She'd been killed in James's kitchen. The scene had been sealed off for the past week, but the police had released it earlier this morning, with my brother's agreement, to Mike. And at nine o'clock, he picked me up from outside the train station.

He'd seemed fairly relieved when I agreed to come with him. I could understand why: in addition to the keys, the police had given him the business card of a specialist cleaning company. When I'd seen crimes reported in the past, I'd never really considered that side of things, but I supposed it made sense. The police weren't going to tidy the place up themselves. So there was that to face and then to deal with – at some point, anyway – but I also imagined Mike didn't really know what to do with the place in general: what was expected of him and what wasn't. For my own part, I was just glad of the opportunity to do something.

I'd laid awake for a long time last night. There was no air conditioning, so I'd opened the window a couple of fingers, and listened to the constant noise of inner-city traffic far below. I'd watched the shadows on the ceiling, attempting to keep horrible pictures out of my head long enough to manage some sleep. Because why would someone steal a girl's body? My mind had come up with several different answers to that question, and it had insisted on showing them to me one by one.

I should have been here.

And now I felt an urge to help in some small way, no matter how little or how late.

As we set off, Mike said. 'I'm sorry about Julie last night.'

'It's fine.'

'I think she was just surprised.'

But I remembered what she'd told me.

'Julie was thinking of you,' I said.

He pulled a face. 'Me? I didn't even notice you were gone.'

I smiled, despite myself.

'That's all right then,' I said. 'But if you had noticed, then I'd have to say I was sorry.'

'And then I'd have to get really annoyed and irritated telling you it was OK.'

I nodded. 'It's a good job you didn't notice then.'

'Notice what?'

We drove in silence for a while, and I felt a little better. Mike had always been forgiving. He was the kind of person to whom you only ever needed to say sorry once. And that's a rare and valuable gift to have in a friend, for lots of reasons, but maybe most of all because we find it hard to grant ourselves that level of leniency. It's why people who are fundamentally good stand out from the crowd. They offer hope to us normal people who are just muddling through.

'So what happened, Mike?'

'Between J and Sarah?'

'Yeah.' I remembered my brother and the way he struck out at the world. 'I mean, he always had a temper, but I never figured he'd do anything like that.'

'I don't know.' Mike thought about it carefully, then shook

his head. 'When they first got together, everything seemed fine. That wasn't long after you left.'

'And afterwards?'

'I guess it was gradual. They started to argue on nights out. We noticed that. And both of them looked really tired, you know? There was obviously some kind of tension between them, but we never realised how bad it was.'

He shrugged helplessly.

'And we lost touch a bit. They stopped coming out as much, and then they stopped coming out at all. We hardly saw them over the last couple of months. I know Julie feels guilty, like we should have done more, or something. That's probably why she took things out on you.'

I watched him for a second, thinking about that.

And then looked away. 'None of us could have stopped it.'

'Maybe not. I don't know.'

I watched the houses flash past. We were nearly there.

'When I saw him—'

That got my attention back. 'What?'

'Yeah. He's on remand until the trial. He can have visitors.' Mike grimaced as he shifted gear. 'You need to phone in advance, but it's no hassle.'

As though I might want to.

There had never been any love lost between us at the best of times, never mind now. I was almost surprised to realise I didn't *hate* him for what he'd done, as though I didn't have any right to, but I certainly didn't have any inclination to see him either.

'How is he?' I said.

'He's totally shit. Broken. I mean, he looks like someone else. Bewildered by it all. You look in his eyes, and it doesn't seem like he can believe what he's done.'

No, I thought. *That sounds exactly like James.*

Mike pulled up outside. We got out of the car, and he gave me the keys, a little hesitantly.

'You up to this?' I said.

He glanced at the house. 'I really don't know.'

'It'll be all right.'

When I opened the front door, there was a sense of decompression: the movement *whumping* gently through the house, touching all the rooms one by one.

We stepped into the hallway. The lounge was immediately to the right. From memory, the hall in front led to the open-plan dining room and kitchen, where Sarah had died.

'Let's get the hard bit out of the way first.'

Mike nodded in response, but looked like he was on the verge of turning around and running back outside. I didn't blame him. It felt unpleasant. It wasn't just knowing that someone had died in here, or even that it was one of my friends; it was more what Mike had said in the car – that they hadn't seen much of Sarah and James over the last few months. I could imagine the house had been sealed up that entire time, with madness festering slowly in the air. As though good emotions had died in this place, one by one, and the atmosphere was now thick with the decay.

We walked down the hall, and then I pushed open the door and flicked on the light. Mike followed me into the dining room, then stopped.

'Oh Christ, Alex.'

'It's all right.'

I said it as calmly as I could manage.

That little thing you can do is to make this easier for him.

So I walked across to the edge of the dining area and squatted down on my haunches, keeping my feet just shy of the kitchen tiles. The floor in there was covered with blood. There was so much of it. More than I'd have imagined possible. It was dried and crusted; in some places, it was a centimetre thick.

A large pool had congealed in the middle, with a long, unnatural ridge at one side of it. It took me a second to work out that it must have been where Sarah's body was lying, the blood pooling up against her. The image made sense of several weak smears across the base of the cabinets. I pictured her fingertips tracing against them lazily, almost curiously, as her life ebbed away.

A panic of dark red footprints swirled from one end of the room to the other. My brother pacing.

I stood up.

There were spatters across the counter, and even on the cream wall behind. The latter flecks were slightly faded now: brown and old-looking, soaked into the plaster. Someone had drawn light pencil circles round them, with tiny feathered arrows pointing to each.

I kept myself still and forced myself to breathe gently and carefully. My heart was fluttering. I'd already known what had happened, and thought that I'd accepted it, but it was obvious that I hadn't. Now that it was right here in front of me, it felt like I was falling away inside.

How could you hurt her, James?

'There's so much of it.' Mike had stayed over by the door. 'I hadn't expected it to be like this.'

'No.'

I took a long, careful breath.

'Me neither.'

Then I remembered what Julie said last night: *Sarah was really hurt by it.* It made me think of something Mike had said in the car on the way over. The silence began ringing gently.

'Mike, I need to ask you something.'

'What?'

'Back in the car,' I said. 'You told me they got together just after I left?'

'Yeah. Not long after.'

I nodded to myself. *J's really annoyed at you for running out.* That was what Sarah said on the day of Marie's funeral. Six months later, I'd run out on her too.

'Do you think it was because of me?'

'No.'

Mike said it immediately. But he was a fundamentally good person, and I didn't believe him.

When I said I needed to be on my own for a while, he looked doubtful. I wasn't sure whether that was because he would feel bad leaving me alone, or if it was what Julie had said yesterday: that I'd relinquished my rights here, and that it was no longer my place to take responsibility. But I pressed it. And in the end, as he often did, he acquiesced.

He left me the keys. After he was gone, I took another brief look around the dining room, then headed through to the lounge.

I hadn't been in this house for a long time, but at first glance very little had changed. James had thrown out my mother's old furniture, painted the walls and put down new carpets, but it hadn't made much of an impact. Every fitting or piece of furniture was *almost* the same colour, or in the same place, as I remembered. It was as though he'd been determined to make the place his own but lacked the budget or imagination to start from scratch. So he'd simply replaced things, one by one, and the end result was all but indistinguishable from the start.

Except in a few places – the orange throw over one chair; the half-burnt candle stubs on the mantelpiece – where I could see Sarah's influence had been beginning to take hold.

I sat down on the settee and put my face in my hands.

You can go mad trying to disentangle the threads of cause and effect and work out where the blame lies. I think that's what happened to me after Marie's death: I looked at them hard, and when you do that it's never too difficult to pick out your own strands. Not just the ones that are there, but all the ones that aren't. The things you failed to do, and the ways you let someone down.

So I sat there on James's settee for a long time, looking hard at the threads. It was impossible to know anything for sure, because I hadn't been here, but that only made it worse. I thought of a hand stretching out for help, and finding nobody reaching back to touch it.

And eventually, I came to a decision. I rubbed my face,

slapped my hands down onto my legs, then went out into the corridor and stood at the bottom of the stairs, looking up at the landing above. It was grey and dead up there.

No, I thought, I wasn't here. I didn't know what happened. So maybe the first thing I needed to do was learn.

Ten

I took it slowly. Starting at the top of the house, there were three bedrooms and a bathroom. There was nothing obvious to see in the latter, so I focused my attentions on the others.

What had once been my mother's old room had been transformed into a makeshift gym. James had stripped the carpets off the floorboards and bolted mirrors up along one wall. There was an Olympic weight bench at one side, and a punch bag at the other. The top was moulded into the rough shape of a man's torso: a head, large shoulders and then a stocky body tapering down to a spring.

When we were younger, my brother and I had both boxed a little, although we were no good at it for opposite reasons: James wanted to hit people too often and too hard, while I never had much fondness for it at all. I'd always liked plain bag-work – it blew away the cobwebs – but Marie hadn't wanted one in our old house because the walls shook and the noise frightened her.

This one here was cracked at the neck. My brother had always swung wide and hard. I jabbed it lightly once, and it creaked back and forth while I glanced around. The room was mostly empty, but I noticed there were actually two sets of boxing gloves over by the radiator: a black pair and a smaller, pink set. So it wasn't only James. Sarah had been working out in here too.

They'd been sleeping in what had been my brother's room

when we were growing up. It was much smaller than my mother's, but maybe he'd felt more at home in here. His childhood showed through on the walls. There were still pale Blu-Tack stains visible on the old paint from where he'd had posters up as a boy. Since moving in, he'd added a badly fitted wardrobe and drawer arrangement that ran the length of one wall. It left barely enough room for the double bed, with two small cabinets at either side.

All right, then.

I started searching, without any real clue what I was looking for. A diary, perhaps? Some kind of note saying 'why I did it'? I didn't know – the only thing I was sure of was that I felt driven to try, perhaps to make some kind of amends, but even just for peace of mind. If I really was responsible in some way, the least I could do now was not run away from it.

So I went through the wardrobes and slid my hand into the piles of clothes, ruffling through the socks in the drawers until my fingers scraped the wood at the bottom. No hidden papers beneath. The cabinet to the right of the bed was obviously Sarah's, but there was nothing interesting inside. Bags of cotton wool, a box of hair dye, a spare pack of contraceptive pills. Nothing else.

Finally, I walked into my old bedroom.

Because I was the youngest, it was the smallest in the house, and looking around now I found it hard to imagine I'd ever fit in here, even as a small boy. Either James or Sarah had transformed it into a makeshift office and even that was cramped. Where my single bed had once been, there was now a desk, with a sleek hard drive resting underneath, amidst a coil of black cables. The shelves above were filled with books and yellow lever-arch files.

On the opposite wall, there were two cheap pine storage units: just open frames nailed together. At the bottom, the old wooden crate we'd kept our toys in as children. Beside that, red tinsel poked out from the top of a battered cardboard box. I recognised that too. It was the decorations my brother and I had unwrapped every December – knelt down together on the carpet – and then back up again after Christmas, always in the same old pieces of newspaper. On the shelves above, there were items that obviously belonged exclusively to James. And then, right at the top, boxes of Sarah's belongings.

Looking at the shelves, they gave a clear snapshot of my brother's life. They reminded me of the layers and sediments you'd see in a cliff face. It would take most of the day to go through it all, and I doubted I'd find anything of immediate interest in there – nothing but a few nasty surprises, anyway, especially from the lower shelves. Memories leaping out like Jack-in-the-Boxes.

I sat down in a swivel-chair.

The computer was an obvious place to start, I supposed, but when I switched it on I hit a password request screen. My fingers hovered uncertainly above the keyboard – and then relaxed. I had no idea, and couldn't even begin to guess, so there was no point wasting time. I turned the machine off and eyed the shelf above me instead.

At the end, there were four books, all the same colour. *Crime Scenes*, it said on each of the spines. Volumes one to four. I plucked the end one down, opened it, and flicked through it a little idly. Unpleasantly, it was just page after page of crime scene photographs, most of them in black and white. There were old police cars parked up, their headlights illuminating bodies in the road, with officers squatting down beside them. White sheets lay on the ground like fallen ghosts, with dead arms reaching out from underneath.

It was hard to tell whether these were related to her work at the newspaper, or the fascination she'd always had with death. Had this been a professional interest, or a personal one?

I replaced the book.

Next along, there was one on forensics. Then a medical textbook. Both were thick and detailed, and came complete with graphic colour photographs throughout.

I frowned, putting them back.

Sarah, Sarah, Sarah . . .

Then I moved onto the folders.

The first lever-arch file contained press clippings of her newspaper articles, each one slipped carefully and proudly into a clear-plastic sleeve. They were in chronological order. Her first ever by-line, from nearly four years ago, was right at the front; I flipped to the back and found the most recent, a short sidebar clipping, dated early February.

POLICE DENY INTERNET LINK TO MURDERED GIRL

by Sarah Pepper

Today, a police spokesman ruled out the suggestion that photographs of murder victim Jane Slater had been published on the Internet.

The local woman's body was discovered on Monday. She had been missing since November of last year.

Claims have been made that a photograph of the crime scene, including an image of Ms Slater's body, appeared online. However, police have been unable to substantiate this.

'These are serious allegations and they have been fully investigated,' a source told this newspaper. 'We have found no evidence to support these claims, but will continue to look into the matter as and when new evidence comes to light.'

Ms Slater's murder is believed to be connected to the deaths of three other local women. Police have faced mounting criticism over their handling of the investigation.

She'd written it roughly four months ago. After that, she'd either published nothing at all, or else hadn't been bothered enough to keep it. Perhaps whatever caused her and James to withdraw over that period had affected her work as well.

I put the file back and took down the next one. This was

labelled 'Research' and it was, again, full of plastic sleeves. The first contained a single printed photograph. But as I realised what I was looking at, something in my chest tightened up.

Fucking hell, Sarah.

The picture showed a skinny, deeply tanned teenage boy wearing denim shorts and an orange T-shirt. Except that it had taken me a moment to understand that, because the boy's body was lying in dry mud at the edge of a dirt road, and it appeared to have been bent backwards, completely in half, so that the base of his skull rested against the calloused edge of his bare heels.

I could tell it was a real human being, but, for a second, my mind refused to accept it. Jesus. Whatever accident he'd been in . . . except there was rope tying his neck to his ankles, so it wasn't the result of an accident at all. Someone had done that to him. There was an inset photo in the top corner: clearly an autopsy shot. It showed the boy's face covered with sore, tender razor cuts crossing the skin.

On the front of the plastic sleeve, Sarah had stuck a small, printed label:

[03/03/08. A2: SMD(i) – email]

I turned to the next sleeve. The label was slightly different:

[03/03/08. A3: TS(i) – email]

Inside, there was another photograph. This one showed what appeared to be a concrete playground, with a low grey building behind it. A headless male body was draped over a swing, with its orange trousers scrunched down at the ankles. The man's head was on the ground a few metres away. It looked like it had fallen from the sky.

But there was also a second sheet of paper in this sleeve. I slipped it out, more cautiously than I probably needed to. It was a newspaper article, printed off the Internet, and the head-line read:

TWELVE DEAD IN PRISON RIOT

Equally cautiously, I slid it back in.

And then turned my head quickly. The landing was empty.

But the small study seemed very quiet, all of a sudden, while the house beyond was now more ominous than when I'd arrived, as though someone had quietly opened the front door and was now standing motionless in the hallway below.

I'd locked the door, of course: the images were just unnerving me. It felt like something had started buzzing next to my heart.

I quickly checked the side of the folder again: 'Research'.

Research for what?

I picked down the folder containing her newspaper articles, and re-read that final one she'd kept:

Claims have been made that a photograph of the crime scene, including an image of Ms Slater's body, appeared online.

Early February.

And the first sleeve in the research folder was dated early March, which meant she'd started collecting the photographs a few weeks after that article had been published. But I didn't see any obvious connection between that and the material she'd been gathering. If it wasn't research for work, what was it for?

I supposed the answer was obvious, just a little unpalatable. If it wasn't professional then it must have been personal. The image of Sarah's face returned to me, but different this time: not the woman she'd become, but the little girl I'd always been able to see below the surface. The one who insisted that death was a monster, that it had to be faced down and confronted.

However, police have been unable to substantiate this.

Perhaps she'd investigated the allegations about Jane Slater herself – maybe tried to corroborate them by visiting somewhere online, and instead of finding the pictures she'd been looking for, she'd found these. Not relevant for the story, maybe. But I thought they would be relevant for Sarah.

[03/03/08. A3: TS(i) – email]

The labels looked a hell of a lot like interview details. Like she'd sought out the people who'd posted these images and got in touch with them.

Sarah . . .

If this was what had occupied her time over the last few

months, it felt like it partly explained the bad taste the house had in its mouth. No wonder the atmosphere here had soured and died. I could imagine her pursuing this, and I could also imagine the rift it would have opened between the pair of them. Her obsession would have become a wedge, driven deeper and deeper into their relationship until it finally cracked apart.

I worked my way through the rest of the folder.

Not all of the photographs were as distressing as the first two, but they were all stark images of dead bodies, and there was something horrific and unreal about each and every one of them. I found myself shaking my head, feeling almost guilty to be looking. With each turn of the page, the room around me seemed to be slowly filling up with ghosts.

And then I reached the final sleeve. It was one of the least graphic shots in the entire folder, but for a moment I could hardly even breathe.

The label read: [20/04/08. A1: CE(i) – f2f]

Oh God.

The labels had started at 'A2', and the numbers, letters and dates had increased from there. So this sleeve should have been at the beginning of the folder. It was the image she must have found first, the one that caught her attention and started her off, but she'd left the interview itself to the very end. Because even Sarah had needed to work herself up to face some things.

It was an innocuous shot, compared to the others she'd collected. The quality was grainy and poor, and it was difficult to make out much detail as the subject was some distance away. At the top of the photo, there was a small black silhouette of a woman standing on an over-pass, behind waist-high concrete railings. Below the bridge, right at the bottom of the frame, a blur of traffic.

The woman's hair was caught in time, half blown-out to the side by the wind, and her face was in darkness. But I didn't need to see that to know it was Marie.

Eleven

The depths of people's insanity never ceased to amaze Kearney. It wasn't the things they were driven to do, so much as the reasons that lay behind them. The intensity of the whirlpool that madness could whip up in a person's head.

Thomas Wells was a case in point. When he'd been picked up that morning, they'd found the interior of his car decked out with curtains. Rebecca Wingate's handbag was in the glove compartment. Three litres of blood had been bottled up in the boot. There was a chilled thermos flask on the passenger seat.

And yet that, in itself, was not what Kearney found astonishing about this man. Inevitably, the vampirism angle had been raised from the very beginning of the investigation. He and Todd had even spent a night at an underground fetish club on precisely those grounds, where Kearney, taken aback by the unexpected normality of the people, had been strangely beguiled.

So it didn't shock him that Thomas Wells thought he was a vampire. It was the absolute *conviction* the man had. This morning, Wells had lost control of his vehicle and bumped an oncoming car, causing the curtains to come down, and, immediately, he'd gone down with them. The sunlight didn't really hurt him, of course, but his own personal myth had become so real to him that it had over-ridden his sense of self-preservation.

It wouldn't have been surprising to find the man slept in a

coffin. But they hadn't found one at his house, and, despite the surge of hope Kearney had felt at the news, they hadn't found Rebecca Wingate either. He'd almost spoken to Simon Wingate upon learning of Wells's arrest, but was glad that he'd held back. That surge of hope had long since faded. It had been replaced by pressure. A feeling of urgency that he was having to fight to keep in check. She was out there somewhere. Almost within reach now, but not quite.

'Do you remember him?' Todd said.

They were walking down the thin corridor to the interview room. Kearney was forced close to the wall. Todd Dennis was a large man. When he breathed, it often sounded like he was grunting, and conversation escaped him in puffs. But the man could march. Every time they encountered a water-cooler, Kearney had to dodge behind slightly.

'Yes,' he said.

'The press are going to have a field day.'

Kearney nodded. They'd interviewed Thomas Wells about eighteen months ago. Back then, he worked the night-shift at the local abattoir. They'd spoken to him there, and then a second time here at the department. And for a couple of days, they'd liked him for it. Wells had seemed nervous and slightly off-kilter with the world – something *not right* about him – and his story was inconsistent enough to set alarms ringing, albeit quietly. But they had no hard evidence against him, and also a large stumbling block that had put him in the clear.

'I remember his prints didn't match,' Kearney said.

Each of the three bodies discovered so far had yielded little in the way of forensic evidence. The only thing that remained was obvious and deliberate: the print of an index finger, pressed against the centre of the victim's forehead. After a tense few hours' wait, they'd learned that finger did not belong to Thomas Wells.

'Yeah,' Todd said. 'We know what that means.'

'He's got an accomplice.'

'Yep. A plague of vampires.'

Todd said it as though he'd encountered such a thing in the past, and it had always proved troublesome. They stopped outside the door and he smiled grimly.

'This isn't over yet, Paul. Not by a long way.'

Kearney thought of Simon Wingate, still sitting downstairs in reception, waiting for news. The sense of urgency was stronger now. The feeling that time was running out.

He fought it down.

'Yes,' he said. 'I know.'

Interview Room One.

The black carpet on the floor was brand new and spotlessly clean; the walls were the colour of fresh milk. In the centre, there was a stainless-steel table, smeared with a distorted reflection of Thomas Wells's down-turned face. His pale forearms were resting either side of it, and he was staring down between them, presenting Kearney with his pitch-black widow's peak: a pronounced crew-cut 'M' resting above a wide, implacable face.

Behind him, the window was covered with dark blinds.

They clicked gently in the slight breeze.

Todd had already started the camera and done the preliminaries. Now, he was settled back in his seat, resting his hands on his belly and staring across the sheen of metal at their suspect. Kearney could tell his partner was impatient because he was chewing his lip, making his moustache roll.

By mutual agreement, Kearney did most of the interviews and interrogations. It was an empathy thing. Whatever you felt inside, you rarely got results in a situation like this by being angry, and they both knew Kearney was far better at being understanding and sympathetic. In fact, other cops often drafted him in to talk to victims, simply because he was so good at it.

For the most part, Todd limited himself to silent, judgemental stares and a vague sense of threat. His own area of expertise.

Kearney leaned forward.

'So. Thomas. We meet again, eh?'

Wells looked up at him. His face was wide, but the features on it were too small. It was like looking down at isolated outposts in a desert, from a height where you couldn't tell if they were occupied any more. But Kearney thought he saw at least a flicker of recognition there. A breeze shifting the sands.

'Do you remember us?'

Wells said nothing.

'Are you comfortable?'

Nothing.

'Have you got everything you need?'

'Yes,' he said. 'Right here.'

His voice was soft and quiet.

'Sorry?' Kearney said.

'I've got them with me right here. That's all I need.'

It took Kearney a moment to understand.

'You mean the women, Thomas?'

Wells nodded once. 'The seed makes the tree,' he said. 'The tree makes the apple. The apple makes the flesh.'

'What does that mean?'

'They're a part of me now. I'm made from them.'

Silence hovered in the air. Kearney felt something inside him slip a little. He thought again about that thermos flask, and realised Wells was talking about consuming a part of the women. Absorbing them into himself.

'I think I understand, Thomas.'

'Like meat.' Wells nodded again. 'Meat for the soul.'

And then, very slowly, he bared his teeth. Kearney forced himself not to respond at all. A moment later, perhaps bored by the apparent lack of reaction, Wells closed his mouth.

'Because the soul is in the blood.'

Kearney said, 'Of course.'

'That's *why*.' Wells looked suddenly disappointed. 'You told me you wanted to understand.'

What? But then Kearney thought back. It was exactly the kind of thing he might have tried in one of the previous interviews: talk to me; I want to understand. Perhaps to coax some kind of confession out of him – or maybe just because it was true. *Kearney needs a reason.*

And so he had it now. The soul is in the blood.

'Thank you,' he said.

Wells nodded once, graciously. *You're welcome.*

It occurred to Kearney then just how much the man had changed since they'd last met. Back then, Wells hadn't been remotely like this. If anything, he'd been scared and confused. Flinching. Unable to look them in the eye. Now, he had come to believe utterly in his own power.

'Thomas—'

Wells interrupted him. 'But I didn't kill them.'

Kearney hesitated. From the fingerprints on the victims, they knew Wells hadn't acted alone.

'Who did, then?'

'Nobody. Aren't you listening? They're alive in me now.'

So he was still on that track. Despite a moment's frustration, Kearney found himself drawn in slightly. His gaze began flicking over Wells's body. *They're alive in me now.* The most terrible thing was that there was some truth to that. Wells hadn't taken the women's souls, of course, but molecules belonging to them had been absorbed into this man's body, literally becoming part of his flesh. In one sense, by consuming them, he really had imprisoned them inside him.

How far would Wells run with the idea, Kearney wondered. If he thought the women really were alive in him, he might be prepared to 'listen' to one of them. Perhaps they could get him to reveal the location of the victims they hadn't found.

Kearney said, 'And what are they doing?'

Wells just smiled.

'Is Rebecca Wingate in there?'

Wells said, 'The blood weakens the body. But it strengthens the spirit. It's better to have a powerful soul, though, surely?' Then he frowned, suddenly unsure of himself, and looked down at the table. 'Everything's a trade-off, though. And it's better to be strong, isn't it? Yes. It has to be.'

Kearney felt Todd shift slightly beside him. His partner had just folded his arms, a familiar signal. *We're losing him here, Paul.* And he thought Todd was right. If so, the fingerprint was the important thing. Kearney thought about it and remembered something from when they'd been researching vampire lore. It sounded like 'aneurysm', but the exact word wouldn't come to him.

'Do you have a helper, Thomas?'

Wells looked up suddenly. The question had caught him off guard.

'What?'

'A human helper?' Kearney said. 'A servant?'

Wells's gaze darted to the far side of the room. His composure had slipped. For the first time, he looked worried.

'I have . . . no. But the thing is, *I don't know*.'

'Someone who helps you with the bodies?'

No reply this time. Wells leaned forward, and then suddenly back again. Then he folded his arms, and one finger began tapping against his elbow.

Kearney said, 'Did he tell you not to talk about him?'

The finger stopped. 'Nobody *tells* me anything.'

'No, of course.'

Wells tilted his head to one side and stared intently at Kearney. He frowned.

And then a sly smile crept onto his face.

'Ha ha,' he said.

For a moment, the man had been floundering – searching for something out of the reams of insanity in his head. Now, apparently, he'd found it. It was infuriating: the man's personality was like a ring of coloured discs, rotating into place across torchlight, one colour after another. Right now, his face was full of stupid cunning.

'Thomas?' Kearney said.

'No.'

'Where's Rebecca Wingate?'

'Who?'

The smile didn't falter. Kearney had a mental flash of her picture and felt his patience falter.

'You know who,' he said. 'Rebecca Wingate.'

'Who?'

To Wells, this was clearly the most intelligent thing he'd ever thought of, and he seemed immensely pleased with himself. His eyes were glittering. Full of sparkle.

'Thomas . . .' Kearney fought back the frustration, and levelled his palms out in front of him. 'This is all over. OK? Why not just tell me? This is a woman's life we're talking about here.'

Wells licked his lips, glanced to either side, then leaned forward conspiratorially, as though he was about to tell a secret. Kearney moved forward, matching him.

'Who?' Wells whispered.

The man sat up again, smiling to himself.

And then he looked bored.

Kearney leaned back slowly. He could feel Wells's silence throbbing in his head. Once again, he had that sense of there being *no time*. His throat was tightening more with every pulse of his heart; he thought he might even be on the verge of a panic attack. The warning signs had become familiar over the years.

And then he thought of his dream, of Rebecca Wingate disappearing backwards into the mist, and the urgency flared up, overtaking him.

We will find her . . .

He scraped back his chair and stood up.

'This is going nowhere. A break.' He checked his watch, his wrist shaking visibly. Then looked up at the black-bulb camera in the corner of the room. 'Sixteen twenty-four. Interview paused. Fifteen minutes.'

Beside him, Todd shook his head once, then pressed the button on the control panel. The red light that had been glowing beneath the camera blinked off.

Kearney walked behind Wells, over to the window. His legs felt weak, like they might give out on him.

We will find her . . .

He wasn't quite sure what he was doing.

'It's too dark in here.'

There was a rustle as the blinds clicked open.

And then Thomas Wells began to scream.

Twelve

Before I left my brother's house, I found an old sports bag in the gym room and took Sarah's folders with me. I also needed to get on the Internet. I called into town and bought myself the cheapest laptop I could find, and, as an afterthought, a pay-as-you-go mobile phone as well. Then I headed back to my hotel room. When I closed the door, it felt like I was sealing myself in.

My heart was thumping.

The wireless link was weak, but good enough to get me online. I paid for a twenty-four hour account with the Cloud, left the laptop open on the narrow desk, then walked across the room, running my hand through my hair.

On the bed, I had the two folders I'd already looked through – the one with Sarah's newspaper clippings, the other with all the photographs – and also a third one, much thinner, that hadn't been labelled but appeared to be additional research material she'd gathered together. I unclipped the contents of that one and spread the pages out on the rough bed sheet.

A bundle at the front contained more print-outs, but these weren't from newspapers. Some looked like academic texts, while others appeared to be screen grabs from websites and forums, each with a URL scribbled at the top for reference. The one thing they had in common was that they were all concerned with death, but at least these were more mainstream. Relatively tame compared to the horrors she'd collated in the '*Research*' file.

Next, I found pages of handwritten notes.

The first contained a series of hastily sketched diagrams. There was a rectangular, slanted 'U'. Then an angled line with a smaller line near the base, like a sword pointing to the north-east. A cross with two middle strokes. And so on: different combinations of lines and circles. I wasn't sure what they were supposed to represent. They looked vaguely occult, but they also reminded me of something else, and I couldn't think what. But Sarah had obviously only been drawing them as a reminder to herself, so she hadn't bothered to explain what they meant.

Help me out here.

The next sheet was more obvious. It was just a single sheet with a list of words scribbled down faintly in pencil, one on top of another:

> <u>redpepper</u>
> A: grudge
> B: buried
> C: graves
> D: burner
> E: ironed
> F: carnal
> G: damage

Sarah's surname was Pepper and she'd always dyed her hair bright red, so I thought 'redpepper' might be an online username. It made sense: the rest all had six letters, so were probably passwords for different websites. The ones where she'd found those photographs, I was guessing.

The next page contained a key.

> A: http://www.doyouwanttosee.co.uk
> B: http://liveleak.com

C: http://ogrishforums.com
D: http://www.rotten.com

And so on.

I cross-checked with the '*Research*' folder, and it was clear enough what she'd done. The photograph of the prison riot was labelled 'A3', for example, so presumably she'd found that at doyouwanttosee.co.uk, where her password would be 'grudge'.

That site was also where she'd found the photo of Marie.

Last of all, there was a stapled, four-page list, with a table of contacts and interview details. The only complete columns were the ones giving computer usernames and a corresponding letter, once again from A through to G. Beside these, there were spaces for 'real name' and 'street address', but the majority were blank. There was a handful of phone numbers, but still not many. Almost everyone on the list was identified only by an email address, and then the date of when they'd been interviewed.

The hotel room felt dark and claustrophobic.

Come on. You can do this.

I checked the label on the photograph of Marie –

[20/04/08. A1: CE(i) – f2f]

– and then referred back to the table.

There it was.

Sarah had conducted only one interview on the twentieth of April. 'CE' stood for Christopher Ellis – username 'Hell_is' – and there was an address for him in Wrexley, which was about ten miles west of here.

I presumed 'f2f' meant she'd conducted it in person.

Checking through, he appeared to be the only person she'd spoken to in the flesh. Of the three other addresses she'd tracked down, two were outside the country and the third would have been too far to travel. They all had 'email' next to them.

Christopher Ellis.

The name meant nothing to me. I was fairly sure I'd never

even heard of this man. But there had to be a reason Sarah had connected these people to specific images, and all I could think was that they'd been the ones to post those pictures online.

And *that* meant something to me.

Come on then.

I went across to the computer and typed the web address into the browser window. Before I could change my mind, I pressed 'return'. The site loaded immediately, and I was faced with the plain front page to a forum. The background was entirely black. There were no fancy graphics, just a simple table divided into three separate blocks of text. The titles of sub-forums showed up in pale red – flesh-coloured, I realised. The date and name of the most recent post in each appeared in grey-white.

A small header at the top right of the screen was like a dare:

do you want to see?

I stared at that for a moment, then turned my attention to the forum below. The middle section was titled 'content', and there were three sub-forums within that: 'images', 'videos', and 'non-gore-related'. I clicked on 'images', and immediately, a pop-up window appeared:

You must be logged in to view that section

Log-in   *Register*

The option to register was disabled. At the bottom of the new window, I noticed a tiny note added in grey:

hell is full – we are closed to new members at present

You don't get rid of me that easily, I thought. Bastards.

I clicked 'Log-in', then entered 'redpepper' and 'grudge' at the prompt. The mouse pointer changed to an hourglass.

And nothing else happened.

I sat there, waiting, and after a few moments I began to have the uncomfortable sensation that someone was peering out of the screen at me. It was ridiculous. But I couldn't get the idea out of my head. I was about to hit a key – wondering if the browser might have jammed – when the screen hiccupped once, and the 'images' sub-forum appeared.

I was in.

The screen showed the forum topics as a vertical list: rows and rows of subjects, ordered by the date the most recent comment had been added. The hottest topic at this point in time was something called 'Pathologist at play', which had nine pages of comments attached to it. Below that, the next line read 'Race driver decapitated'. Then 'suicide by cop'. And so on. The page link option at the top of the table suggested there were another forty-four screens of this.

I decided to use the search function instead. There was no need to wade through all the shit on here, not when I could just sieve it instead: pull out the threads started by 'Hell_is' and see what was there.

But even his username brought up several pages of links. Christopher Ellis was obviously a heavy user of the site. And he was still active too: the most recent post he'd made, at the top of the list, was from only a couple of days ago.

When I saw the title, my heart skipped.

'Dead woman in wood'

Sarah.

The mouse pointer hovered over the link. I kept reading the subject line, over and over again, unsure what to do.

The police think someone else must have found it first.

I hadn't even considered the possibility that one of these people might know anything about what had happened to Sarah, never mind that they might be involved somehow. But now that I thought about it, it wasn't such a huge fucking leap, was it? The kind of person who'd steal a body would probably also enjoy seeing photos of one, which meant they'd end up at a place like this. At the very least, there was an obvious sliding scale there.

I hesitated.

Do you want to see?

I steeled myself, clicked the mouse button . . .

And relief spread through me. It wasn't her. The picture was some kind of leaked police photograph, showing a woman's naked body. She had been stuffed into the entrance of a large waste pipe in woodland, and only her upper body was visible, as though the photographer had captured her in the act of clambering forward out of it. The body was on its front, with the woman's face tilted back, resting on its chin and staring at the camera. The skin was wrapped tightly to the bones, the lips peeled away from a grimace of teeth.

The relief was quickly replaced by revulsion.

But it's someone.

I started to scroll down the comments – but then stopped. The first few were making fun of the dead girl. One even had a smiling emoticon clapping its hands. After reading a couple, I realised I was shaking slightly, as though I'd had one cup of coffee too many. I didn't know if it was caused by the shock from seeing the photograph or the sudden anger I felt towards these people, but I closed the thread anyway.

For the next half hour, I clicked through screen after screen of links posted by Christopher Ellis, scanning the titles without opening them. He was a prolific poster, it seemed: a really committed collector of other people's suffering.

And finally, at the top of the ninth screen, I found mine.

'Bridge suicide – bitch in bits'

I breathed out slowly.

Bitch. I think it was that word, as much as anything – just thrown out like that by a complete stranger. Someone who'd never known Marie or the difficulties she'd had in her life. Someone who was probably glad she was dead just so he could find a picture of it, post it online, and laugh about it.

Do you need anything else while I'm out?

Even now, I missed her so much. I could still feel the lurch of guilt inside me: that terrible, endless drop of a moment when you realise it's too late. That something has been lost, and that you would give anything – anything at all – for it to return. For one chance to do things differently.

Just you to come back to me.

The screen in front of me was suddenly blurred.

I'd come this far now, though, even if I was no longer sure why, so I took a deep breath, and went to click on the link. But then I noticed something else and stopped moving completely.

I'd known it was here, of course. And I'd already seen the picture itself. What I hadn't prepared myself for was where on the site it had been posted. Ellis's thread wasn't in the 'images' sub-forum at all. It was under 'videos'.

Carefully – without really thinking about what I was doing – I got my coat and decided I was going out for a while.

Thirteen

I wandered the late-afternoon streets, moving at random through the crowds of shoppers.

The day was bright and clear, and everyone passing by seemed to be framed in wedges of sunlight. The more I walked, the stranger the people around me appeared: so free of concern and worry, so unaware of how easily life could slip and what would be waiting for you when you fell. I watched them hitching up bags and trousers, tipping back bottles of Coke. Gripping massive plastic carriers full of clothes. I heard music thumping from cars. I heard *laughter*.

And once again, I felt separated from all of it.

You've got to try to hold onto the good memories. That was the thing I couldn't get out of my head now. It was what Sarah had said to me on the day of the funeral. *That's where Marie is now, and you need to try to remember her smiling.*

But I hadn't, and it felt like I'd failed her after her death just as badly as I did before it. The only minds she'd existed in since belonged to the people who visited the bowels of that fucking website. Instead of being remembered smiling and holding my hand, however tentatively, she'd been excluded from my thoughts altogether. In doing so, I'd allowed her to be defined by those last few lonely, desperate moments. Plastered online, like a poster in some dirty, boarded-up basement.

As I walked, everything around me was reverberating in my

head. I circled the city centre for the best part of an hour, moving aimlessly, attempting to escape what I was feeling.

Eventually I stopped, just around the corner from my hotel.

You don't want to see this, I told myself.

The voice was far more appealing now, but I knew it was only offering the bleakest kind of comfort. Because it wouldn't make any difference. The video would always be there, whether I watched it or not, just as whatever responsibility I had for Sarah's death would remain, regardless of whether I chose to face up to it. I could run away. But not looking at something doesn't mean it isn't there.

If Marie had been alive, I would have done anything – anything at all – to go to her. Strangely, standing there now, the fact she was dead didn't feel like it changed that.

So I altered course and bought vodka from the train station.

And then I went back to my hotel room, locked the door, and watched.

Analysing it critically made it easier. The footage had been taken on a mobile phone, I thought, and not one with a great camera either – very obviously technology of the time. The colours were blocky, and whenever the person holding it moved, the clip seemed to swirl and take a second to catch up, as though the phone was drunk and dizzy. The audio – an occasional roar of breeze; traffic like a rustling stream – sounded like it was coming from underwater.

I poured myself a neat vodka. The quality of the clip also made things easier, I told myself. It wasn't like watching something that was actually happening or something that could be stopped.

The first thing I made out was the pavement and a trainer, then a bollard. The mobile swung up, jittered, and I realised the person with the camera was on the next bridge along from Marie. I could hear him breathing quickly.

A moment later, he focused on my wife in the distance.

She was just standing there, barely a centimetre tall on the computer screen. A lonely figure, huddled up beside the shape of her car. Little more than a blur of tiny pixels shimmering.

I moved my face as close as I could. For a few moments, she did nothing, then I had the impression she was glancing behind her. She leaned over the barrier and looked down at the road. A second later, she clambered awkwardly over the railings, one leg then the other, until she was sitting on the barrier. I watched her shuffling slightly, as though adjusting herself for comfort.

Through the speakers, I could hear the man with the mobile phone taking those quick, sharp breaths. Was it panic? Fear?

The small figure extended its arms sideways and tipped its head back. She was staring at the sky. Despite what I had told myself, I wanted to reach into the screen.

Marie, I thought. *Please don't.*

I love you.

She rocked forward. The way she toppled, it was like she was moving in slow motion. But then she was tumbling through the air. The mobile followed her carefully.

'Oh my God. Oh Jesus.'

Even from this distance, the collision registered in the speakers. It was a small, sharp sound, like a stone cracking a windscreen. I knew Marie was gone. That had been her last second in the world. There had been a blur of free-fall, and then she had landed on the back of her head and died instantly. Her body, lying in the road, was crumpled and still.

'Oh fuck—'

The man was drowned out by a screeching noise, as the truck shot out from under the bridge, smoke billowing back from the rows of locked tyres. The driver never had a chance. Both sets of wheels went fully across Marie's body, dragging it along. What emerged out behind made no sense. It looked like three bags of tattered red clothes, flopping across the tarmac.

The truck skidded to a halt and everything settled very slowly. There was a moment of silence that made me think of dust falling gently in the aftermath of an explosion. The second before people start screaming, when everything is absolutely quiet.

All except the man holding the camera. He was still breathing those short, jagged breaths.

I thought I recognised the tone of them now. It wasn't fear or panic. It was exhilaration.

Ellis's video link was the first post in the thread. After that, there were three pages of comments: twenty-seven in total. Twenty-seven people who thought they had something to say about what Marie had done.

The first just had an animated smiling face, nodding, lifting a coffee cup to its lips and sipping. Content with itself.

The next: 'Someone get down there. I think she'll be OK.'

'Selfish fucking skank. What's wrong with pills and a bag?'

I wished an extremely painful death on that user, then scrolled down the screen.

'Wow new to me. Where did you get this Helly?'

Helly. I tapped the mouse button again.

Cute little nickname.

His reply came a few posts below.

'I got it on my mobile,' Hell_is said. 'Just happened to be nearby at the time and saw her up there. Pulled up on the off chance and couldn't believe what was happening. I couldn't wait to share this! Once in a lifetime, I'll tell ya.'

I leaned back in the chair and closed my eyes.

Then tried to rub some life into them.

Psyching myself up to watch the video had sent jags of emotion and adrenalin through me, and now the fall-out was starting to kick in. There was a tightness in my throat, and my hands were trembling. After a while, I stopped rubbing my face and poured myself another vodka. It seemed a more sensible course of action.

It's only a video, I told myself.

A bunch of fucking idiots on the Internet who don't matter.

That was true. Although I was angry with them, I knew the

real target for that was probably closer to home – and also that none of it was particularly useful at the moment. Since finding the photograph at James's house, I'd been in a kind of emotional free-fall. Now I needed to work out what had happened and what to do about it.

Some of the former was obvious enough. While investigating an article, Sarah had stumbled across this clip of my wife's – her friend's – death, and it had led to this research of hers, perhaps the same way a jolt of radiation might awaken a cancer and cause it to grow. As she became more and more obsessed, she dropped away from her friends, her work, and her relationship with James. It had consumed her.

And it really was my fault.

It was a harsh realisation, but there was no escaping it. People are more than happy to make their own mistakes, of course, without any encouragement from others. Sarah and James had both made their own choices along the way. But the fact remained that none of it would have happened if I'd been here. When Sarah had seen the footage of Marie, she would have come to me, because that was the way her mind worked; she would have seen it as 'mine'. But she couldn't do that, because I'd abandoned my post.

I poured myself another vodka, then stared at the screen and rolled the drink around my mouth. *Death has ripples*. I'd failed Marie for the last two years of her life, and then, for two years afterwards, I'd failed Sarah as well. It was like a wavelength.

But that wasn't all.

I looked at what Ellis had written.

Just happened to be nearby at the time and saw her up there.

It was only the image of Marie that he'd stolen on here – I knew that deep down – but someone in the real world had taken Sarah's body. When I'd seen the most recent thread Ellis had posted, I'd thought there might be a connection to this place, and the idea returned to me now. Sarah had interviewed thirty-seven of these fuckers. It wasn't too outlandish to imagine one of them reciprocating that level of interest. Maybe starting to follow her. Maybe even seeing what James did that night and deciding to take advantage of it.

Maybe someone like Ellis. Someone who lived close enough.

That would be a little like a wavelength as well.

So I should go to the police. No doubt they'd already search-ed the house, but even if they'd seen these folders, they might not have understood the relevance. That was what I should do.

I should go right now, in fact.

But instead of getting up, I sipped my drink in the slowly darkening hotel room, and kept staring at the computer screen. Perhaps it was the alcohol – or maybe just the confusion of anger and guilt in my head. Those two emotions shift easily if you let them, one into the other, until you're no longer sure which of them you're feeling, or who's to blame. And like sadness, they too have a way of blurring things, so that *should* begins to look simply like *could*.

So yes, I told myself, I could go to the police. But that was an abdication of responsibility, once again, wasn't it? Sitting here now, I could see the strands of cause and effect and pick out the ones that were mine, which meant that handing that bundle over to someone else was just another method of running away. And perhaps that was even getting ahead of things, anyway. For the moment, the links were only in my head. I couldn't know for sure, because I hadn't been here.

Abandoned my post . . .

I poured myself another drink and stared at Ellis's last com-ment. I kept reading it, over and over, until my hands were trembling. Until, after a while, there wasn't any could or should, only what I knew was going to happen. What needed to.

Once in a lifetime, he'd written. *I'll tell ya.*

Yeah, I thought.

You will.

Fourteen

The garage where Thomas Wells had 'stored' Rebecca Wingate was on the outskirts of the city, at the far end of a dirt track. The path disappeared between a broken-down café and a strangely angled, tobacco-coloured pub, and led to a courtyard beside an old, soot-black viaduct. There was little traffic on the main road itself, and most of the land here was industrial: disused, shadowy factories and grey storage depots. The police vans were parked back at the road to avoid damaging any tyre tracks in the dust of the path.

It was very quiet here, very still. Everything looked slightly bedraggled, as though it had once rained so long and hard that the world was still soaked and heavy with it.

The garage was built into one of the arches beneath the viaduct: a half moon of iron with a padlocked door and a corrugated shutter.

Inside, there was space for a van to park at one end. At the other, there was some kind of half-broken metal table, with leathered restraints sprouting from it in hard curls. Vents crisscrossed the floor, leading to an oily, puckered drain in the centre, which looked to have black hair clogging the grilles. A cracked porcelain sink had been installed on the nearest wall, with a large rubber hose slipped over one of the taps.

Chains were hanging down the wall at the back, attached to a pulley system running on a beam overhead. It looked like something a mechanic would use to swing a car engine across a garage. Except that Kearney guessed most of the old machinery here had been salvaged from the abattoir where Wells had worked.

He and Todd were standing at the doorway while the forensic search team busied themselves within, ghosts in the gloom.

'It's a torture chamber,' Todd said.

He was chewing his lip again.

Kearney said, 'Yes.'

Although actually, he thought his partner was only half right. The conversion work had transformed the garage into a dungeon, and he couldn't begin to imagine the physical and emotional suffering that had been endured in here – but at the same time, that suffering had never been the motivation. This place was simply a way of processing meat for consumption. Human blood. Horrifically, the women and their pain meant nothing to Wells.

Did that make a difference?

A camera-flash illuminated the rusted machinery at the far side of the lock-up. Kearney supposed that it didn't; the result was still the same.

Where is she?

The question was like a steady pulse in his mind. And every time it beat, he felt a throb of panic.

Back at the department, after the blinds had been closed, Wells had changed his attitude and become far more forthcoming. He told them the victims had been kept in this old garage, which was either owned or rented – Wells wasn't sure – by a man named Roger Timms. This man had also helped him dispose of the bodies when he was finished with them. Rebecca Wingate was there right now. He had seen her there the night before last, and she was still alive then. Still in the garage, where he had 'stored' her.

So where was she now?

Todd started to say something, but Kearney turned and walked back outside, edging around the dusty courtyard where more SOCOs were studying the tracks in the dirt. Again, he was struck by how quiet it was here: a little pocket of built-down wilderness on the cusp of the city. On the other side of a fence, black birds were perched in the tree branches, watching him. Kearney stared them out for a moment, and then he felt Todd stand beside him.

'Are you OK, Paul?'

Kearney nodded. 'Yeah.'

'Don't lie to me.'

At forty-five, Todd was ten years older than Kearney, and he'd always had a paternalistic streak to him. Often a gruff one, admittedly, but his advice was usually meant well, and Kearney knew his partner's comments now were motivated by concern. Todd could be belligerent and pig-headed, but he wasn't stupid. Even if he hadn't noticed a change in Kearney's attitude over the past few months – *an unravelling*, he told himself – then his actions toward Thomas Wells had been so out of character it must surely have set off an alarm.

Don't lie to me. But he had no idea how to explain himself.

'I'm OK. Just tired.'

'It's important, Paul. You have to prepare yourself for the fact we might not find her alive.'

'I know that.'

'But we'll find him,' Todd said. They started back up the track, walking along the rocks at the edge. 'Timms, I mean.'

'Yes.'

Wells had been telling the truth about the name: the garage was indeed being rented to a 'Roger Timms'. The team back at the van was tracing the man now, and the door team were on standby, waiting. Even if Wells was lying about some aspects of the story, the facts spoke for themselves. The lock-up was registered to Timms, Wells had a key, and the girls had obviously been kept there. Roger Timms had a case to answer.

But that was troubling in itself. If Wells was telling the whole truth, the only explanation for Rebecca Wingate's absence now was that Timms had learned of his friend's arrest and tried to clear away the evidence. He wouldn't have had time to remove the heavy machinery in there, but he could at least attempt to explain that away. *I had no idea what my friend Thomas was doing.* The one thing he wouldn't be able to explain was the eyewitness testimony of Rebecca Wingate, but, unlike the machinery, there was a simple solution to that.

Todd was right. There was no avoiding it.

You have to be prepared.

Kearney pulled an air of detachment around him as they reached the open side of the comms van. Despite the early evening light, the interior was surprisingly dark. There were three officers, crammed in amongst the equipment: monitors, link-ups, recording devices. The men were little more than dark shadows, partly illuminated by the pale, sickly light of the monitors.

'Hendricks,' Kearney said. 'Anything?'

The nearest man didn't turn around. He was studying the screen in front of him.

'We've just got an ID through, sir.'

Roger Timms.

Kearney sat opposite Todd in the back of a van as it rattled through the streets. They both had small bulky laptops open on their knees. On a separate monitor, Roger Timms's home address was flagged in the centre of a satellite map. Two yellow arrows were converging on it. One was the van they were in. The other was DS Burrows, the sergeant in charge of the department's door team.

The bumps in the road kept jarring and rocking the speeding vehicle. Kearney tried to keep the laptop steady and scan through the data they had on their suspect.

A photograph of Timms stared out of the left-hand side of the screen. Beside it, the basic stats were listed. He was forty-two years old – the same age as Thomas Wells – and stood at six foot, with a medium build. Brown hair, brown eyes . . .

With a sinking feeling, Kearney realised it was a mug shot.

'He's done time.' He checked across. 'Christ. Murder.'

Todd didn't look up, but he raised an eyebrow.

'You mean you don't recognise the name?'

'We've not interviewed him before too, have we?'

'No. He's that artist. I knew I'd heard the name before. The one in the papers. That's all we need. A local celebrity.'

'If he's done time, his prints are in the index.' Kearney clicked through to the next screen. 'So he can't be the one who touched the victims' foreheads.'

Todd said nothing. Beneath them, the van rocked.

The next few screens had some press clippings the comms team had gathered together, and they jogged Kearney's memory a little. He recognised the man now. He'd read about him, but never slotted the name into place.

At the age of twenty-four, Timms had been involved in an armed robbery that went wrong, although 'armed robbery' was perhaps giving him too much credit. He'd tried to hold up a post office, but the gun had gone off, and he'd shot the female clerk in the head. By accident, he claimed. He did eight years. According to the article, the experience had turned Roger Timms's life around: inside prison, he took up painting. He achieved some notoriety, and became something of a cause célèbre in the art world. Following his release, he'd pursued it as a career.

Popular amongst the canapé classes, Kearney imagined, for the frisson of danger he brought along to the parties.

'How the hell is this guy associated with Thomas Wells?'

'Same age,' Todd said. 'Same hometown.'

Kearney shook his head. It didn't seem enough.

'It's the wrong guy.'

'You've not seen the painting yet.'

'What? No, hang on.'

He clicked through until he found the screen Todd was referring to. It was another scanned-in press cutting, this time with two photographs attached on the right-hand side.

The top one was of Roger Timms: a reportage-style snap

taken at a gallery. He'd dyed his hair since the police shot. It was bleached and gathered together in a spiky peak on the top of his head: the short, fashionable equivalent of a Mohican. Beneath it, Timms's face was tanned and healthy. He was smiling, holding a glass of champagne.

The second image was a small photograph of one of his paintings. With the low resolution of the image and the jostling of the van, Kearney couldn't make out much detail, but he could see the vivid colours. It looked like a woman's head, tilted to one side, with a bright red sunset behind. Her mouth was open. The painting was titled *Distress*. Below it, someone had quoted:

'Timms's *Gehenna* sequence has authenticity and bite; it tran-scends the narrative of his own experience whilst remaining entwined with and informed by it'

Kearney had almost no idea what that meant, but it didn't matter. The painting was the important thing. The *portrait*. Even with the exaggerated style and the poor quality of the image, it was clear who he was looking at.

He said, 'That's Linda Holloway.'

Fifteen

Five minutes later, they were there. The two police vans were parked almost confrontationally, nose to nose, one street along from Roger Timms's home address. Kearney was standing by the side of their van with Todd, talking to DS Burrows, the sergeant in charge of the door team.

Burrows was dressed in black body armour, but he would have been solid enough without it. He had a crew-cut, a stocky body and an air of detached physicality. You always felt that, if he wanted to, he could hit you very hard, and in the meantime he was simply presuming you were aware of it.

But then, Burrows had spent most of his career kicking down the doors of drug-dealers, murderers, paedophiles and suspected terrorists. Now he worked in close conjunction with Operation Victor, part of the department's Child Protection Unit. Kearney had walked past it a few times. It was the room where the lights were kept on, and where a screen was often drawn down over the window on the door. Kearney disliked overtly physical men, and he always found Burrows intimidating, but it was the kind of work that would harden anyone.

Right now, the DS had a blueprint of Timms's house-type open on a wireless laptop and was talking them through the inbound.

'These houses are pretty handy for us from the outside. Three main exits. Front and back, here and here, and out through the garage. There's a small window onto the driveway, but it's a worm-hole and it'll be covered.' He sniffed, considering the map. 'Yeah. All good.'

'The interior?' Kearney said.

'Not so great. Four rooms upstairs, three down. Attic via loft panel here. The cellar door is usually in the side of the stairs there. But these houses, it's easy enough to partition things off, move things around. We won't know exactly what we're facing until we're in.' He looked up suddenly. 'Firearms?'

'It's possible,' Kearney said. 'But we have no reason to believe so.'

'But a hostage?'

'Rebecca Wingate.'

Burrows looked down again. Her name clearly wasn't important, so much as the challenge she represented to his logistics. Regardless of whether Timms was armed, a hostage could be used against them in ways that were at least as difficult to deal with as a weapon.

It troubled Kearney as well. He knew the first rule in a situation like this was that the subject was never allowed to leave, no matter what. If the house was contained, Rebecca was the only possible victim. If Timms escaped, other lives would be at risk. So although Burrows would do everything possible to secure Rebecca Wingate's safety, she was not his only objective here.

It was a terrifying situation for her to be in.

The alternative, though, was worse.

'Yes,' Kearney said. 'We hope there's a hostage.'

He and Todd sat in the back of the comms van, watching the door-team's approach on a series of monitors.

The main display showed a basic overview of the house from above – a two-dimensional satellite image, with the GPS locations of officers updating in jerks every three seconds. Every yellow triangle had a small number attached to it. These corresponded to the other screens, which were stacked to the side, illuminated like the windows in a block of flats. Each of these showed the video feed from the cameras attached to the different members of the team. There were ten in total.

Kearney watched the men assemble, piecing the whole scene together from the fractal jigsaw of overlapping images in front of him. On one screen, there was a slanted view of the front door. Directly above, the screen showed a man in black standing by that exact same door. On the monitor to the side, he could see both men. The same actors in the same scenes, all shot from different angles, creating a composite that became self-referential, a series without an end.

Here was the front of the house.

On the top screen, the driveway: jogging backwards and then tilting as the officer flattened against the wall. Kearney could see the small window Burrows had mentioned.

Beside that screen, the camera darted across a back garden, then slid to a silent halt by the side of a patio door, dark green bushes reflected in the glass.

No direct sound: that came through the headset he was wearing, which connected him on the same frequency Burrows and his team were using.

He heard Burrows count down softly.

'Go.'

A metal battering ram swung at different angles on the screens. In his ears, the door went half in with a flat crack, then – a second swing – crunched off its hinges.

'Go.'

All hell broke loose.

Through the headphones: shouting, pounding, calling-out. radio snarls. The monitors became a whirling dance of blue-grey movement. Officers appeared to be everywhere at once, as though the situation was a shattered mirror and the same men were being reflected by the fragments. Kearney watched black-armoured backs huddling forward, caught a snatched glance of a corridor spinning, then – *bang* – a door crashing open into a living-room . . .

'Clear.'

His gaze flicked from screen to screen, from one room to the next: officers fanning out, their duplicates vanishing. He saw a kitchen turning on one screen, this way, the other – 'Clear' – and then cabinets being pulled open one by one.

A black shape flashed past.

Kearney followed it to the next screen, where a gloved hand pushed open a door at the side of the kitchen. There was only blackness beyond it for a second, then a supernova pulse of ghost light that seemed to *whump* in the air, then settle, revealing bright grey dust hanging there like ash. The camera panned steadily over the old wooden racks on the far side of the empty garage. Kearney saw cans of paint, a roll of plastic sheeting.

Wedges of shadows rotated with the camera, smooth and steady, like the second hand of a clock.

'Clear.'

'Empty garage,' Kearney noted. 'Empty driveway too.'

According to the information they had, Timms drove a white Ford transit van. Where was it?

On the satellite feed, the yellow triangles were spreading steadily across the blueprint of the house. They began to overlap, forming stars, as officers thumped up the stairs to the second floor.

Kearney saw the bathroom, the shower-head hanging down, twisted. On the next screen, a black fist punched methodically down at bed sheets. In the corner of that screen, a figure was crouching down. Kearney looked up and saw the area under the bed revealed. Dust and curls of hair resting on sketchily painted white floorboards.

'Clear.'

Fifteen seconds had passed.

Timms's studio was a large room at the back of the house. It was impeccably tidy: the walls clean and white; the floor laid with laminated boards. An easel rested on plastic sheeting beside a folding wooden table covered with plates and bowls and brushes; half-finished canvases were propped against one wall, bulky as paving slabs.

'Clear.'

'He's not there,' Todd said.

Kearney was staring intently at the screens.

Neither is she.

Unless . . .

His gaze travelled back down the stack of monitors. After the frenzy of activity, each of them was now drawing to a tentative standstill, as officers waited in the rooms they'd contained. Only two screens at the bottom were still active. Burrows was leading a second man down into the cellar beneath the house.

Kearney kept his attention on the one that showed Burrows in the centre, ducking awkwardly down the stone steps. They looked very old, as though they'd been carved out of the ground itself.

At the bottom, the camera panned round steadily, giving hints of the huge open space beneath the building. It appeared to stretch across the entire foundations of the house, and had the feel of archaeological ruins. The floor was cobbled, like a Victorian street, and the lights sat in opaque, plastic cases on the pillars. Broken down sections of wall created odd, angled shadows that wavered at the edges.

From the headset, Kearney could hear a cold sound, like wind rushing through a tunnel. Motes of dust hung in the air. It seemed a long time before anyone said anything. When the silence was broken, it was Burrows who spoke.

'We've got something here.'

Kearney tried to see on the monitor, but his eyes couldn't make sense of the image. From what he could tell, there was a pale gap in the darkness – a hole in the wall, like a mouth filled with sharp, crimson teeth. In the centre, there was something a little like a woman's face. *That's an eye*, he thought. But there was only one. Then the camera panned down, played across some dark shapes resting on the floor.

Kearney leaned forward even further, heart beating quickly.

'What is that?' he said into the mic. 'Is it her?'

Burrows's camera didn't move.

'I can't tell,' he said.

*

Down in Timms's basement, Kearney shivered a little at the memory of the interview from earlier. Thomas Wells's soft, quiet words were as insistent and chilling as the draught beneath the house.

They're a part of me now.

I'm made of them.

He and Todd were standing at the far end of the cellar, both of them looking at what Timms had stored down here. The official studio, on the top floor of the house, had obviously been a front: something for the journalists to photograph. Not the whole story. It was down here, in the cold and the darkness, that Roger Timms had produced his real work.

There was a large canvas propped up on a rickety table, flat against the wall of the cellar. This was what he'd seen on the monitor, and it had looked strange because the painting was still a work in progress. The jagged red teeth were actually spreads of background colour, extending up and down around the outline of a woman's head, the detail within only half completed. Timms had only got as far as roughly colouring in the woman's face on the right-hand side. So there was a single, bright, staring eye and some shading around the howl of a mouth, but little else. No hair yet. Just a blank space on the canvas, waiting to be filled.

Yet it was clear to Kearney what they were looking at. The portrait was incomplete, but it was of Rebecca Wingate.

'Tomorrow's going to be a long day,' Todd said. 'We're going to need to get hold of all his paintings. And I mean all of them.'

He shook his head.

'A long day.'

Kearney nodded absently, his face set hard, then looked down at the row of demijohns on the floor by the table. They were dull, ugly shapes. Any shine in the glass had long been lost under the crust of old blood within.

All except one, in fact. The last bottle along was new enough to gleam in the dim light. And despite the swathes of crimson on Roger Timms's uncompleted portrait, it was still half full of blood.

Part Three

Part Three

Sixteen

The next morning, I woke up feeling clammy. Partly it was the vodka I'd drunk the night before, and partly the warmth that had settled in the hotel room as the sun rose. I'd been half awake for a while, the heat growing into a steady pulse that became impossible to ignore.

Over at the window, I opened it wide and breathed in the freshest air I could find. In the distance, above the industrial roofs, a screen was visible on the side of an office block, the display flicking between the day's temperature – seventeen degrees centigrade already – and the time. Half-past eight.

I had a dim memory of how I'd spent the rest of my evening. After deciding I was probably too drunk to go and visit Christopher Ellis, I'd compounded the problem by drinking more, and at some point, I'd begun looking through more of the posts on that website. Not just Ellis's either. I'd clicked on thread titles more or less at random. I wasn't sure why I'd even started, but the more I looked, the harder it became to stop.

The last thing I saw was a video clip of six soldiers in Chechnya, face down in a field, hands tied behind their backs, having their throats cut one by one. By then, the room around me was pitch black, making the computer screen so bright it hurt my eyes. The alcohol was buzzing in my head, and something else was humming in my chest. I'd gone to pour another drink, and, at that point, a sensible part of me had taken the executive decision that I'd seen and drunk enough.

More than enough, I realised now.

I filled the small hotel room's miniature kettle and found a sachet of coffee. Then, while I waited for the water to boil, I made my first phone call on the nice new mobile.

'Mike?' I said. 'It's Alex.'

'How are you doing, man?'

'I'm all right,' I said.

'Good stuff.' In the background, I could hear Josh crying, and Julie *shushing* him gently. 'We've not heard anything new.'

'I didn't think you would have. I was just wondering something. Have you got a couple of hours free?'

Mike paused. I imagined him looking across his front room, probably slightly reluctant, but not wanting to say no. That word had never settled comfortably into his vocabulary.

'Well, I'm supposed to be going to see James at ten.'

James. I remembered the blood Mike and I had seen yesterday in the kitchen, and wondered how he could bring himself to do it.

I said, 'No problem.'

'What did you have in mind?'

'I just wanted to bag a lift to Wrexley. But I can taxi it.'

He thought it over. 'That's not far. It should be all right if we go soon. I can be there in – what – twenty?'

The way I felt, twenty was bad.

I said, 'Twenty's good, thanks.'

We arranged for him to pick me up at the back of the train station. After I hung up, I looked across the room at the laptop, switched off but still open on the desk.

Do you know what you're doing?

The kettle clicked off below a tree of billowing steam, distracting me from the question. There wasn't much time. I poured the coffee and headed for the shower.

At half-nine, Mike dropped me off in Wrexley. We hadn't spoken too much on the way over. I got the impression Julie had been quietly disapproving of this, her boyfriend doing favours for someone who'd lost the right to ask for them, but if so he didn't mention it. He did, however, want to know where I was going and why. I told him as much as I could.

'Whoa, Alex,' he said. 'Maybe we should go to the police.'

'And say what? This is just something Sarah was working on, and I'm interested to see what it was. This guy, Ellis, he's only one of the freaks she was talking to. There's nothing to tell the police.'

'But what if he's dangerous?'

I shrugged. 'The notes are in my hotel room. His address is there. You can give it to the police if anything happens to me. But it won't.'

Mike was silent for a moment.

'And you're not going to do something stupid?'

'No.'

I wasn't sure what I was going to do. Sleep and daylight have a way of knocking all those night-time ideas out of your head, and I was finding it hard to believe Ellis really *was* behind the disappearance of Sarah's body. Then again, someone was. My plan was to confront him with what I knew and see what he had to say for himself. That was all.

I looked out of the window, watching the scenery flash past.

But I hadn't forgotten the exhilaration I'd heard as he'd watched my wife die. Or the thread title he'd chosen for her afterwards. *Bitch in bits.*

'No,' I said again. 'I'm not going to do anything stupid.'

Ellis lived in a large block of flats on the edge of town. Or rather, a block of blocks; there were four of them, one on each side of a central square. Mike dropped me off in the middle. Before leaving, he made me promise to call him when I was done.

'I will.'

'You'd better,' he said. 'I've got your number now.'

'I'll know who to blame those obscene calls on later.'

He grinned. 'Take care of yourself.'

After he'd driven away, I headed across the square, past a

shabby concrete playground. The rusted chains on the swings were tangled around the metal struts, and the seats had been stained yellow and brown by cigarette ends pressed against the plastic. The blocks of flats themselves were similarly unappealing. They'd been painted bright white, but all it had really achieved was to emphasise how ugly the structures were. Each floor was circled by a stone walkway, and appeared to be squinting its eyes closed against visitors. Even the sun couldn't cut through properly; it just slid through at an angle and landed in a thin, broken shard against the far block.

It was very quiet, but I wasn't entirely alone. A group of kids was hanging out in an alcove on the far side of the square, their heads pointed at me, faces barely visible inside the hoods. Three storeys up on that side, a man – incongruously wearing a suit and sunglasses – was leaning on a balcony, watching the world fail to go by.

I made my way to the base of Block C, and then into the stairwell, where the walls were covered with a scribbled collage of black marker pen that couldn't really be called graffiti. According to Sarah's notes, Ellis's flat was on the top floor. My footfalls echoed slightly as I headed up: *chit chit chit*, like a broom sweeping the stone.

Out on the walkway, it was surprisingly cold – just open enough to allow the breeze to cut through. At the far end, washing was hung across, flapping in the wind. Ellis's front door was halfway along, facing out across the square, beside a bent, wire mesh grille over a greasy window.

I knocked on the door, then waited.

There was furtive movement from inside. A second later, I had the impression that someone was looking out at me through the spy hole.

And then nothing.

Someone was obviously in there.

'Hello?' I knocked again. 'Christopher Ellis?'

There was another pause, and then whoever was inside made a decision. I heard the rattle of a chain being pulled back, then a creak as the door opened. It was a young woman who answered. She was wearing tracksuit bottoms and a black crop-top, and her face was drawn, the skin pulled back as tightly as the thin hair she'd gathered into a ponytail.

'He's not here,' she said.

'He does live here though?'

'Yeah.' She snorted, then began fiddling with a roll-up and a lighter. 'Apparently, anyway.'

I was a little surprised. Because of his interests, I'd been expecting Ellis to live alone. It also meant that if he really had followed Sarah and taken her body, he wasn't likely to have brought it here. I supposed that should have been obvious enough from the three flights of stairs.

'Are you his wife?'

She gave me a sarcastic look and I got the message. Girl-friend, perhaps, but not too happy with that arrangement at this moment in time.

She lit the roll-up.

'What do you want with him?'

'Nothing much. A chat.'

'Does he owe you money? Because you'll be disappointed. He hasn't got any.'

'It's not money,' I said. 'I just wanted to talk to him about someone. A mutual friend.'

'Oh yeah? Who? Maybe he's a mutual friend of mine too.'

'Sarah Pepper.'

The woman cocked her head at that, like a predator hearing a click in the undergrowth. It wasn't that she recognised the name. It was simply that it was a *woman's* name.

'Who's she?'

'You might not know her,' I said. 'And "friend" might be pushing it. She was a journalist. She came to interview him for an article, probably back around April time?'

'Yeah. About his computer stuff?'

'Maybe,' I said.

'No, I remember them.' She sniffed and rubbed the side of

her nose, then peered at the lit end of her cigarette. 'They went in the office. I don't know what they talked about though. I don't want anything to do with all that shit he does. I just don't want to know.'

I caught her use of the word that time.

'You said *them*?'

She frowned at me.

'Yeah – girl and a guy. That's who you're talking about, right? She had red hair. I don't know about him. Shaved head, I think.' She pumped her shoulders and chest out. 'Big fucking monkey guy, yeah?'

That was definitely her, and it sounded like James as well, which threw me a little. On one level, it made sense that Sarah had brought my brother along when she came to see Ellis: these were strange people she was talking to, after all. But something must have come between them – hard enough not only for Sarah to leave James, but for him to have amassed sufficient resentment and anger to snap. I'd been imagining her obsession was it, but if James had been involved too then the idea suddenly didn't make as much sense.

'That's them,' I said. 'Look – does Christopher have another place, or anything like that?'

'Yeah, he's got a mansion up the road.' She flicked ash past me, out towards the ledge. Then smiled thinly. 'He'll be down in The Duncan, if that's what you're asking. Pissing away more money we haven't got.'

'The Duncan?'

'The pub. Out on the main road.'

I checked my watch. 'It's open at this time?'

'It's always open. I'd go and drag him out myself, but you tell me – why should I fucking bother?'

'Thanks anyway. How will I recognise him?'

It was an odd question to ask, given the circumstances, but she didn't bat an eyelid. Maybe she was used to complete strangers coming looking for him, or maybe she didn't care.

'Skinny guy. Ginger. About fifty fucking years younger than everyone else in there.'

'Thanks.'

She turned back inside, and said almost to herself:

'On the outside, anyway.'

Seventeen

Back out on the main street, I nearly missed The Duncan. I walked halfway past the place before realising I was there.

The building itself was very old, and looked derelict. From its appearance, it might once have been a grand little hotel, but now it was just a crumbling stone facade with sad, empty arches. A 'FOR SALE' sign hung down near the roof, so battered and worn that it might have been there as long as the building had. There were two doors leading inside, and the signs above them were just wooden boards with the name carved into them. If I hadn't known to look, I'd have assumed the place was stripped down and closed up.

I pulled one of the doors open, and walked inside, immediately hit by a waft of stale tobacco and whisky.

It was just a single large room: a spill of dirty architecture that had pooled around the columns and pillars. The carpet was flattened and tacky, and the air was thick from the blue-grey smoke curling above the tables. I guessed the smoking ban wasn't taken too seriously in here. The bar was along one wall, illuminated by the bright-green bulbs in the beer pumps, while everything else was bathed in dim light that lent the whole pub, from the floor to the ceiling, a miserable orange sheen.

I headed straight to the bar and ordered a Coke, taking the opportunity to look around.

It was surprisingly full, although one look at the residents told me they were probably a constant feature, as familiar to the weary-looking barman as the fixtures and fittings were, and as my request for a Coke likely wasn't. A group of builders in paint-spattered jumpers and boots was standing at the bar, lifting frothy pints and barking laughter. Aside from them, the clientele was almost entirely comprised of elderly men wearing dusty old suits, most of whom looked like they'd drifted back here to haunt the place. The majority were alone at their own tables, staring at their drinks.

I spotted Ellis quickly enough. He was sitting at the far end, where a settee ran along the back of the room, curving into the occasional alcoves. A half-drunk pint of lager rested on the table in front of him.

He wasn't much older than me, although he looked it. He was also painfully thin. The cheap white shirt was too big for him, and the baggy sleeves were bunched at the elbow, revealing freckled forearms that maintained a steady width from his wrist on up. His hair was cropped short and visibly receding. As I looked at him, he was staring down at his hands, picking repetitively at a fingernail, and his lips were moving slightly. He wasn't talking to himself, but he wasn't a world away from it either.

I picked up my Coke and walked over.

You're not going to do something stupid?

This was the man who'd been there when Marie died. If he'd shouted something – caught her attention – perhaps it would have stopped her. Instead, his first instinct had been to scrabble for his mobile phone. *I couldn't wait to share this!* As though he was some kind of hunter and her death had been a trophy to mount on a fucking wall.

I stopped in front of him. The ice in my glass was rattling.

'Christopher?'

He looked up, startled.

His eyes were tiny, and his nose was large and curved. He reminded me of a lizard, how thin and pale and dry he looked.

'Christopher Ellis?'

117

'Who are you?'

It was a bad choice of words. They brought back the memory of a night-time street spinning around me, the rain hissing down. Sarah's face as she opened the door.

Alex, what's wrong?

And I realised I was going to do something stupid.

But something in my expression must have slipped, because before I could do anything at all, Ellis picked up his pint and threw it at me. Instinct took over. I closed my eyes and raised an arm, just as cold liquid splashed across my face and chest. At least the glass missed, shattering somewhere behind me. But I opened my eyes just as Ellis barrelled into me. My foot slid away, and I hit the floor.

'Fuck.'

I glanced around. He was already halfway across the pub, heading straight for one of the exits. For some reason, everyone else in the pub had stopped what they were doing.

I scrambled to my feet.

'Hey!' the barman shouted.

We both ignored him. Ellis slammed the door open so hard it nearly came off its hinges, while I was just running, determined to get hold of him. One of the builders at the bar half-heartedly stepped in my direction, and I palmed him away – 'Fuck off' – then smacked into the door as it slammed back towards me.

I half fell out onto the pavement.

Looked right, then left, and saw Ellis's back disappearing down the street.

I went after him. He was fast, though. His long legs were pounding hard at the ground, like he was running for his life. I did my best to match him, but he was quicker than he looked and began accelerating away.

'Ellis! I just want to talk!'

Obviously, that wasn't convincing. He swerved round the next corner and vanished from sight. I reached it a few seconds later, then caught sight of him ducking into a cobbled alley halfway down on the right beneath a coal-black viaduct. I sprinted across, just in time to see him make another turn at the far side of a skip up ahead. I rounded that, into a smaller, sheltered alley with a spiderweb of dirty metal fire escapes above.

Smash!

Ellis pulled a metal waste bin over as he ran. It rolled down the alley behind him, then stopped against the wall just as I reached it.

Leaping over. Landing OK.

He glanced over his shoulder, an expression of absolute terror on his face, then dodged under some scaffolding and vanished round another corner. A fluttering polythene sheet whipped my arm as I followed.

A large, open, concrete space now. It looked like a factory had been demolished, leaving the ground scarred and pitted. Ellis was cutting diagonally across, heading for a torn section in a chain link fence at the far corner. My shoes crunched on broken glass and rusted bolts as I sprinted after him. I heard the fence *ping* as he clambered through, and then he vanished off to the right.

A few seconds later, I eased myself beneath the sharp edges of the wire, and emerged onto a sandy footpath running along the edge of a canal.

It was empty. Ellis was gone.

My heart was pounding.

The footpath ahead was visible for at least a hundred metres, and there was no way he could have got that far. The dank water was undisturbed. I listened carefully. It was so quiet here I thought I could hear the midges that were flitting off the water's surface.

Slow down. Think.

I walked a little way along. Once I'd got past the end of the fence, there was a seven-foot concrete wall, the top studded with broken bottle glass. No blood, no tears of clothing: he'd not gone over. After the wall, though, the path crumbled away at the side into a stretch of woodland. The trees were standing straight and proud, stuck in a tangle of brambles and under-growth. It looked impenetrable, but I figured Ellis had to have cut into there.

There was no sign of him, but I couldn't see very far into it at all. I listened again and still heard nothing. If he was moving about in there, he was being careful. But maybe he was ducked down. Keeping still.

I took a step in. My heart was still thumping, and now the muscles in my legs were beginning to burn slowly.

'Ellis?'

A pair of birds scattered out from the trees.

'I just want to talk.'

No reply. I made my way through the undergrowth, keeping an eye out for a flash of his white shirt amongst the greenery. I even checked up in the trees. Nothing. If he was hiding, he'd found a good hole to lie in. But it only took a minute of strug-gling before I found a slope leading up to another back street, and realised he was probably long gone.

Shit.

Lost him.

I stood on the edge of the pavement and leaned on my knees, my heart making it clear it would slow down in its own sweet time. Although it was frustrating Ellis had got away, I was more confused by his reaction. Why the hell had he thrown a fucking pint glass at me? Even if I'd looked annoyed, it seemed an extreme response. And when I'd seen his face as he glanced back, he'd been absolutely terrified.

I walked a little way up the street and found the main road.

Yeah, well. I know where you live, you silly bastard.

I started off in what I hoped was the right direction, but then felt a vibration in my pocket. It was Mike ringing me, but when I checked my watch it wasn't much after ten. He must have finished with my brother earlier than expected. I held the phone to my ear as I walked.

'Hey.'

His voice was excited, urgent. 'Alex? You OK?'

'Yeah, I'm fine.'

'How did it go with Ellis?'

I ran my hand through my hair, scanning the street as I went.

'Couldn't exactly pin him down,' I said. 'You?'

'I don't know.' He sounded more out of breath than I did. 'But I asked James about him. About this Ellis guy.'

'What?' I stopped walking. Then started again. 'Never mind. What did he say?'

'He said he'd never heard of him.'

'He's lying.'

'It was strange, though. He got really pissed off when I told him about you coming home.'

'That's not strange.'

'No, but he clammed up. It was different from how he's been. He looked like . . . I don't know, like he'd been *caught out*, or something.'

I didn't think that was particularly strange, either, given the relationship we had. I could imagine how much he'd resent me being here.

'Did he say anything else?'

'He said this was all your fault.'

'Really?'

Even by my brother's standards, that was rich. Feeling a degree of guilt for letting Sarah down was one thing, but I wasn't going to be handed any by him. Whatever I might have done, James was responsible for his own fucking actions.

'Yeah. He said to ask you about a guy called Peter French. Mean anything?'

'No,' I said.

But I stopped in my tracks.

For a moment, I just stood there, feeling my heart knocking against my chest. That was a name I'd not heard in a long time.

'What did he say about him?'

'He said to ask you. And about a letter, as well. He wanted to know if you'd found it yet. What does that mean?'

I thought about it. The only letter I could think of was the one I'd sent Sarah before I left, but I couldn't imagine what relevance that had. *J's really annoyed at you for running out.* Was that it? Was he blaming me for leaving Sarah to deal with what she eventually found?

'I don't know,' I said. 'What else?'

'He was really angry. Do you know a place called the Chalkie?'

I frowned. 'Why?'

'Because he said to tell you to go there.'

Mike paused.

'He said, "to see what he's done".'

Eighteen

When the door went for the second time that morning, Mandy Gilroyd cursed her boyfriend. And not just for the second time. As if she didn't have enough shit to deal with worrying about their finances, she was apparently now expected to be his fucking secretary as well. Christ, he was a bastard. Drowning his sorrows, whatever the hell they were, while he left her here to . . . take messages for him. She had no idea what he thought he was playing at, but it was going to have to stop.

'Hang on,' she shouted. 'Shit.'

She stalked around the front room. The place was a tip. No doubt Chris imagined she was going to take care of that for him as well. There were six empty green cans on the small table, one of them on its side, doubled-up, like a soldier that had been shot; half a takeaway curry, congealed in a tin-foil tray; two bowls over-flowing with cigarette ends – although that was partly her.

The only time Mandy ever felt like tidying was in the handful of seconds after someone had knocked at the door. Since that was impossible, it just made her angry instead. *Bastard.* Refusing to put down her drink, she half-heartedly kicked one of Chris's jumpers to the side of the settee, where it wrapped its arms around the wooden leg.

Bang bang bang.

'I said: *hang on.*'

She skirted the coffee table and crossed to the door.

'Fuck's sake.'

She undid the chain and opened the door. There was a man in a suit standing outside, half silhouetted against the sun. He was looking off down the walkway, but then he turned to her and smiled. He was in his fifties, and had a kind face, but the smile was professional, and she'd seen enough of them in her time to know what he was.

'A cop,' she said. 'Brilliant.'

'Miss Gilroyd?'

'What the hell's he done now?'

Immediately, she felt bad for that. Her personal problems with Chris were one thing, but this was the police. A common enemy. For the first time that morning, she summoned up some solidarity with her boyfriend, and set her expression hard, folding her arms. She forgot about the mug she was holding, which slopped a little vodka-coffee down the doorframe.

The policeman still smiled, although she knew he'd seen.

'That obvious, is it?' he said. 'Here.'

He took out his wallet and showed her his ID. Detective David Garland.

She said nothing.

'Can I come in?'

Mandy shrugged – whatever – then turned away and walked back into the front room. She knew from experience that it wasn't worth arguing. Garland took the hint and followed her inside, closing the door behind him.

'Is Christopher in?'

'Nope.'

'He due back any time soon?'

'Why are you asking me?'

She turned round, expecting him to be annoyed at her tone, but he didn't seem to have even noticed. He wasn't actually looking at her. Instead, he'd wandered over to the bookcase and was peering curiously at a few of Chris's books. The top shelf. Garland ran his finger along the spines there. Mandy knew what those books were. Chris had shown her one about a year ago, as though it was some kind of challenge. She'd shrugged at the time. Then avoided looking at them since.

'Nice little collection,' Garland said.

'They're not mine.' Mandy folded her arms again, remembering the drink this time. 'What do you want?'

'Have you heard of a man called Roger Timms?'

'Nope.'

Garland stared across the room at her, incredulous.

'You don't watch the news?'

She shrugged. 'Never heard of the guy.'

'Does Chris know him?'

'I don't know. And like I said, Chris isn't here.'

'Well, I can wait.' Garland wandered across the room towards her. 'By the way, who was that at the door earlier?'

'The door?'

Suddenly, he didn't look quite so kind any more. A chill went through her. Something wasn't right here. But he was a cop, wasn't he? The ID had looked like . . . well, it had looked like ID.

He was right in front of her now.

'What did he want?'

You've made a mistake here.

'I don't – what?'

But Garland just smiled. Everything froze for a moment, and then Mandy threw her mug at him and tried to dodge past. She was dimly aware of him moving, then the room spun round in a flash, and she was now on her back at the side of the settee. Looking at the ceiling. It felt like she was wearing those old 3D glasses: one of her eyes had gone red. She blinked, and it hurt.

He stepped into view above, tall as a statue, and looked down at her with a blank expression.

By his side – very loosely, as though it was an afterthought – he was holding a gun.

Garland worked his way through Christopher Ellis's flat quickly and methodically. Having already done a damage calculation – nobody had seen him arrive, he'd subdued Gilroyd quietly, and the chain was on the front door in case Ellis returned – he knew there was no need to rush. But he liked to be as efficient as possible. Time was a precious thing: like food and water, you never knew when it might run out. He took it even more seriously when someone else was paying for it.

He searched the drawers and cabinets in the front room, scanning each individual document in turn. Slowly but surely, he gathered together printouts, bank statements and any documents he thought might prove incriminating, and piled them in the centre of the living room floor.

Confidentiality.

All business, Garland knew, was the same below the surface. Someone sold an item and someone bought it – not always an item, and not always with money, but in principle a business was just a market stall. The company Garland worked for was no different. It was just that the stall was set up in a darker corner of the square and the transactions had to be hidden by shadows.

To deal with problems that arose, the organisation employed cleaners. They were men with a natural affinity for the task at hand: usually ex-soldiers or mercenaries, who were intelligent, professional and – when required – at ease with killing.

Problems such as Christopher Ellis.

Men such as Garland.

After he'd swept the front room, he moved through to the makeshift office Ellis had created in the flat's small second bedroom. On the way past, he stopped briefly to check on Amanda Gilroyd. She was lying on her side on the bed, hands and feet cuffed, with a bunched towel knotted in her mouth and tied tightly round her head. Keeping still.

Good.

On a personal level, Garland felt sorry for the woman. The only mistake she'd made was to have a relationship with the wrong man, and what would happen to her today was completely disproportionate to that particular crime. To begin with, he'd watched her asking herself *why*. Garland had seen that response before. People genuinely believed the world functioned on that level. Accustomed to the gently wavering peaks and troughs of everyday fortune, they were often shocked when the graph spiked suddenly downwards, without warning.

Nevertheless, she had been forthright and helpful, telling him everything he needed to know in a small but determined voice. She had convinced herself that co-operating with him would save her life. Garland had seen that response before too.

He turned away from the bedroom and moved down to the office. It had been two weeks since he'd arrived in the country – landing on a private flight to a private airfield – and he'd spent the intervening time evaluating the situation here as it developed. A number of events had forced him to act sooner than he would have preferred, but still: he had been confident everything was now under control, and that dealing with Ellis would be one of the last actions required of him.

But now there was this mystery man.

Turning up here and asking about Sarah Pepper.

Over the years, Garland had become accustomed to weighing the available facts and making calculations, and he knew full well the man was a problem. His arrival had answered one of the few remaining questions Garland had, and yet posed several new ones.

But he pushed it to the back of his mind for now. There was no point. Amanda Gilroyd clearly didn't know, so it would have been unproductive and unfair to talk to her. Ellis wasn't home yet. Therefore those questions had to wait.

He clicked on the light in the spare room.

It was more of a shrine than an office: a temple to Ellis's peculiar obsession. Garland's gaze moved over the items within, taking in the details and assessing what he saw. They were of no interest to him in themselves, only as potential sums of money. As with any business, you salvaged what you could.

A framed reprint of Roger Timms's 'Disgrace' had pride of

place above Ellis's desk. It was the second of the *Gehenna* series – notorious and highly sought-after in certain enlightened circles – but a reprint was worth nothing. Middle-class people hung them on their walls. A devil mask in a glass display case was more valuable, he thought, but it was bolted in place and too cumbersome to move.

Ellis had also collected the standard letters, most of them with prison addresses in the corners. Locks of hair. Vials of blood. Child-like illustrations. Garland recognised several names, but the currency attached to them was of a decidedly low denomination. The mask aside, this was the itinerary of an amateur.

He sat down at the desk and booted up Ellis's computer, hoping the information would be simple to find. It was. Five minutes later, he had logged into several places and destroyed what was necessary. When he was confident that the online files had been removed, he took a USB stick from his jacket pocket, slotted it into the back of the computer and opened the contents up on the monitor. Within a minute, the programs contained on the memory stick had worked their way through Ellis's data and left it ravaged and unreadable.

Almost done.

The final task was to check the drawers in here for additional paperwork: anything that would need adding to the small bonfire he'd accumulated in the front room.

Garland was halfway through that when he heard the front door open, clattering against the chain.

'Mandy? What the fuck – open the door.'

A man's voice. Ellis was home.

Garland pushed the drawer shut, checked his gun with a frown, then walked quietly back to the front room to let the man in.

Nineteen

I didn't know why the older kids had called it the Chalkie. Perhaps they thought it was part of the old quarry. They were both on the south side of Whitrow, close to where the river curled past, but the Chalkie was on the other side of a small road, hidden away between the trees. You climbed a rusted old barrier and then took the vaguest of paths through the undergrowth, never quite sure whether you were going in the right direction or not. Eventually, the weathered, broken-down buildings appeared slowly between the trees, emerging piece by piece, like the fragments of some ruined temple.

I had no idea what it had been before the woodland took it over. All that remained of the original structure was a blackened roof supported several metres above the ground on four enormous, charred timbers, like a giant's table. There were also three overgrown bunkers: little more than doorways leading into thin corridors full of rainwater and pitch-black debris, illuminated by streaks of light from blowholes in the ground above. In places, large wooden blocks rested in weathered piles, with metal ladders bolted to the sides but nothing on top worth climbing them for.

A generation of kids made it their own, then passed it on to the next. Every stone surface was covered in ageing graffiti, broken glass, or ash and burnt newspaper. It was where my brother used to go with his friends. They would drink and smoke weed, have sex and get into fights.

At fifteen, I wasn't old enough – not that James would ever have invited me anyway – but one night I made my way down there. I don't know why. Perhaps I felt some stupid sense of entitlement. That if my brother could go there, I should be able to as well.

It was raining that night, hissing in the air, tapping the leaves above and shining on the dark-green undergrowth. I heard my brother and his friends before I saw them. The first sound was somebody whooping in the distance – and then glass shattering, followed by a collective cheer. Another person, a girl this time, shouted and swore. Then someone belched, and a few people's laughter echoed between the trees.

'Fuck!'

A man's voice. I was still out of sight, but the word came at me like a spear. Full of threat.

Then it came again.

I stopped at the edge of the tree line. It was James, of course. He was standing on the edge of the concrete floor, leaning against one of the pillars, bellowing out at the world. Light from the campfire behind him flickered around the sides of his face, hinting at the contortions of anger there. He looked like he was concentrating on something. Summoning up rage like magic.

Another glass shattered.

Back by the fire, I could only make out shapes and silhouettes: shadows flickering against the back wall. Someone tossed something, and sparks skittered upwards. The flames made it seem as though twenty people were huddled there.

My brother bellowed again.

This time it wasn't even a word, and it wasn't directed at anyone, either, or at least not anyone I could see. It was as though he was trying to make an impact on the trees themselves: to knock them down with his voice. Years later, when Marie died, I would recognise a similar feeling, but back then I looked at him and couldn't understand what I was seeing. He was a stranger.

'What are you *shouting* for?' someone complained.

'Ignore him. He's fucked.'

Someone laughed, and James half glanced behind him, on the verge of saying something. Instead, he lifted a bottle of beer and took a swig, glaring out at the wood again. A moment later, he turned in my direction, and his eyes met mine.

I don't think he recognised me at first. He just saw a strange kid that had turned up at the camp uninvited, then frozen on the perimeter. But when he realised who it was, the expression on his face went utterly blank. He didn't say anything and he didn't need to, because I felt it inside me. The rain pattered down around, and I knew. My brother hated me. He hated me for what I was and for what he wasn't, and maybe a hundred other things that neither of us would ever be able to articulate.

He threw the empty bottle with real purpose, so fast and hard that I barely had time to dodge. It went slightly wide anyway, wheeling past and hitting the tree beside me with a dull clunk, then landing – unbroken – in the undergrowth.

He looked defeated at missing. One more disappointment added to the pile. I was absolutely certain that he'd intended to hit me, and if he had it would have fractured my skull. For a moment, I thought he might even come running at me, but he just stood there, swaying slightly.

I turned around and walked back the way I'd come.

It was another year before I went again, this time with friends of my own, including Sarah. My brother had moved on to the pubs by then, and taken to huddling in corners and shouting with his eyes rather than his voice. He'd been so drunk that night, I was never sure whether he even remembered it.

But obviously he had.

Tell Alex to go to the Chalkie, he'd told Mike.

To see what he's done.

Mike was a sensible man. After he picked me up from Wrexley, he told me he wanted to go to the police. I wasn't a sensible man, so I said no.

When he objected and said he was going to go anyway, I pointed out the inconvenient truth that he had no idea where or what this place was, so he wouldn't be able to tell them anything anyway. Instead of enlightening him, I provided basic directions. Grudgingly, he set off.

'Look,' I said. 'It's probably nothing.'

Mike shook his head. 'Why would it be nothing? And you're seriously telling me you don't know who "Peter French" is?'

I sighed. 'All right, that wasn't entirely true.'

'What?'

'I'm sorry. The name just caught me off guard.'

Hearing it, I'd felt like James had reached out and grabbed tight hold of the front of my shirt. Like he was glaring right into my face. Having had time to think about it, I thought I understood now.

Mike waited for me to explain. It wasn't going to be easy, but I tried my best.

'Peter French,' I said, 'was Marie's stepfather.'

That was probably an exaggeration, but it was close enough to do. Marie's mother was an alcoholic, and she clung to stupid relationships with the wrong people. I didn't think she ever married French, but he certainly lasted longer than most of the men who came into and out of the house. But then, Marie was ten years old at that point, and so he had other reasons for staying.

'When she was eleven,' I said, 'she sat down with her mother and finally told her what was going on. And this woman's reaction was to ask Marie what she wanted her to do. Did she want her to leave Peter French? This fucking woman sat there and asked her eleven-year-old daughter to make that decision.'

And in the end, Marie said no.

'Christ.' Mike looked at me. 'I never knew.'

'Nobody did. Marie had good days and bad days, but it never really left her. I tried to help her as much as I could, but . . .'

I trailed off. It was true: both that I'd tried, and the thing I couldn't quite bring myself to say, which was that it had never been enough. When the depression hit, it was like a steel shell closed around her. But even in better times, I knew there was something inside her that remained completely impervious to anything I said or did, and that it always would.

Mike said, 'But James knew?'

'He shouldn't have. I told Sarah about it in a letter.'

At the moment, I remembered writing, *I'm not sure where I'm going. All I know is that I have to get away. But before I leave, I want to tell you something. Something that you deserve to know.*

'I was trying to explain why I needed to leave. Part of that involved wanting her to know how badly I let Marie down.'

'Alex—'

'Yeah, I did.' I closed my eyes, not wanting to get into this with him. 'And it doesn't matter any more. The point is, he's just striking out. Trying to hurt me.'

I pictured that small, sad figure, extending its arms sideways, tipping its head back, and I felt a jolt of anger at my brother. Throwing that name at me now, just as he had that bottle all those years ago. Only this time, he'd hit.

Tell Alex this is all his fault.

Mike sighed. 'What about this place, then?'

'That, I don't know.' I ran through the story of my encounter there with James, but I genuinely had no idea what relevance it had. 'It's probably just another way of telling me to fuck off.'

Mike thought about it.

'Maybe we should go to the police.'

'Not yet.'

'We could find a body there, Alex.'

That had been on my mind too. As the crow flies, the Chalkie was little more than a mile from the field where Sarah had gone missing. But I'd been mulling it over, and I didn't think it made sense.

'We won't,' I said. 'The police have already found the place he left Sarah's body. James told them.'

'And now it's gone.'

I nodded. 'Yeah, but whoever stole it, that was *after* he'd turned himself in. If it was here, how would he know?'

Mike said nothing.

'The only way would be if the person who did it went in and told him, and then, for some bizarre reason, he decided to keep it to himself. I mean, has he even had any other visitors?'

'No.'

'So whatever he meant by it, it's something else.' I looked out of the window. 'And anyway, we don't even know if the place is still there.'

But it was.

The road reared up ahead: the large, hump-back bridge over the river. Coming down the far side, we drove past the dirt track leading towards the quarry, then a quaint, old building set back from the road – a stables, with old black cartwheels bolted to the outside walls – and then pulled up at the bottom of the hill.

The woodland to the side was thick, but the path was still there. The barrier was too, although so rusted that it had cracked in places and the metal looked as fragile as parchment.

'You should wait here.' I opened the door. 'Just in case. If I'm not out in forty minutes, call the police.'

'Forty?'

I shrugged. 'It's easy to get lost in there.'

Mike nodded, but reluctantly.

'All right. Be careful.'

'Don't worry.'

I gave the barrier an experimental shake and sharp flakes of metal came away on my palms. But it still felt surprisingly solid. I clambered over, my feet landing silently in the thick grass beyond, then dusted my hands off on my jeans and set off.

Could I still remember the way? Within a few metres of the road, the old path seemed to disappear; there was just a vague suggestion of space between the trees, the undergrowth spiralling and curling up to knee height. I found a large stick on the ground, then used it to push the brambles aside and work my way through. I was hoping that either memory or instinct was going to lead me in the right direction.

In less than a minute, the road was out of sight and I was lost amongst the trees. Behind me, the undergrowth had sprung up again, almost indignantly, as though it had been here for long enough now and wasn't going to be kept down by the likes of me. I stopped. The sun was filtering through the trees above, and I could hear the rush of the river from somewhere up ahead, full of quiet purpose. Those sounds aside, I felt isolated. In all directions, as far as I could tell, there were just trees and bushes and darkness.

It took nearly ten minutes to find it. One moment I was wandering aimlessly, pressed at on all sides and beginning to panic slightly in the quiet, damp claustrophobia of the wood – the next, there it was, the old, familiar structures appearing between the trees in front of me.

Wow.

I stepped onto the concrete floor of the central structure and glanced overhead. The timbers were still holding the roof up. At the bottom, brambles had wrapped themselves around the struts, tight and sharp as barbed wire, while grass poked through cracks in the slabs on the ground. On the back wall, the graffiti now looked so old and faded that it might have been part of the stone. The silence was monumental.

It felt like nobody had been here for years, maybe even since my friends and I vacated it. In the time since, the forest had reached out and begun claiming the place back for itself, and that task was nearly complete.

Except that someone had lit a fire here.

I walked across to the far edge of the floor.

There was a small pile of half-burnt wood, with the stone underneath and around it charred black. I scattered the remnants with my foot, breathing in the scent of ash and soot that wafted up at me. It looked and smelled fresh. Someone had been here fairly recently. Sitting out, keeping warm.

I stood still and listened. There was no sound at all now.

It could have been a tramp, I thought. *Or kids.*

It was nice and isolated here, after all, and would probably still make an ideal drop-in centre for any local derelicts that happened to know about it. And it wasn't like the area would have run out of teenagers. At the same time, there wasn't any of the other debris I'd have expected from people sleeping rough or partying. No smashed bottles or crushed cans. No old food.

Check around.

The heavy silence was putting me on edge.

Check around, then get the fuck out of here.

I circled round the back of the building, grateful I had the stick with me, if nothing else, and then ducked quickly into each of the gloomy, old bunkers. They were all empty.

I was heading round the side of the building when I spotted someone slumped in the tree line off to the side.

I froze in my tracks.

It was hard to tell whether it really was a person or not, but it certainly looked like it. Someone was lying there, dressed in blue and curled up in the undergrowth. But if so, they were utterly still.

For a second, I just stared.

'Hello?'

No response.

I made my way slowly between the trees. As I got closer, I realised what it was and moved a little more quickly. It wasn't a person at all, but a faded blue rucksack that had been tossed away into the grass. I reached it and stopped. It was slightly worn at the bottom, but didn't appear to have been here all that long. If it had, I'd have expected the elements to have knocked it into a slightly more neglected shape. Instead, the fabric was crumpled but clean. It was just lying there, in fact, as though someone knew full well where it was and might come back at any moment and pick it up again.

I crouched down in the grass.

Should I open it?

There was a cord drawn tight around the throat of the rucksack. My fingers hovered there.

If this – somehow – was what James had wanted me to find then there might be evidence to think about, and the police wouldn't be too happy with me putting my hands on it. I glanced around. But then, I'd already trampled all over the place, hadn't I? And as things stood, there was no reason to call the police anyway. Without interfering with the scene, there'd be nothing to convince them this was a scene at all.

Which it probably isn't.

So I loosened the toggle and pulled it down to the end of the drawstrings, then stretched the bag open. From moving it slightly, it felt light, but there was at least something inside. I couldn't make out the contents, so, very carefully, I reached in and used my thumb and finger to lift out the first item it came to. It rustled as it came . . .

A sheet of paper, screwed into a ball.

The letter. My heart started thumping. I knew deep down it wasn't, but ever since James had mentioned it, I couldn't stop thinking about it. Had Sarah told him, or had he seen it himself? Did he still have it? It wasn't really important, of course, but for some reason it felt like it mattered.

This wasn't it though. I uncreased the paper, smoothing it out against my thigh, and it was almost entirely blank, except for the top corner, where someone had scribbled a few words in biro. The writing was messy, but I could just make out:

Emily Price
168 Castle View

I turned the sheet over, but there was nothing else – just the name and a partial address, neither of which were familiar to me. Did the rucksack belong to 'Emily Price'? Or was it someone the owner knew, or had maybe been arranging to meet? I peered into the bag again. The only other thing inside was a plastic water bottle. I pulled it out.

Jesus Christ.

My first instinct was to throw it away between the trees. I forced myself not to.

Don't move.

The bottle was old, and had been used so many times that the label had come off, leaving white tufts stuck to the glue. And it was empty, in the sense there was no actual liquid in it any more. But the inside was stained a horrible, dirty crimson colour. There were red and black flakes crusted to the inner ridges of the plastic like scabs.

Blood.

Just as when Mike had told me about Sarah going missing, it took a second to follow the thought to its natural conclusion. Someone had kept a water bottle full of blood in their rucksack. They'd carried it round with them. And then abandoned it here.

Why the fuck would someone do that?

The other thing was that it was empty. There had been blood in it at one point, and now there wasn't. So where had it gone?

One answer came to me like a shiver.

They drank it.

I turned and looked back at the ashes on the concrete floor.

They sat here and drank it.

But even as that terrible image settled in my mind, I began to doubt myself. Rationalise it away. It wasn't blood, of course – that was ridiculous. Despite its appearance, the bag could have been here for weeks. The bottle could have held soup, or maybe some kind of drink. Or anything, in fact. There could be any number of explanations, and there had to be, because . . .

Because what kind of man carried blood around to drink?

I think it might have been all right if I hadn't asked myself that last question. Instead, I'd thrown my mind a shape, and it quietly, expertly, turned it around now until it found the worst possible angle, and the answer that went along with it.

The kind of man, I thought, that steals a body from a field.

And yet what I'd said to Mike back in the car remained true: that didn't make any sense. There was no way James could know about that, and I couldn't think of a single plausible motivation for him keeping quiet about it if he did. So I crouched there in the undergrowth for a few minutes, thinking it over, wondering what to do.

Tell Alex this is all his fault.

James had wanted me to come here to see what I'd done, which implied it would be obvious. But I had no idea what I'd found here, or whether what I was looking at had any connection to my brother at all. This could be random. A co-incidence.

I thought about it some more, and came to a decision. I took out my mobile phone and used the camera on it to take a photograph of the bottle, the note, and the rucksack, and then I replaced the items and took the whole bag round to the other side of the Chalkie, hiding it in one of the bunkers.

Fifteen minutes later, I climbed back over the barrier and dusted my palms off again on my jeans.

'Anything interesting?' Mike said.

'No. Nothing there at all.'

I slid into the passenger seat. I felt guilty for lying to him, but I'd rationalised it to myself. By not telling Mike what I'd found, I was protecting him. If this was a mistake, I was taking sole responsibility for it: nobody would be able to say that he knew and didn't go to the police.

'So what do you think it meant?'

'No idea.' That at least was true. 'Which means I'm going to have to ask him. I'll book in for tomorrow morning. You got the number?'

'Sure.'

Mike fished for his phone. I wondered if James would even see me – but I thought that somehow he would. And he could explain it to me in person. I opened my mobile, waiting while Mike checked his own, and looked at the photo I'd taken of the note.

Emily Price. 168 Castle View.

Until I saw James, there was at least one more thing I could do. But this time it would be on my own.

Twenty

East Street House was located in the heart of the city centre. It rose up between the arched hoardings of high-street shops, dwarfing them: seventeen storeys of glass painted with fractured reflections of the world around. From the pedestrian precinct, looking up, Kearney could see himself in the angled windows of the second floor. Higher up, the building became pale blue. And right at the top – shielding his eyes against the glint of the sun – he saw wispy clouds drifting slowly across, like the building was dreaming.

'No one scared of heights, are they?' he said.

'No, sir.'

The two officers he'd brought with him avoided his eyes a little. Perhaps they were unnerved by how ragged he looked. Well, that was fine; he wasn't particularly in the mood for conversation anyway.

Inside, the reception area was small. The guard signed them in, phoned ahead to Arthur Hammond, and then pressed a button that allowed them entrance to one of the pair of lifts.

The three of them shot upwards quickly, in silence. Kearney stood in the centre, facing the steadily illuminating numbers above the door. Rather than just lighting your floor, the electronic display filled in your progress, like a file downloading. As the only alternative was looking at himself – weary and drained – in the mirrors to the side, Kearney watched as the lift went past the ninth, the light stretching steadily across. The exhibition was on the fourteenth floor. He literally had no idea what was happening on the others. Were they rented by businesses? He'd walked past it a thousand times and never given it a moment's thought.

Ting!

When the doors opened, they were met by a short man in his sixties. He was dressed in a grey suit that matched both his neatly combed hair and thick moustache. He was also wearing a waistcoat and a bowtie. Despite his tiredness, Kearney found himself pleasantly surprised by that; people's eccentricities often delighted him. Todd, back at the department, would probably have stared in horror.

'Mr Hammond?' They shook hands. 'I'm Detective Paul Kearney. We spoke on the phone. These are my colleagues, DS Ross, DS Johnson.'

'Nice to meet you all. It's this way.' Hammond's shoes clicked down the corridor as they walked. 'I'm sorry if I'm distracted. The exhibition is due to open at seven, and we're seriously behind.'

'I'm sorry to hear that.'

'*Seriously* behind.'

Kearney nodded, well aware of this by now. He'd spoken to Hammond earlier, following a difficult morning spent tracking down Roger Timms's artwork. In an ideal world, they would be able to recall every single piece, even the ones from before the murders, but five paintings in particular were most important. The *Gehenna* series.

Those five, in effect, counted as crime scenes.

It wasn't easy. Timms had done the exact opposite to what Kearney would have expected with such personal work. Instead of keeping the portraits for his own gratification, each of the five had been sold. The matter was complicated even further by his tangle of finances. Various accounts under Timms's name showed hundreds of payments, in and out, not all of which appeared to correlate with his tax returns or business records.

Of the *Gehenna* series, they'd traced one painting to a US dealer, whom Todd was still attempting to locate. Another two were owned by separate collectors down south; they'd both been spoken to, and officers were on their way to collect them. And the final two paintings had been bought by Arthur Hammond, a local businessman and arts enthusiast. He was curating this current exhibition, which was due to open tonight, and he was not happy.

Kearney sympathised to an extent. However, the man's disappointment wasn't all that high on his list of priorities right now.

They stopped at a set of double doors.

Hammond said, 'We're still waiting for several pieces.'

'Like I said, we're sorry. It's no consolation, I know, but you're about to have two less to worry about.'

'Two fewer.'

Kearney had enough time to think *did he just correct my grammar?* and then Hammond pushed open the doors and walked into the gallery.

'And those two were already in place.'

Inside, Kearney was shocked by how white everything was. All the walls were clear and clean; the angles, sharp. The effect was emphasised by the large, bright windows that ran along one side, and by the bulbs embedded in the ceiling. The latter were all inexplicably turned on.

'This way.'

Hammond led them through.

They walked past people in overalls, who all seemed to be either heaving packages across the floor or carefully cutting them open with Stanley knives. There was a hum of electricity in the air. From behind the scenes, Kearney could hear hammering and what sounded like someone drilling through plasterboard: an angry, shrieking whine. Hammond rounded a corner. Two students here were minutely adjusting the angle of a bronze statue. As far as Kearney could tell, it wasn't actually moving.

'There,' Hammond said. 'What is currently the *focus* of the exhibition. And will shortly become an empty wall. I suppose the notoriety will at least add something to proceedings.'

Kearney kept a leash on the anger that buzzed inside at that. *Empathy*, he reminded himself. After all, Hammond didn't know the precise reason for the seizure of the paintings. From his point of view, he'd worked hard to put on an exhibition, and now two of his prize pieces were about to go missing.

'The *Gehenna* series,' Hammond said. 'Part of it, anyway.'

The two paintings were mounted on a white wall by themselves. Even from a distance, they were striking, and, as they approached, the effect only deepened.

Both canvases showed the pale face of a woman, tilted to one side, the mouth open in a howl of anguish. Both were surrounded by a hellish, crimson background. On the left, a rough portrait of Linda Holloway. The face on the right belonged to Jane Kerekes. They were stylised, though. Only recognisable if you knew who you were looking for.

Christ, Kearney thought.

This is actually them.

Last night, in addition to his usual activities, he'd done some brief research on the computer. *Gehenna*, as far as he could discern, was another word for Hell, derived from the Hebrew name for some valley outside the walls of Jerusalem. It was where priests had supposedly worshipped strange gods and made child sacrifices. Afterwards, when those practices had been outlawed, the valley had become a garbage dump where the bodies of criminals were thrown. Fires burned there constantly, and the ground crawled with maggots. Some people thought of it as the literal entrance to the underworld.

Just as the seed became the tree, Roger Timms had taken the blood of these dead women and given them a different kind of life. He'd sealed them into an image of themselves, crying out in pain, on these two canvases. And then he'd named his series after a fucking rubbish tip.

Hammond said, 'It is these you were wanting?'

'Yes.'

'It's such fine work. It's a shame people won't see them.'

Hammond was looking at the paintings lovingly. It was obvious that, in his mind, these two paintings were very special indeed. And, of course, they were, but not for the reasons he thought. Looking at them now gave Kearney a chill.

'No.' He turned around. 'It's not really a shame at all, Mr Hammond. We need you to get these packaged up for us so we can get out of your way.'

'Absolutely.' Hammond nodded once. 'Of course.'

If he was offended by the bluntness, he didn't show it, just retreated into the exact kind of polite formality Kearney would have expected from a man in a bowtie and waistcoat. Hammond excused himself, and then the two sergeants separated and paced aimlessly away to either side. Two students began preparing the paintings for transport, lifting the first one down between them very carefully, like a window frame.

Kearney ran his hand through his hair, annoyed with himself for losing his temper. It was just that urgent pressure *beating* inside him. And he was so tired.

It had been after one o'clock in the morning when he'd got home last night. After researching the *Gehenna* series, he'd then sat up even later – stupidly – clicking through his old files, searching online. It had got to the point where he barely even knew what he was looking for any more. Eventually, close to dawn, he'd woken up in the office chair, then dragged himself across to the bed. When he'd woken only slighter later – driven upright by an image of Rebecca Wingate screaming against a red sunset – the yellow man had been lying beside him.

And then was gone again.

Kearney turned on his heels now and walked back across the gallery, seeking out Hammond again.

'Excuse me,' he said. 'I'm sorry if I was blunt.'

'Not at all.'

'This case is very trying for us.'

'There's no need to apologise, Detective.' Hammond passed

a list of papers to someone, then gave Kearney his full attention. 'You do look very tired, if you don't mind me saying so.'

'I am tired, yes. And no, I don't mind.'

Hammond was the second person today to tell him that. When he'd arrived at the department, a little after seven o'clock this morning, he'd felt hollowed out and grey. As early as it was, Simon Wingate had been sitting in reception. Perhaps he'd been there all night. Even though it was the last thing Kearney wanted to do, he'd gone and sat down beside him, and Wingate had said the exact same thing. The concern on the man's face had actually scared him.

Don't worry about that, Kearney had said. *It's my job to be tired.*

He glanced behind him now, then back at Hammond.

'Have you met him? Roger Timms?'

'I have, yes.' He nodded. 'A few times – at events and so forth. And while purchasing those two pieces, of course.'

'What's he like? As a person, I mean.'

'Well, I certainly wouldn't say I *know* him. In fact, he was always quite distant. All part of the persona, I suppose. But very sure of himself – very *astute*, you might say. Charismatic too. There was always that slight element of danger to him.'

Yes, Kearney thought. *There was.*

'Because of his crimes?'

'Yes. It added interest. I suppose that's hard for you to understand.'

Kearney shrugged. That side of things wasn't so complicated. In his experience, people were always interested in violence – attracted to it, even – so long as it wasn't happening to them. There were harder things to understand.

'That was all part of it, obviously. An artist's work . . .' Hammond gestured around, pivoting almost elegantly at the waist, then looked back at Kearney. 'It's rarely just the paintings or the sculptures.'

'No?'

'Not the more interesting pieces. These things are just

objects, after all. Much work is quite ordinary in and of itself. The effect occurs in your head, you see?'

Kearney did his best to smile.

Hammond rested a hand on his arm, leaning in again.

'Do you remember those university students?' he said. 'There was a lot of controversy. They raised funds for their end-of-year project, and had the examiners meet them at the airport. They'd spent all the money on a holiday.'

'Oh. Yeah.' Kearney dimly remembered the photographs in the paper: young people tanning themselves by the pool, drinking sangria and looking pleased with themselves. 'I didn't read it all.'

'They were on the news, in the papers and magazines. Everywhere.'

'Right. And that was "art"?'

'No, no. The reality was that they *hadn't* been anywhere. The photographs and plane tickets were all faked. They were the *objects*, if you like. But the actual *art* was all the coverage they generated. The thoughts and discussions.' Hammond stepped back. 'It was downstairs here. They filled four whole walls.'

It sounded vaguely pointless to Kearney, but he supposed he understood what Hammond meant.

'So knowing what Timms had done gave people something else to think about when they looked at his stuff?' He grasped for the right phrase. 'To *read* into it?'

Hammond nodded, then looked over behind them.

'Just as, I'm afraid to say, whatever he's done now will too.'

Kearney turned around. Across the exhibition space, the two paintings from Roger Timms's *Gehenna* series were now being parcelled up in large brown boxes. One of the students tore a strip of packing tape from the roll with his teeth. For some reason, it made Kearney think of skin being flayed.

And behind them, the walls stood empty. But he supposed Hammond had a point. There was a subtle kind of meaning to be had even in those blank walls. In what had once been there, and now was missing.

Twenty-One

I remembered Whitrow Ridge from when I was a kid. It rose up from the ground, north of the city, like the curved spine of a half-buried dinosaur. After Mike dropped me off, I looked online and found that Castle View was the name of the road that twisted along the top of it. I headed out for a taxi.

'Fifteen quid,' the driver told me.

'That's fine.'

We were out in the country now. On the left of the road, the land spread away slowly and gradually. Open fields were divided by dark hedges, with the airport dimly visible in the distance, and then the edges of the city resting in hazy white mist beyond. There was a pub called the Royalty on that side: popular, despite the drive, with walkers and plane spotters. On the right-hand side, behind the cottages and farmhouses that flashed past, the land fell away much more sharply. This was the Ridge itself, thick with woodland and knee-high patches of dense heath, cut diagonally down by steep, awkward footpaths.

The taxi driver slowed the car to a crawl, and began peering out of the side window, checking the numbers on the houses to the right. He was an old-school cabbie: not only quoting me a price in advance, but determined to deliver me as close to my destination as physically possible without driving through someone's garden.

'That one's 162.' He nodded to the cottage on the right. 'I

reckon you're running out of road, mate. You sure about the address?'

'I think so.'

But the houses were coming to an end up ahead. I was already counting them down in my head. The properties were so large and spread out that it was hard to tell, but I thought there were two left, and then nothing but fields and fences. Which would mean . . .

'No. 166. That's your last one.'

The taxi driver came to a stop just past the final house and shook his head thoughtfully, as if this was a mystery he needed to solve on my behalf or else go home frustrated.

'Well,' he said, 'unless you're after this place.'

I looked where he pointed and saw we'd pulled up by a gravel parking area that stretched back from the road for about thirty metres, I guessed, until it overlooked the Ridge. The car park was half full, with eight or nine vehicles spaced out across the gravel.

Down the other side, there were old, weathered benches. A family was sitting at one, the father pouring hot coffee from a thermos. At another, there was a couple in biking leathers; the man had one boot off and was picking mud out of it with a stick. At the far end, an ice-cream van was parked up, the man inside sitting behind a half panel of grey glass, reading a newspaper.

Just beyond, there was a drystone wall with a break in the middle. I watched as a man followed his dog back through, coiling a lead between his hands.

'That's the Ridge through there?' I said.

The cabbie leaned on his steering wheel. 'Yeah, people come for the view. Plane spotters and walkers and things. Gets some trouble at night, you know? Not that it bothers me. None of my business.'

I didn't have a clue what he meant. Then it clicked.

'What – people come here for sex?'

'Oh yeah. This place is notorious for it. Flashing headlights. All that kind of stuff.'

I turned that idea over in my head. Emily Price. Had the owner of the rucksack arranged to meet her here, whoever she was? Or did the note have a different meaning altogether? Whichever, the knowledge that people came here for clandestine, anonymous sexual encounters seemed to fit. There was something furtive about that, just as it felt there was about the scene I'd found at the Chalkie.

'OK. This'll do, thanks.'

'You sure?'

I handed him a twenty and opened the door.

'Keep the change,' I said.

The engine roared and then faded as the taxi drove away, and the silence that followed closed around me. The place had the same heavy stillness I imagined you'd find at the top of a mountain. I headed into the car park, and the crunch of the gravel beneath my shoes felt like an intrusion. From somewhere over the Ridge, I could hear children shouting, and their voices were simultaneously close and far away, fluttering around like butterflies.

The family at the bench watched me walk past, probably wondering why a lone man would be dropped off in a taxi somewhere like this, or even come here at all without a dog to walk. I was wondering the same thing myself. I had no idea what was I hoping to accomplish here. Or in fact whether there was anything to be accomplished at all.

I crossed over to the ice-cream van.

'Excuse me?'

The guy inside put down the paper.

'What can I get you?'

'Nothing right now. I'm just curious about something.' I tapped a couple of fingers on the small counter. 'It might sound strange, but does the name Emily Price mean anything to you?'

This was my best shot. Unlike the other people in the car

park, I was guessing this man was here most of the time. If Emily Price had any connection to this place whatsoever, he'd be the most likely person to know. I was painfully aware that my best shot was pretty lousy and so, obviously, I wasn't holding out much hope. But he frowned.

'Rings a bell,' he said. 'Why? Should I know her?'

'Not necessarily. I was just curious.'

Rings a bell. Now that he'd said it, it did with me too. I started to say something else, but he interrupted me.

'Is she that girl that comes here?'

He looked troubled by that. I got the weird impression I'd asked him about something that was already on his mind. Something he thought maybe I could help *him* with.

How to play it?

'Yeah,' I said. 'It might be. What does she look like?'

'Not sure to be honest.' He half turned towards the Ridge, then looked back at me and frowned again. 'I just see her up here sometimes. Over there, looking out. She's got long dark hair. Old black raincoat. A bit tatty. Like she's homeless?'

'That sounds like her.'

I had no idea what to say next, but he saved me.

'Why does she do that?' he said.

'What? Stand up there?'

'It's weird. That's why it came back to me then.' He scratched his ear, uncomfortable. 'I look up sometimes, and she's there, standing by herself. And she just seems . . . I don't know, like she's *watching* something. Or waiting, maybe.'

'You've not seen her properly?'

'No. I just notice her every now and then, and the next time I look up she's gone.'

'Right.'

'It started to freak me out a bit. I mean, it's busy up here at the moment, but when it rains, you know, it's pretty desolate. And even then, I've seen her. I was beginning to think she was a ghost or something.'

He said it as a joke, but couldn't quite manage the laugh. I glanced past, towards the edge of the Ridge, and something about the place made it seem not quite so ridiculous as it might have done elsewhere. It was so windswept and isolated: I could imagine a ghost here. Standing with her back to the car park, staring down the hill; silent and sad and full of foreboding. If you walked around the front of her, you'd find that she was somehow still facing away.

Long dark hair. Old black raincoat. A bit tatty.

'Who is she?' the guy asked.

I looked back at him, sorry I didn't have any answers.

'I really don't know,' I said.

The wall looked like it had been there for centuries.

There was nothing holding it together any more, assuming there ever had been. It was just odd-sized rocks, piled waist-high in a long row, and placed in such a way that each one supported the ones around it, with stone stabs added as uprights to either side of the gap leading through. There was a short series of steps beyond.

I walked up and found myself in the middle of a footpath along the top of the Ridge. The wind blasted at my face, and I squinted. It was freezing up here. The sun itself felt hot, hanging in the centre of the sky and beating down hard, but it was wild and exposed, and the wind kept whipping quickly across, swiping any heat away vindictively, like a child would a toy.

Bracing.

To my right, the path had to lean out past the fenced off gardens of the cottages before it curved around out of sight. To my left, it skirted a huge pile of boulders instead, then disappeared into a thicket of trees. A little girl with curly yellow hair and pink boots was perched precariously on top of the nearest rock, hands spread-eagled beside her. A slightly older boy with skinny legs bounded up fearlessly and shouted in triumph. From somewhere I couldn't see, a man shouted at them both to be careful. Although I understood where the guy was coming from with his warning, I also thought he was missing a trick.

Instead of heading in either direction, I walked forward. There was an artificial table built from stone here. On the top, several maps and sheets of information had been sealed in beneath dirty plastic, which in turn had been covered in casual graffiti by generations of idiots.

In front, the Ridge fell off steeply, a carpet of heath and grass, with a third path cutting down from the information point, little more than a rumour in the undergrowth. About a hundred metres below, the woods started. And then, much further down, I could make out the town of Castleforth in the valley. The cottages and factories down there were as flat and still as a tapestry laid out on the landscape. In the distance, beyond them, a cloud was casting an enormous shadow across the fields as it flowed slowly, peacefully across the sky.

I took a glance behind. The ice-cream van was still visible through the gap in the wall, which meant the girl – whoever she was – must have been standing more or less where I was in order for the vendor to catch sight of her. So what the hell had she been looking at? The view was nice, admittedly, but it didn't seem like a place to linger, and certainly not one to keep returning to.

I leaned against the stone table and pretended I was reading the information there. In reality, I was trying to figure out what the hell I was going to do next.

You're here. So now what?

One obvious thing to do would be to take the path in either direction, or else head down the Ridge. But after looking at the map for a moment, I knew that would be a mistake. There was too much ground to cover, and a lot of it would be hard work. It would have been difficult enough if I'd had the slightest idea what I might be looking for, or even where it was. As things stood, I had no idea whether there was anything here at all. The only thing I was likely to get was a good walk.

But I didn't know what else to do.

I was on the verge of phoning for a taxi and getting out of here, when I happened to glance idly at the stone near my left hand and noticed all the graffiti there. Most of it was just names or dates, either chiselled awkwardly into the rock or written in black marker, but at the top left-hand corner someone had drawn something in what appeared to be thin white paint. It was so small it would have been easy to miss. Even if you saw it, you probably wouldn't pay it much in the way of attention.

Not unless you recognised it.

It was an angled line with a smaller one crossing near the base. I stared at it, because I'd seen exactly the same design last night, scribbled on that sheet in Sarah's research notes. For a few seconds, I was as quietly surprised to see it there as I would have been to find a note tacked to the plastic, addressed to me personally.

From beside me, the wind whipped in.

Like a sword, I remembered thinking. Pointing to the north-west. But I lifted my head now, looked at the Ridge falling away below me and reconsidered that.

Maybe it was pointing to the path down through the heath.

Twenty-Two

The Ridge was much steeper than it looked, and I realised straight away that I was wearing the wrong shoes for the job. The path was roughly formed, worn into the ground by centuries of walkers taking the exact same steps, resulting in little more than a series of dry dirt ledges leading awkwardly downwards through the heath. It was precarious terrain, and my trainers were far too flimsy and thin. The slightest misstep and I'd be risking a twisted ankle.

The only advantage to the slope was that I quickly escaped the bitter wind, and, now that I was shielded by the body of the land, the sun felt tentatively warm on my skin. But without the roar of the air, it was even more quiet than it had been at the top. In fact, it was so unnerving I almost preferred the cold.

I was halfway down to the trees. Glancing back up, the top of the Ridge formed a dark line against the sky. Black shapes were moving back along: the family I'd seen, returning to the car park. I watched them go. When they had dipped out of sight, there was nothing up there except grass quivering at the edge.

Keep going.

I set off again.

My mind kept returning to the symbol scrawled on the stone. It wasn't a coincidence. Something *was* here, even if I didn't know what. So at the same time as checking my footing, I was also watching the ground in the hope of seeing another of the painted signs. That was my assumption: that whoever had left the first one would leave a second when it was time to change direction. If not, I'd be going on that long, pointless walk after all.

My heart was humming in my chest. Part of it was nerves, but there was something else to it too. Something almost electrical.

The path led down into the trees, where a cool shade settled across me. The trail still continued at an angle, but the undergrowth had fallen away and the land was almost bare here, the heath entirely gone. It looked as though all the life in the dry, dusty ground had been swept into piles, then gathered and twisted harshly into the gnarled pigtails of the trees. Above me, their branches formed a canopy of scrabbling arms, and as I walked through, it felt like being in an enormous, echoing hall, moving between pillars of oak. Everything smelled of resin and dew and leaves, and, from some balcony high above, the wind created a quiet whispering.

I found the next symbol a little further along the path.

You're right.

The humming in my chest intensified.

As strange as this is, the evidence is right in front of you.

It had been drawn at the top of a long series of wooden steps that led off to the right, straight down the Ridge. Although this one was different from the symbol at the top – just a circle with a dot in the middle this time – it was in the same white paint as before. And once again, I'd probably have missed it if I hadn't been keeping an eye out. Because I had been, it was almost blatant . . .

An idea clicked into place.

When I'd seen the symbols Sarah had sketched in her notes, they'd reminded me of something, and now I realised what it was: the drawings that tramps and hobos were supposed to leave for each other. A secret code drawn on the walls of yards or the gates of houses.

This place is friendly.
Good food here.
Owners hostile.

That was what the symbols were like – especially now I was seeing them out in the wild. They were messages that would mean nothing at all to most people, but relayed important information for those who recognised them. In this case, they gave directions.

But where to?

I made my way down the steps. Unlike the path, these had been artificially carved into the land. Each was about thirty centimetres high, and covered with a strip of old planking. I stopped counting after the first twenty. By then, the fronts of my shins were already hurting, and, looking back, I'd already left the original path high up above. Below me, the steps appeared to continue down for ever, presumably all the way to Castleforth.

Was that where I was going?

But no, it was only a few minutes before I spotted a third symbol on the left. This one had been dabbed casually onto the trunk of a tree: just a slash, but similar enough to the first two for the meaning to be clear, as there was a rough path leading off into the woodland in that direction.

I turned and headed that way.

As I went, I realised something else about the symbols: that they had been placed in an almost offhand manner. Even if someone noticed the last one, for example, they'd have no idea which way it was telling them to go, not unless they arrived here by following the one before it. And so on, all the way back to the top. From the starting point, they made sense and led you inexorably on. But from anywhere else, they'd appear completely random.

The ground began to even out a little.

The trees were larger here, with more space between them. I passed one that had either fallen or been cut down, and the trunk, resting on its side, came up to my waist. The land stretched out between. Towards the top of the Ridge, I was now faced with an almost impenetrable wall of trees. In the other direction, a little further down the slope, there appeared to be a steep drop: a lip pouting on the slant of the land. The further I went, the more the semblance of a path faded, until it seemed to have disappeared entirely and I found myself just meandering between the trees in what I hoped was a straight line.

A couple of minutes later, still watching for any symbols on the trees, I reached a drystone wall. This one looked even older than the one up at the car park. It was small and broken down, with newer concrete posts embedded along it and barbed wire strung between them. The implication was clear. Keep out. It was either private property or dangerous terrain beyond the fence. The undergrowth there was thick and high, the grass forming a solid, unbroken wall.

And no symbols on the pillars.

I had a moment of doubt. Perhaps I was being an idiot.

An idiot in a fucking wood.

It was possible. But then, perhaps I'd just strayed off-course when the path vanished, which I could at least check. So I followed the line of the fence down the Ridge, all the way to the edge of the cliff face there. Found nothing. I went back up again. And a little further past where I'd started, a faint white circle had been painted at the base of one of the pillars.

The strands of barbed wire here had been forced apart to form an eye-shape: one bowing down, the other rising up. On the other side, the undergrowth was slightly broken and trodden down. Wherever the symbols led, it looked like someone else had also followed the trail. How recently was difficult to tell.

I turned around, listening carefully. The wood was vast, open and empty, with sunlight dappling the ground. Beyond the quiet trills of unseen birds, I might have been the only living thing in the world. A part of me hoped so.

Without considering it any more, I turned back to the fence

and stretched the top strand of barbed wire a little higher, then clambered awkwardly through.

Immediately, something was different.

The feeling that wasn't quite excitement spread out inside, reaching all the way to my skin. As I began moving forward, every touch of the grass sent a tingle through me.

Holy ground.

It was irrational, but that was how it felt.

I followed the broken-down trail, watching my footing and taking my time. After a minute, I stopped to listen: I couldn't even hear the birds any more. And that was when I first noticed the smell.

Jesus. What is that?

I breathed in again slowly – gingerly – then immediately wished I hadn't. It wasn't the stench of rotting vegetation, but it was like it. I glanced around at the tangles of grass, expecting to see something obvious, but it all looked green and healthy. And actually, the smell was much worse than that. I started off again, but with every step it became more potent, until it felt as though I could almost *see* it in the air and feel it settling on my skin. It awoke some primal instinct in me.

This is a bad place. Leave here now.

Death, I thought. That was what I was smelling. The rank odour of decay. It was coming from somewhere around me in the grass, or maybe from somewhere up ahead. There was something dead and rotting here, and every step seemed to be taking me closer to it.

Do you want to see?

No, I really didn't. But even so, I found myself moving forward, placing my feet down carefully, anxious not to stand on anything but convinced that, at any second, I would. Yet there was nothing in the grass. I checked to either side of the rough path I was following. Nothing.

No more symbols either. From this point on, I guessed, I was expected to follow something else entirely.

Up ahead, there was a break in the trees.

I lifted my T-shirt and held it over my nose and mouth, approaching cautiously, every nerve in my body singing. The silence was broken here as well: I could hear the gentle trickle of water, so quiet it was almost secret.

The break led into a small clearing, and as I stepped into it the shock hit me, and that hum in my heart fell away, leaving only a solid thudding.

I knew this place.

Oh fuck.

I was standing at the bottom of another cliff face. The rocks looked like the landscape had been formed by shaving small layers of stone away at a hundred random angles. Far above, right on the top, trees stretched even further up into the sky. At the other sides of the clearing, the ground fell away downwards. But my attention was caught by the base of the enormous natural wall to my left, where a large metal pipe emerged from the land, brown and rusted around the rim.

It had been in the most recent photograph Christopher Ellis had posted on his website. 'Dead woman in wood', I remembered – the picture I'd thought might be of Sarah, and then assumed was a police shot. The decomposed body of a girl tucked just beyond the lip of a pipe.

This pipe.

The water I could hear was trickling out of it, spattering on the ground below. The water, slapping the wet mud below, was the loudest sound in the world.

I couldn't quite see inside.

Another step forward revealed a fraction more of the pipe's interior, but it jolted me too. Every little movement here was amplified. There was a power here that made the atmosphere thick and charged, and I remembered my earlier thought. *Holy ground.* In this clearing, away from society and almost within touching distance of the pipe, it felt like standing in a church. Not a modern-day building, but something primitive and old, hand-built from rocks. A real church: one where God was present, numbing the air.

And I realised it didn't matter whether I *wanted* to see. It felt like I didn't have a choice. With the T-shirt still pressed over my nose and mouth, I stepped closer. A stick *clicked* under my feet, the sound immediately hushed, and I thought:

Emily Price . . .

Except the pipe was empty.

I let go of my T-shirt and allowed it to fall back into place.

Water was running along the centre of the metal, and leaves and mulch had built up at the entrance. Behind that, the blackness seemed to stretch back indefinitely into the earth. If this was the right place – and I was sure it was – then it meant her body had been removed.

By the police? I thought.

Or by the kind of person who'd steal a body from a field?

And then I realised something was wrong.

The smell was faint here.

Everything around me became very still, as though the undergrowth had suddenly held itself motionless. Because if that odour really had been death and decay, then it should have been concentrated here, shouldn't it? This was where the body had been. And yet I could barely detect it at all.

So what the fuck had been causing it?

I turned around – very slowly – and scanned the path behind me. There was absolutely nothing to see, but the woods there were suddenly full of threat, and the clearing now felt electric for an entirely different reason. There was no sound except for the spatter of the water.

You're being watched.

I shivered. Even though I couldn't see anyone, I knew that was true. There was someone else here. Back in the undergrowth, that rank thing I'd been smelling, maybe . . .

Maybe something that wasn't dead at all.

There was no way further past the pipes, and I had no chance of climbing the cliff face above them. The only way out of this clearing was to go back the way I'd come.

So that's what you'll have to do.

I forced myself to keep calm and take deep, careful breaths. And then I started off. The path was trodden down, but the undergrowth to either side was thick: walls of grass, punctuated by occasional bramble bushes or solid tree trunks. Difficult to see through. Impossible in places. Anyone could have been there, and as I walked I kept expecting something to leap out from the foliage.

What kind of person would smell like that? I didn't even want to try to imagine. Breathing in now, it remained faint. And listening, the woods were quiet.

Perhaps whoever had been here with me was gone.

I reached the point where I remembered the smell being strongest. It still lingered here, but I thought it was more of the ghost of a scent now. And then I looked to my left and the hairs on my neck stood up.

There was a second trail of flattened grass.

It touched the main path, but led away backwards at an angle. Someone had been there. Perhaps they'd been crouching in the undergrowth at the side of the path. And although I couldn't know it for certain, I thought that, after I'd walked past, they had stepped out behind me.

That new break in the undergrowth filled my vision. I stood there for a moment, half hypnotised by it. And then I stepped forward onto the second path.

It was like triggering an alarm: the terror flared up in my chest, and I heard a high-pitched ringing in my ears. But I forced myself not to step back. Instead, peering carefully to either side, I moved a little further in. The trampled-down undergrowth curled around, forming a path that ran parallel to the one I'd arrived on.

It didn't go far. Barely thirty seconds later, I stepped out onto a precipice of rock. In front of me, looking over the tops of the trees below, I could see all the way out to the fields at the horizon. At my feet, the rock face seemed to go almost vertically down, its hard angles fuzzy with moss and looped with roots. I couldn't see how far it was. The ground down there was lost in the trees.

It looked all but impossible for someone to have clambered either up or down it, but I couldn't see any other explanation. And whoever the man was, he had definitely been here: there was still a trace of the smell in the air. But it was fading now, and I realised I could hear the birds again. The woods seemed to be returning to life, as though something awful had been here for a time, and the world had been keeping still until it was gone.

My heart was returning to normal as well.

I turned around. Headed back.

What the fuck is going on, James?

Because this must have been what he wanted me to see. For some reason I couldn't fathom, he knew about the bag at the Chalkie, and he'd expected me to come here afterwards. What I didn't understand was why.

I looked around the wood, then started up the steps.

James would be able to answer my questions, of course, but I couldn't see him until tomorrow morning. In the meantime, there were at least two other paths I could follow. One was to try to find out more about Emily Price. The second was to get hold of Christopher Ellis and wring some fucking answers out of him.

Whatever was going on here, Ellis had to be the link. I knew he'd posted the photograph of the dead girl online; and I knew Sarah had been to interview him, and had a copy of the symbols noted down in her research. It seemed reasonable to believe those two facts were connected: that Ellis had known about them, and, for some reason, he'd told Sarah.

But knowing that wasn't any real comfort. Because the real question was why there was a trail of symbols up here in the first place. Who had left them, and, even worse, who the hell had been meant to follow them?

I emerged back out of the treeline and glanced up. Above me, the top of the Ridge formed a ragged black line against the sky.

I was beginning to think she was a ghost or something.

I half expected to see a girl standing up there, staring out at this desolate patch of land. But like the pipe back in the clearing, the Ridge was now empty.

Twenty-Three

The instructions he had been given were relatively simple, but, just to be on the safe side – and because he was sure he must be missing something – he read through them again now.

Head north along the ring road, the instructions began.

Half mile, right onto Winchester Lane.

Quarter mile, right onto Winchester Pass.

And so on.

That was the straightforward part: no problems there. Morgan was basically a glorified delivery boy, and he was used to going places for his boss – although normally it was warehouses, and he got directions from an A-to-Z, rather than a neatly typed piece of paper.

But anyway, he'd followed the various junctions that were listed, gradually leaving the centre of town and heading out into the wilds of the nearby countryside. The directions had eventually brought him here, to a curl of road on the outskirts of Castleforth.

There is a lay-by on the left-hand side of the road.

All he'd been able to see at first was the sheer face of the Ridge, but he'd spotted it as he rounded a corner. A dirt track, little more than the width of the car, angled up and disappearing around a cluster of rocks. He'd slowed the car and driven up, the tyres undulating gently on the hard clumps of dry mud.

The track led to an elevated patch of gravel and yellow sand, with the road out of sight below and to the right. Morgan had pulled ahead, so that whoever he was supposed to meet could fit in behind him, then *cricked* on the handbrake.

Wait for the delivery to be made.

And so here he was, sitting patiently, listening to the soft click and buzz of the woods, the almost subliminal background music of birdsong.

Waiting.

After a few minutes, he rolled down the passenger window and peered out. He was at the base of an enormous cliff. The Ridge itself seemed to have stepped back a few ancient paces to accommodate this small parking area. Directly to his left, there was a thick wall of trees and undergrowth, and then the rock began some distance beyond, rising sharply. He could see birds, tiny and black, and the silhouetted outlines of distant trees at the top.

The road he'd left wasn't busy, and the few cars he did hear sounded subdued and far away: part of another world. The trees and undergrowth were louder, and the slight breeze brought a musty smell from somewhere deep between them. Midges fluttered lazily around the car.

His sheet of instructions was balanced on top of the map he'd been told to spread out – somewhat theatrically – across the steering wheel. The intention was to allay the suspicions of anyone else who pulled in here, so that Morgan would look like just another lost traveller, unsure exactly where he was, checking the route.

It was ridiculous, of course.

But then, so was the next instruction on the list.

Do not under any circumstances get out of the car.

What the hell was that supposed to mean?

Morgan didn't like it one bit. He had a vague idea what he was here for: that it would involve meeting someone and picking up a package. That was what his job generally entailed. Usually he was expected to hand something else over in exchange, but this time his employer had clearly made other arrangements to pay for what he was getting. That was OK too. But he'd never dealt with people who provided instructions like these.

Do not under any circumstances get out of the car.

It was the type of advice you'd give someone if there were wild animals around. What was it – was some kind of bear going to pad up to him with a parcel in its jaws? It was rural around here, but it wasn't that fucking rural.

Coming up on three o'clock, which was supposed to be the time of the meet. Morgan alternated between checking his watch, the sheet of instructions and his rear-view mirror. Behind him, the lay-by was slightly distorted and completely deserted. Every time he heard a car approaching, somewhere out of sight on the main road, he expected to see it come bumping up behind him. But there was nothing. And then . . .

And then he noticed the smell.

It was insidious and it was vile. Slinking into the car inside the pine aroma of the woodland at first, then becoming stronger and more potent within just a few seconds of him noticing it.

Jesus.

One time, back in his student days, he'd moved into a flat but hadn't had time to sort out a full shop, so he grabbed bread, a roast chicken and spare ribs from the market. The bag of leftovers had ended up piled in the hallway, forgotten amongst all the empty cardboard and bin bags: the harmless stuff there was no rush to get rid of. It had been over a month later, suspecting he had a gas leak, that Morgan had tracked the smell to the corridor. He'd lifted away an old box and found the blood-stained bag pulsing and writhing, with twenty or thirty maggots poking through the white plastic skin like acne. Malformed flies, black and dead, had been trapped in the fuzzy curls of the old carpet.

The smell wafting into his car now was like that. It wasn't just the odour itself, but the slow realisation that you were smelling something horribly wrong, and then you found it: *oh my God, it's that.*

Slowly, Morgan turned his head to face the woodland.

And then quickly turned it back.

The map slid to one side as he gripped the steering wheel with both hands, repeating the instruction to himself, over and over. *Do not under any circumstances get out of the car.* On a primal level, it now made total sense.

He wasn't even sure what he'd seen. Something crouched at the edge of the treeline, folded over itself as though bowing in prayer. Impossibly thin. And it appeared to be naked, the nubs of its spine standing out.

Morgan kept facing forward.

A moment later, the side of his face began itching. He was sure it was because the thing in the trees was looking at him.

It's just a man, he told himself.

Some kind of man, anyway. And even though that must have been true, it didn't make him feel any better. He began nodding gently to himself, as though listening to music only he could hear. Breathing through his mouth.

What did a man have to do to smell like—

He caught movement out of the corner of his eye, and he jerked his head round, expecting to see something right up at the passenger window, staring in.

But the man was gone.

There were just the trees now, their leaves shivering gently, the branches bobbing. Some way back, between them, darkness began. When he risked breathing in through his nose, Morgan realised that awful smell was fading a little. The man had come out of the forest and then retreated back within.

His heart was pounding.

Something had been left for him. It was at the base of the tree where the man had been squatting – praying, or whatever the fuck he had been doing. It looked like a bag. A red and gold sports bag, slumped at the edge of the undergrowth.

Do not under any circumstances get out of the car.

So he sat there for a while, calming himself down. When he checked his watch again, it was twenty past three. The lay-by remained empty. It was naïve to hope that the delivery he'd been instructed to pick up hadn't already been dropped off, but a part of him was stubbornly clinging to the idea. Deep down, he knew. He hadn't been supposed to get out of the car until the delivery had been made. Now that it had, he was safe to do so.

Eventually, he fumbled for the instructions.

Confirm receipt (Mr Garland).

Confirm collection.

Do not open package.

That was it. Morgan took a deep breath, opened the driver's-side door and stepped out into the sun. The sand crunched slightly underfoot. The air was cool on his skin; without noticing it, he'd broken out in a sweat.

It was only five metres to the tree line. He walked round the back of the car, and kept a close eye on the undergrowth as he approached the bag. But the birds were singing – brightly, happily – and the air smelled clean and fresh again. Within the trees, nothing was moving.

The bag was small – a child's sports bag. The zippers were secured in place with a black plastic tag, one that would have to be cut in order to be removed. Morgan picked it up and it was much lighter than he'd expected, barely weighing anything at all. Whatever was inside felt fragile and weak, like a bundle of broken sticks, poking against the fabric.

Do not open it.

There was no danger of that. He didn't know what was inside, and he didn't *want* to know; he just wanted his pay-check and then to forget about what he'd seen here today. Instead, he took it back to the car. One phone call to confirm receipt, a call to his boss, then a short car journey, a shower, and he was done.

The bag went in the boot, out of sight. As he closed the lid over, Morgan thought of something and paused, looking down at it. *Praying*, he'd imagined. But it occurred to him that it hadn't been like that at all. It was more like the thing in the woods had been crouched down and embracing it.

Holding it close, and saying goodbye.

Garland folded his mobile shut and stood in the hallway for a moment. The man who'd called him had sounded a little . . . disturbed. But then, Banyard did have that effect on people. Garland didn't have much fondness for the man either, but his talents were indispensable for some tasks. Just as the organisation employed cleaners, it also required caretakers. They were usually local men with a natural affinity for the job at hand. Banyard was both, but he had a longer and more distinguished pedigree than most.

It was done anyway. The exchange had been made. All being well, at two o'clock tomorrow afternoon, this would be over. Then he could get out of this country and away from these people.

In the meantime, there was still a lot of work to do. The mystery man back at Ellis's flat had been asking about Sarah Pepper, and now he had a name to go along with that. Alex Connor. But he still needed to know where to find him. Garland slid the phone back into his suit pocket, and stepped through the doorway, back into the lounge.

'Sorry about that,' he said. 'Colleagues pestering.'

Julie Smith was sitting with the baby on the settee.

'It's fine,' she said, 'honestly.'

Garland leaned against the doorframe and smiled.

'Anyway,' he said. 'As I mentioned, it's your boyfriend I really need to speak to. What time will he be home?'

Twenty-Four

Kearney stood on the top-floor balcony of Block Three, Parkway Heights, looking down at the square below him.

About twenty years ago, there had been riots here. That was before his time, but he remembered watching the smoke and fires on the news: reporters in the thick of it with the police. The corridors had looked like the boiler room of a steam ship. Since then, it had been renovated and cleaned out – which really meant the people. Despite the council's best efforts, community spirit had failed to arise. Kearney doubted the square below had seen such a gathering of residents, not to mention emergency vehicles, since the bad old days.

Three fire engines were parked close up to the block. Two ambulances a little way back. Four police cars and a van. When he and Todd arrived, the thick smoke hanging above the block had been casting a shadow over the square, but it had cleared slightly now, and the red and blue flashing lights were weak in the sun.

Evacuated residents had joined the gawpers from the other blocks down below. Some of them were staring up, shielding their eyes against the sun so that they appeared to be saluting him. Those whose expressions he could make out looked more excited than concerned. But then, things always seemed like that on a sunny day, in the same way that a house felt more threatening at night. Nobody felt afraid.

Kearney turned his head to the right and watched another

police van enter the square, curling steadily around until it came to rest beside the concrete playground. Then he looked up, squinting. The sky was so bright, the colour there so intensely pale, that he could see little sparkles in his eyes, like the air was sweating light.

To either side, everything was black and wet. The attentions of the fire crews had transformed the walkways and stairwells into temporary waterfalls. When the breeze picked up, it brought with it the scent of old bonfires and petrol, and just a trace – faint but unmistakable – of the two people lying dead in the blackened flat behind him. But if you didn't breathe in, and didn't look at the sludge on the floor, the sound of dirty water trickling down was soporific and almost peaceful, like being in a forest.

Todd leaned on the balcony beside him.

'Jesus.' He puffed up his cheeks, then breathed out slowly. The longest sigh Kearney had heard from him in a long time. 'It's a mess in there.'

'Yes. What do you think?'

'I think the Incident Commander is right.'

Kearney nodded. 'Arson.'

'No need to be rude about the guy, Paul.'

Kearney raised an eyebrow at him. Todd smiled in return, but he could tell his partner's humour was forced.

'Deliberate ignition, then.'

The fire had been under control when they arrived, but they'd had to wait for the nod before they could come upstairs. When the structure had been deemed safe, the Incident Commander had briefed them on the situation. The blaze had been mostly confined to the top floor, but had licked along most of the flats here. The damage was worst in the rooms directly behind them now, where the fire crew had found the remains of a can of lighter-fluid near the door.

The flat itself had been gutted, first by the flames, and then by the high-pressure jets of water that had arced up from the fire engines below. Now, it looked more like a dark, dripping cave than the home it had been. The furniture was reduced to charred wreckage, with only a few burnt scraps of fabric still clinging to the blackened frames, and the floor was thick with mud. Old papers and shrivelled books were scattered in the sludge, and the air stank of ash and paraffin. In the far corner of the room, the television had melted like a candle. Yet it was so cold when Kearney had first stepped inside, his feet slopping through the filth, that he'd shivered. Now, ice-cold water was *slapping* down from the ceiling above, as steady and insistent as rain from a broken gutter.

The two bodies – believed to be those of Christopher Ellis and his girlfriend, Amanda Gilroyd – were lying, face to face, on the crusted metal bed frame. The heat had scorched and tightened them, baring their teeth so they resembled tiny, blind boxers squaring up for a fight. Angry. Then Kearney had noticed that Gilroyd's feet were curled over, almost delicately, like a newborn's.

He hadn't needed to cross the room to see the handcuffs binding their wrists and ankles. He also hadn't wanted to think too much about what they meant. It was both obvious and horrible. You wouldn't leave handcuffs on dead bodies.

He supposed there was at least one positive thing to hold onto – as far as they knew, the couple were the only casualties. The fire alarm for this level was next to Ellis's front door, and someone had activated it. They'd already spoken to the dead man's neighbours. When they'd heard the alarm and emerged from their flats, there were no initial signs of a blaze. The logical conclusion was that whoever had started the fire had also sounded the alarm.

Kearney lifted his arms off the ledge and turned round to face the doorway.

'Why set off the alarm?' he said. 'Why risk being seen?'

'Because he didn't want to kill anyone else.'

'Maybe.'

Kearney knew he was exhausted and finding it hard to think straight. It was mysterious that someone could have the will and . . . *detachment* to tie two people up and burn them alive, yet also feel the need to alert others, possibly even saving their lives.

'Then again,' he said, 'it means the alarm's going off and everyone's panicking, heading downstairs as quick as they can. They wouldn't be paying as much attention, would they? Maybe he figured it would make him harder to remember.'

'Also possible,' Todd conceded. 'But why burn the place at all?'

In this scenario, the usual reason was to cover up what you'd done so that a murder looked more like an accident. But the handcuffs ruled out that motivation.

Kearney said, 'Trying to hide something.'

'Evidence of *something*,' Todd agreed.

'Something he couldn't be sure he'd found, so needed to make certain was gone.'

That was at the heart of what bothered him. The fire alarm – whatever interpretation he put on it – didn't indicate sloppy thinking. Nor did the handcuffs. Nor did the thoroughness of the job. All things considered, there was something coolly professional about this. Something organised.

He said, 'But how does Roger Timms fit into this?'

Two leads on the Butterfly case had brought them to what remained of Christopher Ellis's front door.

The first was that Ellis seemed to have acquired a painting from Roger Timms at the end of last year. There was nothing exceptional about that, but they'd not been able to find any record of *what* Ellis had bought. In addition, the amount Ellis had paid – five thousand pounds – was considerably greater than Timms's minor artworks generally fetched. So it must have been a privately commissioned piece. That in itself intrigued Kearney. Timms wasn't well known for accepting commissions from the general public. And for a man in Christopher Ellis's financial bracket, five thousand pounds was a huge figure to pay.

The second, and more important, connection was that Roger

Timms's phone records had been analysed, and Ellis's number had turned up a number of times over the past eight months. The pattern was interesting. There had been a degree of contact between them at the end of last year and the beginning of this – presumably arranging whatever Ellis had purchased – and then nothing at all until this week, when Timms had made a single, late-night call to Ellis's flat.

It was the final item on the account. From the evidence they had, Christopher Ellis was the last person Roger Timms had spoken to before he'd gone on the run.

Now, Ellis and his girlfriend were dead.

And *something* had been destroyed.

Todd said, 'I don't buy Timms for this.'

'It's not a coincidence.'

'Well, they do happen, Paul.'

Kearney was unconvinced. Todd gestured at the gaping doorway of the flat.

'Why would Timms be involved in this?'

'I don't know.'

'He wouldn't. What's the point? Imagine that Ellis is involved somehow. Let's say he knows something about the murders. Perhaps he's even the guy with the fingerprints we're after.'

Kearney said, 'Why would Timms care?'

'Exactly. It's not like we don't have enough on the guy.'

Even without what had been found in his basement, the evidence of Timms's involvement was hanging on walls in at least two different continents. Kearney couldn't see a single reason why he would waste time trying to cover his tracks right now.

'I agree,' he said. 'Timms is running.'

'As fast as he can.' Todd nodded to himself. 'So let's get crime scene into this shit-hole and then sub it off to someone else. Fast as *we* can.'

With that, he began walking back along the scorched concrete walkway, his shoes leaving tilted footprints in the wet sludge. But instead of following, Kearney stayed where he was, staring into the remains of the flat.

'Maybe he wanted his painting back.'

'Not good enough, Paul.'

Kearney almost smiled. This was a standard part of their routine. Just as Todd generally left the interviews to Kearney, he also recognised his partner was better at teasing out the connections. This was precisely the kind of challenge he often laid down. *Come on, convince me.* Despite the dismissal in his voice, Kearney knew what Todd really meant was: *I'm frustrated here; although it pains me to admit it, I need your help.*

A fleck of paper fell silently from the door frame.

'OK,' he called over. 'What about a third party?'

Todd stopped at least. But he didn't turn round.

'Go on.'

Kearney took one last glance into the flat, then sloshed up the walkway towards his partner.

'We've got Wells and Timms. But from the fingerprint, we know at least one other person is involved.'

'Yeah,' Todd said. 'Wells, Timms and Mister X.'

'So what if Ellis isn't Mister X?'

Kearney reached him, and they set off walking together.

Todd said, 'So what you're suggesting is we know about Wells and Timms, but not Mister X, whoever the fuck he is. And he's the one who came here and killed Ellis?'

'Yes.'

'What about your good friend Mister *Why*?' Todd pushed open the heavy fire door. 'You're forgetting about him.'

'Because Ellis knew who he was?'

They started down the sodden concrete steps, Todd leading the way. He didn't say anything, and Kearney wasn't sure whether that meant he was thinking the scenario over or if he'd not done well enough and Todd had dismissed it for the moment. For himself, the thought felt right but unfinished.

What did Ellis know that had been so dangerous? Nothing

about Timms, because they already had everything they needed. So it had to be someone else's identity.

Had to be.

Because what else could Christopher Ellis have said that would be worse than what they already knew?

Of course, Ellis wasn't going to tell them anything now.

Back out in the square, the reality of that hit Kearney. The air down here was fresh and clean, but he suddenly found it hard to breathe. He didn't seem able to get enough of it into his lungs.

Something in his head began to thump.

A panic attack. The realisation came with a lurch that only made things worse. They came on at odd times. He didn't need to be thinking about anything specific. They just bubbled up from the anxiety seething deep inside him.

It began with this frantic feeling, like a spider was trapped in his windpipe, tapping its legs.

Calm down.

He forced himself to take slow, steady breaths, and tried to distract himself by scanning the crowds across the square, deliberately emptying his thoughts. But each person there seemed to be looking directly at him. Their faces reminded him of the children from his dream. Demanding answers. Resolution. Before it was too late.

We aren't going to find her.

The more Kearney fought it, the worse it became. He closed his eyes and stood very still, sweat beading on his forehead. More than anything else right now, he needed that familiar image of Rebecca Wingate not to come into his head. But trying not to remember something only makes you—

Then he thought: *wait.*

Something was wrong.

A second later, he realised it had been something in the crowd of people. He opened his eyes again and looked back at them, trying to work out what it was that he'd seen.

A few of them *were* looking at him, but most were just standing there, either talking, or else staring up at the remains of the flats behind him. His gaze flicked from face to face, and he couldn't find it. But now he felt more certain.

He'd recognised someone.

He started walking towards the crowd.

If he couldn't see the person, he could find him. His mind gave him a sense of the man's appearance, rather than an actual image. Long, blond hair. A rough beard. Tanned skin. Eyes that had been looking directly back at him for the split-second their gazes had met. Whoever the man was, he'd recognised Kearney too.

Where was he?

'Sir? You got a second?'

Shit.

Kearney caught himself mid-step, turning to face the uniform who'd just spoken to him. She was young and pretty, and he knew her vaguely, but only because Todd had made a comment about her once. And he couldn't remember her name either. Kearney glanced over at the crowd again – frustrated – then settled himself.

'This gentleman has something to tell you.'

From her tone of voice, she was obviously more than a little dubious about it, and when Kearney focused on the man standing beside her, he understood why. He was about seventy years old, wearing a baggy, old-fashioned, tweed suit with a stained grey jumper underneath.

Kearney could see the alcohol before he smelled it. It was there in his face: in the deep lines and pink eyes, and in the faint hint of jaundice to his skin.

The yellow man, he thought. That brought another irrational flush of panic, but this one was more easily contained. The old man in front of him was about as far from the threatening creature in his nightmares as it was possible to get.

'Yes, sir,' Kearney said. 'How can I help you?'

'I saw him.'

The voice came out through a web of phlegm, and the old man's eyes were gleaming as he jabbed a finger up at the block of flats.

'The lad up there. I saw him this morning.'

'You saw Christopher Ellis?' Kearney said. 'Or someone else?'

The man shook his head. '*Chris*. We all did.'

'Where?'

'We noticed it, because there was trouble. He was in the pub with us, and there was trouble.'

Suddenly, this was more interesting.

Kearney nodded a *thank you* at the uniform, then stepped closer to the old man, giving him his full attention. The panic was still there, but he did his best to pull himself together.

There was still time. He had to believe that.

'What kind of trouble?'

Twenty-Five

Ellis was dead.

I made my way out of the square as quickly but as carefully as I could manage – not wanting to draw attention to myself, but needing to put as much distance between myself and that policeman as possible. I knew him, but I couldn't remember where from. I was fairly sure he'd recognised me as well.

I reached the main street and glanced back. Nobody was following me. Up above, an enormous plume of thick, black smoke was drifting away in the sky, like something slowly migrating. When I'd first arrived, it had looked as though an entire corner of the city had been set alight. Once in the square itself, it had been obvious where the blaze had started. Or been started.

And then I'd seen the policeman.

It came to me then. I'd spoken to him after Marie died. When he'd first sat down with me, I thought he was some kind of victim liaison worker, simply because he was so sympathetic compared to the others. He waited with me, talking quietly, and it had felt like what happened had genuinely affected him too. It wasn't until afterwards that I learned he was actually a detective.

I reached the entrance to The Duncan.

It would only be a matter of time before the incident from earlier was reported to the police. Someone had set fire to Christopher Ellis's flat, and the last time he'd been seen he'd been running for his life. They'd get a good enough description of the man chasing him, and the policeman I'd seen would be able to fill in the rest. If he couldn't remember my name now, I was sure it would come back to him.

Which meant I was running out of time.

Time for *what* was a question without an answer right now, because I knew deep down I should turn around and go back: tell the policeman what I knew, even if I had no idea right now what it meant. But something inside kept me moving. My chest was tight and my heart was fluttering.

You were right, I'd told Sarah. *You have to face up to these things.*

I hadn't done that, but I was doing it now. And I was determined to carry on, for as long as I could. To figure out what had happened and what it meant, and to take responsibility for whatever part I had played in it.

When I got back to my hotel room, I turned on the television, found a twenty-four hour news channel, then sat down at the desk and booted up the laptop. As the machine flickered slowly to life, a report about Sarah came on the TV, and I turned to watch.

There had been a press conference while I was out, and the report showed clips from it now. Three policemen were sitting at the end of a hall, with large blue banners stretched down behind them, and glasses of water and microphones on the table in front. The man in the middle wore a suit, and was reading from a sheet of paper, occasionally looking up for emphasis. Camera bulbs *chattered* in the background. When he explained that they believed Sarah's body had been moved from the field, the sound intensified. It looked and sounded like a flock of birds had begun pecking hungrily at him.

A handful of questions followed. Yes, the detective repeated, they believed Ms Pepper's body *had* been in the field, and it had since been removed by person or persons unknown. No, there was no obvious connection with the arrest of Thomas Wells at this time, although police were pursuing a number of possible leads. Any members of the public who had been in the vicinity were being encouraged to come forward. And so on. The report cut to the field, and then back to the talking heads in the newsroom.

There was nothing I didn't already know.

As it finished up, I turned my attention back to the computer, which had finally managed to boot up. I opened the browser and navigated to doyouwanttosee.co.uk. There was still a small possibility – one I was clinging to – that I was misremembering what I'd seen last night. I'd been sober when I saw the photograph Ellis had posted, but more than a little drunk afterwards. Maybe the fog in my head had obscured what I'd really seen. Made me imagine a connection that wasn't there.

I searched for 'Hell_is' again.

When the screen came up, the same posting was still at the top: 'Dead woman in wood'. I clicked it open, willing it to be different. But, in the centre of Ellis's last post, there was now only a small white box with a red cross inside it: a broken link. The image had been stored somewhere, and the page was failing to find it where it expected to. Error.

Just like the body itself, the photograph had been removed.

And Ellis's flat had been burnt out.

'Emily Price,' a woman said.

I jumped. The voice startled me so much it took a second to realise it had come from the television. A reporter – a prim woman in a grey suit – was standing outside the Crown Court in the city centre.

'But police are still questioning Thomas Wells over the disappearance of twenty-eight-year-old Rebecca Wingate.'

The red banner at the bottom:

MAN CHARGED WITH 'VAMPIRE' MURDERS

'They also wish to question this man, Roger Timms, an artist local to the area.'

The screen changed to show a man with a rugged, tanned face, and dyed blond hair stroked into a ridge on top of his head. He was smiling and shaking someone's hand while photographers leaned in around him. There was a brief cut, and then he raised a glass to the camera. The reporter continued the voiceover.

'Police are asking anyone with information as to his whereabouts, or that of his vehicle, to come forward. Rebecca Wingate remains missing.'

Fears for missing Rebecca.

I remembered that front-page story from the taxi two days ago; I'd scanned it briefly, but been more interested in finding the article about Sarah. Up at the Ridge, I'd thought the name 'Emily Price' was familiar. That was where I recognised it from. The fucking news.

I opened a fresh window on the computer, searching for 'Thomas Wells', 'Emily Price' in Google News.

Over three hundred results.

I sorted by date and opened the most recent. Emily Price's name was in the last paragraph.

Wells is also charged with the murders of Melissa Noble, 22, and Emily Price, 27. Their bodies have never been found. Today, a representative of the Noble family stated: 'We hope that, if nothing else, the arrest of this man will soon allow the families of all his victims a sense of closure'.

I read it again. Just to be sure.

Their bodies have never been found.

But Christopher Ellis had posted a photograph of her online, which meant that someone had found her. And there was a trail up on the Ridge: a secret path that led to the place her body had been left. You could only follow if you knew what to look for. The trail was hidden, but it was meant to be followed.

I went across to the bed, and scattered Sarah's research notes until I found the sheet with the symbols drawn on it. My hand was trembling as I picked it up.

I wasn't imagining this. But why would anyone want to . . . ?

I glanced across at the laptop.

Do you want to see?

Something began crawling inside my chest.

Was that possible? That people might share this information, in the same way they posted photographs? Rather than trading images, they went out into the real world and looked. Ellis had known how to find Emily Price's body, and when Sarah spoke to him, he gave her the map.

What had he said about capturing Marie's death on camera – he couldn't wait to share it? And I'd noticed he was a heavy user of that site, keen to show off. Maybe he hadn't been able to resist telling her what he knew. That was probably a part of it, but I wondered if there was something else: if Sarah's fascination with death had been as obvious to him as it always was to me. Perhaps when Ellis looked at her, he had recognised a kindred spirit of sorts. Different sides of the same coin. I didn't like that idea very much.

I looked back at the television again. They'd moved onto a different story now, but I remembered what the reporter had said. They were still looking for Roger Timms. And they were calling these things 'vampire' murders. That fit with the bottle of blood I'd found – so was it his rucksack I'd found at the Chalkie?

Christ, had James sent me there expecting me to run into Timms?

It was another idea I didn't like very much, and I was still considering it when my mobile vibrated against my hip.

A call. I was expecting it to be from Mike, but when I picked the phone out of my pocket, the screen said [number withheld].

I paused for a second, then accepted it anyway.

'Hello?'

'Is that Alex Connor?'

It was a man's voice. Unfamiliar.

'Who is this?'

'This is Detective Paul Kearney.'

I sat down on the edge of the bed.

Kearney. That was his name.

I pictured him now, and remembered him being very direct and intense. Very *involved*. He was only a small man, but there was something about his physical presence that could be either reassuring or intimidating, depending on how he wanted to use it. His eyes, too. Looking at him had been like being hypnotised.

I waited.

'Alex?' he said. 'Are you there?'

'Yes.'

'We need to talk to you. I'm sure you know that already.'

'How did you get this number?' I said.

'We're the *police*, Alex. Don't be naïve. We need to talk to you about the deaths of Christopher Ellis and Mandy Gilroyd. I understand you were at their flat earlier today. Is that right?'

I thought about that.

'Yes,' I said eventually.

'But we've also been speaking to your brother. He had quite a story to tell, and, to be honest, I'm not sure what to make of it. It seems very far-fetched on the surface. He told us you might have information that could help us make some sense of it.'

I glanced at the papers on the bed, still thinking.

'Where are you?' he said.

After a moment, Kearney lost patience.

'This isn't a *request*, Alex. I'm not asking you for a favour here. You're currently a suspect in the deaths of Mr Ellis and Ms Gilroyd. Do you understand that?'

The room felt closer and more claustrophobic than ever.

My mouth was dry. Time to make a decision.

'Yes,' I said.

'Where are you? A hotel?'

'No. I'll be back there in about half an hour.'

He sighed.

'Where you are now? I'll have someone pick you up.'

'No,' I said. 'The things you want are in my room anyway. Give me half an hour and I'll meet you outside.'

It was Kearney's turn to be silent for a moment.

'This is me trying to help you, Alex,' he said. 'Don't mess me around. There's a young woman's life at stake here. You know that, don't you?'

'Half an hour,' I repeated. 'It's the Everton Hotel, behind the train station. I'm in Room 632. You can ring up and confirm it with reception.'

Another pause. He was writing something down, and I thought I heard him click his fingers at someone.

'I'll be outside,' I said.

'OK, Alex. Half an hour.'

I cancelled the call.

Then went to the bed and started gathering Sarah's research notes into a pile and jamming them into my rucksack. My heart was thumping. Thirty minutes wasn't long. I doubted I even had that.

We're the police, Alex. Don't be naïve.

Naïve was one thing, but I hadn't given my name when I bought the mobile. The only person who could have told them the number was Mike, and I couldn't imagine why Kearney hadn't just said so. Not to mention how he'd had time to find that out. Even if he'd remembered my name, it couldn't have led him to Mike that quickly.

But that wasn't even the main thing.

I understand you were at their flat earlier today, he said. The phrasing there was all wrong. We'd stared right into each other's fucking eyes, whereas he'd said it as though someone had told him second-hand.

I tried Mike's mobile. There was silence for a second, followed by a series of beeps in my ear, like an alarm. Unavailable. I tried his home number instead. It rang and rang, and nobody picked up.

Keep calm, Alex. You don't know anything's wrong.

Except I did. I tapped out a quick search on the Internet and found the last number I needed.

'Hello,' the woman said. 'Whitrow Police Dep—'

'Detective Paul Kearney, please.'

She paused. 'Transferring. One moment.'

Another two beeps, and then the number was dialling.

'Kearney,' a man said.

The voice was different.

'Did you just phone me?' I said.

'I'm sorry – who is this?'

I hung up. Not the same voice, and the confusion in it was genuine. That hadn't been Kearney on the phone. I disconnected the laptop and tossed it, still powered-up, into my bag. The cable could stay. I patted my pockets. Wallet. Phone. Passport.

According to my watch, I still had twenty minutes until the man I'd spoken to turned up. Except I was quite sure that I didn't. There was a wooden wedge by the door to my room, and I jammed it under, as hard as it would go, then walked back across to the window. It was small, but large enough to fit through.

I took the fire escape.

Twenty-Six

The Wetherspoons pub was at the back of the train station, and the main entrance was from the concourse. I was sat by the open glass doors there. From behind me, I kept hearing the chatter of the large black screens, as yellow letters fluttered into place, updating departure and arrival details. Occasionally, it was all interrupted by the bing of the tannoy, and then a calm voice would announce a train had been delayed.

The first thing I'd done was to call the police from one of the payphones out there and give them Mike and Julie's address. Something might have happened to them, I said. To speed them along, I said it was connected to the murder of Christopher Ellis.

Even now, I was still hoping I was wrong.

Christ, they've got a baby.

That was the last thing I told them, and I'd felt something fall away inside as the words came out of me. Until then, I'd actually forgotten.

After hanging up, I found myself a nice, innocuous seat in here. Parked myself up at this flimsy metal table. And waited.

It was heaving, and there was some comfort in that. The bar itself was thick with men: forcing their way in and then, more carefully, out again, with pint glasses and bottles gripped between splayed fingers. On the wall, muted plasma screens showed silent dance videos.

My attention was focused on the far end of the pub.

It was glass-fronted there as well, but this side faced out onto a patio area at the back of the station. Metal chairs glinted in the early evening sun and, at the edge of the pavement, people stood with clumps of luggage, waiting for taxis or lifts. Beyond all that, across a curl of road, was the entrance to the Everton. And from this safe distance, occluded from return view by panes of glass and at least fifty people, I sipped my drink, and watched as the three men came back out of my hotel.

I know you.

I'd sat down just in time to see them arrive, pulling up in a smart, black BMW. All three were neatly dressed in suits; I didn't think they were policemen, but they had a quiet air of authority about them. Two were young, dark-haired and dark-suited, and solidly built. They wouldn't have looked out of place jogging alongside a presidential cavalcade, fingers touching their ear-pieces. The third was older, and he wore a grey suit that matched his thinning hair. He had the same sense of physical power as the others, but seemed more relaxed about it. More casual. The first two moved like they knew they were stronger than you, whereas the older man moved like it wouldn't matter.

And I recognised him – or I thought I did anyway. He looked a hell of a lot like the guy I'd seen earlier on, leaning on the balcony in the block of flats opposite Ellis's, watching the world go by.

Or maybe scoping the place out.

The chain of events came together from there. He'd seen me call at Ellis's. Afterwards, he'd gone over and killed them both. But before he did, he must have asked them about me, and, although I hadn't left my name, I'd been asking about Sarah Pepper and James Connor. The link after that was missing, but somehow those names had led him to Mike, who had told him who I was and given him my phone number.

I watched them walk back out again now. The grey-haired man led the way. The other two headed straight back to the car, but he stopped on the pavement instead. He looked around, turning his head slowly from one side to the other. It was frighteningly clinical – like a security camera doing a steady sweep of a room. When his eyes fixed on the large windows of the bar, he stopped.

I felt a chill run through me.

He was at least a hundred metres away, and there was no way he could see me: the sunlight would be turning the glass into a mirror, so that even the people sat closest to it would be invisible. Never mind me, right at the back. But I shivered anyway. Because he understood exactly what I'd done, and he knew I was here somewhere, watching him. As much as I could make it out, his expression was blank and impassive. Coolly weighing up the options. Deciding on a strategy.

I stared back, waiting to see what he would do.

Who were these people?

If I was right, this man had killed Christopher Ellis, and I was guessing he'd also taken down the photograph Ellis had posted of Emily Price. I wasn't quite sure *why*, but one explanation occurred to me now: that the information Ellis had shared around was intended to be kept private.

There was certainly something secret about the trail up on the Ridge. For Emily Price's body never to have been found, it had to be that way. So it was forbidden knowledge, designed to be spread discreetly around.

Here. Do you want to see this?

Back in February, Sarah had been investigating rumours of another victim – Jane Slater – appearing on the Internet. Maybe there had also been a trail of symbols leading to her body, and Ellis was the one who'd posted that photograph as well. He'd taken it down for some reason, but not been able to resist for ever. Couldn't keep it to himself. He hadn't been content with just seeing; he'd needed to show, and perhaps that was what had cost him his life.

It made a degree of sense. When I caught up with him in The Duncan, he'd clearly been terrified. While it was flattering to imagine I was that intimidating, my guess was that he'd mistaken me for someone else.

For one of these people, whoever they were.

My drink rattled as I lifted it and swallowed a mouthful.

I watched as the man in grey walked back to the car and got in. Then, a moment later, the vehicle sped away. But it wasn't remotely reassuring; given everything, I suspected they might circle around, park up somewhere out of sight, and come inside to check the bar. For some reason, even with all these people here, it didn't feel like I'd be safe.

I put my glass down and headed out, joining the throng in the station.

As I walked, I passed the payphone I'd called the police from, and thought about Mike and Julie. If something had happened to them, I was to blame. I should have gone to the police. Instead, I'd been so determined to take responsibility for my past – to face it head on and deal with things myself – that my actions might have put them in danger.

Tell him this is all his fault, James had said.

I was beginning to think that he was right.

I was still thinking about it twenty minutes later, sitting on a train, rattling away south from Whitrow. Where I went right now wasn't so important. My plan was to pick a stop at random, and then wander until I found a hotel. It was as close as I could get to losing myself. I needed to go to ground for a while and work out what I was going to do.

I didn't want to go to the police. It wasn't anything to do with making amends this time, or owing it to Sarah to find out what had happened. It was simply practical. The man who'd phoned had not been Paul Kearney, but he had known about him. As far as I could remember, neither Mike nor Julie could have told him we'd ever met. Which meant this man had other connections, possibly within the police themselves, and that I was looking at real organisation here: people who could gather information quickly and efficiently, and then act decisively within the space of a few hours.

Until I knew what was going on, I didn't know who to trust.

That was what I was telling myself. But there was also something else, and I couldn't quite pin it down. Strangely, it was Kearney my thoughts kept returning to. The memory of his eyes, and the way he'd looked at me. I had the feeling that if I stared back into them for long enough, I'd work out what was bothering me.

But instead of probing the idea, I looked around the train. It was a cheap, local service, and the carriages seemed to have been assembled from the old parts of disused buses. The floor here was lined with rubber and the seats were faded and tattered, crammed in tight and facing one another, like booths in a dirty café. The whole thing rocked from side to side as it clattered along, as though it might fall apart at any second.

We passed into a tunnel, and the rattling of the tracks whipped away into a hush. I saw a pale, yellow reflection staring back from the window, but for a second, it didn't look like me at all. It was slightly different, in the same way that the city had felt. My absence had changed me too. And as I looked at myself now I found it hard to work out what was wrong.

Who are you?

I blinked. But then we shot out of the tunnel again, and the stranger was replaced by the green static of an embankment, blasting backwards.

Who are you?

I didn't know. I didn't know if I wanted to.

Running had never really worked: that's what I'd thought back in Venice. That I'd never been able to leave the bad things behind me. But an awful feeling was coiled inside me, and I wondered now if maybe I'd been wrong.

If there was something I really had managed to forget, and which, through the shape of its absence, was coming slowly and irrevocably back into view. A punch that would knock me flat if it landed. One which I could no longer move quickly enough to slip.

Twenty-Seven

The house was dark when they arrived.

The early evening sun was still hazy in the corner of the sky, and Kearney thought he could see a hint of light through the closed curtains, but the building still looked grey, as though it was full of mist, pressed up against the windows. It wasn't a matter of illumination; it was something else, something that was missing. The life in this house had simply gone out, like a broken bulb.

'Side door's open,' Todd said.

His partner's voice sounded grim. He was feeling it too.

'You take the front,' Kearney said.

'You sure?'

But Kearney was already heading down the drive, turning sideways to edge between the red-brick wall and the white saloon that was parked up beneath the car port. Sheltered from the sun, he began to shiver. Not just from the temperature. Adrenalin.

Maybe something else too. In the back of his mind, the headache thud was growing louder and faster. He felt frantic. Desperate.

Round the front of the house, Todd banged on the door.

'Mister Halsall? Could you open up, please? Police.'

Kearney pushed the side-door further open with the back of his fingers. It moved silently, only creaking as it came to a halt. A kitchen. Dark. Empty. He opened his mouth and listened carefully, hearing nothing but the heavy pressure of absolute silence.

He stepped inside, turning slightly.

'Police. Anyone home?'

Nothing.

He heard Todd knock again, louder this time.

The kitchen was long and newly fitted. There were clean pine cabinets under a polished granite counter, and others fixed on the walls. The last person to wash up had left a pink dishcloth folded neatly over the arched spout of the tap. At the far end of the room, a water-print of Kearney's own face stared back from the black gloss front of the oven. Beside it, the light-blue time pulsed softly in the gloom.

18:08.

It ticked over suddenly: 18:09.

Kearney blinked, then moved further in, checking behind the door: *clear one room at a time*. But there was no obvious place for anyone to be hiding in here. He'd seen someone cram themselves into a cabinet before, but these were too small. The door to the pantry was hanging open though. Just mops and a lawnmower, the blades clumped tightly with grass.

A doorway had been cut into the side wall. Through it, Kearney had an angled view of the lounge. He could see a neat, beige carpet, stretched across the floor. The back and shoulders of a plump, leather armchair. A plasma screen. The edge of the curtains, with a dagger of white light at the side, where the fabric didn't quite meet the wall.

Kearney stepped around the island in the centre of the kitchen and saw—

Feet.

Two pairs of feet, a little splayed out, their heels resting on the carpet. One was in black shoes. The other was bare, the toenails painted purple.

Todd banged on the front door. The feet didn't move.

Kearney shouted, 'Round here, Todd.'

Then he moved cautiously into the front room.

Oh God.

There were two bodies on the settee, dreadfully quiet and still. A man and a woman, resting shoulder to shoulder, their hands in their laps. The woman's head was tilted back, her mouth half open, while the man's had lolled to one side, as though he was staring down at her shoulder. There was what looked like a gunshot wound in the middle of his forehead, and his eyes were closed. Behind him, the top of the sofa was saturated.

Mike Halsall and Julie Smith.

Kearney breathed in and caught the scent of burnt air. It was the aroma of old gunpowder. Behind it, a trace of the blood that had been spilled in here.

Neither of them appeared to have fought or resisted. Was that because . . .

They have a baby.

The panic flared, just as his partner arrived beside him.

'Oh Christ,' Todd said.

Kearney set off across the living room.

'Paul – what the hell are you doing?'

'They've got a kid, Todd.'

'These two have been *shot*. We need—'

'There's a little boy in here.'

Even as he stepped past the bodies, he knew Todd was right. It was possible the gunman was still inside the house. In the corridor, perhaps, or waiting quietly upstairs. If so, he was putting himself at risk.

He moved into the hall anyway, and then started quickly up the stairs, not even hesitating. The thudding in his mind was accelerating. *There's a little boy in here.* The thought drove him upstairs. On the landing, he smelled talcum powder and shower gel.

The main bedroom was obvious. The bathroom too. Kearney went to the final door along. As he pushed it open, his heartbeat was racing, and the pulse in his head was keeping time with it.

The room was dark and silent. At the far side, there was the fractured, shadowy shape of a mobile hanging down above a . . .

For the first time, Kearney paused.

The crib was like a wooden cage. Through the bars, he could see a white cushion and blankets, and the ridge of something beneath them. He stepped closer, then finally rested his hands on the top of the wood. Within the crib, he could see a baby's head, turned to the side. The cover rose slowly, then settled. Then again. The baby was sleeping.

Something flipped inside him, and for a moment he thought he was going to collapse. Instead, he rested his forearms across the top of the crib and took deep breaths.

'Paul?'

'It's OK.'

As he heard Todd's footfalls on the stairs, the baby stirred slightly, and Kearney looked up at the wall behind the crib. It was covered with stickers. Some of them were peeling away, as though they'd been too old to stick on properly in the first place.

Stars, he realised blankly. *Fluorescent stars.*

They threatened to overtake him.

'You think it's the same guy?' Todd said.

He spoke quietly. They were outside waiting for extra units, standing by the car. Kearney was holding the baby, wrapped in a blanket, and staring at the dark house in front of them. The child had flopped against him and didn't seem unduly concerned by what had happened. Now that it was over, Kearney himself was shaking enough for both of them. He had tunnel vision. The only way he could control the feelings inside was to fix his attention on the house.

Unravelling . . .

'Paul? The guy that called you?'

'I don't know, Todd.'

The phone calls had come in relatively quick succession, and his mind kept returning to the man he'd seen outside Ellis's flat.

195

The same man with long hair and a tan that had apparently been seen chasing Christopher Ellis from The Duncan earlier in the day. Kearney had told Todd about him, and he couldn't shake the idea the guy was the key to all of this, but—

'He asked for you especially the first time.'

'Yeah,' Kearney said. 'He thought I'd phoned him.'

'But you hadn't?'

'You were there with me.'

'And you've no idea who it was?'

Kearney didn't answer. The feeling of recognition was stronger than ever, but he couldn't place him. It was like the man had *changed* somehow. Not enough to obscure him totally, but just enough to confuse the part of Kearney's brain that was normally so good at recalling people.

Todd began chewing his fingernail nervously. He didn't like it when Kearney got lost; it made him uncomfortable. After a moment, he nodded at the house.

'No obvious connection to Christopher Ellis.'

'The man on the phone said so.'

'That doesn't mean anything. No handcuffs. No fire. And socially, these people are a world away from Ellis and Gilroyd.'

Kearney didn't reply. He knew Todd was waiting for him to provide the usual answers, or at least come up with a theory, but he couldn't. The only thing he was sure about was that these people *were* connected to Ellis somehow. It might not be obvious, but when he figured it out everything else would fall into place. And he needed to make the connection. Needed to make it now.

Kearney closed his eyes and rocked the baby very gently. He could smell the child, and it was a warm smell. The scent of *care*. He tried to use it to focus his thoughts.

'Are you OK, Paul?'

'I'm trying to think.'

And right then, Todd's mobile phone started ringing.

Kearney kept his eyes shut, but something inside him swung away. Was this it? There was no way he could know for sure, but he had a feeling it was. For the last six months, he'd been expecting it. Every time he saw Burrows in the corridor, or walked past the curtained door of Operation Victor, he'd felt it coming towards him. And yet every night, he'd continued. Unable to stop.

Because, by then, it was too late anyway.

He wanted more time.

'Shit,' Todd said. 'It's White.'

DSI Alan White: their boss. There was a beep as Todd accepted the call. Kearney tried to ignore it. Tried to think.

Come on, Paul. You need to make this connection now.

'Sir?' Todd was silent for a moment. 'Yes, sir. He's with me here.'

After that, Todd didn't say anything for a while. Perhaps it was only thirty seconds, but it felt like a lifetime. And the answer just wouldn't come. In its place, all he could think of was an image of Rebecca Wingate, reaching out to him. Almost within touching distance, but then – suddenly – gone. He'd failed her.

Kearney opened his eyes.

Todd slid the phone into his pocket. He was looking at him curiously.

'White says you need to head back. He says straight away.'

Kearney nodded.

'What's going on, Paul?'

'You know what the worst thing is?' he said. 'I promised him we'd find her.'

'What?'

'Simon Wingate. I promised him.'

Todd stared at him, not understanding.

'It's just like Anna said,' Kearney explained.

'Paul?'

His ex-wife had told him that the worst thing about his affair was not the fact he'd done it, but that he'd continued to say 'I love you' when it couldn't possibly be true any more. Promises that he knew could never be kept.

We will find her.

All the frantic mornings came back to Kearney now. The way he'd woken up full of fear and shame, wishing he could take it back, determined not to let it happen again. But then, each night, it had. And yet he'd spoken to Simon Wingate, making promises that would inevitably turn into betrayals when the truth came out. That was the worst thing of all. It was better to say no words at all than to have the ones you did turn to poison.

Todd looked almost panicked now.

'Paul?' he said. 'What have you done?'

'I'm sorry,' Kearney whispered.

He had no idea who he was talking to.

Half an hour later, he'd regained at least some sense of calm.

DSI Alan White was in his early fifties, but looked younger: his hair was receding but still dark, and he had the confidently muscular build of a man who played squash three times a week and could pound the streets for hours without troubling himself. In fact, Kearney remembered, he'd run a marathon recently, hadn't he? Last year, maybe. Or perhaps the one before.

It didn't matter, of course, but his thoughts kept jumping everywhere. White was sitting on the other side of his large oak desk, and was clearly finding this conversation difficult. Strange that someone who usually had so much authority could be reduced to this.

'Paul . . .'

But he trailed off.

White had never called him by his first name before. It had always been surnames, like a school teacher. It wasn't hard to find alpha males in the police force at the best of times, but White in particular never let you forget who was in charge. He prowled and glared. Sometimes, trapped in his office, you imagined he might forget himself and hit you. Many officers were terrified of him, but today he was so subdued it was almost eerie.

He doesn't know how to handle this.

Kearney actually felt sorry for him.

'Paul, something's been brought to my attention.'

There was no point denying it. He'd been following the case from a distance and heard some of the site names that had been floated about. They were familiar to him. Every time Burrows and his team went out on a knock, he held his breath. He'd never had any doubt this would come out eventually.

The worst thing.

'Yes, sir,' he said. 'I know.'

White's gaze flicked up. Common wisdom held that it could strip paint, but what Kearney saw now was closer to confusion. Hurt, even. Kearney's thoughts turned briefly to Simon Wingate, who was probably still sitting down in reception right now. But that was too painful. It was better just to get this over with.

'What is it that you *know*?' White said.

'Operation Victor, sir.'

'Go on.'

'As part of that investigation, I believe my credit card details will have been found.'

'Where?'

'On websites,' Kearney said. 'Private websites.'

'Jesus, Paul. That's one way of putting it, isn't it?'

'I know what the others are, sir.'

White shook his head. There was a printout on the desk in front of him, and he took a few seconds, ostensibly reading it over.

'DS Burrows,' he said, 'is at your house right now. His team have a warrant to search the premises and seize various materials, including, but not limited to, any computer equipment they find there. You will not be going back home tonight.'

'I understand that, sir.'

'And you won't need to call me that any more.'

'I understand.'

White rested his elbows on the desk and began rubbing his eyes. He kept his fingers straight the whole time.

Had he seen the videos, Kearney wondered. Probably not, if Burrows was still at the house. But he would have been told what they were; there would surely be records of what had been downloaded by whom – access logs, and so on. Kearney's collection was only three videos in total, but the quantity was irrelevant. This type of material was categorised between one and five, with five being the most serious. He knew that all three of the clips on his computer would be ranked four.

And he also knew that, in a moment, White was going to ask him to explain. The prospect made him feel sick.

The reality was he really didn't know. It had started earlier this year, when he'd been investigating the reports of a photograph of Jane Slater appearing online. That photo had not been there, but he had found others instead. And once he began clicking through, he'd been unable to stop himself looking.

And then he'd found something else. Just a brief aside in a comment trail.

Let me tell you the worst thing *I've* ever seen . . .

What followed wasn't a video or even an image. It was simply a phrase, but it had lit a fire inside him. When he'd first read it, his heart had tripped, stumbled – and then begun beating hard and fast. A cold sweat had prickled on his face. He wasn't even sure what the story meant, but it was certainly the worst thing *he'd* ever read as well. And from that point on, he'd been lost. Driven to *comprehend*.

After a moment, White moved his hands down and stared across the table at him. Kearney saw that the confusion in the man's expression had been replaced by barely concealed disgust. He felt that mirrored within himself. A sense of the purest shame he'd ever known. He was dirty. Revolting.

'Why, Paul?' White said.

And Kearney was about to explain – to tell White at least part of it – when something inside him suddenly hardened, resisting the idea. His emotions clenched up like a fist.

No. You're not going to do this.
You're not going to tell him anything.

And it didn't matter anyway. A man like White wasn't interested in the why. He wasn't even prepared for it: the fact that the question was its own answer; that asking *why* was like directing a video camera at a television. You got the same image, repeating to infinity, smaller and smaller. It happened all by itself, and it formed a tunnel that, once you started to look, you could do nothing but fall deeper and deeper into.

So Kearney said nothing.

Twenty-Eight

Dan Killingbeck watched his son disappear out through the back door, chasing the dog. Sam was still dressed in shorts and a T-shirt – probably still sand in the creases – and he was little more than an enthusiastic flap of thin limbs. The boy was so uncoordinated recently, he thought. Eleven years old now, his body was growing up faster than his mind could keep track of.

A part of Dan was glad he was still a boy at heart, though – that Sam was as excited about picking Barney up from the kennels and bringing him home as he had been about the holiday they'd just been on. As he was about everything, really. It was nice to see.

A lovely kid.

That's what people said when they met him. He was sweet and good-natured. Secondary school was probably going to kill him.

'Watch yourself out there,' he called.

'Yeah, yeah.'

The words drifted back in on the cool evening air, more breathless than dismissive. But Sam would be fine out there with Barney. God help anyone who messed with his son with that dog around. Even Dan himself was second when Sam came to visit. That was fine too.

He shook his head and threw his car keys down on the kitchen table; they clattered, skittered to a halt. At the far end of the room, beside the door, the blinds were open. In the pitch black square of the window, he could see a blurred, yellow reflection of himself, and he watched as it shrugged off the leather jacket it was wearing, and hung it, down out of sight, over the arched back of the kitchen chair.

Then he ran his fingers through his hair and turned away. Stretched his back. It had been a *long* drive today, and in some ways he was glad to be home; but there was always something bitter about returning. He got Sam two weekends a month, which was OK, but the highlight of the year was always the long week he got in the summer, which was the week just gone.

For the last few years, after Joanne finally agreed, he'd taken Sam to a campsite in France. Just a simple place, really. There was the two of them, a tent, and a double cooking stove that he made Sam take half charge of. In the daytime, they sat and read, or drove to the nearby castle, or took the path down to the beach. In the evenings, they caught films at the open-air cinema. Most important of all, they talked. There were times when Dan felt he had so much he wanted to tell his son, and other times when he just wanted to listen and think: *Jesus – isn't he just fucking great?*

It took at least two days there and then the same back, and Sam loved staying in the bed and breakfasts too. On the radio, they alternated favourite CDs and his son laughed at his attempts at singing. Outward bound, Dan drove pretty quickly; the way home, he stretched it out a little. Even today, with Sam mostly asleep against the passenger window, his son's face reminding him of the baby he'd once been, Dan had slowed the journey down. As though it wasn't the time they had together, but the distance.

Now that he was back, habit took him over to the fridge for a beer. Bathed in the light, he paused. He wouldn't normally drink with Sam here – it was sort of an unwritten law he had, designed to contradict any of Joanne's propaganda. But then he shrugged to himself. One wouldn't make much difference, and Sam was getting older now.

At the time of the divorce, when things got quietly nasty, his own father had given him the best advice he'd ever had. *Just don't play a game*. Never say anything bad; just be a good father, as much as you can. Because the only worry he had was losing Sam's affection. And even if he was momentarily swayed, his son was smart: the way most kids were. Dan had lost touch with his old man as a teenager, convinced of all kinds of things, but only really on the surface, where his mother had needed to see it. His father had soaked it up quietly, confident that Dan had always known the truth deep down. And, of course, he had. Sam would too.

So he twisted off the cap.

And that was when Sam, still out in the back garden, began screaming.

They collided at the kitchen door.

'Sam?'

His son pressed himself tightly against him; Dan could feel his heart beating as he put his arms around the boy. But even as he tried to hold him, Sam twisted and pointed out into the dark garden.

'A monster! It's killing Barney!'

'A what?'

'A monster!'

Dan gripped his son's shoulders.

'Sam. Go inside now.'

'It's out in the field.'

The boy started crying, so Dan physically turned him around and moved him back into the kitchen. Tried to make the hold on him a more reassuring one for the second before he released it.

'It's OK. Just stay here.'

'Be careful.'

'I'll be fine.'

Dan glanced left and right and found the torch sitting on top of the fridge. He'd got it out when he was packing last week, estimated that the battery wouldn't last, then dug out the smaller one from upstairs instead. Now, he pressed the rubbery button and weak light illuminated the grass at the edge of the lawn. It would do.

'Just stay here.'

He stepped outside, then reached behind him and pulled the kitchen door closed. Whatever was happening, he didn't want Sam to see it. He had an unpleasant feeling about what was going on at the far end of the garden. Barney's enthusiastic scrappiness was endearing when he was playing inside; when he got out in the field and crossed paths with the local wildlife . . . less so. One of the neighbours' cats had been found dead a month or so back, and he'd had his suspicions. The neighbour had too, but nobody could prove anything.

Not again, he thought.

Please God, just let it be a . . . fox or something.

Dan followed the flagstones up, training the torchlight at ground-level, and then raising it as he reached the fence up ahead: just posts with barbed wire strung between them. Beyond it, the tall, wavering grass of the field. Far back, the trees were like black clouds against the dark-blue night sky.

He couldn't see a thing.

'Barney?'

But he heard something. It didn't sound much like a fight. Barney was snuffling, growling a little. He called his name again and the dog barked eagerly in response, but didn't come as he'd been taught. Too distracted by something.

At least he didn't sound hurt.

Dan stopped at the end of the path and moved the torchlight methodically along the ground at the base of the fence, shivering in the breeze. He wrinkled his nose. Something smelled bad, he thought. Not terrible, but . . . *off*.

His hand stopped moving as the light fell on a section of fence close to the corner post. Barney was there, his hindquarters low down and shuddering. Struggling with something.

'*Barney.*'

He said it sharply. Maybe because of the light, the dog took notice this time. It let go of whatever it was working at and turned to look at him, a reproachful look on its face.

Dan glared back.

'House.'

The dog trotted to one side, and the light fell on what it had been fighting with. Dan froze. His hand began trembling. He didn't even notice it when Barney slunk past him and padded back towards the house.

Which suddenly felt a long way behind him.

His first thought was that Sam had been right. It was a monster. The face was vaguely humanoid, but swollen and pale, the features lost apart from a single, huge black space where an eye should have been. The thing was completely still. Dead. The skin on its arm was mottled, and it appeared to be pointing at him.

He swallowed. There was no such thing as monsters, of course, and after that first jab of shock he realised exactly what he was looking at. Barney must have smelled it, run into the field, and then dragged it back here as best he could.

God, the face . . .

He recognised it from the newspaper.

Part Four

Twenty-Nine

The next morning, I woke up early. The miniature kettle on the table beside the bed rumbled and clicked as I made myself a piss-weak coffee, and then I sat cross-legged on the end of the bed, in the light from the small television, waiting for the local news to come on.

The first item was a double shooting in the suburbs.

I sipped my coffee slowly, trying to work it past the knot that was tightening in my throat. When they went to the reporter on scene, he was standing outside Mike and Julie's house.

I nodded to myself. In my heart, I'd already known that something had happened, but there was still something shocking about seeing it on the television screen in front of me. The building now looked even more unfamiliar and strange than it had when I'd first turned up there.

I waited.

The reporter said, 'Police have also revealed that a baby was found at the house. The child is apparently uninjured and is currently being cared for by trained officers.'

Josh. At least that was something.

But then I remembered Mike and Julie and realised that it wasn't. It really, really wasn't.

You shouldn't have come back.

The voice had been right all along. Everything here seemed to have stemmed in one way or another from my leaving in the first place, and now my return had made things even worse. I didn't understand it all, and it was true that I *never meant* any of it, but neither of those facts seemed to matter any more. Perhaps they never do.

Regardless, I'd already decided what was going to happen next. My passport was out on the bed beside me; everything else was packed. I was going to leave. Maybe it was another mistake, but sometimes you have to make them, just because that's all there is on offer. And if you're going to end up damned by your actions, it's better for it to be the things you didn't do, rather than the ones you did.

I sipped my coffee.

Besides, there was nothing else I could do.

I certainly couldn't go to see my brother. The missing link in the chain had come to me last night. How had the man in the grey suit moved from a mention of Sarah and James at Ellis's flat to talking to Mike?

I mean, has he even had any other visitors?

That was all I could think of: that Mike had been the only person who'd been visiting my brother in prison. Yesterday evening, I'd wondered how well-connected the men I'd seen at the hotel were. They obviously had some kind of contact within the police, and now this indicated they had access to prison visiting records as well. So they would know about my appointment.

I tipped back the dregs of my coffee and nodded to myself again. All that was entirely true.

And yet I couldn't shake the feeling I'd had last night on the train, and I knew the idea of going to the prison had brought something else along with it. It wasn't just fear of these men. It was the same small curl of panic I'd felt in Venice. And even though I tried to ignore it, I wondered about that.

I wondered if maybe what I was running away from was not the man in the suit at all, but something James might tell me, and that I would finally be forced to see.

*

At just before ten, I walked up along the wide, curving driveway that led to the prison's reception area.

It was another nice day. There was a warm, gentle breeze, and the air smelled of cut grass from the neatly trimmed verges on either side of the drive. Up ahead, the prison itself looked like a castle from a children's story: a solid old building covered with turrets that stood out against the blue sky and the white, comforting tufts of cloud behind. It was almost tranquil here.

But the knot of emotion remained in my throat, growing tighter with every footstep. The voice in my head was adamant that this was a huge mistake, for several different reasons, and that I really didn't want to do this.

And that was the point.

You were right, I'd told Sarah. *You have to face things.* Ever since I'd returned here, I'd been telling myself I was taking responsibility for my actions: that I was dealing with the repercussions of what I'd done. But perhaps I hadn't been. In fact, I thought that coming here today might be the first thing I'd done right since I arrived. The fact I didn't want to was evidence of something.

But with every step, that feeling increased.

You shouldn't be doing this.

The glass doors at the front of the building slid open, and I walked into the reception. There was a single guard sitting at a desk, concentrating on paperwork. To my right, an area of plastic seats, where the people were waiting quietly, minding their own business, like patients waiting to be seen in a surgery. In one corner, there was a woman in her twenties, with a little girl curled up asleep on the seat beside her. Several older people were staring into the mid-distance; some young people were slouched out, arms and faces folded. Nearest the door, a woman with tired eyes was ignoring the child in front of her, who was banging toy bricks together.

None of them paid me any attention.

I gave my details at the desk, fished out some ID, and then took a seat with the others. No alarm went off. Nobody looked at me. The only sound was the little boy with the bricks; every time he *clacked* them together, my heart jumped a little.

Just after ten, another guard came to collect us. We were taken down a corridor and through security. It was too late to back out now. From there, we were led into a large room. It had the smooth, polished, wooden floor of a school gymnasium, and the folding tables were set up like desks for summer exams. Every small noise – the scuff of feet, quiet coughing – echoed around. Down one side, there was a long, makeshift counter loaded with clean cups at one end and used ones at the other. A woman in the middle was pouring out teas and coffees from black plastic urns.

I picked a table and sat down.

Ready for this, whatever it might bring.

A few minutes later, they brought the prisoners in from a door at the far end of the room. The men trooped along in a line, then dispersed amongst the tables, seeking out the mothers, wives and families that had come to visit them. They were all dressed in casual clothes – jeans, T-shirts, jumpers – but had bright orange bibs tied around their chests, which made them look like labourers coming in for a break from work.

No James.

Out of everything I'd anticipated happening, I hadn't prepared myself for the most likely eventuality of all – that my brother would decline my visit.

After a minute, the door echoed shut. Everyone around me was settling down, leaning forward, the air full of conversations that mingled into a single, complex murmur. I was left very obviously alone. Upright and awkward in a room full of people huddling together.

I was wondering what to do when I noticed a middle-aged man in a suit and small, round glasses. He was standing at the side of the room, whispering to one of the guards. Both of them began peering around. When the man's gaze hit me, it stayed.

So that was it then.

I looked back at him and waited. There didn't seem any point doing anything else. A moment later, he began to thread his way between the tables towards me, and when he reached mine he leaned down, speaking quietly, so the people around us couldn't hear.

'Is it Mr Connor?'

'Yes.'

'Would you come with me, please?'

The man escorted me back down the corridor, and introduced himself as Charles Peterson, explaining that he was the prison's Family Liaison Officer. He'd left instructions at the front desk for them to call through when I arrived, he said, but for some reason it had been missed.

At this point, as he apologised to me, I understood that I wasn't being arrested. But that was about all I understood.

'Can you tell me what's going on?'

Peterson nodded, but didn't. 'We'll talk in my office.'

He led me inside. It was small and tidy; there was a window at the far side, and little more than a desk, chairs and potted plant in between. He closed the door behind us and gestured for me to take a seat. Something was humming, and it was too warm in the room. As I sat down, Peterson sighed gently to himself and began adjusting buttons on an AC unit by the window.

I lost patience. 'What's this about, Mr Peterson?'

He gave up on the AC and sat down on the other side of the desk. Then rested his forearms on it and looked at me.

'I'm sorry to have to tell you,' he said, 'that your brother died last night.'

His voice was serious and professional, with just the right amount of sympathy underlying the tone.

'OK,' I said. Then I shook my head, leaning forward. 'Sorry, what did you just say?'

'Your brother,' he said. 'James Connor. He was found in his cell yesterday evening. He was taken to the infirmary, but they were unable to resuscitate him. I'm really very sorry to be telling you this.'

Keep calm, Alex.

I noticed my heart thudding in my chest and was almost surprised by it. James was dead. But at the same time, he couldn't be. Because those were just words, and I couldn't get the idea itself to settle in my head. Everything in the office felt hyper-real: saturated with colour. Was I dreaming this?

I swallowed.

A moment later, an image of James came to me. But he wasn't throwing a cushion, or throwing a bottle. The image was of a small boy wearing shorts, kneeling on the front-room carpet with his legs tucked underneath him. I was sitting beside him, and we were surrounded by open scraps of newspaper and snow-capped baubles. James was smiling quietly to himself, as though he'd just unwrapped something he wanted to like very much, and was cautiously allowing himself to do so.

My brother. I closed my eyes.

And something terrible occurred to me.

You got what you wanted.

I really was cut off from my old life now: everyone was gone. Leaving had never accomplished it, but returning home again had. I was now totally alone, exactly the way I'd always wanted. The thought was a sharp, vicious twist inside me.

Tell Alex this is all—

'I'm very sorry to have to tell you this,' Peterson said.

That phrase again. It cut through the mist, and I had a sudden urge to reach across the desk and make Peterson very fucking sorry indeed. Because someone needed to be, and I didn't think I could bear it all myself.

Instead, I clenched my fist in my lap.

'What happened?'

Peterson told me that James had been attacked early yesterday evening. The two men responsible were caught on CCTV entering his cell, and guards were immediately alerted, but didn't arrive soon enough to prevent the injuries he sustained from being fatal. The two individuals in question were both hardened lifers, and it wasn't fully understood why they had chosen to pick on James. Both were in custody over the incident and would be questioned shortly.

They wouldn't be talking, I thought, and I didn't need them to. The men I'd seen at the hotel last night wouldn't have been able to get to James in here, but they'd have been able to pay someone who would. A lifer, for example, with nothing to lose, but maybe a family to provide for.

They got to James as well. They got him too.

'Can I get you anything, Mr Connor? A glass of water?'

'No.'

Peterson leaned back. 'As I said, the police are here, and you can talk to them in a moment. And I'm afraid there will be some paperwork to attend to. I'm sure you have some questions too, but I appreciate this has come as a huge shock.'

'I need some fresh air.'

'Of course.' He walked round and opened the door for me. 'You'll have seen the benches out by the main entrance. When you're ready, ask for me at reception. And, of course, if you need anything in the meantime.'

'Thank you.'

Back in reception, the doors slid open, and I walked outside, blinking against the sunlight.

My chest felt hard and heavy, as though it had been beaten over and over until it clenched itself into a ball. I barely heard the glass panels whispering shut behind me: just faltered forwards a little, unsure what I was going to do.

And then a hand gripped my elbow.

'Alex Connor,' the man beside me said.

Thirty

Detective Todd Dennis was standing in the mid-morning sun at the side of a field on the edge of town. Farm-land, technically, but this area lay fallow and untended right now, and the grass, fed by a hot summer, reached his thighs. He was looking down at a dead man. Not just a dead man. A real problem.

'An estimated time of death would be helpful,' he said.

'Yes. I understand.'

Do you?

The pathologist, Chris Dale, was squatting on his haunches, his black rubber boots bowing out at the shins and buckling at the foot. His head kept tilting as he inspected the livid bruising around Roger Timms's face. Taking his time.

Do you understand?

They'd been working on the assumption that it was Timms who had taken Rebecca Wingate. That he was *running*. If he'd been dead for longer than a couple of days, that was impossible.

And he had been.

Todd didn't really need the pathologist to confirm that.

The artist's naked body was lying belly down near one of the fence posts, its head resting on the lowest of the strands of barbed wire strung between them. It was as though the corpse had crawled through the grass, encountered this obstacle and not been able to make it any further: just put its chin down and stopped.

Horrifically, it was facing into the garden of a man named Dan Killingbeck. It was Killingbeck who had found the body last night. Or rather, his dog had. Timms appeared to have been dumped much further back in the field, but Killingbeck's enormous, fuck-off German Shepherd had tried to drag the body home by the wrist. Then given up, leaving the ravaged, swollen arm draped over the wire, pointing towards the house like an accusation.

Dale shifted his weight, moving around to peer at the underside of the corpse. Its bloated hips were gleaming in the undergrowth.

Todd began chewing his lip.

Behind him, scene of crime officers were moving through the swaying field, looking for clothes, footprints, evidence of any kind left by the man who'd brought Timms's body here. Forensics would spend hours sifting through sweet wrappers and cigarette ends. Not because it would tell them anything, but because they had to be absolutely certain it wouldn't.

Above, the sky was blue and clear. The slight breeze made the grass swim gently. And yet Todd could feel a silent and sickening bloom of emotion hanging in the air. As though, despite the sun, this place now had a weight of darkness to it.

That's a Kearney thought if ever there was one.

Dale stood up. 'On first appearances, it's a male, looks to be in his forties. Cause of death is most likely the gunshot wound to the head.'

'How long ago did he die?'

'Hard to tell.' Dale squinted up at the sky, like it was an enemy on the horizon. 'Decomposition is quite advanced, but you know the weather we've had.'

'Just an estimate.' He was getting desperate now. 'Please.'

'Two, maybe three days.'

Todd closed his eyes, breathing slowly to keep himself calm.

On the cusp, then. Nevertheless, he was sure that Timms hadn't been the one to take Rebecca Wingate from the lock-up. Instead, he himself had been taken. Someone had kidnapped him, beaten him, executed him. And that same unknown person must now have Rebecca Wingate.

Mister X.

Todd opened his eyes. In the distance, the field dipped down. Beyond it, bright under the sun, was the spread of the suburbs. The houses were almost hazy in the heat. A silent car glistened. Quiet and still.

'Thank you,' he said.

He stepped away, leaving Dale to continue the examination.

The car in the distance made him think about Roger Timms's missing van. It still hadn't been located, which was bad in some ways, good in others. In its absence, he could hope that, when they did find it, they would also find Rebecca and the man responsible for her abduction, and that she would still be alive when they did.

Small hope, Todd.

The way the situation kept deteriorating, he expected they'd shortly find the van parked up by the roadside. Empty. Adding nothing to the investigation except another layer of confusion. Another layer of shit for him to wade through.

Behind him, at the fence, the dead man was keeping his secrets. To the extent that his features remained, Timms had an almost stupid expression on his face. Looking at him now, Todd felt a sudden desire to run back over and kick that pointless, silent thing. To stamp at it and keep stamping.

What happened to you?

Who did this?

Why?

But that question reminded him of Paul again, and it killed his anger. He knew that a lot of the impatience and frustration he was feeling now was because of what had happened.

White had called him in yesterday evening, after he'd returned from the crime scene at Mike Halsall's house, and laid the situation out plainly and cleanly. Paul was downstairs; he'd been arrested and was giving a statement. The evidence was strong, and he wasn't disputing the allegations against him.

Paul had used his credit card – his own name and card – to access and download hardcore child pornography involving young boys. Todd was unsure, as things stood, whether his partner would do time. Probably not. But there was no question of him keeping his job. Effectively, his life was over.

'Stupid bastard,' White said.

'I just don't understand, sir.'

'Neither do I. But you know what he's like, Dennis. He'll have just been "fascinated by it". *Needing to understand*. Like one of those fucking look-at-me rock stars.'

White was disgusted.

'It's all the same, of course.'

And it was. Kearney had paid for membership and downloads. Justifying it as 'harmless interest' would still have cost him his career and possibly his freedom, but there were degrees even when it came to this sort of filth, and Kearney's fascination had a price. It put money in the pocket of the scum who produced that shit. By providing his demand, he had fed the supply.

Obviously, the news had gone through the department like a bullet. When he'd arrived this morning, Todd could sense the emotion in the air. Anger. Confusion. Disgust. Other than White, nobody mentioned it directly, but he'd sensed everyone watching him too, as though he was tainted by association. Paul had betrayed them.

Todd was angry with him too. And yet he'd still wanted to grab each person he saw this morning by the throat and shake some of the crap out of them.

What? What have you got to say?

Because the hardest part was that he *understood* why Kearney would have done it: that was the tragedy. It was too easy to imagine his partner – his old partner, now – getting drawn in by that sort of material. Paul would have sat there for hours, poring through the sludge, digging pointlessly for answers. And yet he must have known he wouldn't get away with it. He was a cop for fuck's sake. It didn't make sense.

At least it explained the way Kearney had been behaving recently. How distracted he'd become; how tired and panicked. The way he'd looked like a sword was hanging over him. Hell – even the way he'd charged upstairs at Mike Halsall's house yesterday, like he almost wanted to get shot.

Fucking idiot, Paul.

You stupid, fucking idiot.

Todd made his way around the fence, back up through Dan Killingbeck's garden. His car was parked at the front of the house. Once inside, he closed the door, grateful for the solid *whump*, and then the contained silence of the vehicle's interior.

He took out his mobile phone.

You know what he's like, Dennis.

Yes, he did. And deep down, as much as he hated to admit it, he also relied on it a little. There had been animosity between them on occasion, and Kearney had often infuriated him with his constant need to understand – but that was part of how they worked. So as much as he couldn't help feeling betrayed, he also felt abandoned now too. Lost.

Todd checked for missed calls or new messages. None. Then he opened his list of contacts and scrolled down until he found Paul's number.

In the early days, when their hunt for the killer had been in its infancy, they'd needed to read a lot of supernatural bullshit – there were still a few embarrassing books dotted around the office. Todd remembered one in particular. It was something he'd seen while flicking through at random, but this had really happened. Some villages used to have 'sin-eaters'. They were men who lived apart from the community, shunned by it, until someone in a household died. The sin-eater would be invited in, then, and given a huge feast. In exchange for that food, they were supposed to consume the sins of the deceased, so that the dead could enter Heaven unblemished.

Kearney's absence reminded him of that, as though him asking those questions meant others didn't have to. And whatever answers he'd found over the years had often seemed to provide him with an insight that Todd always lacked.

His finger hovered over the dial button for a few seconds. He wanted to ask Paul what the fuck he thought he'd been doing. But even more than that, he just wanted to . . . make sure he was OK. See where he was and if he needed anything.

He pressed the button, and held the mobile to his ear as it dialled. But it went straight to voicemail; Paul had turned his phone off.

Todd cancelled the call and slipped the mobile back into his pocket. Frustrated. And worried now too. He kept remembering the way Paul had been last night, outside Halsall's house. Mentally, he'd been teetering on the edge of something, and Todd felt an urge to find him, to stop him from falling. But there was nothing he could do if Kearney wanted to hide.

Where are you, Paul?

He started the engine and drove away.

Thirty-One

'I'm surprised you remembered me,' I said.

I was sitting across from Detective Paul Kearney in a small café. When I turned around and saw him, back at the prison, I'd expected him to arrest me. Instead, he'd decided to drive me across town and call in here for breakfast.

The place was called The Rubber Duck, which only added to how bizarre the situation felt. It was the size of an average front room, with space for six circular tables inside, and three more directly outside the glass window behind us. The owner was now bustling away in the kitchen, where I could hear something sizzling and spitting. Metal clattering against metal.

There was nobody else in here and we'd already got our food: two full English breakfasts sat in front of us. Kearney was tucking into his quietly and efficiently, as though he hadn't eaten anything for a very long time. I was ignoring my food. He was ignoring me.

'Kearney?'

Nothing.

The chairs were made of wicker. Mine creaked as I leaned back, watching him eat. Something was very definitely wrong with him. I remembered him being intense, but he looked different now – exhausted and deflated. His suit was crumpled, his hair was messy. In fact, he reminded me of someone mentally unhinged. The kind who would stop you in the street and

grip your shoulder, determined to make you understand something *important*.

And his eyes.

I was struck by that feeling again: that if I stared into them
for long enough, I'd understand something very important.
That whatever was missing in my head would come back to
me. I'd been scared to. But those eyes, when he looked at
me at all, were baggy and tired, and not how I remembered
them. Whatever answers I'd been worried about, they weren't
there.

'Kearney—'

'I didn't at first.' His knife and fork continued working
delicately, and he didn't look up at me as he spoke. 'I recognised you at Ellis's flat, but I couldn't place you. It came back to
me last night. I searched for "Mike Halsall" online and found a
quote from him in an article about Sarah Pepper's murder. That
made the connection for me.'

I frowned, unsure for a moment what that connection might
be. But then it came to me: the article would have mentioned
James Connor, and he would have got the surname from there.

He said, 'It *was* you who called last night, wasn't it?'

I nodded.

'Which means,' he said, 'you're now involved in at least two
separate murder enquiries. First, we have Christopher Ellis and
Mandy Gilroyd. You attacked Ellis. We know that.'

'Technically,' I said, 'he attacked me.'

Kearney ignored that. 'Secondly, Mike Halsall and Julie
Smith. You were friends of the victims, and you called it in.'
He shook his head. 'I think you're in a lot of trouble, Alex.'

'Why haven't you arrested me, then?'

Why are we sitting here in a fucking café?

Kearney considered it.

'Because I'm not sure what kind of trouble yet.'

Then he lapsed into silence again. I watched him eating, and
thought about his odd manner. No, I decided, that wasn't the
reason. He was trying to hide something from me. I had the

impression that if I stood up and walked out of here right now, there wasn't a thing he could do to stop me. His dishevelled appearance, his behaviour . . . but I couldn't quite put my finger on it.

Even so, the way I saw it, he had at least one thing going for him. Whoever was behind this seemed to have access to police files, but if Kearney was involved then he'd surely have called me last night himself. Which meant I could trust him. To an extent, anyway.

I said, 'I had a phone call last night, as well.'

'Oh yes?'

'From someone pretending to be you.'

That caught his attention. He looked up.

'Me?'

I nodded slowly. 'But Mike's the only person who had my number. They turned up at my hotel. Three guys in suits.'

'Three?'

'Yes. I saw one of them earlier on at Ellis's flat. They killed Ellis, and then they killed Mike and Julie. And then they came looking for me.'

Kearney stared across the table.

'I'm listening. Why are they doing this?'

'I don't know for sure,' I admitted.

But I told him what I suspected. Sarah had been research-ing something in the months before she died: online footage of death and murder. In doing so, she'd spoken to Ellis and learned something she shouldn't have. Something these men were determined to keep a secret.

Kearney frowned. I expected him to ask what that was, but instead he said, 'When did she start? Researching, I mean?'

'Earlier this year.'

He put down his knife and fork and used the napkin to dab at his mouth.

'Why?' I said.

'Because I spoke to her back then. In a professional capacity. She phoned up and talked to me around the time Jane Slater's body was found. Probably back around January. There had been some rumours at the time, about some kind of photograph turning up online. We'd already looked into it.'

'And you didn't find anything?'

For a moment, Kearney didn't reply. Then he picked up his cutlery and started eating again.

'No,' he said. 'Anyway. What do you think Ellis told her?'

I thought about it.

Then I picked up my knife and fork and started eating.

'Tell me about Thomas Wells and Roger Timms.'

It was a direct challenge: some way short of walking out on him, but not by much. I was curious to see what he would do. If he wanted to arrest me, he could get on with it. If he didn't, the information needed to flow both ways. So I gave Kearney the same top of the head treatment he'd given me, and waited while he came to a decision.

Eventually, he leaned back in his seat.

'All right.'

He began with what I'd already seen on the news, but then went into greater detail. Thomas Wells had murdered the girls, while the artist, Roger Timms, had been helping him, and taking some of the girls' blood as payment.

'Timms used the blood to seal a part of the victims into his canvases. So that people would be looking at a portrait of a dead girl painted with . . . part of her, I suppose.'

He looked disgusted, and I didn't blame him. But the idea also chimed with me a little. It reminded me of what I'd thought when I'd seen Marie online.

'It was like they were being watched,' I said quietly. 'Over and over again.'

He looked confused.

'What?'

'OK,' I said, 'not "watched". But it's similar to . . . videos I saw online. When I looked at them, it almost felt like I was replaying the actual event. As though those people were stuck there in a loop, dying again every time someone pressed play.'

Kearney stared at me, but I thought the confusion had shifted slightly. It was like something had just chimed in his head as well, only not as clearly as it had in mine.

After a moment, he frowned and looked away.

'Your turn,' he said. 'What was Ellis's secret?'

I took a deep mental breath.

'I think it was a kind of map.'

'A map?'

'To Emily Price's body.'

I told him about the photograph Ellis had posted online and the symbols I'd found up at the Ridge. Kearney was as outraged as I expected him to be.

He said, 'Why the hell didn't you call the police?'

There was a flash of anger in his eyes – a brief glimpse of that old intensity – and a memory fluttered into my head. *Talk to me, Alex.* Then, just like that, it was gone again. But whatever it was, it had just started my heart thumping badly.

'Alex?'

'I didn't know what it meant back then.'

'Jesus—'

'Look,' I said quickly, 'what's important is where the symbols led. You never found Emily Price's body, did you?'

'No. We never did.'

'Well, *someone* did. They left that trail so other people could find her too. The body's gone now. The photo too.'

Kearney looked away. He stared at the remains of his breakfast and didn't reply. Whether he was disgusted with me, or simply thinking everything over, I couldn't tell.

Probably both.

'Kearney?'

'Let me *think*.' He glared at me. 'Ellis bought something off Roger Timms earlier this year. We thought it was a painting – a private commission – but we never identified it.'

I nodded to myself. That made sense. Forbidden knowledge wasn't something you just gave away, after all. Not when there were such risks attached. You'd need reassurance: something that gave you a hold over the other person, and a reason why they wouldn't tell the police.

I said, 'Ellis was buying a map.'

'No, Alex—'

'I looked on *one* website, Kearney. There were thousands of users in that place alone, all of them wanting to see terrible things happening to other people. Some of them were really getting off on it.'

And even the ones that weren't – they were still obviously drawn to that sort of material. I'd experienced it myself, and the effect had been much more powerful and pronounced on the Ridge. The place had a kind of dark electricity to it.

I said, 'It's not a massive stretch to imagine a handful of those people might seek out *more* than just a photograph. Maybe a few of them are willing to pay enough to make it worth the risk for everyone involved.'

Kearney remained silent.

'So Timms takes the cash,' I said. 'And he gives people just enough information to find the scene.'

'We found a fingerprint on the bodies. An index finger. The same one each time.'

'Jesus,' I said. That was a macabre idea: that someone wouldn't just pay to look at a body, but actually touch it. 'Leaving a calling card. Like a signature to prove he was there. Make himself part of it.'

Kearney started to say something, but then stopped. Instead, he just shook his head – *you stupid fucker* – and whispered something to himself under his breath.

'What?' I said.

'Art.' He shook his head again. 'It's never just the painting on the wall. The context is always part of it. That's what interests people.'

I frowned. 'Listen—'

'No, you listen.' Kearney stood up and leaned on the table. 'Have you still got all these research notes you mentioned?'

'Not with me, but they're in a safe place.'

'That's good enough. I want you to call the police and ask for Detective Todd Dennis. You can trust him. Wait for him here, and then tell him everything you just told me.'

'But—'

'Just do as you're told.' Kearney headed for the door. 'He can help you, Alex. I can't.'

I opened my mouth – but he was already outside, running off in the direction he'd left his car.

'Fucking hell.'

The situation had felt odd enough before; in a split second, it had just become completely surreal. I looked around the café to make sure that Kearney really had just got up and abandoned me here. Yes, he had.

Detective Todd Dennis. You can trust him.

I took out my mobile and held down the green button. It took a couple of seconds to turn itself on.

The display lit up.

But instead of calling anyone, I sat there, thinking it over. Was this the right thing to do? Even if I trusted Kearney, I wasn't sure how much confidence I had in his judgement right now. Not to mention the fact I still had no real idea what was going on. If Timms had been selling the information, who the fuck were the men in suits? And how did James know about the bag with the note and the bottle of blood? And . . .

Talk to me, Alex.

The memory surfaced again. It was Kearney saying those words, staring right into my eyes. And it hadn't been at the hospital, either. His eyes hadn't been as kind or understanding as they had back then.

Tell me where you really were.

I swallowed.

When he'd told me the article on Sarah Pepper had made the connection for him, it hadn't been James's name that had brought him to me. It had been hers.

Don't make her lie for you.

For a moment, there was only my heartbeat.

And then the mobile started ringing.

I picked it up slowly. The display said [number withheld], the same as last night. The man from last night.

I accepted the call. 'Yes.'

But it wasn't him. It was a girl that came on the line.

'Hello?' she said. 'Who's there?'

The voice drifted to me, sounding lost and far away. My hairs stood on end. It was the sound I imagined a ghost would make, and after all this time I still recognised it without even having to think. It was *speaking* I had to concentrate on now.

'Sarah,' I said.

Thirty-Two

Confidentiality.

The first sign the organisation had a problem in Whitrow was a newspaper report written earlier in the year. It claimed a photograph of Jane Slater's body had appeared online, and that police were unable to substantiate the rumour. Garland had investigated the matter himself, with the same result. However, he was less inclined to leave the matter there. From a distance, he'd ordered surveillance to be increased.

After a while, he almost began to relax.

But then, towards the end of May, he was told that someone had been spotted at Whitrow Ridge. Banyard was the caretaker for that particular exhibit, and he'd seen a woman returning to the area on several occasions. Once, she'd been close enough to Emily Price's body to indicate she knew about it. Most of the time, she simply stood at the top of the embankment, looking out, as though trying to decide what to do with the information.

Garland had the girl followed – carefully – and discovered who she was. Two days later, he and his team arrived in the UK. By the time their small plane touched down, he knew almost everything there was to know about Sarah Pepper.

He knew she was the journalist who had written the original article. The only explanation he could think of was that she'd investigated the matter, and had more success than either he or the police had. It also meant the breach of confidentiality was a serious one. This woman had gone looking for Jane Slater, but someone had told her about Emily Price.

Garland needed to know who.

Time had therefore been spent following Sarah Pepper's movements and trying to work out *how* she knew. Ideally, Garland would have simply acquired her and asked, but he considered that too risky. While his police source insisted Pepper had not contacted them regarding the whereabouts of Price's body, Garland remained cautious – in his experience, sources only knew what they were told. Sarah Pepper might be working with the police. Or another journalist. And he was reluctant to show his hand until he fully understood what was happening.

He was also curious about her intentions.

From his research, he knew about the murder of her mother, then the father's suicide and the child's subsequent finding of his body. And as an adult, she worked as a crime correspondent at the newspaper. Now, she appeared to know at least a little about the organisation, and yet hadn't reported her suspicions to the police. Instead, she kept going back to the Ridge.

Garland wasn't remotely interested in the objects his company dealt in, but he was familiar enough with the customers to recognise their mindset. Taken all together, the information he had about Sarah Pepper was suggestive. For either personal or professional reasons, she was drawn to them. From experience, he suspected the former motivation. Justified by the latter.

He was observing the situation carefully when three things happened that forced his hand. The first was that Sarah Pepper, with the help of her boyfriend, made her intentions completely clear.

Attempting to draw them out with scraps of information – the gate, the bottles of vodka – was smarter than she probably realised, and under other circumstances it might have worked. Any experience would have needed to be arranged swiftly, but it had certainly been done before. Pepper might have been able to photograph or even approach a few key-players.

The mistake she'd made was imagining they didn't already know. Garland had, briefly, felt sorry for her. He'd even toyed with the idea of leaving her wild to see what she would do. He couldn't imagine what she thought was going to happen, even if her plan had been successful. He suspected that she didn't know either. She was just compelled. To try to see.

But then two other events occurred and he'd been left with no choice. The first was that Roger Timms contacted them to let them know a new victim had been taken. And then the photo of Emily Price appeared online. At that point, there was too much attention. Too many unknown variables. Too much risk.

When the chess board becomes crowded and awkward, you clear away pieces. So the first thing Garland had done was grant Sarah Pepper her wish.

He took the phone off her now and moved back out of the small cell. He had two men with him in case she attempted to fight, but she didn't even move: just stood in the centre of the small, dark room, watching them go. It was what he'd expected. She had been this way since they picked her up, as though she knew that questioning gaze of hers would unnerve him far more than flailing hands.

One of the men closed and locked the heavy steel door. Finally, Garland turned his attention to the phone. The reception was poor because he was underground. He hadn't wanted to take Pepper up to the warehouse floor.

'Mr Connor,' he said.

There was a pause before the response came.

'Detective Kearney.'

Garland almost smiled at that.

'Listen to me,' he said. 'I'm going to give you an address.'

'*Put her back on.*'

'No. Shut up and pay attention. Rose Avenue is on the edge of the Balders Estate. You'll go to number seventeen. You'll understand what to do when you get there. Take the footpath.'

'What—'

'You will be there in an hour, and you'll bring everything with you. Her research, her files. Everything. If you're not there, the letter that was in her possession will be sent anonymously to the police.'

'But—'

And then Connor shut up.

'You remember what you wrote in that, don't you?' Garland said. 'About what you did?'

There was silence on the other end of the line. But he was still there, Garland could tell.

'One hour's time,' he repeated. 'Or she's dead. And I'll have to come looking for you myself.'

Then he cancelled the call. The encoded, untraceable connection crackled away into nothing as he slipped the phone back into his suit pocket.

That was that.

Garland stepped across the thin corridor and looked through the grille on the door of Sarah Pepper's cell. It was dark both inside the room and out here in the corridor, but she was just about visible through the mesh. As he'd anticipated, she had remained standing in the centre, arms down by her side. Looking out at him, her face totally blank.

From the beginning, he had been reluctant to hurt her. Not because she was a woman, but because he had sensed it wouldn't work: that some part of her was missing. Despite everything that had happened, she did not appear to be afraid.

Fortunately, he hadn't needed to resort to persuasion. She had answered every question he put to her – only lying once, as far as he knew, when she claimed not to know the real identity behind the username 'Hell_is'. And she often responded with questions of her own. It was those that made him uncomfortable. Even when she didn't ask them out loud, he could see them there in her eyes.

It's about money, he wanted to tell her. *That's all.*

It always came down to business.

The organisation he worked for had been able to flourish precisely because it took confidentiality seriously. In order for the transactions to take place, both the clients and suppliers needed to be assured of absolute discretion. The buyers had to know the experience they paid for was safe, while the sellers needed to know their freedom would not be compromised. Everyone involved had something to lose. If either side lost confidence in the company's high standards of privacy, the business would collapse.

And so the organisation had only one rule: all transactions were conducted through it. Roger Timms had been very well rewarded for providing them with access to his victims; in return, he was expected to be loyal. The company could then sell that information on with confidence to interested parties. To ensure Timms's *own* safety, clients were vetted to ensure eligibility. Having money, by itself, was not enough. It was when people forgot that and became greedy that problems arose.

Problems like Christopher Ellis.

Problems like photos appearing online.

Timms hadn't proved quite as forthcoming as Sarah Pepper. Fortunately, Garland hadn't had the same qualms about persuading him to talk.

Now, his work here was almost done. Timms and Ellis were dead. James Connor had been silenced. The final stage of the salvage operation was to be completed within the next few hours, and then this branch of the organisation would be closed for ever. He would be gone by nightfall.

In the cell, Sarah Pepper remained standing where she was, looking out at him.

Garland stared back.

He had been right about her, but not completely. The letter had confirmed some of it. *Death is contagious*, Alex Connor had written. *You have to face up to it*. And the way he wrote that suggested the sentiment had been the driving force behind her whole life.

Yet she was different from the regular clients.

When he was younger, Garland had worked at an illegal game reserve. There, he'd watched fat tourists pay to gun down the antelope that were kept in a small pen. All they had to do was point and pull. Afterwards, they went away flushed and nervous from the experience, imagining that they were hunters. It was laughable. But it was also good business, and Garland had become adept at hiding the contempt he felt.

His current work was similar.

But Sarah Pepper was not like that. It seemed like she had gone out hunting in the wild with nothing at all to protect her; she had snuck into the pen to stare back into the eyes of such people. There had been no safety net there.

Alex Connor, too. Not afraid to get his hands dirty.

Which reminded him.

Garland shifted slightly, intending to leave. But the movement must have been noticeable from within, because something changed in Sarah Pepper's expression. It was almost imperceptible, and her face was blank again now, but he hadn't imagined it. For a brief second, the mask had slipped.

She was afraid, he realised. In fact, she was so scared that if she allowed herself to feel it she might tremble and collapse. But at the same time, whatever was left inside her was absolutely determined.

You have to face up to it.

Garland looked back at her for a second longer, and then he closed the grille and walked away.

Thirty-Three

After the man hung up on me, I sat there in the café for a while, staring into space. And then I rested my elbows on the table, put my face in my hands. My body was trembling.

If you're not there, the letter that was in her possession will be sent anonymously to the police.

You remember what you wrote in that, don't you?

About what you did?

Yes. I remembered now.

Back in Venice, I'd thought that running had never allowed me to escape the bad memories. But that wasn't true. There was something I really had managed to forget. Just pretending doesn't work, so my mind had been clever and gone one better than that. Rather than trying to erase this thing, it had hidden it. And the best place to hide something black is always in the darkness.

I'd convinced myself I left because of the guilt and regret I felt over Marie's death. Every time a shadow fell, I moved on quickly, telling myself it was simply because she'd died and I'd been unable to deal with my failure. That it was too painful to bear. That was only part of why I'd left, but it was threaded through it so inextricably that the excuse felt true if I didn't examine it too closely.

And that was what had gone wrong.

You don't want to remember how bad it was.

When I read the newspaper report about Sarah, I'd thought

236

of everything I'd lost without seeing clearly why it was gone. I'd allowed myself to feel lonely without understanding I deserved to be. And I hadn't listened carefully enough to that voice. I'd thought it might be safe to come back, because I'd forgotten the real reasons why I left.

The things you forget are invisible by definition, noticeable only by the space they leave between the memories they touch. When you stay turned aside from them, it works. When you finally turn back, the memories around come into focus, and the shape of what's missing inevitably appears. It gets harder and harder to stop yourself from seeing.

Before I leave, I want to tell you something.

Something that you deserve to know. I want to tell you about a man named Peter French.

That's what I wrote to Sarah in the letter.

I want to tell you what happened that night I turned up at your house in the rain.

And now, finally, I saw.

The weather that summer had followed a predictable pattern. For days on end, it would be unbearably hot and bright, the sun beating down so hard you imagined that paving slabs might split. People left the doors and windows of their houses open like tents. At lunchtime in the city centre, they sprawled flat out on patches of grass, fanning themselves with magazines.

But every so often, there was a breaking point. A cool breeze picked up and grey clouds began to gather; the air would smell of ozone and the horizon grumbled. Huge droplets of rain would patter down, tapping at first, then growing faster and faster, until the rain fell in savage sheets, washing the heat from the air.

I'd just learned about Marie's insurance policy and what it meant, and I'd been drinking most of the day. By eleven o'clock, when the pubs banged their doors shut, I was drunk. I went back home and paced back and forth. And then at some point, the heat became too great, and I broke in the same way as the weather.

Just before one o'clock in the morning, I was standing with my back to The Cockerel, my attention totally focused on that house across the road. Rain was slashing down in between, swirling in the gutter. No cars: not at this time. I was wrapped in a slick black coat, unsteady on my feet. It felt like I'd arrived here either by magic or by accident, much as it had on the day of Marie's funeral. But this time Sarah was not there to save me.

I crossed the street to that innocuous house. Just a square, red-brick semi, with the curtains shut tight and the paint peeling from its old front door. I walked up the path through the unkempt front garden, and knocked twice.

An upstairs window filled with yellow light. I glanced up, rain pattering into my face, then back down at the door, and waited.

Footsteps on the stairs.

A moment later, the light came on in the hall.

At that point, the anger and grief was swirling inside, riding the waves of the alcohol, and I no longer had any real idea why I was there, or what I was planning to do.

If Peter French had leaned out of the window and asked what the hell I wanted, it would have been different. If he'd even just opened the front door a crack and kept the chain on. Instead, he opened the door wide and stood there, framed by the light, like a fat, fallen angel.

For a second, neither of us did anything. There was just the insistent hiss of the rain all around me. I looked at him, seeing not only the person who'd destroyed Marie's life, and then mine, but an impatient man: angry at being disturbed. It would have been different if I hadn't realised Peter French had absolutely no idea about what had happened to my wife. He probably didn't even remember her name. He wouldn't know or care that in the privacy and secrecy of her heart she had replayed what he did to her, every single day, in a place I must have never tried hard enough to reach, and now never could.

It would have been different if he had.

Instead, he looked at me and said, 'Who are you?'

And I thought about that question now.

At the time, I'd been a man unable to deal with the guilt inside him. Afterwards, I'd been that same man: running away from what he'd done. But who was I now?

I wanted to believe I'd come back because I was lonely, and missed my friends, and because I felt guilty about not being here for Sarah, the way that she'd been there for me. I wanted to believe I'd come back for the *right* reasons, not that a part of me had simply used them to hide darker, more selfish motives behind.

But I wasn't sure.

He wanted to know if you'd found it yet.

The letter. My brother thought that was the real reason I'd come back. He knew what I'd done two years ago, and so it was natural for him to think I was returning now to cover it up. To make sure that letter didn't fall into the wrong hands. And maybe he was right.

Because I remembered sitting on the steps in Venice and thinking: *she was living with him*. Then, after I arrived, I'd searched the house from top to bottom, with no real idea what I was looking for. Later on, when I suspected Ellis might have taken Sarah's body, I'd gone to see him myself, rather than call the police. Even when I found the rucksack at the Chalkie, I'd rationalised not going to them. Perhaps I hadn't been facing up to my responsibilities at all. Maybe what I'd really been doing was tracking down that letter – my guilt, set in stone – so that I could keep it hidden.

The worst thing was that I couldn't tell any more. Both explanations used the same language. Responsibility. Guilt. Pain. Regret. It was what my mind had done so successfully for two years, and looking back over the last few days, I realised it had become impossible to read between my own lines.

But I wanted to believe.

'You OK, love?'

I looked up suddenly. The owner of the café was standing beside me, smiling pleasantly. It felt like I was half asleep. The memory of what I'd done had crushed me half conscious, and I didn't feel remotely capable of whatever I was supposed to do next.

'Fine,' I said.

It didn't sound convincing, but she nodded. 'May I?'

'What? Oh.'

I leaned back so she could clear the plates away. As she went about it, I moved the mobile phone to one side.

Sarah was alive.

One hour's time. Or she's dead.

The voice that wasn't a voice began speaking then, and it told me that I needed to leave. That going to meet this man would accomplish nothing, because Sarah was going to die anyway, and there was no point me getting killed too. Not like Ellis and Mandy Gilroyd had, like Mike and Julie and James. None of those deaths was my fault, anyway, the voice said: people make their own mistakes, and they live or die as a result of them. I'd kept my passport in my jacket pocket. I could go to the airport and be out of the country in the space of a few hours.

With time, the voice told me, I might forget even this.

But Sarah was alive.

Everything kept leading back to that. It was insistent, like a pulse in my head. If I walked away now it felt like something inside me would die along with her. It was one thing to abandon the dead; another thing entirely to walk away from the living. Perhaps I would be able to forget in time, but I thought it would require giving up more than I could afford to lose: cutting so much of myself away that there was nothing left worth keeping.

And I remembered: *if she was still alive, I would have done anything – anything at all – to go to her.*

It was just before I watched the video of Marie's death. I'd thought about that endless drop of a moment when you realise something has been lost, and that it's too late to save it. When you would give anything at all for it to come back to you. Anything at all for just for one chance to do things differently.

Sarah was still alive. I had that chance now.

I closed my eyes.

After a while, I thought: *we're always there for each other. If it was the other way round, you'd be there for me too.*

Thirty-Four

Forty minutes later, I was standing outside number seventeen on Rose Avenue, wondering what was supposed to happen next. *You'll understand what to do when you get there.* But I didn't.

The street was a main road that traced the edge of a run-down estate. Number seventeen was a post-office. It was the last shop on a small stretch of concrete, squeezed in beside a bookies, an off-licence and a set of blue, graffitied shutters down over what had once been a card shop. A few local kids were hanging out at the far end, beneath the card shop's tattered awning: a teenage girl sitting with her legs flat out; a scraggy boy on a bike curling back and forth in aimless circles; another boy occasionally kicking the shutters. When I walked past them, they'd asked me to buy them alcohol, and then laughed at me when I said no.

This was definitely where the man had told me to come, but I was missing something. He'd said to take the footpath, but there wasn't one. Behind me, the road was busy, so I didn't think anyone was coming to meet me here. It was too exposed. Too public. But I couldn't just hang around here for ever.

So now what?

For the second time, I walked round the corner of the post-office. The view here wasn't any more edifying than out front. The road continued into the Balders estate, curving between flat, grey houses. Even in the sun, the buildings looked pale and sick: half of them either dying or already dead. The untended grass verges were bigger than the gardens. And there wasn't a footpath in sight. I'd already checked, but I did so again now. Nothing.

I turned round to head back out front. And then stopped. Someone had painted a small white arrow on the side of the building. I hadn't noticed it the first time I looked.

It was about three metres up the wall, and the paint looked very old and faded. But now that I'd seen it, the sign was unmistakable. And it was pointing into the estate.

Now I understood: this wasn't my destination at all; the man was being careful. If I'd gone to the police and given them this address, it would have achieved absolutely nothing, and now it would be obvious if I was being followed.

You shouldn't do this.

But I was well past the point where that was an option. Instead, I looked down at the plastic bag full of papers in my hand, and then took a deep breath and set off.

I thought I understood what had happened now. Like the symbols, it was a trail that was hard to follow unless you had the starting point and knew what to look for. But, when you did, you could trace it clearly from one end to the other, and the signs along the way became obvious in hindsight.

The starting point was that Sarah wasn't dead. James hadn't killed anyone. Instead, the pair of them had been shuttered away together over recent months. I'd imagined a festering madness in the air, as Sarah's research created a wedge, driving my brother to drink and then Sarah away from him. There clearly had been a kind of madness – it was the only word for what they'd done – but instead of driving them apart, it had brought them closer together.

What Ellis revealed to Sarah had fed her obsession. She would have become fascinated with these people, but also conflicted about what she should do. I pictured her returning to the Ridge, time after time, staring out at where Emily Price was lying unfound. But at some point when she was up there, she must have decided what she was going to do. *Black hair, tatty coat*, I remembered. I'd seen the box of hair dye in her bedside cabinet, but been too preoccupied to pay attention. It made sense in light of what she'd done. Bright red hair wasn't going to help her lie low.

Similarly, I'd written off the books I'd seen – the photos of crime scenes and forensic textbooks – as being part of her fascination with death. They were, but not in the way I'd thought. I hadn't considered that she might have been studying them – painstakingly, methodically – not so that she could dwell on those scenes in particular, but so that she and James could convincingly manufacture one of their own.

So that she could meet these people.

And finally, my brother's actions.

I'd worked hard to convince myself he might be a killer, but in my heart I should have known he wasn't capable of that. In reality, James really had done something absurd and unbelievable, and wrong too, but not because of his temper, or because Sarah was going to leave him. He had enabled her obsession by lying for her, to help her achieve what she thought she needed to do. He'd done it because he loved her.

I could understand the resentment when he knew I'd come back. Why wouldn't he hate me? I was the brother who'd never been able to do anything wrong, and who then ran away the first moment life became difficult. The one who'd left Sarah with that letter and the knowledge it contained. He'd been dealing with the fallout from that ever since. And now I'd come back, perhaps in an attempt to hide those things for ever and disappear again.

Tell Alex to go to the Chalkie. To see what he's done.

I think what he expected me to find there was Sarah. The Chalkie was close to the field, and I suspected she must have camped there when she wasn't keeping watch. The items in the rucksack, I thought, were leftovers. It would have taken weeks to collect the amount of her blood necessary to fake the scenes, and it would need to have been kept somewhere in the mean-time. The note too. Both items grabbed in a moment of haste at the last minute. And then flung into the undergrowth when these people came and took her.

That was what he'd expected me to find, only by then it was too late. But whatever happened, I was going to find her now.

To begin with, the estate was just everyday rough – squat, scowling houses with smeared windows and concrete lawns – but the further I walked, the more beaten and broken-down it became. There was rubbish, bagged and abandoned in the cracked, flagstone gardens, and more and more windows and doors were boarded up. The buildings increasingly resembled prize-fighters, bandaged and black-eyed.

The road curled steadily onwards, then shifted suddenly, as though startled, and rose up at a steep incline. It was here, at a junction with a smaller street, that I found a second symbol daubed on the edge of the kerb. A circle with a dot in the middle, like the view through a sniper's rifle.

I took the turning, and found the next symbol little more than twenty metres along, where another street led off to the right. I followed it, heading deeper into the heart of the estate. Way up ahead, a woman was meandering along, dressed too far down even for this hot weather. She passed the shell of an old car, stripped to its chassis and resting on breeze blocks, and then turned the corner and disappeared.

I looked around. I was now totally alone.

It was so quiet here. Some of the houses were obviously deserted, but even so: there were no children playing, no other sounds of community. I could hear a dog barking in the distance, but the noise was plaintive and lonely, as though the animal had been left somewhere and didn't expect to be heard.

I passed the car, and reached a crossroads. Bits of wood were scattered across the centre, as though a packing crate had been dropped from a plane. The next symbol, a white slash that crossed two of the slabs in the pavement, told me to head right, and so I did.

The signs looked older than the ones I'd found on the Ridge. I was guessing the man who'd phoned me had decided to use this set because it was most convenient; he'd skimmed through the database and found somewhere that suited him. So where had they been originally intended to lead? Was I following a map to the other missing victim of Thomas Wells and Roger Timms, or was this something else entirely?

How many fucking routes are there?

A few minutes later, I got at least some kind of answer. The 'somewhere' I was heading was about half a mile into the estate, at the end of a cul-de-sac called Suncast Lane. The street finished at number ten, an abandoned house with the windows and doors secured by perforated metal sheets, bolted into place. In the corner of the downstairs window, someone had painted a small white semicircle.

It was obviously deserted, but the house still had a presence. I could feel some kind of energy humming in the air, like when you stand close to a pylon. This was a destination: a place of power. I wondered what I would find if I went in. From everything I'd heard, it didn't seem like the kind of place where Wells and Timms would have left a body. All their other disposal sites had been out in the open.

Regardless, it was clear enough what I was supposed to do now. The promised footpath was at the side of the house: narrow and tight, with six-foot wooden fences on either side. It carried on straight for a time, and then bent sharply off to one side, like a broken bone.

I set off.

It was barely wide enough to walk down. The slatted wooden fences bowed in at me in some places, leaned back in others. I reached the bend in the path, and turned to the right. There was a section missing here; the corner had hidden it from view. Too late for me to stop, someone grabbed hold of my arm and yanked me sideways through the fence.

I sprawled forward into wasteland, swung by one man, and caught a flash of another man's fist –

Then shook my head, blinking. I was on my side in a patch of long, dirty grass, with dampness on my face and hands. My left eye was numb . . . and then it began *thudding,* in time with my heartbeat, and everything pulsed red.

Fuck.

'—et him—'

Barely heard through the ringing in my ears.

I wasn't sure if I'd been knocked out, or just knocked down, or what had happened. I told my body to sit up, but then felt pressure on my arm stopping me.

'—ott is thi—'

The man in the grey suit. Except he was red now, silhouetted against something green, and his head had about six crimson auras echoing around it. I stared at him, mesmerised, as he slowly came into focus and the colours drained out.

'What is this?'

He was squatting down on his haunches beside me, framed by the bright green trees behind him. I saw the leaves rustling, and then felt the breeze on me.

'I said, "What is this?"'

He was flicking through the empty folders, newspapers and magazines that I'd been carrying in my bag.

'An insurance policy,' I said.

He nodded to himself, his expression blank. Then he looked up and around, and I had the impression that he was weighing up various options, calculating the most efficient course of action.

He tossed a magazine to one side and stood up. In his other hand, he was holding a gun with what looked for all the world like a silencer screwed onto the barrel.

'Get him to the car,' he said.

Thirty-Five

Kearney drove past the house slowly, making sure he had the right address, then carried on up the road and turned around. He pulled the car up onto a grass verge, out of sight behind a four-by-four, and killed the engine.

On his right-hand side, across the thin country lane, there was a low, twisted hedge, thick with spiky leaves and dotted with red berries. In the distance, over the fields that lay behind, drystone walls stood in crumbling lines. A nice view. With the window down, the breeze felt warm and clean.

On his left-hand side, the houses.

He was in the suburbs to the west of the city. They were affluent and quietly distinguished. This far out into the country-side, the straight lines and sharp angles of the city streets were smoothed away beyond recognition; the roads curled and stretched out on their own, like children running off and exploring the green fields. You could drive a mile before meeting a junction. The houses were large and wide, and some of them were probably better classed as mansions. They all rested behind neat lawns and arched hedges and cobbled driveways. In the garden beside Kearney's car, there was an old red telephone box. In the next one down, someone had actually installed a well.

It was a very desirable postcode. Also a very private one.

He thought Anna, when they were together, would have dreamed of retiring somewhere like this. It had the illusion of being a nice neighbourhood, but in reality it was just expensive. The truth was that it wasn't actually a neighbourhood at all. Certainly not a community. Sitting there now, his arms resting on the steering wheel, it felt to Kearney more like a place to ostracise yourself. To secrete yourself away. A place where everyone kept their distance. Where the houses were far apart, so that nobody could hear what was happening through the walls. And where the only people who might were other rich people, who were probably doing similar private things themselves.

Keep yourself together.

Yes. He stared blankly ahead, trying to do just that. His mood had been erratic today. His mind was having difficulty holding onto thoughts without running off with them and getting itself lost. If he didn't consciously keep a grip, everything began to drift, as though some central hub had been dislodged, and nothing was holding him in place any more.

He peered down the lane at Arthur Hammond's house. It was even more opulent than the ones around it. The size and privacy of it unnerved him. You couldn't really see in at all. The hedge at the front was effectively a wall, broken only by a double gate topped with small, subtle spikes. All that was visible above it was an angle of the top floor of the house, and a single blank window. It made the building look furtive. You couldn't see what it was doing with its hands.

What are you going to do, Paul?

He had no idea.

What Connor had said in the café had set him moving, but he didn't have a plan, and he wasn't sure of anything. His intentions kept shifting, back and forth. Perhaps he was simply here to ask for Hammond's advice. After all, the man clearly had things to say about the matter in hand. About the nature and collection of *art*.

Then again, perhaps he suspected something else altogether.

But now that a decision was needed, he couldn't make one. There wasn't much justification for either course of action. If he walked up and knocked on the man's door, he didn't know what questions to ask. If he kicked it down, he couldn't imagine what would happen next.

Frustration built up inside him. After a moment, it coiled itself into the familiar shape of self-hatred, so that his skin began to feel like it was hurting him. Like his entire body was held at some painful angle and there was no way of stretching that would relieve the ache.

Maybe it would have been different if the investigation was over – if they had found Rebecca, even if she was dead. Or if he hadn't woken up in his hotel room from a nightmare of the yellow man, to see the children watching him. Demanding something of him. Mike Halsall. Sarah Pepper . . . and then the name *Peter French* was in his head, like a gift they'd brought for him.

There it is.

Now what are you going to do?

The question hadn't changed.

See if Arthur Hammond was home, he decided. Listen to what he had to say. Maybe look around a bit, whether he liked it or not.

Kearney supposed that the events of yesterday evening had done something for him, at least. No longer a policeman now, he could simply do what was necessary. He could ask whatever questions he liked. Only one thing mattered. Perhaps the promise he'd made could never be kept, but he had nothing to lose by trying. He would find her.

He held down a button and the car window slid up. As he opened the door, he heard a *screech* and then a *scrape*, and he paused. The sound of metal rasping over concrete drifted up the quiet lane. The gate leading into Hammond's little estate was opening slowly inward, catching on the ground.

Kearney closed the car door slowly, and then waited.

A few moments later, the nose of a car edged out from the driveway. Kearney ducked down in his seat. He stayed out of sight until he heard the same *scrape* return – fainter now that it was muffled by the closed door – and risked sitting up again.

The back end of a battered old car was disappearing down the lane. It was dark crimson, but he couldn't make out the model. Instead, he concentrated on the back window, trying to see who was inside. The driver and one other person, he thought. The second man appeared to be in the back seat, like he was being chauffeured.

Was it Hammond?

Kearney couldn't see enough to be sure, but he thought so. Up ahead, the old car rounded a curve in the road and dis- appeared. The property's automated gate crunched back into place.

Kearney sat there for a moment, wondering what to do. Should he still try the house? There hadn't been any guarantees before, and now there were at least two less people home. *Fewer*, he reminded himself. But he was also a little unnerved by what he'd just seen. A rich man in a battered old car. On the surface, it was innocuous . . . but there was also something hidden about it, wasn't there? Something secretive and underhand.

Where are you going? he wondered. *In your disguise.*

Kearney came to a decision and started the engine. For at least the first few miles, he was going to have to be careful. Hang back slightly. Hope for the best.

He was going to need a little luck.

Thirty-Six

'What was that house?' I said.

I was in the back seat of the car, sandwiched between two men. Both of them were young and utterly implacable: holding me in an efficient, professional manner, but otherwise paying me no attention at all. They were just staring idly through the tinted glass at the streets outside. A third man was driving, his hand resting lightly on the steering wheel.

The older man in the grey suit was in the passenger seat up front. I could only really see the back of his head. It was bullet shaped and his grey hair was thinning, with rough, leathery skin visible underneath, as though he'd spent a lot of time in hotter climates with the sun beating down on him.

'What was there?' I said.

'Nothing.' He sounded so uninterested that I wasn't even sure he was talking to me. 'It's one of our older places. That's all.'

'Who the hell are you people?'

He cocked his head slightly, but didn't reply.

A minute later, I said, 'Where are you taking me?'

Nothing. None of the other men seemed interested in talking either.

Not yet, at least.

I put that thought out of my head.

The car rocked gently, the driver's hand barely moving. We were going at a slow pace, doing nothing to draw attention to ourselves. As much as I could, I watched the shops and houses we passed and saw people strolling along the pavements, sunlit and unconcerned.

It reminded me of reeling through the city centre two days ago, back when things had still felt – on the surface – under my control. Back when I should have gone to the police. Before these men had killed Mike and Julie. Before they'd killed my brother.

We drove for about twenty minutes, and I was shivering by the time we arrived. The car pulled up a slight incline, then paused as a yellow barrier ahead of us lurched upwards. After we drove in, I heard it *clank* down behind.

I had no idea where in the city we were, but this was some kind of industrial complex. The car moved forward, rounding a corner, and I caught sight of rows of other vehicles parked up ahead. The older man paid them no attention, but the men on either side of me peered out with interest, as though curious to see who was here. We left those cars behind, then took another corner, the tyres crunching over glass, then another, and I realised we were slowing down, circling round to the back of a row of buildings.

Halfway up, there was an open garage door. It looked wide enough for three or four cars. Another man in a suit was standing beneath it. His hands were up on the shutter there, and he was leaning out, like a mechanic on a cigarette break. When he saw our car approaching, he let go and stepped out, then waved us in past him.

'What's going on? Where is this place?'

No reply.

We drove into what appeared to be the back of a warehouse – some kind of large loading bay. There was a series of cranes and hooks attached to rigs in the ceiling, and a ramp leading up at one side. Thick pipes ran down the walls. Everything was pale green, and the paint looked to be about an inch thick in places, with veins and clots where it had run and stuck.

The only other vehicle was a small, battered, white van, tucked in next to the ramp. We pulled in just past it.

The handbrake *cricked*, and then the engine cut out.

I could hear my heart beating in my ears.

'What the fuck is this place?'

Nothing. But I noticed other noises: distant clanking and scraping; something that sounded like a buzzsaw whining angrily through timber. Like there was a metal workshop next door.

All of it echoing around, but my heart remained loudest. And I felt sick. My breath would hardly come. These men had killed so many people, and now they were going to kill me, and Sarah, and . . .

Just keep a grip on yourself.

The doors opened to either side and the man on my right pulled me out that way. I didn't resist. He rested his fingers on my shoulder, the heel of his palm in my back, ready to push me forward. The second man came round the car.

A huge screech filled the air. The shutter was rolling slowly down towards the ground, rattling in its runners. A wedge of sunlight on the concrete floor was retreating towards it.

I was about to be trapped in here.

No.

I went for the man on my left first, simply because it was a right-handed shot. His eyes clenched shut as the hook landed, and he made the same noise I'd heard in the video of soldiers having their throats cut – just a quick grunt of fear, surprise and pain. The impact shattered his teeth and knocked him to one side.

The second man reacted fast, and his punch slammed my left hand back into my face. I couldn't even see him, so I just curled under and threw an uppercut somewhere I hoped his head would be. It caught him under the jaw and snapped his head back. Not hard enough. Rather than knocking him down, he just took a recovery step to the side, tightening his guard.

But it gave me a clear run to the garage door.

Ten metres, a dive and a roll, and then that one guy who was still out there. And I'd be away.

Maybe I could have made it. But the punches had lit a fire inside me, something hot that burned all the way from my heart to my skin. Instead of running, I went for the man again. Threw a jab that landed on his fists, and then the hardest right hook I could manage. I put my whole body into it. My brother had always been the one with the strength, and I wished for some of that now. No finesse. I just imagined the head of that old punch bag cracked at the neck, and clenched up every muscle . . .

It landed hard and felt good.

The man stood it, covering himself, but it had rocked him. I threw mad, random punches at him then, and he staggered backwards, desperately guarding. My breath was coming out thin, like I had a reed in my windpipe, but an absurd thrill ran through me as I landed another and the man stumbled over his own feet and went down. Every single blow felt like solid *hate*.

'For God's sake.'

The man in the grey suit sighed. I looked across. He hadn't even taken his gun out of his jacket. The driver had moved across to the garage door and was standing there now, arms folded, but neither of them looked concerned.

The older man was closer, so I walked across and went for him. A stupid, diving right. He leaned away from it, then palmed me hard in the side of the head, knocking me off balance. I had time to think *you didn't have a chance*, and then my wrist was turning against itself. My body went with it, completely out of my control, moving instinctively away from the lock. He shifted his body slightly, using my wrist as a pivot, taking me all the way to the ground. Face down.

Fuck.

I had a view of the loading bay. The first guy I'd hit was still bent over, leaning on his knees, spitting blood onto the floor. The second was standing up now, stunned. His face was bright red, as though he'd been slapped and didn't know what to do.

It was nothing, but still – it felt like something. Even if it was just taking some of the emotion inside me out on someone else. I could have gone for the door, and perhaps I should have done. But right then, I didn't care.

A second later, somewhere out of sight, the garage door crashed once against the ground and then was silent.

Thirty-Seven

Kearney had lost them.

He smacked his hand on the steering wheel in frustration.

It had been difficult to keep track of Hammond's vehicle on the country lanes, simply because there was so little other traffic that he'd needed to keep his distance. Every time he reached a junction, he was trusting his luck a little: hoping that at least one direction offered a clear enough straight for him to make a choice. If the battered old car *wasn't* visible on a clear run, he took the other route, accelerating quickly to make sure he was right, then hanging back again.

In theory, that should have been the hardest part. And once they'd got back on the main roads, heading towards the city, he'd been able to slot a few other cars between them and relax a little. He could see the turnings Hammond's driver took far enough in advance to follow. It had started to go wrong when they'd skirted the centre, heading into a largely residential area.

He'd turned the corner just now and they'd vanished.

A long, empty road ahead of him.

He slowed the car and pulled in at the side of the street, leaving the indicator flashing. Rubbed his forehead, grimacing. Then opened his eyes with new intent.

Come on. You've not lost them.

It was mainly houses here, all facing right up to the pavement with their chests out. On the left-hand side, there was a wall of trees, then more houses further up. No driveways that he could see, and Hammond's car wasn't parked up on the street.

So there must be something else.

Kearney killed the engine and got out, closing the door behind him with a clap, and then he walked up the road, checking either side as he went. He found it a little further along on the left. The trees had been partially obscuring it: a yellow barrier across a tarmac drive. It was actually wide enough to fit an articulated lorry down.

The pavement curled around the side of the barrier. Kearney took one last look around before he followed it, but there was nowhere else they could have gone.

The drive led into an industrial complex, and it was much larger than it appeared from the road. He walked past single-storey warehouses and factory units, their walls and inclined roofs all made from corrugated iron. There was a printer's yard. A bridal warehouse, with wedding dresses covered in cellophane on racks outside. A half-open metal shutter. He looked inside and saw fridges stacked there like bared teeth.

And then, up ahead, a row of parked cars, slotted in at angles. Most of them were cheap, but a couple were polished and expensive: black and glinting in the sun. Hammond's old vehicle was pulled in at the far end. The driver was still inside, reading a newspaper draped over the steering wheel. The back seat was empty now.

Kearney strolled along, as casually as he could manage. The building to the left, where the cars were all parked up, was one of the largest in the complex. It was painted entirely black, with an arched sign over a set of double doors, one of which was wedged open with a rusty metal box. The sign itself was old, the paint there faded and faint, but he could make out a red hammer with a wooden block drawn below it. The white lettering was scratched: barely visible beneath the static of time.

Tooleys Auction Rooms.

A chalkboard was bolted to the metal beside the door:

2pm. Small Items.

Kearney stepped into a tiled hallway that smelled of tobacco and old clothes. He had no idea what he was going to say if he encountered Arthur Hammond, but fortunately the man wasn't in sight. There were just a few groups of older men here, faces weathered and grim.

At the end of the small hallway, a door led into a larger space, where Kearney could see chairs laid out in rows, many of them already filled: again, mostly with men, their arms folded over pot bellies. A low, constant murmur was coming from the room, like people in church waiting for the service to start

To the right, another door. The sign above said: *Viewing Room*.

Kearney checked his watch: it was nearly two o'clock, but not quite. A couple of stragglers were still in the viewing room, but there was no sign of Hammond. Kearney wandered in, as much to avoid being seen as out of interest. One of the other men in here was elderly, clutching his stapled catalogue in both hands behind his back as he stalked, perusing the wares. The other was short and squat: wobbling from leg to leg, his bottom lip quivering.

Neither seemed particularly excited, and at first glance Kearney could understand why. There was little here of obvious value – or at least, not to him. Ugly porcelain figures. Old, arched pipes. Sets of china cups with ornate handles. Several clocks, one of them fashioned like a doll's house. None of it looked the sort of merchandise that would draw a collector like Arthur Hammond, even if his tastes were as innocent as they might be.

Does he own the place?

That was a thought. Kearney had no idea. But it seemed like the kind of business opportunity a man like Hammond might associate himself with.

So perhaps he was wasting his time here. He was still pondering the question when a thick-set man in a black suit leaned into the room.

'We're beginning, gentlemen.'

The other two headed for the doorway.

You're here now, Kearney thought.

He manoeuvred himself between the pair and followed them through.

Thirty-Eight

They left me sitting down at the far side of the loading bay, my legs splayed out along the ground. My hands were cuffed behind me, around the back of one of the thick pipes that ran from the ceiling down into the stone floor.

After securing me in place, the man in the grey suit squatted down in front, resting his hands on his thighs. His knuckles were enormous, and I was convinced he was going to punch me. Instead, he just looked at me curiously, tilting his head slightly, as though he couldn't decide what it was that he'd caught. The anger I'd felt before was fading now, like the effects of a pill. In its place, there was pain and there was fear.

'Where is she?'

It was all I really wanted now.

But he shook his head, then stood up and walked away.

The men I'd fought with had recovered and were standing a little distance back, by the van, the second of the two staring at me with unconcealed hatred. I forced myself to stare right back. *Fuck you*. But the older man put a palm on both of their chests, forming a solid 'W' between them.

'Not now,' he said.

And then they left the loading bay through a side door, heading towards the front of whatever building we were in.

Aside from that distant clanking noise, the room was now still and quiet. The car we'd arrived in was a few metres away from me, *ticking* slightly as the engine cooled. The van was far across the bay. Both of them might as well have been in another world.

I tested the cuffs as much as I could, but I wasn't going anywhere. Not least because of the pain in my wrist. He hadn't broken it, but something had torn, and it was getting worse by the second: a soft thudding, growing louder. Even lifting my hands made it flare. There was no real point in injuring myself for the sake of it, I supposed, but I tried anyway: gritting my teeth, pulling against the cuffs . . .

Then collapsed.

Behind me, the pipe was vibrating gently: a soft, quiet rumble against my spine. It was cool at the moment, but I had the disturbing impression that it might become scorching hot at some point. Better not to think about that.

Over to the side, the garage door was sealed tight. There wasn't even a trace of sunlight creeping underneath. One of the men was outside anyway – but still, perhaps someone else might pass by, or maybe by the other door that led further in. There might be people close enough to hear.

'Hey!' I shouted.

The word echoed around. It felt dangerous, the way it didn't land on anything and seemed to just hang in the air.

'Can anyone hear me?'

No response.

I tried again, this time shouting as loud as I could:

'Hey! Is anyone th—'

But my voice gave way slightly, and the words disappeared. I coughed, my throat catching. Fought against the despair. I was about to try again when I heard it.

A single muffled scream.

I stopped moving.

It had been an animal noise, but I knew straight away that it had come from a human being. A person in such distress they could hardly even breathe properly. It made my heart bounce.

And then a second later, I heard a terrible *thumping* noise. It sounded like someone panicking: fighting for their life, unable to move properly. But it was all obscured. The sound was being deadened by something.

'Sarah?'

I looked across the loading bay, one end to the other, but I couldn't see anything. The noise was coming from this room, but there was nobody here. Then my gaze fell on the white van and stayed there, locked in place. The vehicle's chassis was trembling slightly, bowing at the wheel arches. Someone was in there, struggling madly. They'd been in there the whole time, in fact, but my shouting had woken them up.

The person began hyperventilating. It was a desperate noise: gathering in as much air as possible, so that they could—

They shrieked again. Again, it was muffled.

Roger Timms's van, I thought. A chill ran through me. When I'd watched the news back in my hotel room last night, the reporter had said the police were still looking for it.

Fears grow for missing . . .

'Rebecca?'

There was no reply from within the van, but whoever was inside continued screaming, and the van was now rocking frantically. *Christ.* If it was her she'd been missing for days, tied up in God only knew what conditions: maybe even in there the whole time. No wonder my shouting had panicked her.

'It's all right, Rebecca.'

It was a stupid thing to say, but I felt a desperate urge to reassure her somehow. It didn't have any effect. Either she didn't believe me or she was past the point of being able to feel anything but terror.

I tried the cuffs again, more recklessly now: twisting my hands against them, testing the angles, trying to find . . . something. But then I collapsed back down, my wrist burning and my vision starring over.

There was a knot in my throat as I called out again.

'It's going to be OK.'

But my words simply hung there, and the van continued to scream.

Thirty-Nine

Garland found himself a seat at the back of the hall, and watched as the auctioneer Hammond employed took his place at the podium. The man was extremely elderly, but well-practised in the art, and he'd dressed for the occasion in a black, double-breasted, pinstripe suit with a crimson rose puncturing the lapel. Behind him, there was a screen, where the projectionist would shortly display photographs of point-less, inexpensive items, which the men in here would then squabble over, often with the intention of selling on at a greater price in the weeks and months to come.

To Garland, it was the equivalent of betting a pound on the horses. And yet everyone here took proceedings so seriously. Pandering to them, the auctioneer's face was set suitably grim.

Garland folded his arms, scanning the audience.

Searching them out.

Before he came to the employ of the organisation, he'd been a soldier for a time, and then a mercenary for hire. He'd worked with a small team of like-minded Americans fighting in the former Yugoslavia, killing for money. On one occasion, they'd had to search a small village for a handful of soldiers they'd been tracking; the men had discarded their uniforms and hidden themselves in plain sight amongst the farmers.

It had taken Garland only a few minutes to identify them. After they'd been separated from the civilians, the men had been lined up on their knees in a dirty field and shot in the back of the head. One by one, but quick and professional; a second, at most, between each. Some had cried, others had just knelt there shaking, unable even to knit their hands behind their necks. But none had seemed surprised. They had hidden themselves, exhausted, in the village without any real hope of success, knowing that even in the pervading mist of beaten-down despair, they stood out. Some uniforms couldn't be taken off. Men like Garland could smell their own.

As always, it was simply about money; he hadn't hated them. In fact, he felt a certain degree of respect. That they'd trembled and cried didn't diminish them in his eyes, because who wouldn't? It hadn't saved them, but they understood the consequences of their actions. Each of them, in turn, was a killer himself. They had fought hard to arrive at their deaths. And so the brief music that cracked across the field that day had not been out of tune.

Dotted around the auction room now, these men – and one woman – were entirely different. Garland would have had no trouble spotting them, even if he didn't have their faces committed to memory. They were simply angled differently to the other people in here. Even so, they imagined themselves disguised. They thought that if they sat there, the uniform alone would be enough to keep them hidden.

That wasn't entirely their fault, of course. It was part of the myth that had been peddled to them. The myth of safety.

But it was the main thing that set them apart from the men in the field, and it was what excluded them from his respect. Those men had dirt under their nails, while these people had nothing. They liked to think of darkness and death, but never with consequences. They probably saw their damp interest as profound – that they were explorers – when in fact they lived in cocoons and paid for bundles of evil to be left beyond the membrane, so they could admire it from a position of safety. And then, afterwards, they would wash their hands and go back to work, imagining themselves distinct and powerful.

Like the game reserve he'd worked on, it was laughable.

But good business.

He concentrated on that now, keeping his expression blank. It was the same whenever he dealt with clients. Any disgust he felt was buried deep. What he thought of these people was irrelevant. He was paid to be here.

The thought of money . . .

His gaze picked out the back of Arthur Hammond's head.

Nearly over, Garland reminded himself. His job had been to tidy up the mess in this particular branch, which had involved spreading it out first of all, so he could see what had caused it. Now, everything was clear. Timms's greed was the root cause, but Christopher Ellis had not been the only one to exploit it. Before he died, Timms had offered up another name, a more high-profile one, perhaps in the vain hope that it would save his life.

Garland investigated the claim through his police source, and it was true: a fingerprint had been found on the forehead of Jane Slater. That was a sign Hammond had visited the scene, but the experience had not been officially arranged.

People being greedy.

He checked his watch. In a few hours, he would be on a private plane, leaving all this behind. It couldn't come soon enough.

The auctioneer batted his hammer down three times to signal silence. The raps echoed.

'Ladies and gentlemen. Welcome to Tooleys Auctions, for our weekly small-item sale of treasures and collectables. Those intending to bid, please make sure you've registered at the desk for a paddle.'

Garland stifled a yawn, glancing to his left down the back row. He noticed the man at the far end, recognised him immediately, and then turned back to face front as though nothing had happened.

The policeman. Paul Kearney.

Except Garland knew from his contacts that Kearney wasn't a policeman any longer. What was he doing here?

Possibilities clicked past in his head.

The only thing that made sense was that Kearney had followed one of the clients. Hammond, presumably, since the others had travelled from too far afield.

Garland performed a few more calculations. He had no reason to believe the police suspected anything. Even if they did, they were unlikely to have sent Kearney here, given his current status. Which suggested Kearney was here on his own account.

Interesting.

What did he know, and what did he expect to achieve? Nothing illegal was going to take place during the auction itself. When it was over, Kearney certainly would not be allowed through the door at the back of the room, which the other clients would casually drift across to and enter. There was no real danger of him interfering or causing a scene.

In fact, although Garland would rather have avoided the scenario, even the police would have problems. Discounting Banyard, who was otherwise engaged, he had only six men in the building. However – when they were paying attention, at least – those men were an entirely different type of animal than the police would be accustomed to dealing with. All heavily armed as well. If it came to it, nobody was going to stop them leaving. Not unless the army were drafted in.

Garland took another brief, sideways glance and then followed Kearney's gaze to the front of the room.

Yes, he was looking at Arthur Hammond.

Interesting, Garland thought again.

But little more than that.

'Lot Number One,' the auctioneer said.

He signalled to the projectionist. And, as a photograph of a silver tray appeared on the screen behind the man, Garland leaned back in his chair and stifled another yawn.

Forty

I couldn't tell how long it was before they returned. It felt like at least half an hour, but it was probably longer. The man in the grey suit led the way, and he was followed in by five people I hadn't seen before. There were four men and one woman, all of them dressed casually. Two other men in suits came in last. They closed the metal door behind them, then bolted it shut and stood like sentries on either side of it.

The man whose teeth I'd smashed in was conspicuous by his absence – perhaps he'd been considered too messy for this class of company. Even though the five newcomers were dressed down, they all had a certain air about them. The kind of quiet confidence and sense of entitlement that came with wealth and power. They all looked as though they were used to having their orders carried out. I didn't need to see their wallets or everyday wardrobes to feel the money that had just entered the room.

None of them noticed me at first. They were too busy hurrying to keep up with the man in the grey suit. He led them to the back of the van, and they formed a semicircle around him.

I looked from one face to another. There was no real point in memorising them, but for some reason I was determined to try. There was a tall, pale man with a neat brown crew-cut and bobbled acne-scarring on his cheeks. The man beside him was shorter, with a tan and a neatly trimmed beard. Next, there was a bald man who looked like a scientist, with small, round glasses and furrows lining his forehead. The woman was stocky and had a plump face; her hair was parted in the centre and sprayed into a solid grey cone that rested on her shoulders. Finally, there was an older, almost aristocratic man. He had a moustache and a waistcoat, and was dabbing at his forehead with a handkerchief.

And all five looked nervous. Despite the power they might normally have, I could tell they were a little out of their comfort zone here. But perhaps that was part of the experience. Perhaps, I thought, they were *exhilarated*. They were all eyeing the van, and I had no doubt they knew exactly who it had once belonged to and what was now inside.

It's not a massive stretch to imagine a handful of people might seek that out. People willing to pay enough to make it worth the risk.

But when I'd said that to Kearney, I'd been talking about looking at the dead. This was something far removed even from that, and I couldn't imagine what must be going through their heads. Some of them had expressions on their faces like children. What did they do out in the real world, I wondered. Did any of their families or colleagues know what they did when they were out of sight?

'Ladies and gentlemen,' the man in the grey suit said. 'We arrive at the final lot of the day.'

Some time before they came back, Rebecca Wingate had fallen silent, but the sound of the man's voice now started her screaming again. It must have sounded even more horrific that close to the vehicle, but the woman standing beside it actually smiled. There was a flash of ice in her eyes.

The man in the suit patted the side of the vehicle once.

'I know that all of you have been following Thomas Wells and Roger Timms over the years. Some of you are connoisseurs.' He looked between them. 'Others are collectors. However, you'll all be aware that their careers are now, regrettably, over. As valued clients, we have invited you here today for the offer of one final experience.'

He paused, glancing at the van. But he kept his face blank and professional, and gave no indication he was aware of the sound or movement coming from inside.

'For the collectors amongst you, this might be seen as a particularly unique piece: a work-in-progress. For others, it will simply be a once-in-a-lifetime opportunity. The sale price will include the original registration plates. And, of course, all of the vehicle's contents at the time we acquired it.'

Some of the bastards actually smiled at that. They were visibly relaxing now: the man in the grey suit's patter was reassuring them. He looked from one to the other, and said:

'I think we'll begin the bids at fifty thousand.'

None of them moved.

'Do we have fifty thousand to start with?'

The scientist nodded almost imperceptibly – and then a second time, more strongly, as though the movement had gone wrong at first and he'd needed to try again.

'Fifty,' the man noted. 'Do we have sixty?'

It was the woman's turn. She moved her fingers down by her side. A queen, signalling someone's execution.

'Seventy?'

The pale man nodded.

'Eighty?'

They were auctioning her. It was clearly happening, right there in front of me, but I still found it hard to believe this was happening. Even from across the bay, I could hear Rebecca Wingate struggling inside the van. Yet these people were bidding, calm and uncaring, for the right to . . . own her. Simply because she was Roger Timms's last victim.

They were going to allow her to die so they could watch, so that they could feel part of something larger. To touch her murder, just as one of them, I presumed, had pressed a fingertip to the foreheads of the previous victims.

'One hundred thousand?'

It was almost incomprehensible.

But it carried on.

The pale man dropped out at two hundred. The woman and the bearded man battled the scientist back and forth up to two-thirty, but then they fell silent as well.

'Two hundred and forty thousand?'

At this, the small man in the waistcoat nodded. He was the last of the five to join the fray and he appeared the most nervous: still mopping at his face with that handkerchief. His skin was glinting under the lights, and his expression was pale, deadly serious. Was this his first time, I wondered. Or did it just mean so much more to him than it did to the others?

'Two hundred and fifty thousand?'

A pause. It took a moment for the scientist to nod.

'Two hundred and sixty?'

The small man signalled immediately, more confident now.

'Two hundred and seventy?'

A longer pause this time. Then the scientist nodded again.

I watched them fight it out. Despite the reticence, the bids stretched all the way to three hundred and thirty. When the man in the waistcoat went ten higher, the scientist was visibly fighting with himself.

The whole time, I could hear Rebecca Wingate struggling in the back of the van.

'Three hundred and fifty?'

The man in the grey suit looked between the members of the group, giving each of them one last chance to come in if they wanted. None of them did; they'd reached their limits. The little man in the waistcoat was staring at the vehicle now.

Focusing on it intently.

'Anyone?'

'Here.'

My voice echoed round the bay. The group turned, almost as one, and noticed me for the first time. For a second, the little man was so startled I thought he might bolt for the door.

And then they began clamouring:

'What the hell is this?'

'Who is that?'

'What do you think—'

The man in the suit held up his hand, attempting to placate them. He didn't even glance in my direction.

'Everybody,' he said. 'Please relax.'

'What are you trying to pull here, Mr Garland?'

It was the little man in the waistcoat who'd spoken. In fact, he'd actually stepped forward, his face flushed. He'd seemed timid before, but something had risen up in him quickly, his temper flaring indignantly, like a struck match.

The man in the suit – Garland – looked down at him.

'Please don't use my name, *Mr Hammond*.' He let the moment pan out. Then turned to look at me. Again, that blank expression. 'None of you need to worry about Mr Connor. He won't be discussing today's events with anyone.'

'Three hundred and fifty,' I said. 'Seriously.'

'Is that legitimate?' the scientist said.

Garland held my gaze a little longer. He'd read the letter. Not only had I written about Peter French, I'd also told Sarah all about the insurance money I received from Marie's death, and I was hoping he remembered that part too. I thought he did. His expression seemed to have shifted slightly. It was closer to the look of curiosity I'd seen when he cuffed me to the pipe.

A moment later, he turned back to the group.

'Do we have three hundred and sixty?'

Hammond was flustered. 'This is ridiculous. We've come here in good faith, with credentials. What—'

'Hey, fuck you,' I shouted.

'Mr Connor does have the money,' Garland said. 'It is up to him what he does with it.'

'But money isn't enough!'

Garland considered that. 'He has other credentials.'

It was obvious Hammond wanted to protest further, but he looked from me back to Garland, and saw the implacable expression return to the man's face. Up went the handkerchief again. His hand was trembling slightly.

Good, I thought.

'Do we have three hundred and sixty?'

Hammond nodded. 'Yes.'

'Do we have—'

'Four hundred thousand,' I said.

'For *God's* sake!'

'Mr Hammond.' Garland actually pointed a finger at him this time, and the little man flinched. He lowered it again very slowly. 'Remember where you are, and who you are talking to. You will observe house rules. Do you understand?'

'Yes. Of course.' Hammond glanced at me for a second, then looked at the van. 'Four hundred and fifty.'

'Five hundred.'

I had no idea what I was doing. I thought I knew what Garland meant by my 'credentials', but he'd also said it was up to me how I spent my money, and there was a certain implication to that. I was never going to walk out of here with Rebecca Wingate. But even though Hammond was glaring at me with unconcealed hatred, he was clearly squirming below the surface. And I liked that.

'Five hundred and fifty?' Garland said.

Nothing. I kept Hammond's gaze.

'Mr Hammond?'

Then Hammond took a deep breath and looked back at Garland. He nodded once, emphatically.

'Five hundred and fifty.'

That was out of my price range. I could have carried on regardless, just to spite the little man some more, but when Garland looked across at me I decided not to. Maybe it was just that, for some stupid reason, it felt important to be honest. It wouldn't save me, but it would at least differentiate me from these people in some small way.

'Mr Connor has reached the end of his funds.' Garland turned back, giving the other members of the group a chance to intervene. 'Is anyone else willing to continue?'

It was clear they'd passed their limits long ago; Hammond and I had left them far behind. I stared at him, willing him to look at me. But now that he'd won the lot, his attention was focused on the van.

'Very well,' Garland said. 'The item is sold for five hundred and fifty thousand pounds. Congratulations, Mr Hammond.'

The scientist clapped Hammond on the shoulder, and then the others stepped in, one by one, to shake his hand. As it continued, he began to look relieved. The victory was sinking in. I watched him smile and thank them, but it was obvious he was distracted. His gaze kept drifting back to his prize.

As the others began to move away, shaking Garland's hand on their way to the door, Hammond reached out to the side of his vehicle. His hand touched the panel there gently, almost with a sense of wonder.

'Congratulations,' I called over.

And he jerked back a little, as though it had shocked him. Stared at me again. I did my best to communicate with my eyes how much I'd like to get hold of him right now.

Garland walked back over to the van and held out his hand.

'We still have the issue of payment to address, Mr Hammond. If you'd just like to . . .'

He trailed off, but the meaning was clear. Over by the door, one of the other men had opened a laptop on a small table. Hammond looked at me, but then he took in the sight of me properly – chained to the pipe – and he realised I was no threat to him. It was his victory: he was the one who'd be driving out of here shortly, and I'd remain where I was right now, waiting for it to be over.

'Yes.'

Hammond smiled at me unpleasantly.

'Of course.'

Forty-One

Todd was surrounded by the ghosts of children.

Except these were children that had never even lived. He was sitting in the offices of the Child Protection Unit, the hub of Operation Victor. On the shelves around the walls, there were several PCs running on separate monitors and servers, and each of the hard drives had a white sticker on the front, with a different name scribbled on it in marker pen. Every name represented a fake child. An imaginary identity that did not exist anywhere in the real world – only inside these computer cases, and the thoughts and dreams of men sitting in dark rooms around the country.

By way of contrast, the lights in this office were always turned on. It wasn't a health and safety issue. Todd understood the rationale perfectly: you didn't want to sit in the gloom and stare into a bright monitor, not when you did this kind of work. The screen would start to feel dangerous.

He was sitting with an officer named Robert Cole. Cole was half reclined in a swivel chair, holding a pen close to his mouth, occasionally tapping it against his teeth. He seemed totally at ease, and not remotely unnerved by the soft hum of activity going on around them. There was a poster above his desk: a painting of a tobacco pipe, with the words '*Ceci, ce n'est pas une pipe*' written beneath. *This is not a pipe.*

'So,' Cole said. 'What can I do for you, Detective Dennis?'

'It's about Paul. Paul Kearney.'

'Yes. I thought it might be.'

Todd leaned forward, feeling awkward. He didn't really know why he was here, or quite what he expected to gain from this.

He said, 'I realise it's ongoing. I just . . .'

'It's just that he was your partner.'

'Yes.'

'Well, like you said, it's ongoing.'

'I realise that. I was just wondering where it might be right now.'

Cole nodded once. 'I can tell you a little, in confidence, but you should be aware that none of it's, well . . .'

It was his turn to trail off, but he gestured with his hands slightly and Todd got the message. This was off the record: a professional courtesy that would not be mentioned again, not until the information they'd gathered had been analysed, set in stone, and charges settled upon.

'I understand.'

'We've been monitoring a number of sites here, at various stages. It's a delicate operation. I can tell you that Kearney's credit card details were used at several.'

Todd rubbed his hands together. Did he want to know this?

'When did it start?'

'Around the beginning of the year. His use appears to have steadily increased over the last six months. To the point where he's recently been spending several hours online every evening.'

'Becoming more and more obsessed with it?'

'It's a pattern we notice a lot.'

'But he only downloaded three clips?'

Cole *clacked* the pen once. Didn't reply.

'I'm not excusing it,' Todd said.

'Only three,' Cole agreed. 'But they were three files he had absolutely no right to possess, and which he paid money to access. Thereby—'

'Increasing demand for supply,' Todd said. 'I know.'

That wasn't what was bothering him. There was no

argument against what Cole had said – Kearney was totally in the wrong. But the behaviour concerned him. Something had set his partner off scouring these sites, and he seemed to have become more and more desperate as time went on.

And yet he'd only actually downloaded three files. It was as though he'd been searching for something. Paul had always asked *why*, of course, but this time the question felt more specific than it had in the past. He hadn't just been staring at random atrocities, trying to understand them. He hadn't been collecting anything and everything. It had been more . . . targeted.

'The three files,' he said.

'Yes.'

'Were they similar?'

Cole stared at him for a second. Another *clack* of the pen.

'Please,' Todd said.

'Yes. Different boys, but part of the same series.'

'Series?'

'I agree. It sounds horrible. But we hear rumours of these things all the time, and every so often we find them.'

'What was in this one?'

'Are you sure you want to know?'

Todd wasn't.

'Yes,' he said.

Cole put the pen down on the desk and leaned forward.

'The MO for these particular videos was normal, everyday children being targeted at random. Boys were abducted off the street and abused horribly, in each case by the same individual, and that abuse was captured on film. The boys were then returned close to the place they'd been taken from, as though nothing had happened. The camera captured that as well. They showed it in place of credits.'

Jesus Christ, Todd thought.

'When was this?'

'It depends who you listen to. Allegedly, there were several instances in the late seventies and early eighties. Nationwide.'

'You say "allegedly"?'

'Yes.' Cole nodded. 'Until recently, we only knew about the films through hearsay. People have mentioned this series in the past, but only the same way they talk about snuff films. They saw it at someone's house once, but can't remember where. A friend of a friend saw it. The story gets passed around.'

'Some fucking story.'

'Yes.' Cole blinked. 'I agree totally. But this one turns out to be real.'

Todd shook his head and looked down at the floor, still rubbing his hands together. It had begun to feel like he was washing them.

He'd known it was going to be bad, but somehow it was even worse than he expected. If nothing else, it confirmed his suspicions. This sounded like the exact type of thing Paul would have been fascinated by. He would have seen it, been appalled and then become driven to look into it. Searching out examples of absolute evil so he could try to figure out *why*.

Todd said, 'And that's why he only downloaded three.'

'Yes. Obviously, examples are very difficult to find. But that's what he had: three videos of *The Yellow Man*.'

Todd looked up. 'Sorry?'

'The offender who appears in the clips,' Cole said. 'That's how people always referred to him and it's where the title came from. The series is known as *The Yellow Man*.'

Forty-Two

The number plates on the white van had been changed.

Even so, as he watched it pull out of the industrial complex, Kearney knew what he was seeing. It was Roger Timms's missing vehicle, disguised so as to pass unnoticed amongst the other cars on the road. Just as Hammond and the others had been dressed down, scattered amongst the crowd at the auction.

And Hammond was behind the wheel now.

Kearney kept his face turned downwards, moving his hand around near the car stereo, and the white van went past him. There was no sign Hammond had seen him.

Preoccupied, are you?

Kearney gritted his teeth. The driver who had brought the collector here had already left, heading off alone in a different direction. And now Hammond was disappearing away with his prize.

After the van had taken the corner, Kearney started the engine. He presumed Hammond was going back to his mansion, but needed to be sure. There was oncoming traffic, but he ignored it, swinging the car around in the road. A horn sounded, and he saw someone gesticulating at him. Furious. Kearney blanked him. Just shifted into gear and then headed off after the van.

The van, and what was inside it.

We will find her. I promise you.

He caught sight of the back of the vehicle, approaching a

roundabout about a hundred metres ahead, and decided he was going to pull it over. He no longer had the authority – not officially – but Hammond probably wasn't going to know that. The longer he left it, the greater the chance of harm coming to Rebecca, assuming she was still alive.

Assuming she was actually in there.

After the auction itself was over, Kearney had loitered as carefully as possible, moving from the main hall to the corridor outside, and then back again. He'd seen one man approach a doorway at the far end of the room, and been allowed through it. He hadn't seen Hammond go that way, but, looking around, the man wasn't there any more either, and he hadn't come out the front way.

Two men in suits stood to either side of the back door.

Kearney hadn't wanted to draw attention to himself by forcing his way through. Not before he'd figured out what was happening. Instead, he'd gone back outside, and walked around the side of the buildings.

There was a thin drive running up behind them, then waste ground bordered by a fence. No other obvious exit from the complex. Up ahead, at what he estimated was the back of the auction house, a metal shutter was pulled down; another of the men in black suits was standing outside it, talking on a mobile phone. Looking the other way for the moment.

Kearney had retreated before he was seen, then returned to his own car to wait.

Hammond had gone backstage with the others. A little later, he'd emerged with Roger Timms's van. And so Rebecca *must* be in there. The old man had . . . bought her, and now he was taking her home to complete whatever fucking collection he was building.

The van took a right at the roundabout.

Kearney reached it a few seconds later, but couldn't pull out straight away: too many cars were sweeping past him, all of them going too quickly to risk pushing out.

'*Come on*,' he said.

A break in the traffic, and he took it: screeching out too quickly, and nearly losing it as he circled round. There was another angry blare from somewhere behind him. Now he was on the long, straight hill that Hammond had taken. But the white van was far ahead of him now, shining in the sun, with perhaps ten other vehicles separating them. And here, the oncoming traffic was so close there was no chance of overtaking.

Calm down and pay attention.

Hammond took a left at the next roundabout. At first glance, he was reversing the route his driver had used on the way to the auction, which meant he was almost certainly taking Rebecca to his house. But if he wasn't, Kearney was going to lose him.

That sent a jag of fear through him. Suddenly he was bumper to bumper with the car in front.

Twenty painful seconds later, he reached the roundabout. When he turned left, the van was nowhere in sight.

The road that led out towards Hammond's house was coming up on the right. As it approached, Kearney made his decision: he couldn't risk making a mistake. The road was wider here, so he pulled out and accelerated away, overtaking the line of traffic. He knew where Hammond's house was, and he could take another right further up if he needed to. But he had to be sure the man wasn't heading somewhere else.

As he shot up the middle of the road, one hand holding the wheel steady, he got his phone and flipped it open. Turned it on and waited. Kept his eye on the white lines flashing underneath his car. Brake lights kept flicking on to the left. More horns *whining* past him to the right.

He speed-dialled the number for Todd's mobile.

Car after car . . .

If Hammond hadn't turned off, he should have seen him by now. *Shit.*

'Paul.'

'Todd – listen to me. I think I've found Rebecca. I think Hammond's got her.'

A pause.

'You mean *Arthur* Hammond? Paul—'

It would take too long to explain. He interrupted.

'Look, I *know* he's got her. Todd, please. You need to get people to his house now.' The next turning was coming up. He slowed, indicated. 'I'm following him now. He's taking her to his house.'

'You shouldn't be following anyone, Paul.'

There was something wrong with Todd's voice, he thought – but then, he should have expected that after everything he'd done. Kearney shook his head. Right now, he just really needed Todd to *fucking listen*.

'Listen to me: Hammond is driving Roger Timms's van.' A break in the traffic. He swung the car around, hitting the kerb as he went. The chassis rocked, and then he was off again. 'The number plates have been changed, but I'm sure it's his. And he's got Rebecca in the back.'

Silence on the line.

He said, 'Are you there?'

'What's the reg?'

Thank God. Kearney read the new plate from memory.

'He's taking her home. Back to his house.'

'OK. Don't do anything stupid.'

'I'm sorry, Todd,' he said. 'I'm so, so sorry.'

'Paul—'

But Kearney cancelled the call and tossed the phone onto the passenger seat. He needed to concentrate now. There was a right turn up ahead. The tyres shrieked again, and then he had both hands on the steering wheel, and his foot to the floor.

Forty-Three

Garland wasn't taking any chances with me. Two of his men held me in place as he released the handcuffs from round the pipe, and then clicked them shut again behind my back. They lifted me to my feet and kept a tight grip on my upper arms as he walked off to one side and took the gun out from underneath his jacket.

Examined it.

With everyone gone, the loading bay itself was now silent and empty. There was only that same distant *clanking* of metal. I could feel the space where the van had been. The sense of what was missing.

'Why are you doing this?' I said.

'It's just business.'

'Business.' I tried to laugh, but couldn't.

'Of course.' He frowned to himself, then finished checking the gun and looked up at me. 'Your friend asked the same question. I'm sorry to disappoint you both. We're just facilitators. All we do is arrange an experience for people with the appropriate funds. That's all there is to it. I don't understand it any more than you do.'

'You trade people for money.'

'Not living people. Not usually, anyway. When people act professionally, we're probably the only business in the world that doesn't hurt anyone.'

'Rebecca Wingate was alive,' I said. 'She's a human being.'

He shook his head.

'You don't understand what's happening here.'

'I know you're a killer.'

'Only when I have to be, Mr Connor. And besides, so are you.'

'No.' It was stupid, but I denied it anyway. 'I'm not.'

'Yes you are.'

With his free hand, Garland reached inside his jacket and pulled something out of the pocket. It was a single piece of A4 paper, folded into quarters. He rubbed it open between his fingertips. There was writing on both sides. My letter.

'Your friend had this with her when she performed her stunt,' he said. 'She obviously thought it was important.'

I didn't say anything.

'You know what this is?' he said.

And even now, I still couldn't admit what was there; I could feel myself wanting to refuse it. It was ridiculous. *You were right*, I'd told Sarah. *You need to face up to it.* I'd written those words as I prepared to do the exact opposite, and I was still doing it now.

I said, 'Yes.'

'It's a confession, isn't it?'

'Yes.'

But the truth is, it was something even worse than that.

So you were right. Death really is a monster, and you need to face up to it. If you don't, it spreads. It contaminates every-thing around you. I didn't face it, and that's exactly what happened.

When I learned how long Marie had been planning what she did, I couldn't deal with the knowledge. I couldn't bear to accept how badly I must have failed her. How could I not know? And so I ran away from the responsibility and tried to pin it on someone else. I convinced myself it was that man's fault. A part of it really was, but that's not why I went to his house and did what I did. I was blaming him simply to avoid blaming myself.

But what she did was my fault.

You shouldn't have told the police I was there with you that night. I asked you to when you didn't know the truth, and that was wrong of me. You have a right to hear that truth now and change your mind. Which is why I'm leaving you this letter. There is more evidence in the rental space the police will be able to find under my name. It's up to you what you do with this. Whatever decision you come to will be the correct one.

Most of all, you deserve to know that you were always right.

I appreciate everything you've done for me, and how you tried to help me. I hope you can understand and forgive me for this.

Alex

I remembered the perverse sense of self-sacrifice I felt when I wrote that. *Whatever decision you come to will be the correct one.* When I sold the house, I packaged up my belongings and put them away in storage, where I wouldn't need to see them. The letter was just another example of that. All I'd done was brush my guilt into a tidy little pile of words, and leave it for someone else to deal with. So that the responsibility didn't belong to me any more. So that if I didn't turn myself in, it wouldn't be my fault.

So that I could leave unencumbered.

Garland folded the letter up and slipped it back into his jacket, then nodded at the two men. They stepped away and he moved in beside me, placing the barrel of the gun against my side.

The pressure was light but it tingled, as though there was an electrical charge to it. At the same time, he gripped my arm. Again, only the lightest of touches, but it tilted me off balance.

'Tell me something,' I said. 'If I'd out-bid that guy, Hammond, would you have let me win?'

'No.'

'You were just letting me raise the price for you.'

'It's just business.' He shrugged. 'And my job here is salvage. That's all there is.'

The pressure on my arm increased slightly, and then the gun went into my side a little harder. This was it, then. I wanted to close my eyes, but I decided that I wasn't going to.

'Now move,' Garland said.

Forty-Four

He took me into the cellar of whatever building we were in.

It was strange down here. The walls and floor were made of stone – roughly hewn blocks – and the ground was moist, almost mossy in places. From somewhere, I thought I could hear water trickling. The corridor was dark, illuminated only by weak, inadequate bulbs hanging down from nooses of cable. It felt like a natural underground structure, partly adapted for purpose, rather than man-made foundations. For some reason, it made me think of haunted houses, built on top of old grave-yards.

We turned a corner, and I smelled petrol in the air.

There were large, steel kegs lining the sides of the corridor here. Drums. Panic flared inside me, and I faltered slightly. He was going to burn me alive down here. But the gun nudged me in the back, and I started moving again.

'Look—'

'Quiet.' He lowered his own voice. 'We're here.'

On the right, there was a break between the barrels, and I realised the space had been left to provide access to what looked like a door. It was made of dark metal, and the outline was lost in the gloom, but there was a panel at face-height. Garland reached up and pushed it across with his fingertips, revealing a steel mesh, the kind you'd stub a cigarette out on.

'Your friend,' he said.

For a moment, I didn't move. Then I realised what he was allowing me to do, and I stepped closer.

Sarah.

She was lying down on a mattress at the far side of a small cell, wearing dirty blue jeans and a black blouse that merged with the darkness around her, making her appear half formed. Her long arms were slightly brighter: tucked up together to form a pillow she could rest her head on. Her face was mostly lost beneath a tumble of jet-black hair, which itself was only really discernible by the pale skin between the tangles. But in those spaces, after a moment's confusion, I saw enough to know that it was Sarah.

She was asleep.

Tears blurred my eyes. I thought of the photograph in the newspaper, when she'd looked so young and unguarded. Smiling, tilting her head slightly, and leaning back against me. This was still the same woman, but she had changed in the same way everything had. I think it was the fact she was sleeping that bothered me most. She looked peaceful, as though being in a dirty little cell was all she'd ever known.

You were always right.

When I'd written that, I was thinking of that young girl Sarah had told me about, and the lessons she'd learned and taken through her life. I think I wanted to offer her some reassurance. But it was only ever selfish. I should have realised that Sarah would hold those words close to her heart, like an ache. Because saying you should have listened to someone is only ever a way of telling them they should have spoken louder.

I'm so sorry, I thought. *So, so sorry.*

'Why haven't you killed her already?'

Garland thought about it.

'When she first turned up at one of our displays, we needed to know who she was. And then there were different reasons at different times. If it makes you feel any better, you were one of them. If I hadn't seen you at Mr Ellis's flat yesterday, she would be dead by now.'

It didn't make me feel any better.

'You just said "our displays".'

'Did I?'

'And back in the car, you said "one of our places". Plural.'

Garland didn't reply.

I think I'd understood already, but his choice of words confirmed it. This wasn't simply about Thomas Wells and Roger Timms. If people were prepared to pay to see their victims, they'd be prepared to do so for the victims of other killers too. Clearly, there was money to be made from offering this kind of 'experience', and Garland's organisation had built up enough resources – over only God knew how much time – to expand. The murders here were just one small part of their business, and for various reasons they'd been compromised.

'So what was it?' I said. 'Was it because of Timms?'

'Because of greedy people. We always paid Mr Timms well, but apparently that wasn't enough. He put everyone at risk, and we can't have that – not for ourselves or our clients.'

I nodded. 'So this is salvage.'

'It's what happens when you're forced to close a branch of your organisation. You tidy up carefully. You save what can be saved. You cut out the dead weight.'

Dead weight. He was talking about everyone he'd had to remove to keep this covered up. My brother. Mike and Julie. And me, I supposed – me and Sarah.

In the cell, she was still fast asleep. I found it hard to breathe as I looked in, but her body was rising and falling gently as she slept. Oblivious.

Perhaps that was for the best.

'You're forgetting something,' I said.

'What?'

'I still have the research Sarah collected.'

It was all I had. And Garland didn't look impressed.

'Neither of you really knew a thing.'

'I wouldn't gamble on that.'

'I don't gamble on anything.' He shook his head. 'My work

here is finished. Mr Hammond's money has disappeared into a large number of foreign accounts and will never be traced. This place will burn to the ground. And in less than two hours, I'll be on a private plane.'

'What about the police?'

He shook his head again. 'They'll have the only answers they'll ever bother looking for.'

There was an air of finality in the way he said it, and I realised we'd almost come to the end of the discussion. It felt like I should panic: flail about again, maybe, or attempt some kind of heroics. But I looked in at Sarah and my throat was tight. I just wanted this to be over now. I wanted not to feel this any more.

Garland reached into his jacket and pulled out the letter again.

'I want you to tell me exactly what happened with Peter French,' he said. 'And where we can find this "evidence" you mentioned.'

'Why?' I said. 'What does it matter?'

For a moment, Garland didn't reply. At first, it seemed that he wasn't quite sure of the answer himself. But then I realised he was simply choosing his words carefully.

'Mr Hammond said that money wasn't enough, and he was right. Part of what allows us to operate is that everyone involved has something to lose. It's just business.' He paused. 'And I think you have the credentials, Mr Connor.'

I turned slowly to look at him.

'That's why I want you to tell me,' he said. 'Because I want us both to understand the exact terms of the offer I'm about to make.'

Forty-Five

Arthur Hammond went through to the kitchen and poured himself a Scotch. The ice chinked as he swallowed the whisky, then rattled emptily in the glass. A bead of condensation ran down his wrist, tickling beneath the cuff of his shirt like a spider.

He poured himself a second.

His hand was trembling. He'd been so excited on the drive back here that it had been difficult to focus on the road. As he sipped the drink, savouring the silk and burn of it, the silence in the house was thumping with its own quiet heartbeat. It was an ominous sensation, like something huge and heavy was approaching from the distance, the pulse in his ears measured by the beast's enormous stride.

He'd almost missed out.

The ice rattled at the memory.

He was still *furious* about the man who'd been there. He owned that auction house; he'd only permitted Garland to use it today because the bastard had offered him a special, one-off payment. One he knew Hammond wouldn't be able to resist.

Emily.

If he'd known what would happen – that he'd be made to pay over the odds for something he wanted even more – he'd have refused. Not even what he *wanted*. He *deserved* to have it . . .

Hammond shook his head.

At least Garland would be dealing with that man now. There

was some small measure of consolation to be had from imagining that. Nothing extravagant, of course; Garland was a businessman first and foremost. So it would be a bullet into the top of the head as he walked casually past. A puff of bloody, burnt smoke. Gone. Garland probably wouldn't even look behind him.

That could have been you, Arthur.

Yes, it could. A smile cracked his face. A sensation of relief. There had always been a danger that Garland knew about his unauthorised dealings with Timms: the violation of the indirect purchasing system. He imagined the repercussions would have been harsh. But he had gone anyway. Risked it. Partly because he wanted this piece so badly, but also because it was the nature of the experience. Part of the seduction of selling your soul was that the buyer always had the power to take it if they preferred.

The drink was finished. He put the glass down on the kitchen counter, where it refracted the blue lights from under the cabinets. He might pour himself another when he was ready. In the meantime, there was work to do. He opened the side door and moved through to the garage. He had to get the new piece installed with the others, in the gallery beneath the house.

It didn't take long. The metal box was resting on makeshift runners in the back of the van, and slid out easily onto the waiting trolley. Heavy in itself, but simple to manoeuvre once he got it onto wheels and put his small weight behind it, pushing it across to the elevator that had been built into the corner.

In the contained, amber space of the lift, he took a moment to look at the box. It was the shape of a coffin, although slightly larger, and with a mesh of air holes drilled into the centre of the lid. He scratched at it with his fingernail, and the box responded by *thudding* inside and then screaming. As they descended, he realised he could smell her: that she'd soiled herself. It both revolted and excited him. In the early days, there had often been revulsion, but it had always been overtaken by fascination. He'd had to force his way through it sometimes, but it remained important and he made sure he paid attention to it. Every doorway, after all, was a part of the room beyond.

One level below, the thick doors slid open and Hammond pushed the gurney out, his body at an angle to it. And then he rolled it along, the wheels clicking and screeching.

The floor plan down here was hammer-shaped: it was basically just a long corridor with a large room at the far end. A number of smaller rooms jutted out to either side as you went down, but they were reserved for individual pieces – single works – with the exception of one at the end where a shower unit had been installed. Each had a separate light switch. All now rested in darkness as he passed them, moving under the single bulbs that illuminated the corridor at intervals, leaving half of it in darkness, half bathed in light.

The décor was shabby. He'd never attempted to turn this into one of the clean, white spaces he maintained in his public galleries. When he'd bought the house, this level had been bare floorboards and peeling wallpaper; it had reminded him of a forgotten floor in a hotel. Aside from adding the elevator, lights and atmospheric controls, he'd left it that way. It felt right: you came down in the lift and entered another world, entirely distinct from the polished, modern sheen of the house above.

'Shhh,' Hammond told the coffin.

It had no effect. He wheeled it down to the larger room.

At one end, there was a large projector screen and a single seat where he could watch his collection of movies. Various pieces rested under mounted spotlights around the walls. The newest was a sports bag, small and slumped, the security tag still in place. Hammond turned the trolley awkwardly, rotating and positioning it against the wall beside the bag.

Then he stood back.

Weighing the difference between the two – the contrast between the large, solid metal of the box and the tiny, crumpled bag. He felt a thrill run through him that couldn't be articulated in words. An understanding. You couldn't explain it; it was something you could only get from standing here and seeing this.

And so he did just that, holding himself quiet and still, listening to the thumping noises from within the box. The air was tingling. His throat, still scorched from the whisky, was now almost too tight to swallow.

It was the sound of a human being, in pain and terrified of dying. For a moment, Hammond felt the familiar tug of society: the insistent voice that told him he must *care*. But empathy was only a learned response, and there was power from overcoming that. He already knew the trivial lessons they taught in schools, and the knowledge on offer in this room was of a different, more honest kind. It couldn't be gained any other way. You had to touch it. When you did, everything on the surface felt safe, but everything inside tilted to a perspective you had never even dreamed was possible.

A drink.

But he couldn't wait. He needed to see her. He needed to touch his fingertip to her forehead, and become part of this momentous thing.

His hands shook as they reached out to the lid. Hammond spread his arms to grip it at either end. Thumbs on the front; fingers down the side. It was terribly heavy. He had to get beneath it and *push up* with his whole body weight to heave it open. As the hinges turned, the smell from within wafted out in a thick, terrible cloud, and the tone of Rebecca Wingate's desperate keening became clear.

Hammond stumbled backwards in shock.

He realised two things very clearly. The first was that Garland hadn't allowed him to get away with anything. The second was that Rebecca Wingate's screams had not been motivated solely by a terror of death after all. But also by the rank thing that had stowed itself away with her, and was now stretching itself upright.

Forty-Six

Kearney couldn't hear any sirens as he pulled up outside Arthur Hammond's house. The country lane was as empty and silent as it was when he'd been here before.

Were they even on the way?

He certainly wasn't going to wait around. Rebecca was in there right now, and he wasn't leaving her alone for a second longer. The nearer he'd got, the more he'd felt a *pull* inside him. It was as though his heart was connected to hers by a stretch of emotional fabric, and – now that he was this close – he could feel both of them beating inside his chest.

He abandoned his car at an angle across the grass verge. Left the indicator blinking and the driver's door open, a curve of metal wedged deep into the turf.

It was a warm, hazy afternoon, the air blurred softly by the heat. Kearney approached the gate and took hold of it. The painted metal was rough against his palms. It seemed surreal. The house beyond looked so ordinary now, with its row of potted plants outside, its arched doorway and wide windows. Somewhere up in the enormous hedge, there were even birds singing.

Some things were so horrific that you expected them only to happen in darkness, or in dank places like the lock-up Timms had rented. Dirty old houses. And when they weren't happening directly in front of you, where it was impossible to deny them, the mind turned away from them, embracing the apparent normality.

Are you sure . . . ?

But he was. It didn't matter anyway. He shook the railings, pushing them backwards into the driveway, and knew he wasn't acting on reason any more. The image of Rebecca's face filled his mind. He had been given one last chance at finding her, and he was going to take it, no matter what.

As the gate scraped backwards, a connection was broken and he felt a slight buzz. No doubt it meant an alarm would be sounding inside the house. He would have to move quickly.

There was a large double garage adjoining the house on the left-hand side, but the metal was sheer and tight to the ground. Probably opened by the same remote control that was meant to operate the main gate. Kearney headed across and tried the front door instead, unsurprised to find it locked. It looked too heavy to kick down, and he didn't want to break his leg trying, so he stepped back, picked up one of the potted plants and heaved it through a downstairs windows.

The explosion shattered the peace and quiet, the sound full of sharp angles and tinkling points. When it faded, Kearney was left with the anxious, high-pitched twitter of the house alarm.

If the police weren't coming now, they soon would be.

The remains of the window formed jagged glass teeth around the edges. Inside, he could make out a dimly lit lounge. The pot had come to rest against the base of a red settee, and the cream carpet was now scattered with earth and flowers and glass. Kearney picked up a second pot and used it to knock shards of glass from the frame, and then he hoisted himself quickly inside.

The alarm was much louder in here. The sound vibrated intensely, thick in the air, so that it felt like you were standing inside it. Beyond the lounge, the dark corridor was flashing with red light.

'Hammond!' he shouted. 'Where are you?'

But he could barely even hear himself. As he moved out into

the hallway, where the noise was pure, he winced and covered his ears.

'Hammond?'

The room at the end of the corridor was brightly lit, so he made his way down there, then edged around the doorframe. A kitchen. It was all neat and clean, full of polished, space-age appliances. The counter was glowing with soft blue light. Kearney noticed the open bottle of whisky on the side, next to a squat glass with some half-melted, clear pebbles of ice at the bottom.

Toasting himself.

'Hammond. I'm coming for you, you sick bastard.'

Although he could have been anywhere in the house, Kearney's instincts took him to a side door hanging ajar at the far end of the kitchen. It led through to the back of the garage, where bulbs in the ceiling were casting cups of light down onto Roger Timms's white van.

Both of its back doors were open. Kearney crossed to the vehicle and checked inside. There was nothing there but a series of metal racks, bolted to the base of the interior, a little like a set of ladders. Something had clearly been resting on there: positioned to be rolled out for ease of access.

Rebecca.

Where had he taken her?

He looked around – then spotted the silver door built into the corner at the back of the property. Kearney's gaze moved from the closed metal surface to the smooth tarmac beneath his feet.

Just like Timms, Hammond liked to keep his unnatural interests buried under his house. A physical basement for an emotional one.

There was a single button to call the lift. It glowed orange as he pressed it. There was a slight rumble from below, and then the clank of machinery in the wall as wheels and chains hoisted the contraption upwards.

Is there another exit?

If there wasn't, then Hammond must still be down there.

The door slid open to reveal the empty metal lift. Narrow but deep. Kearney stepped inside. There were only two buttons, and he pressed the lower one.

The door closed and the lift descended.

In the seconds it took, images bloomed in his mind. The burned bodies of Ellis and Gilroyd, her feet curled like a baby's. The way Mike Halsall's head had been tilted to one side, gazing down. The gunshot wounds. Handcuffed wrists.

Simon Wingate's clasped, praying hands.

Rebecca's face.

The door slid across again. An empty corridor.

Kearney stepped out, moving into a thick slab of air that stank of mildew and wet, peeling wallpaper. It was damp and unpleasant down here, like slipping your hand into the mulch of a forest after a heavy rainstorm. He half expected to see plants curling up the walls, but there were only small patches of rot. A hiss of mould that might have been sprayed onto the ragged paper.

'Hammond?'

No reply.

But it wasn't quiet here, he realised: there was some kind of noise coming from the room at the end of the corridor. It was muffled and frantic. After a moment, he recognised it was a woman trying to scream, and his heart jolted like a starting gun. Before he could think, he was running down the corridor. Past dark alcoves. Under the lights that buzzed and faded as he sprinted beneath –

We will find her . . .

– and into the room, slowing down just as he reached it, but not soon enough to stop himself.

Stupid.

He turned as he entered. Too late, but scanning for movement anyway. There was none. It was empty.

He saw Arthur Hammond immediately. At the far end, the man was slumped in a single chair with his back to the rest of the room. Everything in here was lit up by orange bulbs on the walls, and Hammond's body was silhouetted against them, like he was sitting in front of an open furnace, roasting alive. A part of his head was missing; the rest was on the floor and the side wall. One hand was in his lap, and the other dangled uselessly, resting against the wooden legs of the chair. Kearney could smell the gun smoke in the air.

He looked around him. Along the base of the walls, there were exhibits on small display pedestals.

The crying was coming from the opposite end. Ignoring Hammond for the moment, Kearney approached that end of the room. A metal coffin. The lid had been hefted backwards and leaned against the wall behind.

When he looked inside, his vision of her was immediately blurred by tears.

I promise you.

Rebecca Wingate was alive, but she couldn't see him. There was black masking tape wrapped around her eyes and then the lower part of her face, beneath the nose. A small slit had been cut through where her mouth would be. Her hands were bound on her lap, and Kearney could see there was a terrible injury on her right arm. It looked as though something had taken a bite from the crook of her elbow, nearly severing the limb. But the skin around the wound seemed burnt, and he could smell it. Not a bite at all. It was the single small point at which blood had been taken from her, now stretched wide by infection.

But she's alive.

'You're going to be OK,' he said. She jumped from the shock of his voice. 'I'm a policeman.'

She stopped crying, but her body was trembling. He needed to call Todd again, get an ambulance here.

'You're going to be all right. I promise.'

Then he heard a slight *click* from behind him.

Kearney froze.

Another smell reached him: strong and somehow even more vile than the odour of Rebecca's wounded arm. He was aware

300

of another presence down here now. Something was standing a little way behind him. He could feel it there.

Stupid.

He'd been so desperate to get down here – to Rebecca – that he hadn't checked any of the blackened alcoves he ran past. And he hadn't thought carefully enough about Hammond either, he realised. It looked like suicide, but the man's hands were empty and there had been no gun on the floor. Someone had staged the scene to look that way. And the lift had still been down here when he arrived, which meant the *someone* was too.

Turn around?

The Yellow Man.

That thought was irrational, but it came anyway. And it felt true. Maybe it wasn't the same man standing there right now, but that didn't matter. They were both shadows: cast by different objects, perhaps, but standing in front of the same fire.

Do you want to see?

For the last six months, he'd been driven to do just that. *Let me tell you the worst thing *I've* ever seen.* He'd read the description of the Yellow Man series that followed, and something good had fallen into shadow inside him. Something had fled, and a sense of horror had crawled in to take its place. At first, he'd tried to resist – told himself not to – but it was hopeless: once he knew of these videos' existence, something had compelled him to seek them out. And why? Even now, he wasn't sure. In three examples of the Yellow Man, he'd still not found the answers he was searching for, but it had only made him look harder. And like a video camera pointed at a television, the question had become a tunnel. He had fallen into it, and it had led him here.

Turn around then, he told himself.

And he started to. But then he realised, now it had come to it, he no longer wanted to. Whatever answers might be there, he wouldn't allow them to be his final thoughts in the world.

Instead, Kearney looked down at Rebecca Wingate. He smiled at her.

At least there was this, he thought.

At least, in the end, he had found her too.

Kearney closed his eyes and waited.

Forty-Seven

'This is the place?' Garland said.

I nodded.

We'd parked up by a small office on the outskirts of the city. I was in the first of two cars, both of them black with tinted windows, and I was sitting in the back seat with Garland. There were two men in the front, but neither were the ones I'd fought with back at the auction house. Perhaps they were in the second car, which was pulling in behind us now.

Sarah was in that one too – not that I could see her through the glass. Back at the auction house, I'd already been confined in this one by the time they brought her out. I watched as best as I could. She walked calmly across the floor of the loading bay and clambered easily into the vehicle, without a care in the world.

After I'd agreed to Garland's offer, he'd taken me back upstairs, and they'd brought out the laptop again in order for me to make the payment. Four hundred thousand pounds in exchange for the life of my friend.

As I'd keyed in the information required of me, I'd wondered briefly whether I was making a mistake. Garland could just kill us both anyway and have done with it, which would make things far easier and simpler for him. But then, if he wanted the money, I was sure he'd be able to extract it from me without much effort. And if he was going to kill us, nothing I did or didn't do was going to stop that from happening.

There was also the small detail of the figure we'd agreed on. Not five hundred thousand, but four. He wasn't taking everything, and that suggested he was leaving me – leaving us – with enough money to run.

All that aside, I didn't have any choice but to trust him.

The strangest thing was that, as the money vanished into the ether, I wasn't expecting a bullet in the back of my head. And I didn't get one. Garland watched the screen carefully, making sure the transfer had gone through, and then nodded to the man operating the computer. It was shut down. Then, without another word, Garland took me to the car to wait.

And then we had driven here.

Pro-Storage UK. Just an innocuous building with benches outside, a reception within, and then, out back, a large number of garage units. One of which contained everything I'd kept after selling the house I'd shared with Marie. It was the second time I'd been here today. The first had been earlier on this morning, before heading to the prison, when I'd dropped off the laptop and Sarah's research materials. That was what we were here to collect, but it wasn't all that we were here for.

'Yes,' I said. 'This is the place.'

'Well, then.'

Garland opened the door on his side, leaving me to get out on the other by myself.

It was a main road: there was traffic shooting past, and people outside a café a short distance up the street. I could have run or fought – caused a scene and tried to get out of this. But once again, there was no point. Garland still had the gun, slipped inside his jacket, and the other men were all armed as well. I wouldn't achieve anything by fighting except getting Sarah and myself killed, and maybe someone else as well.

And if that was still going to happen anyway, better for something I didn't do than something that I did.

A minute later, after I'd signed us in, we were standing in a small garage at the back of the complex. It housed everything I hadn't thrown away when I sold the house. The remnants of my old life. Never entirely gone, just pushed in here, of sight.

'Quickly, please.'

I nodded.

The money had only been the first part of our deal. The second, as with all his customers, required something less tangible.

Everybody involved has something to lose.

I suppose you could say it required a soul.

I pulled down a small box from the top shelf. It was very light. As I opened it, Garland stepped back slightly and put his hand inside his jacket, ready to retrieve his gun if it was needed. It was understandable. After all, I'd told him about Peter French now, so he knew what was hidden inside this box, and what I was capable of.

Apparently, anyway. But as I stared down at the knife, it seemed absurd to think I'd done what I had. I reached down and picked it up, and my hand seemed to have no memory whatsoever of holding it before. It was a mystery to me, as was the blood still crusted slightly on the blade.

Beneath it, an old raincoat.

I remembered Peter French's eyes clenching shut, like he'd been shot at close range, and then the way he'd crumpled down in the hallway. He laid there on his side, the blood stretching quietly, inexorably, across the carpet from the centre of his chest. I realised what I'd done immediately. There had been no sense of satisfaction or relief. Instead, a trickle of cold had begun to spread through me.

I shook my head.

'I'm surprised you kept them,' Garland said.

'I didn't at first.'

I remembered running off in a blind panic, taking turnings at random. The knife was in my coat pocket; they were both covered in blood anyway, so it didn't matter. *Marie.* I couldn't get her out of my head. *I've let you down so badly.* At some point, I found myself near some waste ground, and I stuffed the coat and knife into an old tyre, and so I only had a T-shirt on when I ended up at Sarah's house.

I went back for them the next day. They were upstairs in my house when Detective Kearney called round to make his enquiries. I think that had been another attempt at absolving myself from blame, the same as writing the confession to Sarah. All he'd needed to do was ask to look round. I'd have said yes, and it would all have been over. But he never did, and so it wasn't my fault.

Garland had brought a briefcase with him. He laid it on the ground now, opened it, and took out a large see-through zipper-bag. He handed it to me.

'Put them in there. Carefully.'

I did as I was told, then passed it back to him.

He took the letter out of his jacket – the confession – and placed that in the bag with the knife. I wasn't sure how much legal weight the two items carried, but I suspected it would be enough. That was my soul then. As he placed it in the briefcase, I thought: *that's what it looks like*.

He snapped it shut.

'And this research material?'

The laptop and Sarah's folders: they were still in my bag, on the bottom shelf. I slid it out and handed it to him.

'Thank you, Mr Connor. We're nearly done.'

'Good.'

'This is what will happen next. After I leave, you will wait here for one minute. Then you will go outside, where you'll find your friend waiting for you.'

'I understand.'

'Before that, I want to remind you of the situation. You have two options. The first is that you can go to the police and tell them what you know. They won't believe you. Even if they did, I can promise you they will never, ever find us.' He gestured at the briefcase. 'And in addition, they will receive the evidence in my possession.'

'I understand.'

306

It wasn't just proof against myself I'd given him. The letter implicated Sarah too, confirming that she'd lied for me. Although, if it came to that, the police were going to have far more difficult questions for her to answer.

'The second option,' Garland said, 'is for you to run.'

He reached inside his jacket again. When he brought it back out, he was holding a passport. He handed it to me.

I took it and checked the back page. Sarah's photo. She had bright red hair in it, just as I remembered. I had no idea whether passports were cancelled automatically, or if people really paid attention when you showed them, but perhaps we could get away with it. Maybe not at an airport, but possibly a ferry. A hundred thousand pounds and our feet on foreign soil. It was a slim chance, but it was something. It was enough to run.

'What happens next is your responsibility,' he said.

'Yes.'

'She's . . . damaged. So you have to make her understand what's necessary. That might be hard, but *she's* your responsibility too. Do you understand that?'

'Yes.'

Garland looked at me for a second longer, then picked up the briefcase and the bag and walked past me without another word.

I checked my watch.

One minute.

While I waited, I looked around the garage. There were haphazard boxes of belongings here. Most of them were Marie's. Clothes, books, jewellery. It had been easy to discard my own things, but I'd agonised over the shared possessions, and the items that had been solely hers. Looking around now, I was surprised to find I could remember the contents very clearly.

But that was part of the problem, wasn't it? They were packaged up and stored away out of sight, but whether it's boxes of belongings, or a video clip, or even simply a memory, just because you don't look at something, it doesn't mean it isn't there.

Marie.

I checked my watch again. It was time to leave.

As I headed back out, I took one last glance behind me, and then turned off the lights and locked the door.

Sarah was outside, waiting for me. Just a small girl dressed in black, sitting at one of the benches, huddled up, as though protecting herself against a cold that wasn't to be found in the air. I sat down opposite her, and she looked up at me.

Damaged, I remembered.

She seemed to be half asleep, peering at me through the haze of a dream, but after a moment she smiled. Only slightly, but it was there.

'Alex?' she said.

'Yes.' I tried to smile back. 'It's me.'

And then I reached out and carefully placed my hand over hers.

Forty-Eight

Todd Dennis walked down the corridor of the hospital, running his big fingers through his hair, attempting to stem the frustration inside him.

She was probably going to be all right.

That was the main thing. They had found her.

But it wasn't the whole truth. He had been able to see Rebecca Wingate through the meshed window of the prep room. She was nothing more than a thin shape moulded from a bed sheet, with a plastic mask obscuring most of her face, and a fan of lank hair on the small pillow. The doctor beside him explained that her condition was serious, and she was in no position to be spoken to for the time being. They would be operating shortly. She was certain to lose her right arm.

So it wouldn't be true to say they'd found her in time.

You didn't find her at all.

He wanted to slam his hand into the wall.

Todd had moved quickly after Paul's phone call, but not fast enough. And now that it was all over, he kept questioning himself. Could he have got there sooner? Might it have played out differently? He remembered how desperate Kearney had sounded, and he wasn't sure there was anything he could have done. Because Paul would always have got there first. And he would never have waited.

But he still had no idea what had made Paul so certain about Hammond, or what had happened in the time leading up to both of their deaths. Which meant there must be something he had missed. Something he would never know that he could have done.

He couldn't think about that now. Not yet.

Todd stopped at a drinks machine and bought himself a coffee. When it emerged, he stared at it in disgust. The cup was tiny, and made of beige plastic so thin that it burnt the tips of his fingers. He blew on it gently as he walked.

A minute later, he stopped outside a small consultation room just down from the main reception.

Simon, he reminded himself; that was the man's name.

While Kearney had spent the last week talking to him each morning, Todd had always been careful to avoid him. He didn't fancy it much now either but, with Paul gone, it felt like that particular baton had been passed.

'Simon.' Todd closed the door behind him, and did his best to smile. 'How are you doing?'

Simon Wingate was perched on the single bed at the side of the narrow room, the black of his suit contrasting against the pale green bedclothes and the white paper sheet rolled out along the bed. He was clutching the edge, his knuckles hard and white, and staring at the small trolley across from him. When he looked up now, Todd didn't think he'd ever seen a man look so exhausted and eaten away. Not even Kearney. But there was also a kind of light inside him. A sense of validation, perhaps. He looked like he'd been outside in the freezing cold for a very long time, waiting patiently for a warmth that nobody else had believed would ever come.

'How is she?' Wingate said.

'You've not seen her yet?'

'Through the window. And they told me . . .'

He trailed off. Todd nodded as sympathetically as he could manage. That was something Paul had never understood when he sat down with people like Simon Wingate. There was nothing you could really say. Even in the rare moments like this, all you could offer was the meagre comfort that, as bad as things might seem, they had beaten the odds and come out incredibly lucky.

'But she's alive, Simon,' he said. 'Don't lose sight of that.'

'I know.'

'You must have feared the worst.'

Wingate frowned. Then shook his head.

'No,' he said. 'He promised me you'd find her.'

It took Todd a second to realise that Wingate was talking about Paul. He said nothing.

'Where is he?' Wingate asked. 'Detective Kearney, I mean?'

Todd felt himself grow blank. *Not now*, he reminded himself.

'You haven't heard what happened?'

'No. I'd like to thank him.'

His first instinct was to dodge the question. For one thing, it was too early to be sure exactly what had taken place in Arthur Hammond's basement; for another, the conversation would be out of place. What stopped him was the knowledge that Kearney, if he'd still been alive, would be sitting down beside this man now. And, rightly or wrongly, he'd be telling him the truth.

Todd leaned against the opposite wall.

'I'm not sure what to say.'

In the end, he told Simon Wingate what they knew, and a little of what they suspected. About Thomas Wells and Roger Timms, and their motivations for abducting the girls, and about Arthur Hammond, who had been involved with the pair on some level. Rebecca had been found at his house. In addition, they had found the remains of what appeared to be another victim. He didn't say that the body had been gathered up and crammed in a sports bag, like a handful of litter.

Detective Paul Kearney had learned of Hammond's involvement and confronted him at the property. In the course of what followed, it appeared that Hammond had shot Kearney and then turned the gun on himself.

As he explained that, Todd found himself wondering about

Paul's final moments in Hammond's underground gallery. The last six months had seen Kearney desperately searching for something. The events unfolding from that compulsion had ultimately led Paul to Arthur Hammond's house; they had saved Rebecca's life. Todd hoped that, before he died, Paul had at least had the opportunity to know what he'd done. That he'd kept his promise.

He didn't tell Simon Wingate any of that, though, just as he didn't explain that Kearney had no longer been a police officer. If Paul hadn't quite redeemed himself by his actions – if there was even such a thing as that – then he'd at least earned the right for this man to remember him well.

So he just told him what was important. Rebecca Wingate was alive. And that was because Paul Kearney had looked for and found her.

Forty-Nine

Every so often, my thoughts return to that early memory I have of my brother, the one in which James is red-faced and shouting, losing control of himself and throwing the cushion at our mother.

And I remember this:

I am three or four years old, and I'm crying as hard as, at that point, I imagine I ever will. After James storms out of the room and slams his door, my mother puts her arm around me and holds me tight for a moment. Then she gives me one extra squeeze and goes upstairs to my brother's bedroom. She talks to him, so softly I can't make out the words, but I can hear that he's crying, and perhaps she is too.

She doesn't leave me alone for long, but it's long enough to notice that I *am* alone, and that I shouldn't be. The emptiness downstairs feels heavy.

There is something missing.

After a time, I sit down on the living room floor and then pick up some toys and start *clacking* them together. One of them is a red Lego car, and I remember, for a second, being outside in the driveway. A familiar man was in the car in the driveway, and I was standing on the doorstep. James was by the car beside the man, and he was sobbing, holding onto the door by its open window. My mother was trying to pull James back, but it wasn't working.

I *clack* the toys together curiously.

The man took James's fingers calmly off the door and then the window came up. And I remember the car reversing. There was a screech, I think, but I'm not sure where that came from: whether it was from the car, or from something else.

Something makes me put the toys away again: back in the wooden box as I've been taught. And then I go and clamber up onto the settee and curl up. A few minutes pass before I notice the emptiness for a second time. There is something missing, but I'm not quite sure what it is. I do know that I'm terribly upset with James for losing his temper and throwing the cushion, so perhaps that's what it is.

I decide I don't want to play with the red car again, although I don't frame it to myself in exactly those terms. In the end, I don't think it ever gets thrown away, but it sinks to the bottom of the wooden box through lack of use. And there are always enough things on top for me not to see.

When I met Sarah outside the storage unit, she was dazed and forgetful, and not quite sure what had taken place, as though she had just woken from a long dream, and was unable to remember where or when she fell asleep. She spoke very little. As we left that afternoon, she simply followed me, determined to keep close by my side. In terms of our travel plans, she asked me where we were going, but not why.

It was a full two days later, when we were in Venice, before she first mentioned James.

We had been walking for most of the afternoon, nowhere in particular, just losing ourselves amongst the crowds, and found ourselves pausing on a flat stone bridge. The canal snaked off in front of us. The water down there looked dark and meaty, pressed between the buildings on either side. A small boat was moored there, bobbing slowly on its leash and nosing the water. Further up, the canal expanded out into something sunlit and blinding, although it wasn't immediately clear how you might reach it. We just leaned on the stone side of the bridge and listened to the lap of the water.

And then Sarah said, 'I miss him.'

I turned sideways to look at her. She was staring at the water in the distance, a few strands of jet-black hair wavering in front of her. Her expression was tight and pained, like someone wincing against a strong, icy wind.

'I know,' I said.

'What happened, Alex?'

'You don't remember?'

She shook her head, but I wasn't sure whether she was saying yes or no. I thought about it.

I understood a lot of what had happened, but not everything. And I wanted to. I wanted to know what Sarah and James's plan had been. It was clear a kind of madness had overtaken them and that, sealed in the house together, their mutual need and support had built up layer upon layer of foundations for what they did. But I wasn't sure how they'd ever expected it to be resolved: what they thought would happen afterwards.

I did wonder if, somewhere back at the house, there was another letter, one that they'd written together and hidden somewhere – at the bottom of a box, for example – which I hadn't looked hard enough to find. One that perhaps explained it all and, just in case anything happened to Sarah, laid bare her own responsibilities for the events of the past few weeks. And I wondered if at some point in the future she would feel compelled to return, either to destroy it for ever or to confront the truth of what was written there: to face the evidence of the terrible ripples that death had cast.

For the moment, though, I thought she needed something else.

I turned back, and flicked a small stone off the side of the bridge.

'You were investigating an organisation,' I said.

'Yes. I remember that.'

'And you got too close to them.' I thought about it, then said, 'They abducted you, and they killed James. They held you captive for a few days, the whole time trying to work out how much you knew about them.'

She didn't say anything.

'And in the end,' I said, 'it was OK. I came to find you, and they decided to let us both go.'

I looked back at her.

'But it means we can never go home.'

She nodded, and then began to cry softly at that. After a moment, I put my arm around her. It wasn't quite right, and I knew it wouldn't always be enough, but what I'd just said was something. It was the bare bones of a story I could keep telling her, fleshing it out as we went, until it was written indelibly over the real narrative and the parts that were missing no longer showed through.

And every word of it was the truth. The best place to hide something black is always in the darkness.

In the week following our arrival, I kept checking the international papers for coverage of what had happened. Sarah's disappearance continued to make the news, but the space accorded to it gradually decreased. James's death was reported, and Mike and Julie's was, although the press did not connect the two stories. But with no real developments to go on in either case, the media began to lose interest.

The focus remained on Rebecca Wingate.

I learned that she had been found in Arthur Hammond's mansion, following his suicide. She remained in a critical but stable condition, and was expected to recover. One paper carried a few brief comments from her husband, who paid tribute to the efforts of Detective Paul Kearney in finding his wife, and expressed sadness at his death.

I read all the coverage carefully, attempting to keep myself calm. It was believed that Kearney had been shot by Hammond, only seconds before the businessman took his own life, and the papers were calling Kearney a hero: a policeman murdered during the course of active duty.

There was only one report that differed from that stance, implying that he'd been suspended and was under investigation over unspecified allegations at the time of his death. But no explanation was given, and that side of the story was dropped the following day. It fitted with what I remembered, from meeting him that day in the café, but even if it was true I thought the overall tone of the coverage was right. Whatever he was under investigation for, when someone dies they deserve to be remembered for the best thing they did, not the worst.

The police also uncovered a number of other incriminating items from Hammond's house, including several illegal videos, and they confirmed that his fingerprint matched that of one recovered from the victims of Thomas Wells and Roger Timms.

And in his basement, they also discovered the remains of Emily Price. I kept thinking about Emily, and how I must have come very close to finding her that day, or meeting the man who took her. I was glad that, in the end, she had been found: returned to her family so that they could lay her to rest and receive a level of peace from that.

Of course, I knew the official story wasn't true. It had all been Garland. Even if I didn't quite understand how it had all been accomplished, it was clear that his *salvage* operation had been successful; and like he'd told me, the police knew everything they would ever need to. The facts might be twisted, and parts might be missing, but as long as nobody looked at it too closely, it was enough. It would hold together.

Sarah and I would stand behind it, rightly or wrongly, and remain obscured from view.

But there was one thing I realised I couldn't leave alone. Garland had described the house on Suncast Lane as being one of their old places. I didn't know exactly what he'd meant by that: whether he was saying the place was empty now, or if something or someone might still be there, lying forgotten, no longer of interest to his customers. I fought the idea for a time – told myself I would be putting us both at risk – but after a while

I decided I couldn't ignore that possibility, or perhaps that I shouldn't.

So one day, I left Sarah alone in our hotel room, and went out into the city streets. There was an Internet café just around the corner from where we were staying. I paid for an hour and found myself a seat at the back, where nobody could see.

After setting up an anonymous email account, I searched online and found an email address for Whitrow Police Department, then sent a message marked for the attention of Todd Dennis. I mentioned Kearney's name and told him he should see what was inside number ten, Suncast Lane. In case I'd mis-remembered the number, I told him he'd recognise it from some graffiti on the shutters.

Before I could debate it any more, I pressed send.

I was about to get up and leave, but suddenly I had a strange idea. So, instead of logging off and disappearing, I opened a new window in the browser, navigated to doyouwanttosee.co.uk, and logged in using Sarah's old details.

When I searched for Ellis's posts, I received the same list as before. After scrolling through for a time, I reached the page where the footage of Marie had been posted.

'Bridge suicide – bitch in bits'

I opened that post, and the footage was gone.

It had just occurred to me that when Garland removed the image of Emily Price, he might simply have wiped all of Ellis's stored files in order to save time. And he had. So the video had been deleted for ever.

I nodded to myself. It was another of those things that didn't really matter, not now, but at the same time I was glad. Nobody would ever watch that again. If Marie existed any-where, it would be in my head, and I'd do my best to remember her well.

Finally, I logged out and left.

That afternoon, to be on the safe side, we moved on.

*

I still do my best to think of Marie that way. I try to remember her at Coniston, and the way she held my hand then, or else at some other happier time, when my presence might not have been enough, but at least it was something. And I try hard not to blame myself for what she did because that, if nothing else, was not my fault.

Even so, there are times when I lie awake at night, unable to sleep, and I think back to the last time I saw her – properly saw her – on that day in the kitchen when she left me and did not come back. And on those nights I think:

I wish she could have seen how beautiful she was.

I wish she could have just seen that.

Fifty

Suncast Lane.

Even in daylight, the name wouldn't have been appropriate. It conjured up images of fields with lazily swaying grass, and bright white cottages and streams – not these flat, grey houses, with pale, ghostly faces. Everything around looked dead: tombs of brick and perforated metal. Suncast Lane was in the middle of the estate, and Todd had the impression that something had died here, and then the poison and decay had seeped out into the neighbouring areas, spreading slowly and destroying everything it touched.

He closed the car door and listened: the slam echoed and faded, and then there was nothing. No sound here at all. Looking around, there were no lights in any of the houses. They were all long-abandoned, of course: destined to be knocked down when there was money to be made: when the details were finally pulled out of whatever dusty old council file they'd been lost in. In the meantime, the street appeared forgotten, like a bricked-up room in an old house that had long since changed owners.

Johnson was waiting by the front of the house, holding a torch; Ross was standing a short way down the footpath that disappeared off by the side. Both of them looked a little freaked out by what they'd found inside. Todd hadn't given the email he'd received too much attention, but the person who'd contacted him had mentioned Paul, and so he'd sent these two along to see what, if anything, might be here. Even now, after they'd been inside the place, he wasn't quite clear what that was.

'You two OK?'

Johnson nodded, but didn't look too sure about it.

'Yes, sir. There's a bad feeling in there, though.'

'Yeah, well. There's a bad feel out here too.'

Todd stepped around Johnson, and looked at the building. From the front, it looked as though every conceivable entrance and exit had been sealed up with grilles of metal, all of it bolted solidly into the brickwork. It took him a moment to see the white mark that had been daubed there. A small half moon. It wasn't exactly obvious, and he wouldn't have noticed it if the email hadn't mentioned graffiti. As it was, he had no idea what it was supposed to signify.

'Any word on the last known occupier?' he said.

'Banyard,' Johnson said. 'Francis Banyard. But that was years ago.'

Todd nodded. 'And what am I meant to be looking at?'

'Round the back. The window's been . . . messed with.'

'I meant inside.'

'Well, there's something weird in one of the downstairs rooms. But the main thing's upstairs. First door on the right. That's where it looks like this person's been sleeping. There's rubbish everywhere and it stinks.'

This person. Todd looked back up the street, thinking it over. He was a little impatient with Johnson for getting spooked so easily: all the two officers had found was evidence that someone had been living rough inside. And yet, he felt it himself. Everything around here was deserted and almost deathly quiet. The house was the one mentioned specifically in the email. And it was the only one, as far as he could see, that had been singled out by white graffiti on its shutters.

A breeze picked up. Somewhere out of sight he heard a can rattle along the pavement.

He turned back and held his hand out for the torch.

'Right,' he said. 'Thank you.'

'Be careful, sir. The stairs are half rotten.'

Todd glanced at the house again. In the dark, with the windows shuttered over, it made him think of a corpse with pennies over its eyes. He still didn't like this woolly thinking, but Johnson had been right. Something about the place felt bad.

'I want you two to keep an eye out,' he said. 'Whoever's been sleeping here, we want to speak to them, OK? Whatever this is, we're not losing it.'

'Yes, sir.'

He clicked on the torch and moved through the small garden at the front of the house. The paving slabs had long since been stolen, he noticed – this place might have been forgotten, but not before it had been stripped bare of anything that could be salvaged and sold. Around the back, he scanned the rear of the house, quickly finding the window Johnson had mentioned, then stepped awkwardly over some debris, and shone the light around the edges of the frame.

Todd frowned.

Someone had added hinges at the far side of the grille.

He took a moment to examine them, confirming not only that they were really there, but also the work that must have been involved. The hinges were made of different metal to the main sheet, and had been soldered onto it. There was some slight damage to the walls where the original bolts must have been levered out; the only ones that remained were on the right-hand side, and they'd been sawn off. They were just long enough to keep it snug to the wall, so that a couple of light turns would release them.

Which meant that someone had come here, removed the metal sheet blocking the window and transformed it into a carefully-disguised door.

Why on earth would someone do that?

Todd shivered slightly, feeling a tightness in his chest. As he pulled the grille open, then breathed in the stale air from the room beyond, he had that impression again: that someone awful had been staying here, drawn to the place because it matched them. The tightness came because they were out now – prowling somewhere in the dark – but might return at any time, like he was about to enter a monster's house in a fairytale, one where a pot had been left bubbling softly to itself on the stove.

Come on.

He clambered inside, a little awkwardly, using the torch to make sure of his footing. The room within was empty and bare, but flaking pipes on one wall suggested it had once been the kitchen. Now, it was cold and smelled of mildew and earth. His torch ran across a doorway at the far side. The light switches in the corridor beyond had been stripped away, leaving wires twisting out from ulcers in the plaster.

Todd made his way straight into the hall. The torchlight cast a shadow of ribs above the staircase which slowly rotated as he walked down the corridor and then shone the light up at the landing above. Then he started up them. Johnson had been right about the rot, as well. The steps were too damp and soft to creak, but they gave slightly under his weight, like the rotting hull of an old ship.

There's rubbish everywhere and it stinks.

It was the first door on the right, he reminded himself – but he would have recognised it anyway, as the rubbish was spilling out of the doorway there. Curled, yellowing newspaper pages; swollen black bags; old, crusted food cartons. Stained clothes. Todd grimaced as the torchlight played across the whole mess.

And it did stink, he realised. It really did. A nasty, unhealthy smell. Like rot, but somehow more *alive* than that. He didn't think it was coming from the refuse on the floor, either – more that it was lingering from the presence of whoever lived here amongst it, as though the person had spent so much time in contact with decay that they'd caught it like a disease. It was awful in the same way the house itself felt tainted and awful. There was something *unnatural* about it that made you want to back away.

But it was familiar, too.

That idea nagged at him. He thought he'd smelled this before, or perhaps just a hint of it, but he couldn't quite remember where.

Todd stepped cautiously over the rubbish, searching out a small, bare patch of floorboard to place his foot down on. The torch light cut into the darkness, revealing a blue sleeping bag lying unzipped in the far corner, surrounded by empty bottles and packets of food. Beside them, the thick stubs of candles, their wicks scorched black. A row of old books was balanced upright on the floorboards.

Who was living here like this? It could be a derelict, he supposed, but for some reason that didn't seem right. For one thing, the graffiti on the shutter bothered him: it marked the place out. And as squalid as it looked, this room gave the impression of being someone's *home*. He couldn't explain it, but it felt as though the person staying here had picked this house in particular, out of all the others, because it held special meaning for them, or had done once. They hadn't just bedded down here at random.

What was the last occupier's name again?

Todd moved the beam of light along the back wall, picking out more bin liners, more piles of clothes, a sports bag. A magazine with a child's face laughing on the cover. Dirty crockery, some of it broken . . .

He stopped.

And then slowly moved his hand back, allowing the light to return to the sports bag again. It looked relatively new compared to the other items in the room, and appeared to have been placed down carefully, as though the contents were more valuable to its owner than all of his other possessions combined.

Todd stared at it. The zip was secured in place by a thin strip of black plastic, just like the bag they'd found in the room below Arthur Hammond's house. The one that had been opened to reveal the remains of Emily Price.

Melissa Noble, he thought. Her body was still missing.

Suddenly, the air in here felt like it was tingling.

Todd took a step back, out of the room.

The sight of the bag made him remember where he'd noticed the stench before. He'd been distracted and upset at the time – standing over Paul's body, surrounded by Hammond's collection of dead things – but it had been down there: just the faintest trace of it, hanging in the air in the old man's basement. And then fading away. As though something even more horrible had been down there, only minutes before they arrived, but had slipped away just in time.

He kept the light trained on the bag. As he looked at it, something Paul had said returned to him.

So what if Ellis isn't Mister X?

He'd been right about that, of course. It was Hammond's fingerprint that had been found on the victims' foreheads, and it was Hammond's basement that both Rebecca and Emily Price had been discovered in. It had been him who had shot Paul, then taken his own life. But then . . . what if Hammond hadn't been their Mister X either? What if it had been someone else altogether?

Someone else . . .

That reminded him of what Rebecca Wingate had said. When they'd finally been able to interview her, she'd not been able to tell them very much about those last few moments, aside from dimly remembering two loud gunshots. But she had also said something else. Something that hadn't made any sense, and which, at the time, Todd had decided was likely due to her being blindfolded and delirious, her mind half-burned away by fever.

I think there was someone else in there with me.

His skin began to crawl.

Someone else. The more he thought about it, the more certain he felt. The man who had been sleeping here – beside that bag – had also been in Hammond's basement. He'd never been as intuitive as Paul – never able to put the pieces together as quickly or nimbly – but they were there, and he could see the beginnings of one picture they might make. And as connections began to appear, he felt a sense of resolve hardening inside him.

Banyard, he thought. That was the name of the last person who'd lived in this house. Francis Banyard. So was it him that had been staying here? Come back to his old home for some reason? Well, they would track him down, wherever he was. They would stake this house out – this whole fucking estate, if they needed to – and they'd see who came back.

We'll get this man.

He played the light across the rubbish, thinking about Paul again. At first, it was the image of his partner's body, lying on the floor of Hammond's basement – but then he shook his head, ridding himself of that memory. Instead, he concentrated on the intensity that had always been there in Paul's eyes. The determination. The pledges he'd felt compelled to make. The fact that, against all the odds, he had followed that and found Rebecca Wingate. And as the beam of light settled back on the sports bag again, Todd thought:

Whoever this man is. We'll get him.

It sounded a lot like a promise, but he made it anyway.

There's something weird in one of the downstairs rooms.

He would have to get forensics in to examine the scene upstairs, and he also needed to start orchestrating the surveillance side of things. But, on his way back outside, Todd decided to quickly check the other thing that Johnson and Ross had found. As he stepped through the doorway into what must once have been the house's lounge his thoughts were already running off through the logistics of the long night ahead of him. When he saw what was there, those thoughts tripped slightly.

Like most of the other rooms, this one had been stripped bare. But it wasn't what was missing that stood out. It was what had been added afterwards. On one side of the room, an old, faded mattress rested on the floor. It was stained in places, as though coffee had been spilled on it, and the springs inside were visible, pressing against the thin fabric like half-crushed cola cans. Green mould speckled the sides. At the opposite end of the room there was a tall-legged wooden stool and, on top of that, a video camera.

And that was all. There was nothing else to see: just a revolting, makeshift bed with a camera pointed at it. But the scene was incongruous because it felt staged. It reminded him of a room in a museum, in fact – one of those exhibits where the original desks and chairs and clothes had been collected and placed down carefully, recreating the bedroom or study of someone famous and dead. A room where people came to see, to get a hint of what it had been like to be present at the time.

A moment preserved.

Todd thought about the graffiti outside. And then the man who'd been sleeping upstairs.

Is this why you chose to stay here?

He crossed to the wooden stool. It wasn't a video camera, he realised. It was much older than that: mechanical and sturdy. The sides were made of bobbled black plastic, with circular loops of metal jutting up from the top like rabbits' ears. All of it was coated in dust, as though it had been here for a very long time. There was no tape in the reels, but a snipped trail of frames had been left on top of the machine.

He rummaged in his pocket –

Tweezers . . .

– and then picked up the tape of cells. It was impossible to see what was on them in the dark, so he moved the torch beam behind to illuminate the tiny images and the rest of the room collapsed into blackness. And as he saw what was on the film, his hand began to tremble.

'Oh God,' he said.

The first frame was a simple, innocuous shot of a street. It was a winter's day, the air white with ice and fog. A boy was in the centre of the frame, wrapped up in a duffel coat and staring straight at the camera from several metres away. He was only eight or nine years old, but Paul Kearney's features were already clear on the boy's face. You could see the blueprint for the man he'd become, as though the most important part of him – the essence – had been frozen in place at this moment right here.

The boys were then returned close to the place they'd been taken from, like nothing had happened.

Todd ran the torch down behind the strip, creating a stuttering animation. The camera moved back quickly – someone had filmed this from a car or a van as it sped away. In the centre, the boy stood still and receded into the distance, as though he was being yanked backwards into the mist. He was still staring straight ahead, his expression like a question, right up until the moment he disappeared entirely.

The camera captured that as well, Todd thought blankly.

Showed it in place of credits.